3⁵⁰

Critics Praise Holt Medallion Winner Kathleen Nance!

ENCHANTMENT

"*Enchantment* is a wish come true for fans of genie romance. Ms. Nance creates a world as exotic and intriguing as the characters who inhabit it."

—*Romantic Times*

"*Enchantment* was a wonderful reading experience, [with] a great set of characters and a wonderful setting. I cannot say enough about this book except I have a fervent wish for a sequel."

—*Romance Reviews Today*

MORE THAN MAGIC

"*More Than Magic* is an undeniable treasure trove of pleasure, bursting with magnetic characters and a bewitching plot that's sure to capture the imagination of fantasy and romance readers alike."

—*Rendezvous*

"An astonishingly original story in a world which contains far too few paranormal romances, *More Than Magic* is more than satisfying."

—*Affaire de Coeur*

WISHES COME TRUE

"Kathleen Nance has penned a supremely enticing tale with laughter, intrigue, the paranormal and, of course, a passionate steamy love that comes across in spades."

—*Rendezvous*

Wishes Come True is "a story of magic, wishes, fantasy, and . . . a lot of spice. Ms. Nance is wonderful in her debut novel. Fantastic! 5

More Rave Reviews for Kathleen Nance!

THE SEEKER

"With tantalizing plot twists and impossible interference, the path to love is a heck of a lot of fun! The fresh premise . . . characters, and complexity of plot result in a sparkling romance!"

—*The Midwest Book Review*

"An exciting story filled with romance, magic and mystery!"

—*Romance Reviews Today*

THE WARRIOR

"An exciting tale interwoven with a fun premise."

—*Romantic Times*

"Kathleen Nance puts a refreshing twist on paranormal romance. . . . Well-executed with amazing romantic and sensual tension."

—*Romance and Friends*

THE TRICKSTER

"*The Trickster* is a magical tale that is fresh and captivating. Kathleen Nance has weaved a story unlike anything I have read before and for that I applaud her. She is a true genius."

—Scribesworld.com

"Kathleen Nance spins a unique and clever tale. *The Trickster* is warm, funny and tender."

—*Romantic Times*

A BOLD CLAIM

"Madeline," he said, setting aside his oud and rising from the pillows with a languid movement. Just her name, but he made it a symphony in three syllables.

"Magic," she whispered, her insides growing cold.

"We call it ma-at."

"We?"

"I am djinn."

The blood left her brain, and her knees lost their strength. Madeline sank onto the mound of pillows, then immediately shot back to her feet. "The pillows moved," she accused.

"They do but adjust to support you," he answered mildly.

She gave him a wild look. "You think you're a genie."

"Djinni," he corrected, giving the word a softer beginning and a lilt at the end. "And I not only think, I am."

She shook her head. "Genies are bald guys who come from a lamp and grant wishes."

"I do not grant wishes," he said, his low voice suddenly dark and menacing. "Only a spellbound djinni can be so commanded. And do I look like I could live in a lamp?"

Her mother and stepfather dabbled in the occult, held some strange beliefs, but she'd never seen any evidence that their magic worked. She'd been cynical about the world of mysticism, believing only in what she could taste and touch and smell.

Well, here stood that evidence, six feet three inches of near naked glory.

Other *Love Spell* books by Kathleen Nance:

ENCHANTMENT
THE SEEKER
THE WARRIOR
THE TRICKSTER
MORE THAN MAGIC
WISHES COME TRUE

KATHLEEN NANCE

Spellbound

LOVE SPELL

NEW YORK CITY

LOVE SPELL®

June 2003

Published by

Dorchester Publishing Co., Inc.
276 Fifth Avenue
New York, NY 10001

ISBN 0-505-52486-4

Printed in the United States of America.

In memory of my sister, Pat,
who lit our world with her determination, courage,
giving heart, and boundless spirit.

Spellbound

Chapter One

Kaf, the realm of the djinn

The birds were growling.

No, not again! Zayne leaned over his oud, his fingers dancing across the strings as the song swelled from him. He was the sole Minstrel of Kaf; no others shared this trust. His music wove into the harmonies of his world, balancing the elemental powers of *ma-at*. His *ma-at* and his music *could not* be the source of the chaos.

Yet, as his voice grew in richness, so did the unrest of the birds grow louder. Their tumult held a mirror to the ferocity inside him. To the battle between his *ma-at* and the strange force fueling his song.

His listeners, sprawled on cushions scattered across the night-cooled sand, murmured restively, but he paid them no mind. His passion was for the beauty and the clarity of music. Only the oud and the voice, which gave substance to song and soul, mattered. Only the strength of his *ma-at*, the elemental fuel of his harmony, mattered.

His powerful *ma-at* wove through the music, enchanting all the senses, a counter to the strange force rising within him. The taste of honey heightened each note. Scents of sandalwood and green melon gave way to the spicy intoxication of clove and mimosa. Fierce arousal shot through him, hardening his body and demanding release, and he shared that erotic need through his song.

The seductive lure of the strange force captured him, and at last he submitted to its call. His lyrics told of dark deeds and darker hearts.

A bolt of lightning slashed across the sky. No thunder followed, but the wind rushed through the circle with a moan. Moments ago the oasis had been filled with sunset and the pleasures of a quiet eve; now the night held fire, the hot sirocco, and the growl of birds. Even the brilliant moon of Kaf hid behind roiling clouds.

Still, he sang, denying the unthinkable. As the feral song grew, the sparkle of djinn emotions danced on the edges of his vision. White and gold deepened to red, purple, and blue. The murmurs of the audience grew in volume. *What was this eerie melody from their Minstrel?* He could almost hear the questions. Yet he did not look at his listeners; his auburn hair shielded his face from view, as it always did when he played.

Flame encased him, a shimmering blue spire that encircled but did not scorch. Instead it pulled at the air and heat, as though fed by his thrumming blood and his powerful *ma-at*. His fingers flew across the strings, aching with the need to release the building alien power, while his *ma-at* fought against the intrusion.

Lightning crackled and danced in whips of blinding whiteness. Wind tore at the linens and silks of his audience. Scarlet geysers of lava burst from spreading cracks in the sand. All were outward manifestations of his inner battle.

Someone from the audience screamed, and several

others scrambled to their feet. A single, eerie screech cut through the night. The birds were silent before the might of *ma-at* and the violent unrest of Kaf.

Minstrel, what do you do? The deep masculine voice of the Oracle of Kaf dared to pierce his absorption. Zayne's glance shot upward, but he saw not the shadowy figure of the powerful djinni. Only the faces of his audience—lit with fascination and fear, shock and need—surrounded him.

I feel the unrest of Kaf here in the Tower Lands, Alesander added.

For a moment, Zayne considered ignoring the question. No djinni could read another's thoughts, only send his own.

Zayne? The voice could not be ignored.

I but sing. His fingers slowed as he struggled to rein in the tumultuous song and the accompanying chaos. He could no longer deny that his music and his tumult had created the strange disturbances, but he dared not admit that to Alesander.

No, your song is never that simple. Music feeds the soul of Kaf, and you are the only Minstrel. You keep our harmony.

Do you think I could forget that?

Your responsibility is to the people and the land.

I know. Abruptly he broke off the conversation, fearing that further contact would reveal his cursed malady.

Note by note, he fought against the tumultuous force. Beat by beat, he slowed the driving, foreign melody. Each time he sang, though, the task grew harder. The indigo silk of his shirt stuck to the perspiration coating him. With agonizing care he transformed the music, locked away the turmoil, and reestablished the harmony.

The fires waned, and the land settled. Wind gentled to a breeze, lightning disappeared, and once more pleased djinn emotions sparkled through the night. A lively, charming air replaced the dense song. The audience's collective sigh of relief was almost a palpable thing.

The new song was light as air, fresh as a breeze off the cool oasis. With his *ma-at* he added the scent of laurel and the taste of lime, suggested misty images of palms and grass and an intertwined couple.

He wove his *ma-at* with song, with the motion of a finger and the unvoiced chants of his power. He restored the harmony. Yet, even now, the winds threatened to lift, while desire and wildness still beat against his throat and chest. Ruthlessly he ignored them to intone the words that would soften the memories of his audience and soothe their disquiet.

He was unable, however, to soften or soothe himself.

The song ended on a single, clear note which faded into the night. Zayne pushed to his feet, acknowledged the applause with a simple incline of his head, slung the strap of his oud over his shoulder, and then strode away into the desert. He sought the solitude and luxury of his tent, which was pitched a little distance away from the others.

A woman stepped into his path. He felt her heat before he saw her shadow. Neheri. She had given him her name earlier, when he had first entered the tiny village and she had brought herself to his attention.

"Minstrel, after such a performance, do you wish solitude?" Her voice was low and seductive.

Urgent heat shot through him again. As always, the music left him aroused and feeling each sense keenly, but lately this awareness had become a sharp thirst, undeniable and unquenchable. Maybe, for a few unrestrained hours, she could relieve his pressing needs and he would give her the pleasure she craved.

"Come closer," he commanded, drawing her near with only the music of his voice. She leaned against him, all willowy curves, and his fingers threaded through her dark hair. He rubbed the downy strands between his forefinger and thumb, then captured her chin and lifted her face to his brief kiss. It was all he could risk for the moment, lest the wildness overwhelm him. And Kaf. "Is this what you want?"

"Yes," she breathed. "No, I want more, Minstrel."

Not *Zayne,* only *Minstrel.* In seeking his identity, he had lost it. Zayne smiled, sensually, ruefully, without humor, though she would not realize it. He released her. "Go, Neheri."

"I can satisfy you." Her hands ran down his back and curled around his oud.

"Do not touch my instrument," he warned, his voice gentle but implacable.

Her arms dropped away as though burnt, but she recovered quickly. "Could I touch another instrument, then?" she cooed with coy seduction.

"Are you sure?"

It was a warning, but she heard it as an invitation. "Yes." She slid her hips across his. "I know your need."

"This is the need of the Minstrel." He bent to the kiss again. It was the kiss he needed to give, the release he craved. He was ruthless, violent even, demanding all of her with the touch of his lips and teeth, with his *ma-at* and his seething emotions.

She pulled away with a murmur of protest.

He let her go, knowing to his soul she was not the one he needed. "Go, Neheri," he repeated, his voice a mere sigh. This time she did not demur, but disappeared into the night.

Zayne entered the tent and stripped off his clothes, leaving only a loose cord around his neck. From the woven cord hung his round turquoise tablet—the symbol of his djinn status—and hidden beneath it rested a second, half tablet. The sole possession of his youth. With a wave of his hand and a quick chant, he cleansed his clothes and body. Exhaustion grabbed hold of him at last, and a mound of pillows beckoned him to rest. First, however, there was a task he must perform.

Naked, he knelt before the circle of stones at the center of his tent. He stretched out his hands and chanted a brief incantation. Flames ignited at the center of the stones.

Zayne fingered the smooth warmth of his turquoise tablet. He was Minstrel of Kaf. His songs fed the fire and air of Kaf; he was part of her energy and her harmony. He could not stop singing—voice was as vital to him as breath and drink—nor could he deprive Kaf of his Minstrel's touch. There was no other to take his place.

But this strange new power became part of every song. It fought with his *ma-at* and brought disharmony to the land and the people he was sworn to nurture. Yet the dark beauty within it was as compelling and mesmerizing as any he had felt. The songs it fueled could not be denied.

He had to master this power. Or he had to eliminate it. A wrong choice would be disastrous for his music and for Kaf.

He thought he knew the answer. Although few djinni united in the soul bonds of *zani* and *zaniya*—male and female as one—Minstrels had always taken a *zaniya*. The *zaniya* of a Minstrel was a great chanteuse, whose voice blended with his in the harmonies of Kaf; she was as vital to him as his *ma-at* or his song.

In this, as in so many other things, he was different, for he had never found such a woman, and he was well past the age when other Minstrels had found theirs. No longer could he leave such an important matter to the whims of fate. He must find his *zaniya*.

So this evening he would perform the ritual of divination, seeking guidance. A divination was not a ritual to be performed lightly. It could not reveal the future, for the future was shaped by the choices of free will. Instead, it provided a path to follow, but often the path was murky and the divination difficult to interpret.

He took a deep breath, the rhythm of his heart hard upon his chest. Who was the woman to be his *zaniya*? He *had* to find her. Once he did, there would be no barriers to returning the harmony and balance to his song. For what woman on Kaf would refuse the Minstrel as *zani*?

Intoning the incantations, he picked up a vial of oil and sprinkled seven drops on the fire. Purple flames shot upward; the heat beat against his face and chest. The tent filled with the scent of violets. Still chanting, he spread his arms outward, and a whirling wind circled across him, twisting the flames downward to a knotted inferno.

A plume of smoke rose from the center, and in its heart a face formed. A woman's face. A woman he did not know.

Eagerly he sought some clue in the visage. Nothing about her was familiar. Something about her seemed almost . . . alien. Her hair was cut close to her scalp—perhaps she pulled it back?—and she had a firm jaw, eyes and brows that tilted up, an unsmiling mouth, a sensual full lower lip, and a rounded nose. She decorated her ears with three round gems at the bottom.

Hers was an intriguing face, with the contrast of smooth hair and flashing eyes, of serious mouth and kissable lips, of soft cheeks and determined chin. As he studied her, his body hardened and rose to life.

Zaniya? Was she to be his *zaniya*? His body said yes, but—

"Who is she?" he whispered.

Madeline Fairbanks. The plume of smoke curled around his neck and ears and whispered out the odd name. *Madeline Fairbanks.*

No djinni on Kaf had such a name.

No djinni on Kaf. The smoke whispered in echo.

"No," he hissed. His soul was connected to his world, the source of djinn *ma-at*, and as Minstrel his connection was stronger and deeper than that of most of the djinn. His *zaniya* must also be of Kaf. The smoke began to break apart as he denied what his eyes saw and his instinct accepted.

He added another drop of oil, replenishing smoke and flame and violet. "I need more. Where do I find her?"

Images danced through the fire: a jungle of twisted trees and thick brush, stagnant dark water beneath and around the roots, the ripple of an armored reptile as it swam through the swamp. The scene shifted to hard walls and impossibly tall buildings, people everywhere, crowded and hurrying. His lip curled with disdain. Everything about the land was foreign.

At last he saw a sign. *New Orleans*, the letters read.

This was Terra. Or Earth, as the humans called their world.

A world his mother had detested and taught him to despise.

He recoiled from the flames. An impossible thought. No woman of Terra, no matter how mesmerizing her voice, could be *zaniya* to a Minstrel of Kaf. A Terran had not the rhythms and harmonies of Kaf in her soul. Yet he could not deny the instinctive response of his body, nor the guidance of the divination.

He looked again at the face of Madeline Fairbanks. Perhaps the path was not as direct as he'd first surmised, and Madeline Fairbanks would provide the answers. Would she guide him to the djinni destined to sing with him?

"Is she my *zaniya?*"

The divination did not change.

"Show me what I must do," he begged.

Only Madeline's face remained. The divination had shown him a path. It was up to him to choose what to do with it.

"How am I to find this woman?"

Her face faded, replaced by a second, brief image. Another woman, much older, but this one he knew. Tildy Maehara, the Terran woman who had helped raise Isis, the *zaniya* of the Protector of *Ma-at*.

He had met Tildy on Kaf a few times, and to his surprise he had liked the Terran woman. Once, he had even gone with Isis to Tildy's house, his single visit to Terra, but he had left very quickly, uncomfortable with the strange forces of magic on the alien world. Yet go to this world he must, for through Tildy he would meet Madeline.

Zayne watched the divination fire until it died, then rose to his feet and stretched. He would rest tonight, make his preparations tomorrow. Then he would go to Terra and discover the answers he needed.

Madeline Fairbanks stared at the news release taped to the podium. The sun beat against her scalp. Her heart pounded, her vision blurred, and her voice froze.

Blindly she gripped the edges of the podium, willing herself to inhale the sticky New Orleans air. Willing the panic to pass.

She could do this. This wasn't a stage performance, just a brief, routine announcement. She didn't need to read the words; she knew what they said, she'd written them. Three simple announcements to the press: Feydor Blaze's newest release in the Dorian Justice mystery series had hit the *New York Times* best-seller list, a new series of occult mysteries was to be launched, and there was to be a party in three weeks celebrating St. John's Eve and the start of summer.

An announcement. Simple to do.

Impossible to start.

Sweat, which had nothing to do with the oppressive heat, caked her skin, and bat wings of fear beat against her ribs. She cleared her throat and heard the sound reverberate through the microphone in front of her. The murmuring crowd of reporters, who milled around the grass of Feydor's home hoping for a glimpse of the reclusive author, quieted. Waiting, expecting her voice.

She *had* to do this. She loosened her death grip on the podium long enough to touch a hand to the sleek knot of her hair, assuring herself of her tidy competence. Between the panting breaths, she inhaled deeply and looked up, hoping for a steadying glimpse of her friend Natalie, a reporter for the *Times-Picayune.*

Big mistake.

Faces. All she could see was faces. Faces watching her. Faces with avid eyes and grinning teeth.

I know these people, some for years. I spoke to each one of them on the phone, invited each one here. She tried to begin, failed. Nausea rolled inside her, and the unrelenting stab of a headache pierced between her eyes.

Fear—and humiliation over that fear—warred within her. Neither let her open her mouth and do her job.

"Give me the mike," growled the smoke-roughened voice of her employer from behind her.

Blindly she fumbled for the microphone and passed it to Feydor, who stood hidden within the door alcove. Succinct and blunt, he made the announcements, then shoved the microphone back to her and disappeared into the house.

Thank you for coming. She couldn't even croak that into the microphone. Without another look at the mass of faces, she fled into the house, where she leaned against the closed door, letting the cooled air dry her sweat and the darkness take the sunshine spots from her eyes. She drew in long breaths, letting her heart settle. At last the fear dissipated.

That left only the humiliation.

"Maddie, my office," snapped Feydor, who'd been waiting for her to collect herself.

She hated the nickname Maddie. For once, though, the automatic correction didn't come. Instead, she followed him into the jumbled cave he called an office. He poured Jack Daniels into a glass, lit a cigarette, and then posed himself in his chair.

The familiar actions steadied her. As did being away from the microphone. She plucked the glass from his hands, tossed the whiskey out an opened window, and then poured water from the bar into the glass. After clearing the tibia, thumbscrews, and jar of leeches from the desk, she set the glass at his side.

"What the hell is going on, Maddie?"

"Madeline, sir. Call me Madeline. It's five o'clock. You told me not to let you have alcohol before seven."

"That's not what I meant, and you know it. That scene out there was an embarrassment, we both know it, and I don't *ever* want to have to put myself forward like that again. What the hell happened?"

She glanced over and saw the cigarette dangling between his fingers, the set of his shadowed jaw, the narrowing of his dark eyes. He wasn't going to drop this. "I'm not very good at public speaking," she said. "Lots of people have a fear of it; it's next to the fear of death."

"Yeah, but most people don't look like they're going to vomit on their shoes. And they get through it. You couldn't. Why didn't you tell me?"

"All I had to do was . . ." Brushing a spot of dust off her skirt, she fought the humiliating fact that he was right. "I thought I could . . ." She stopped, faced him. "I'm sorry, you're right, I should have said something."

"You haven't always had this." He eyed her thoughtfully.

"Things change," she said shortly, nipping that line of questioning. "Next time let your publicist handle the announcements."

"My publicist is in New York, like my agent and my editor, where I prefer to keep them. I need a presence locally, here in New Orleans. I wanted you to do this, Maddie," he added gently.

"I'm better behind the scenes." She neatened her sleeves. "Now, I've finished those last translations and typed them for you. Your correspondence has piled up again, so I'll start answering that. I set up a signing—"

"No, don't start on the correspondence. Don't start on anything." He took a swallow of the water, grimaced, and then set it down on his desk with a clunk. "I have to let you go, Maddie."

"Excuse me?"

"I'm firing you."

"You're joking."

"I wish I were."

He was dead serious. She sank into the nearest chair. "Just like that? Why?"

"Your employment was temporary, you knew that."

"Yes, but I thought . . ." She bit her lip. A six-week stint had expanded to six months. He had hired her to translate some documents and books, because she was fluent in both Russian and French—thanks to a Russian-born mother and secondary years at Ecole Classique, the French immersion school. But they'd found an easy rhythm in working together and she'd gradually taken on other tasks, other responsibilities.

"Remember I said I needed a personal assistant?"

She'd hoped his offhand comment meant he'd offer her the job. "Filing, managing your calendar, ordering flowers for your dates. I do all that."

"If you're my personal assistant, your job is to do whatever I need." He gestured with the cigarette. "You disappointed me out there, Maddie."

She sat back, stung. She prided herself on a job well done, on exceeding expectations. "Madeline," she corrected automatically, trying to quell the very real fear that he was firing her. "For those announcements, someone could come in—"

"I already let you talk me into hiring a researcher."

"Virginia's doing a good job."

"Damn straight she is." He stubbed the unsmoked cigarette out in an ashtray and leaned forward. "You, me, Virginia Krumkowski, a cleaning lady. Too many people already wandering around the house; I don't like it. Three's my limit."

Feydor Blaze was a fanatic about keeping his house private. Parties, press announcements were all held outdoors. Even his multiple affairs he conducted at each woman's house; none of them had ever breached Feydor's front door.

"Let Virginia do the announcements, talk with the press." The suggestion was a desperate one, and she knew it.

He gave a snort of derision. "PR needs presence. Virginia is dog-ugly. I know it; she knows it; you know it."

"Virginia's a sweet girl." Her stomach tightened into a knot.

"Sure she is, and I love her for it, but the reporters would eat her alive. Dealing with the press needs flash and glamour." He lit another cigarette. "I don't need a PA just to answer letters. Hell, I could hire a service for that. I need someone who can interview a research subject, answer media questions, or put together a party for my new release with equal ease."

"You want Archie Goodwin to your Nero Wolfe."

For the first time, Feydor cracked a smile. "Yeah, except I weigh a hell of a lot less. Point is, I don't do public appearances. My PA will have to, and will have to live up to my image."

"What image? The reclusive writer?"

"My detective, Dorian Justice, is suave, virile, a creature of the night. So is his creator."

"Dorian Justice is a vampire. You're not."

"Are you sure?" He smiled, showing the face on the back of his books, the one that made his readers wonder how much of this vampire business was real, and for one single moment she almost wondered as well. Then he leaned back and drank the water, and the image was lost.

"My rep needs that wit and charm, that suave sophistication," he continued. "Flair is *sine qua non.*" His glance ran down her tailored brown suit. "I've been trying to get you to modernize for some weeks now. I thought you knew."

Her brows knit. "When?"

"Stephanie suggested you go to the hairdresser. Megan asked you to go shopping. Belinda offered to do your nails."

"Your *girlfriends?*"

"I asked them to help."

The thought of him discussing her with each of his string of paramours hardened the knot in her stomach. "Well, I didn't want my hair turned purple, my clothes to look like I belonged on a Bourbon Street corner, and my nails glittery talons," she retorted, anger starting to rise along with the distress.

"Okay, so they weren't the best role models. But you need to loosen up a bit, Maddie. I even thought about a sweaty, no-commitments-wanted, mind-blowing affair."

Her jaw dropped open in shock before she snapped it shut. "Oh, God, Feydor, you aren't suggesting that you and I—"

"Hell, no!" he assured her. "But remember, last month, I sent you to interview Richie Aquina for me."

Richie Aquina was the smoothest voice to hit the R&B market in years, even if he was a complete misogynist. "What does that have to do with—"

"You did a phone interview."

"He told me to wear something easy to tear because he wanted to, and I quote, 'loosen me up with a piece of man that would have me howling like a bitch.' I wasn't flattered." She gave Feydor an incredulous look. "Was that what you thought I needed?"

"I didn't realize Aquina was so crude; he has a reputation as a lover. I must admit, though, your prudish streak shocked the hell out of me, considering—"

"Considering my family background." Considering she'd lived with media attention most of her life. Anger spread through her veins.

She was tempted to walk out right then except for a couple of very big reasons. One, Feydor Blaze was generous. He paid her twice what anyone with a recent degree in classical literature could expect, and with the bills for her mother's care, she needed cash. This permanent job would pay even better. Two, with the exception of the past fifteen minutes, she genuinely liked her boss. Granted he was egotistical, brusque, and opinionated, but he was also brilliant and interesting. Most of all, he was straight with her, and she valued that. He dealt with everyone the same. Expected a lot, returned a lot, but fail to meet his demands and you were out.

He'd told her what he wanted, a PA with flair, charm, and wit and capable of handling the occasional publicity demand.

Well, she wasn't charming or witty, and she paid no attention to modern fashion. She was straightforward, disciplined, and classic, but she could look at a few fashion magazines, make some changes to her hairstyle. As long as she dealt with the press in a professional manner, Feydor would end up happy. Only one thing stood in the way.

Her debilitating stage fright.

One-on-one, she dealt with people fine. With large groups, though, being in front and on stage, she failed. She couldn't even perform in a classroom. The limelight terrified her and had since she was fifteen.

She leaned forward. "Give me a chance at the job. Everyone has a weakness; mine is appearing at a podium or on stage. But I have a lot to offer. I know a hell of a lot of people, I can learn the flair thing, and you're never going to find someone you can depend upon more."

He gazed at her, unblinking. "Is this job what you really want?"

"Yes." It was what she needed. What she wanted was no longer possible.

"All right," he said at last. "The St. John's Eve party. There's going to be an announcement."

Already her stomach started to clench with nausea. She ignored it. "What am I going to announce?"

He shook his head. "If you're successful, I'll get someone else to make the announcement."

"Successful at what?"

"Finding Cyrus Cromwell. I want him at the party, and I want him to agree to a no-holds-barred interview."

Cyrus Cromwell. Her breath hissed in. Fresh anger—so potent and foreign it almost frightened her—raced across the numb resignation, and she felt a distinct kinship with the White Knight Burgers employee who'd left his boss tied up naked in the freezer.

"Feydor, you're a bastard."

"Only my mother disagrees."

"Is that what all this job nonsense was about? A set up to reel me in with Cyrus?" She'd sworn she wouldn't be drawn back into that world of music and magic again.

He lit another cigarette, inhaling deep. "Yes, if you gave me the opening. And you did."

"Damn it, Feydor." She jumped to her feet.

"But I'm giving you a real choice; I don't play games. I need a PA, a representative, and I want her to look sophisticated and vogue. You don't," he said bluntly. "I also want Cyrus, and this is the only way I know to get him. You've got grace and classic looks, Maddie, so if you bring me Cyrus, I'll adjust."

"Thanks a lot."

He ignored her sarcasm. "What's your choice?"

"I'm not doing some version of *Stepdaddy, Dearest* so you can write a scene in your book."

"In this new series of occult mysteries, my detective is a renowned warlock. Cyrus Cromwell is the closest this town has ever come to the genuine article." Feydor leaned forward. He picked up the thumbscrew on his desk and rotated it. "I've got to know what makes him tick. He's got secrets, Maddie, and I want them all, including how he took your mother from an obscure classical pianist to a rock sensation, whether he had anything to do with her collapse, and where he's been the past year."

Talk about all your nightmares in one assignment. But she was determined to prove she could do this. Madeline straightened. "All right. When I get you the interview, though, I want a permanent job and a raise, and you'll hire a local PR person. And you'll call me Madeline."

It was Feydor's turn to hesitate.

"Cyrus Cromwell has never been photographed, never been interviewed," she pressed. "Even I don't know where he is right now. But I'm the only one who could get him for you, and you know it."

"The PR firm never comes inside the house. You deal with them. And you'll stop wearing tailored suits."

"A big raise."

"All right. You've got three weeks. St. John's Eve. If you don't have Cyrus Cromwell, then don't come back."

Madeline smoothed her brown skirt and tucked a loose hair into the twist on her head. "Oh, don't worry, Feydor. I'll be back."

Chapter Two

Anger carried Madeline all the way home. She didn't have the remotest idea how she was going to manage this assignment.

Sweat slicked every inch of her skin as she trudged the final blocks from the bus stop to her apartment. May in New Orleans was the head of the beast, hot and humid with air almost too thick to breathe. The heat sapped the anger from her, leaving only questions and problems: Cyrus, stage fright, and flair.

As she collected her mail, she waved to Leila Montgomery, her neighbor around the corner, who was pushing a shaded stroller. Now, there was a woman for whom flair was innate—her long, dark hair was glossy, and the blue of her shirt set off to perfection the turquoise in her intriguing necklace. Sweat wasn't part of her vocabulary.

"Hi, Leila," Madeline called. "How's the plant business?"

Leila stopped. "Hello. My business does well, and thank you for watching Phillip last week when I was called away. He was quite fussy, from what Jack told me."

"He was fine. Arsenic hour isn't the best time for any baby."

Leila drew back, horrified. "Arsenic? Is that not a poison?"

Madeline kept forgetting English wasn't Leila's native language, although she never had found out exactly where Leila was from. "I just meant he's colicky this time of day. Cranky."

"Ah, yes. Cranky. That he is." There was obvious love in her tone as she looked down at the stroller. "Walking helps."

Madeline peeked into the stroller to see the drowsy, chubby-cheeked boy. His hair was as fair as his father's, but his skin held his mother's natural tan. "He's such a cutie."

Just then, Phillip opened his eyes and began to fuss. Leila crooned to him in a foreign language, but the child refused to quiet. "I am sorry," she said, appearing flustered for the first time since Madeline had met her. "It is walking or his father's voice that soothes him at this turn of the day. And Jack will be home soon."

"Please, don't let me stop you."

Leila nodded, and a moment later she, the stroller, and the calming baby rounded the corner and disappeared from view.

Madeline unlocked her door. She liked her tiny apartment, one of six strategically placed amidst palms, hibiscus, and azaleas. It was close to the Magazine Street bus lines, and they let her keep her two cats, Bronze and Silver. Inside was cooler. She threw down the copies of *Vogue, Mademoiselle*, and *Elle* she'd picked up, then stooped to pet the cats twining about her legs.

"Do you fellas think I can be sophisticated and vogue, with a touch of flair?"

The cats purred an encouraging answer. Or maybe they just purred a "we want dinner."

Catching a glimpse of herself in the hall mirror as

she rose, she tried to see what Feydor was talking about. Eyes an indeterminate color, brown hair. She shook her hair out of its knot. Healthy sheen, okay length, although it needed a trim. Her daily exercise regimen kept her toned, and an erect posture had been drilled into her since she was five.

The rest, though. . . . Neat brown suit and emerald blouse. At least it didn't have a bow at the neck. Serviceable, some people called such an outfit. She preferred the term classic, and there was nothing wrong with brown. Brown was the color of chocolate, after all. She liked chocolate; she liked classic; she liked grace and elegance.

She closed her eyes, then opened them, looking with a fresh view, and her lips pressed together. Who was she fooling? Panty hose, buttons, polyester, and shoulder pads. Classic and chocolate? Admit it, she'd turned into brown and serviceable.

Feydor might be a bastard, but he was an accurate one.

This was not who she'd once envisioned herself to be. Suddenly, anger reared again. Anger at herself and what she had allowed to happen over the years.

With a jerk, she tore off the jacket and unfastened her blouse, sending a button popping to the floor. Her skirt followed her blouse to the floor. Kick off the sensible shoes. Strip off the panty hose. Down to bra and panties.

Her arms poised, and her muscles flexed. The ingrained memory of countless phrases of music and movement drove her. Glide left, chassé right. Toe pointed. Arm held to a perfect ninety degrees. Keep the form. Comfort came with mechanics.

No! Don't look in the mirror! She squeezed her eyes shut, erasing the reflection of soulless technique. Back bends. Pirouettes, five wild spins. A sketch of dance. Form and virtuosity don't matter. Just feel. Feel.

Familiar panic beat inside her like the quick flutter of feet in a petit battement. Her muscles cramped in refusal, sending a shot of pain down her leg. A sob rose in her throat. Sweating and panting, she dropped to the floor and braced her fists against the hard tile.

She couldn't do it. Couldn't soar. When had she lost all pleasure in the dance?

When her breath and heartbeat slowed, when her tears dried, she pushed to her feet and once again studied herself in the mirror, seeing the flushed cheeks and tousled hair. Better. She finger-combed back the loose strands, but left them down.

She'd turned her back on those dreams, first out of cruel necessity and then by choice. She didn't *want* to be drawn back into Cyrus's world of performance, music, and magic. That world hurt too much: manipulation, exploitation, longing for what she could not do. But, dear God, all these years when she'd danced in private, she'd kept the discipline and the denials—*exercise, don't eat that beignet, give yourself class, mind your form and posture*—and she'd leeched out joy.

She wanted back that *joie de vivre.* If she could not find it in dance anymore, then elsewhere. Flair and style didn't mean bizarre, trendy clothes, just as classic elegance didn't mean mousy neatness. Flair she could do. She *would* do.

Her shoulders drooped. She'd put on a show of bravado to Feydor, but the truth was that finding her stepfather and getting him to agree to a no-holds barred interview was as big a problem as the debilitating stage fright she battled. Finding a little style paled in comparison.

* * *

After a quick shower and changing into shorts, Madeline sorted through her collected mail—bills, advertising flyers, a letter from her rental company. She slit open the letter, read it, and let it flutter down. What else could go wrong on this beastly day? They were raising her rates when her lease expired next month.

The apartment was expensive before; this made it astronomical. Between the rent she already paid and the nursing care for her mother, she was stretched to the limit, and her savings were nonexistent. If she lost this job . . .

Add *Find a cheaper apartment* to the to-do list. And soon. Relocating her mother wasn't an option. Familiar surroundings were the only reference point her mother had, the only thing that kept her from losing touch entirely with the real world.

The doorbell rang. When she opened it, she found her friend Natalie waiting. *My day for women with flair*, Madeline thought with a grin. Whereas Leila was graceful elegance, Natalie Severin was a shag-haired, leggy blonde with a knack for combining odd bits of clothing into an avant-garde style that somehow worked when she wore it. Today that meant a '40s pencil skirt, a lacy top, and a loose silky jacket.

Natalie exchanged hugs, then shook her head at Madeline's offer of a drink. "My boss wants to see me about a story I'm working on. I just wanted to see how you were."

"I'm fine."

"What happened at that press conference? You looked as gray as Spanish moss."

Best get the explanations over fast. Natalie looked airy, but on the trail for info she was as unstoppable as an avalanche. "I've got a phobia about public speaking."

"You? I never knew that! You never said anything before."

"Off the podium, I'm fine—and I'll bet you have some fears you don't blab about."

For a moment, Natalie's jaw tightened, making Madeline wonder what secrets her friend hid, but quick as it came, the expression vanished, replaced by an easy grin. "Then I'd better change my plan to rope you in as auctioneer for the One Night Out fund-raiser," Natalie said.

Not even for the battered-women's shelter where they both volunteered would Madeline do that. "Put me down to handle ticket sales." She hesitated, then asked, "Natalie, you investigate stories. How would you find someone who didn't want to be found?"

"Follow the money. Charge cards, purchases of favorite items."

"I don't have access to his bank statements."

"There are ways. The best bet is to talk to people he knew. Somebody always knows something; the key is getting them to tell you. Who you trying to find?"

"Cyrus Cromwell. Feydor wants to speak to him."

Natalie's face stiffened. "Be careful, Madeline. Anyone involved in that magic stuff is dangerous. Don't trust them."

The flat warning sent a frisson jetting along her spine. "I'll be careful."

After Natalie left, Madeline fixed a chicken salad sandwich. As she munched, she listed Cyrus's contacts and was in the process of prioritizing when the doorbell rang again. She was sorely tempted to ignore it, not wanting to fend off a solicitor or face another friend, but it rang again, and a woman's voice called, "Ma-de-line. I need to speak with you."

Madeline couldn't help but smile. Tildy Maehara, Leila Montgomery's aunt by marriage, lived in a shotgun house down the street and was well known as the block's resident eccentric. Tildy looked and sounded like an antebellum Southern lady, but she had two unique hobbies: magic and debunking fake psychics. When Madeline opened the door, Tildy breezed in, a flurry of chiffon and floral perfume, her skin protected from the ravages of the sun by a wide-brimmed hat and white gloves.

"Hello, dear." After bestowing a kiss on Madeline's cheek, Tildy bent to pet the cats. "Ah, my precious ones. You smell Vulcan, don't you? You must visit him, but only if you promise not to torment Khu. In fact," Tildy continued, rising and adjusting the spray of eucalyptus Madeline kept by the door, "I hope you bring them over quite soon. Tomorrow, to be honest, for I am in quite a pickle."

It took Madeline a moment to realize Tildy was talking to her and not the cats. "What's the problem? Would you like to come in for some tea? Or a cold drink?"

"No, thank you, I cannot stay. Did I tell you I would be gone an extended period this summer?"

Madeline nodded. "New Mexico, wasn't it?"

"Yes. I am studying with a shaman and have agreed to look into a little matter of a woman who claims to channel for departed spirits." Tildy's sniff expressed her opinion of the likelihood that the woman was legitimate. "I hired a Tulane summer student to stay at the house. An empty house is an invitation to thieves." The rose on Tildy's hat bobbed in vigorous punctuation. "Well, my student got mononucleosis. Mono! She's dropping out of school to go home and get well."

"I'm sorry to hear that. Will you have to delay your trip?"

"I feared so until I conducted a scrying, looking for answers. To my surprise, your face appeared in the mirror. Could you house-sit for me, my dear?"

Madeline blinked, startled by the silence that followed Tildy's question. She was still back a sentence figuring out what *scrying* was. "House sit?"

"Yes. I will, of course, cover the mortgage and utilities. I just ask that you be there and pay for any long distance calls you make. You may bring Bronze and Silver with you. I will be gone until autumn." She looked expectantly at Madeline.

Madeline recognized a golden opportunity when she heard one. "I'd be glad to. They just raised my rent, and I was thinking of moving. This gives me some breathing room to find someplace else."

"Then it's settled. Come over tonight after dinner. I'll show you where everything is and give you the key. I'm leaving early morning, so you can move in anytime tomorrow. Is that satisfactory?"

"Sounds good." She had the time to move. After all, she had the next three weeks without Feydor expecting her at his office. *Prudish streak.* His accusation whispered through her mind. "Tildy," she asked abruptly, "do you think I'm old-fashioned?"

Tildy patted her on the hand. "Yes, and it's a lovely trait, my dear. Gives you a pure, ethereal quality too many young ladies lack these days."

Great. A seventy-plus woman who wore gloves thought *she* was old-fashioned.

"Oh, there are just a couple more things." Tildy paused in the doorway, settling her hat firmly on her head. "Many of my books and talismans contain powerful magic. When you choose to experiment, do be careful."

"Not much worry about that."

Tildy gave her a gentle smile. "Scrying doesn't lie, it's just misinterpreted. Also, I'm expecting a visitor. He'll stay in the guest suite when he arrives."

Probably some elderly widower. "Don't you want him to house-sit for you?"

"Zayne? Oh, no, he's not suitable. You should do quite well together."

She exited, leaving Madeline to wonder exactly what Tildy thought she'd seen in the scrying.

Madeline woke up confused and startled by a cat pouncing on her toes. What was Tildy's pet Vulcan doing here? Then she fell back to the pillows, remembering. New bed, new room, new house mate for the next four months. Last night she'd moved into Tildy Maehara's home, lock, stock, clothes, and cats.

Bronze and Silver joined Vulcan in the Toes-As-Mouse game. "Okay, you cats, fun's over." She rolled out of the bed, rubbing her hands across her scalp. Throwing on a pair of frayed denim shorts and an old, oversized T-shirt with the yin-yang symbol, she stumbled to the kitchen, switched on the coffee pot, added food and water to the cats' bowls, fed the bird, and then ran through her morning stretches, breathing in the heavenly scent of brewing coffee. As soon as she could, she poured herself a cup, then wandered through the house, acquainting herself with her temporary home.

Strange sounds caught the edges of her hearing. A sigh, a creak, a snap. Normal house-settling sounds, she assumed, but ones she wasn't used to. The scent was different, too. Powder and floral overlying a hint of something exotic and rich. Incense maybe. Despite these foreign sensations, the house seemed almost inviting. It whispered, not with words but with a lure that drew her inward, toward a heavy closed door.

Tildy's room of magic.

Madeline took a slug of coffee, burning her tongue in the process. What fanciful notions had brought her here?

No, it wasn't fancy, but curiosity. Tildy had pointed out the door yesterday. She hadn't opened it, but she had told Madeline to feel free to explore with care.

Not bloody likely. Magic fascinated her mother and stepfather, but Madeline never trusted the idea. Unlike Natalie, she didn't hate it, but give her the physical—sweat, sore muscles, and a hard floor—any day. Irena and Cyrus were successful because they worked damned hard and held a wealth of talent.

Still, she pushed open the door, which moved easily and without sound. The exotic scent was stronger here, she found, and the room was cool and shady. In the center, beside a stuffed chair, was a table with a mirror and a red candle. Flanking it were stacks of books, shelves of brown bottles, and a jumble of the arcane—candles, a silver wand, feathers, a crystal ball. She opened an aromatherapy bottle labeled Nocturna, took a sniff, and was surprised as heat spread throughout her, like the first flush of desire.

Quickly she stoppered the bottle. That was one potent scent.

There was a CD player on one shelf, and she turned it on, starting whatever CD was in the player. It turned out to be *Song of Magic* by Irena Cromwell. Madeline's favorite of her mother's releases, with its haunting melodies and strange rhythms.

Swaying to the beat, she turned to the shelves of

books, picking up first one, then another, glancing through them. The subjects covered a wide range of topics from exposés of fraudulent psychics to the cabala.

One book piqued her interest. *Powers*. It was an unassuming paperback, with only the succinct title on a tattered blue cover; no author or editor was listed, yet something about it caused her to sit in the chair and read. She had not known there were so many nuances to magic powers. How to steal the power of a wizard. How to wash away power. How to acquire new powers.

A vivid illustration on the bottom of one page caught her eye. It was a tormented-looking man surrounded by blue flames.

She read the caption beneath it: " 'Beware, oh foolish one, to be so bold. For the fury of a genie is mighty and his retribution fearsome to behold. Protect well thyself, for offenses cannot be undone except by purification in the Ordeals.' Whoo, that's dire," she laughed, then glanced to the page top and read, " 'To Spell Bind the Power of a Genie, weight a blue cloth with seven rocks, each the color of magic: white, green, red, yellow, orange, brown, and black. Use three candles of purest wax. Inside the Circle of Power walk backwards thrice around and chant these words.' "

As she spoke, the hairs on her arms rose, as though the air were charged with electricity. From some hidden vent in the room a breeze flicked at her hair. Her voice died, and she sucked in a deep breath. Even though she knew that genies came not from lamps but from the imagination of gifted storytellers, there was a power to words. A power she respected and would not invoke.

She flipped through the pages until another ritual

caught her eye. "The Power for Charm and Assurance." Now, this was more like it. A spell to take away her debilitating fear of appearing before an audience.

"A mirror, a lock of thy hair, a candle of pure red wax. Say these words. 'Spirits of Light grant me this strength. Mind and soul together.' Sip of the bitter brew. As the heat spreads, so shall the power." She downed the last of her coffee as she read the words. No heat spread here—the bitter coffee was cold. The only sensation was a faint tingling running up her hand holding the book.

She closed it with an abrupt snap. Much as she accepted Tildy's right to her beliefs, magic wasn't part of Madeline Fairbanks's life.

She glimpsed herself in the hand mirror lying beside her and brushed off a strand of hair that had fallen onto it. Her face didn't look any different. There was no dashing sparkle to her eyes, no mischievous tilt to her lips, no stunning mystery to the familiar lines of her features. No magic spell from a tattered book would—

The notes of a melodious harp, one single unidentifiable phrase, echoed through the house, startling her. She shot to her feet. Did assurance and charm come in by harp? Only when the music was repeated a moment later did she realize what it was. Tildy's doorbell.

Maybe assurance and charm came in by the front door.

The sound rang a third time. An impatient visitor, likely the unsuitable-for-house-sitting Zayne. "I'm coming," she shouted, and to the accompaniment of the repetitious tune answered the door.

A man, dressed in an indigo sleeveless silk shirt and tight pants made of soft leather, leaned against the house and studied the bell button with fascination. His waist-length auburn hair blew across his face, hiding it from her view. Without looking up, he pushed the doorbell again, then cocked his head, listening to the tune. "Tildy, I pushed this button for seeking entrance as you told me was your custom, but will the tune not change? Pretty as that one is, it must be annoying always to hear the same phrase." He looked up then, and his smile faded, replaced with a smoldering sensuality as his gaze took in the curves and planes of Madeline's throat and face. "Ah, but you are not Tildy."

Madeline sucked in air at the sudden rush of heat that spread like a brush fire from low and deep inside her. She'd asked for assurance and charm. Had she forgotten to mention she wanted them for herself?

Breathtaking was a term to be taken very literally with this stranger, for he radiated energy and sexuality, and his voice carried a lilt that was nearly music. She had known men for whom fitness was a religion, but this man carried height and hard muscle and curved definition with elegant ease.

She couldn't guess his age. He had smooth bronze skin, eyes as dark green as a magnolia leaf, and classic bone structure saved from extreme beauty only by the nose, which was slightly large for his face. That one odd feature took him from merely handsome to unforgettable.

"I'm Madeline," she stammered out at last.

"Yes, Madeline," he murmured. "And I am Zayne."

Oh, hell. So much for her picture of the houseguest as a traveling widower with sturdy shoes, an umbrella, and a well-worn guidebook. Instead, she was going to be sharing a house with this hunk of gorgeous humanity?

"Have I pushed the button on the wrong house?"

"Ah, no. I'm house-sitting for Tildy."

"House-sit?" He glanced upward, as though expecting to see a chair on the roof.

"I'm living here while she's on vacation. She said she was expecting you. We'll share the house."

"Mmmm." A flash of assured fire sparked in his eyes. His smile returned, knowing and interested, as though he'd discovered a delightful surprise.

She'd seen a lot of smiles in her life, but she'd never seen one as genuine. Or as seductive.

"I shall miss seeing Tildy, but she has given me a most intriguing companion for my stay."

Heat rushed through her again as his voice seduced her.

He couldn't have meant that the way it sounded. Get a grip, Madeline. You're an embarrassment, lusting like a teen in heat. She pulled in a long breath. "There's a guest suite that Tildy said you could have. Where's your luggage?"

"Here." He reached down and lifted two bags that Madeline had failed to see. One was a soft-sided duffel, the other looked like an instrument case.

"Do you play guitar?" she asked, nodding to the case as she led him through the house to the back.

"It is an oud."

"An oud? What's that? I've never heard one."

"Then soon I shall play, just for you," he murmured, "and perhaps when I do, you shall sing."

Madeline flushed, then gave herself a mental kick. From his accent, she guessed he spoke English as a second language. She was imagining the subtle double entendres. Wishful thinking.

"I don't sing," she muttered. And, judging by her scintillating contributions to the conversation, she was afraid that assurance-and-charm thing was all wish and no substance, too.

* * *

As he followed Madeline, the lingering energies of a strange *ma-at* teased at Zayne like a wisp of fragrant smoke. The differences haunted him, too formless and elusive to identify. Either the ritual was conducted some time ago, or whoever had called upon the powers was unskilled.

Were the energies simply a part of Tildy's *ma-at*—or magic, as the forces were called on Terra? Or was Madeline a practitioner of the ancient arts of magic? She did not look like a powerful wizard, but appearances were often deceiving.

He gave Madeline a curious glance, his body tightening again. Her elemental appeal had taken him by surprise. The divination smoke had not revealed that her hair was not a single color, but streaks of gold and red and sand, nor that it reached past her shoulders. The smoke had concealed the way her fascinating eyes changed color with her thoughts and emotions: green when she first looked at him, hot gold when he allowed his *ma-at* to touch her with his unexpected and sudden desire. The divination had not shown she would be wearing a slip of blue fabric cut to reveal the shape of her legs or a symbol of the unity of male and female on her chest, or that her breasts and hips would sway with enticing summons when she walked.

His blood rushed low. He would have no trouble performing those functions of a *zani*, he realized with a touch of amusement. But he must be very sure she was the one before he said, or did, anything.

"I hope you like cats." Madeline's comment pulled him from his thoughts.

Three felines escorted them, twining through his feet, whiskers twitching and noses sniffing. He paused to pet them—one black and scarred, one of orange fur, one especially glossy—and crooned a small tune. The orange one and the glossy one purred loudly. The scarred one licked his paws and eyed Zayne with caution.

"That's Vulcan, Bronze, and Silver. They seem to like you."

He straightened. "Animals know with instinct the harmonies of the Minstrel." Or the unbalance.

"Ah, right. Where are you from?"

"Kaf."

"Hmm, never heard of it."

"It is very distant. A place of desert and rock and beauty." He smiled and was gratified to see Madeline's eyes flash gold before she turned away.

"Are you here on business?"

"Partly. Partly my pleasure," he murmured, entranced by the grace of her walk.

"Well, there's lots to do in New Orleans. This is the guest suite where you'll be staying." Madeline opened the door to a sunny room. "There's a sitting area at the end of the bedroom, and the bathroom's there too."

Curious about Terran abodes, he explored the rooms. He tested the sleeping platform—he would have to add more pillows. Who slept with but two and a hard box beneath? Overhead a fan circled, and the windows opened to the fresh air, he discovered when he tested one. The air coming in was as hot as Kaf, but it contained more water. He sniffed and wrinkled his nose. The smell was not pure, but at least there was a breeze and the garden outside added a hint of flowers.

"You'll have to keep the windows closed," Madeline said, "so the air-conditioning doesn't work too hard."

"I prefer a breeze." How did humans tolerate the confinement of solid walls and stale inside air?

Still, the room was pleasant enough, he decided, if

he got used to solid walls that neither shifted nor swayed with a breeze. He came to her side, then slid his fingers beneath hers. He lifted her hands to his mouth and kissed their backs. Ah, by Solomon, more fascinating contrasts. Smooth skin, a musician's hard fingers. And she smelled like rich vanilla. "Thank you. This will suit."

"Don't thank me. This is Tildy's doing."

"But you share the conditioned air with me." Oh, her eyes were of such beautiful colors.

Slowly she pulled her hands from his loose grip. "Okay, well, then, I've got some work to do, so I'll leave you to your own devices." She sidled backwards to the door.

"Is there food?" he asked softly, delaying her.

"Yeah, sure. Tildy left things stocked, so no grocery trip's needed right away. We share the kitchen." She perched in the doorway. "I'll make lunch for us, give you some time to get acclimated. Turkey and cheese sandwiches okay?"

"I would prefer only cheese." To sit beside this woman, whose husky voice held both reserve and excitement, to share bread, to learn her secrets, would be a greater pleasure than he'd anticipated. He smiled at her.

Madeline backed out the door, a delightful pink tint shading her cheeks. "Couple of hours, then."

He had no idea how much time must elapse to fill a couple of hours, but it should be enough for him to prepare and protect this room, to see to his comforts before he drew Madeline Fairbanks into the spell of a djinni.

First he must attend to the basic protections of any djinn place where pillows were laid. And the special protections that would help shield him from the pricking of the vast, untapped magic of Terra, which flowed like a deep river beneath the surface.

He held the door for the cats to leave, then firmly shut it. Finding a suitable open spot on the floor near the sleeping platform, he pulled from his sack the stones he'd brought from Kaf and arranged them in a circle. Now for something to burn. There were no twigs or leaves, but in the room she had called a bathroom he found a roll of fragile, white cloth. He placed it in the center of the stone circle, then removed his garments.

Naked except for the turquoise tablets, he sat cross-legged on the wooden floor. He sprinkled tiny blue crystals over the cloth, then chanted the words that would protect against entrance except by invitation, that would warn of intrusion and ill will, that would repel magic. The thin cloth burst into flames of gold and violet. The chant in his throat deepened, weaving the impenetrable shields.

The flames wavered, then grew higher and more opaque. The smoke thickened with soot as the cloth collapsed. Without warning, a high-pitched shrieking erupted above his head. It battered his ears and shoved his heart against his throat. Zayne leaped to his feet, arms outstretched.

The power of *ma-at* shot from his hand.

The smoke alarm! Madeline's cell phone clattered to the counter, and she covered her ears against the raise-the-dead din. The three cats streaked out of the kitchen.

Not the kitchen alarm; she wasn't cooking. It was—Zayne!

She hurried toward his room, flung open the door just as the alarm turned off, and then halted. Zayne stood stark naked—except for a neck cord with a pendant—facing her, hands outstretched.

His perfection wasn't limited to his face.

Moisture left her mouth. For a moment, she thought she saw a lightning-sharp light spin about the room, but it was gone so quickly, she decided it was a trick of her eyes. A ghastly odor emanated from a circle of stones on the floor, and overhead the now-silent smoke alarm was a mass of shattered plastic. The nine-volt battery hung forlornly from its cables.

Averting her eyes from the magnificent sight of Zayne—he didn't seem to have a smidgeon of modesty, but she did—she waved her hand in front of her nose. "Whew. What were you burning?"

"I burned what I found, some sheets from the roll of cloth in the small room attached."

For a moment, she forgot herself to gape at him, then quickly she switched to the mass of ash. "You were burning toilet paper?"

"I needed a medium through which the spells of protection could spread throughout the room."

She pressed a finger against the bridge of her nose to ward off a headache. Okay. She had a magic-practicing nudist with violent tendencies towards smoke alarms living in the house with her.

"Why do you not look at me?" he asked.

"I'm not used to seeing a naked man in my house."

"Ah. Is this better?" he asked after a moment.

Madeline gave him a sidelong glance, to discover he'd donned his leather pants.

Not better, but definitely safer. "Thanks. What did you do to the smoke alarm?"

He looked up. "It was simply alerting you to the smoke?"

"You don't have smoke alarms in Kaf?"

"No. Why does it screech at the smoke?"

"To wake you up. In case of fire."

"I see, the hazards of solid walls."

Madeline had the distinct impression that conversation between the two of them was an exercise in futility.

"Miss Tildy," Madeline whispered into the cell phone.

"Speak up, dear. I can't hear you."

Madeline hesitated, and glanced at Zayne's closed door. He had shut it firmly behind her after the smoke-alarm incident. God knows what he was doing in there now.

She spoke a little louder. "Miss Tildy, about that guest—"

"You've met Zayne?" Tildy sounded delighted.

"Does the Zayne you expected have long auburn hair? Play the oud?"

"Stunning face," Miss Tildy purred. "Toe-curling voice? Yes."

No doubt about his identity.

"Is there a problem?"

"Is he all right? I mean, he seems a little . . . odd."

Tildy laughed. "Zayne is fine. Quite sane, and really quite intelligent. So what has the man done?"

"He destroyed a smoke alarm."

Tildy's response was another chuckle. "He's not familiar with our amenities. But you're such a steady woman, you'll manage."

Madeline gripped the telephone. "He practices magic, Tildy!"

"Of course. So do I. You know, I would appreciate it if you could take him in hand, Madeline. Show him around. He might be able to teach you a few things, too."

And with that she hung up, leaving Madeline to her nudist, magic-practicing, amenity-challenged houseguest.

Chapter Three

Zayne stood in the middle of the room. He had completed the spells of protection, then added the comforts he enjoyed. The room had no pool, but he had discovered a plentiful waterfall in the attached room. He had even discovered that the water came with the twist of a handle instead of a chant. If he must stay for some sunrises, he would at least have his basic pleasures. Nonetheless, he felt strangely ill at ease.

However much he made his surroundings look familiar, they did not *feel* familiar. There were strange energies in this house, in this city, on this world. Energies that plucked and pulled at him with uncomfortable persistence. And he had naught to counteract them.

On Kaf, his *ma-at* and his music filled his days. He traveled the lands of Kaf; he sang; he enjoyed the pleasures and responsibilities of being the Minstrel; he grew in skill with his *ma-at*. Here, he was adrift in a strange world with stranger customs. He picked up his oud. For a moment he caressed the smooth wood and ran a finger down the taut strings, delaying the moment of testing.

Had coming here made a difference in his problem?

A door at the end of the room caught his eye, and when he opened it, he found a small garden, the source of the flowery fragrance that came in through the windows. Tildy had a rich jungle of plants and flowers, like an oasis in the middle of the starkest desert. He sat down on a bench of stone, shifted on the uncomfortable hardness, then snapped his fingers and brought out one of the pillows from his room.

Much better. He sat cross-legged on the pillow, his oud in his lap. The heat of the air surrounded him; the sounds from beyond the walls seemed muted. A bee buzzed near his ear, greeting him, the only sign of activity beyond the tinkle of the fountain. The fertile scent of rich soil, so different from the sands and rocks of Kaf, added to the redolent mix of flower and leaf. The magic of Terra was particularly strong here, shimmering along the edges of his *ma-at*.

His mind echoed with the songs he had sung, and his throat swelled with the ones he had yet to give voice to. Still, he did not pluck the notes or sing, only stroked the oud restlessly. He was afraid, he realized. He had little reason to believe that simply coming to Terra and meeting Madeline would immediately alter his difficulty. If she were his chosen, the bonds between them must be strengthened and sealed. They must sing and blend voices, make love and share intimacies.

It would take time, for she was not of Kaf and would not understand. If she were the one, he must woo and seduce her, for she must be willing to join with him. He could use no coercion, no trickery; she must want him as much as he needed her.

But he had so little time. While he was here, Kaf and her people were without a Minstrel. The Kafian moon was just beginning its cycle. If he did not find a solution before the start of the next cycle, if he could not sing to balance the *ma-at*, the natural forces of Kaf would be thrown into disarray.

The music inside him would not be denied. He must sing or go mad with the loss.

Hope and desperation were potent motivators. He bent over the strings and plucked first one, then another. Just the instrument, no voice. Outside, the world of Terra still went on. No geysers of fire erupted. No birds howled.

There were no warnings from the spells he had set on Kaf before he left, spells that would tell him whether his music here on Terra was felt on Kaf.

Music welled from deep inside him, and he began to sing, driven by the strange, wild power, a power growing more familiar by the note. This power gave shape to gravelly tones and flowed with the cool power of the flood. His fingers flew across the strings, and the notes melded with his voice in perfect harmony. He sang softly. Volume was unnecessary to express power; a whisper could contain as much force as a shout. He gave free rein to the new beckoning power.

It swelled and flowed through the music with a rush of air and a crackle of fire, demanding its rightful ascendancy.

The trees around him rustled, disturbed by a rising wind. A twig snapped, sounding like a crack of thunder in the quiet garden. Heat scorched his skin as a tiny ball of flame popped into view, then disappeared in a flash of red.

He snatched his hands from the oud and pressed his lips together, cutting off the song. The sharp silence cut through him like a blade. Nausea roiled in his throat.

His warning spell from Kaf had come. The ball of flame told him, as clear as a voice in his ear, that his singing still affected Kaf. The warning was undeniable. Meeting Madeline had not been the simple answer. He had more to accomplish, and he had until the start of the next moon cycle to finish.

Madeline closed the cell phone with an irritated snap. Not that she'd expected to find Cyrus with a few simple calls, but she'd hoped for more than the proverbial dead ends and blank walls. No one had seen or heard from Cyrus Cromwell in the past year. Not since his wife Irena's very public break from reality onstage at the Orpheum Theater. No one had any leads as to where he might be or what he was doing. The man had simply vanished, leaving Madeline to put together the pieces after her mother's collapse.

"If you do hear from him, let me know," seemed the eager general consensus. Cyrus Cromwell was a manager and promoter, the best the industry had seen. He'd taken a classically trained, temperamental pianist and not only married her, but made her into a phenomenon. He guided Irena Cromwell to becoming the top-selling rock female vocalist in the world, and he'd kept her on top for almost nine years, a lifetime in the mercurial music business. Everyone wanted a piece of his magic. Producers wanted his knack for detecting the next hot act. Performers wanted him to guide them into the fame Irena Cromwell had held. An ex-lover just wanted him.

A few of the people Madeline called had asked why she wanted to know—her split with her stepfather was no secret, even if all the reasons behind it were. Others had put out tentative feelers asking if her mother would ever return to the performing she had adored. Madeline had given them no more information than they had given her.

The phone rang, and she flipped it open, hoping it was a reply to one of the messages she'd left. Instead it was a guy she'd dated last spring—until she found out he was researching a book about Irena and Cyrus. Now he hoped to renew their acquaintance, offered to buy her dinner at Commander's if she'd answer a few questions. She told him no and hung up. If he'd approached her honestly from the first, she might have been willing to help. She had no trouble with the concept of mutual back-scratching. It was manipulation and deception she hated.

Madeline drummed her fingers against the counter, staring at her open address book and the scribbled, useless notes she'd made. Some personal visits were in order.

Her stomach grumbled, reminding her it was past lunch and she'd promised Zayne a cheese sandwich. She assembled the makings for lunch, then glanced at his closed door.

Engrossed in her search, she'd barely registered the muted activity inside. Now she recalled the occasional flash of colored light, the odd thump and swish. At least whatever he was doing hadn't involved smoke detectors this time.

Her curiosity was aroused. *Just poke your head in and invite him to lunch.* At his door faint scents tickled her nose. Cinnamon and cedar. She paused, hand outstretched, unable to curl her fingers around the doorknob. A faint tingling ran up her arm, from fingers to shoulder, lifting the small hairs. She snatched her hand back, shaking it to relieve the lingering electricity, then stared at the door.

Nah, had to be her imagination. Nobody put a charge on their bedroom door.

Still, she didn't reach again for the knob. Instead she gave the door a sharp rap. "Lunch time."

There was no answer.

She knocked again, then heard a snatch of music from the garden. He must have found the door leading out there from his bedroom. She crossed the kitchen to the second garden entrance, ready to call him again, but stood in the doorway instead, mesmerized.

She had been raised with music, by one of the most talented classical pianists ever to grace the stage and the most sought-after manager in the business. She couldn't sing, but her ear recognized talent, and she'd never before heard anything so beautiful.

He sang in a foreign language, one in which she recognized no words. One that held no combination of familiar sounds. Yet, his music was universal.

His auburn hair fell across his face, shielding him from her view. He wasn't looking at her or at anything, and she recognized that complete focus. Only the music mattered.

The notes wove around and through her, filling her heart with poignant longing. A tale of star-crossed lovers. She could almost taste the coffee and pastry shared as they said adieu at the foot of a mountain. The wind turned cold, an echo of the cold years they would face because they would not compromise. A tear formed in the corner of her eye, but, spellbound, she could not move a finger to wipe it away.

The crack of a twig and a flash of light sliced through the spell that his voice wove. Abruptly the music ended. The image and taste and scents disappeared with a snap. Madeline blinked, startled to find herself in Tildy's garden.

Zayne remained motionless, bowed over his oud, and her words of praise vanished. Whatever emotions his music had brought to her, his talent brought him no joy. Though she could not see his face, in the set of his shoulders she saw sadness and in the clenched hand resting on his knee she saw anger. Her heart went out to him, even though she didn't understand the cause.

Lightly she cleared her throat. When he didn't respond, she said softly, "Lunch is ready."

"I shall be with you in a moment."

She hesitated, debating about giving him privacy for whatever pain he carried, but she had seen too much to ignore. She went to him and sat beside him. "I've never heard anything so beautiful, Zayne."

"You have never heard a Minstrel."

She smiled at the touch of arrogance. "True. But I grew up around some very talented people. Do you perform in your own country?"

"I did."

"Don't let whatever it is that's bothering you stop you from singing." She laid a hand on his arm. "You've got too great a gift not to share it."

He was silent a moment; then he lifted his eyes to hers. His eyes were as hot and liquid as molten emeralds. He rested his hand atop hers, then twined their fingers. "The next time I play, Madeline, it shall be for you alone. We shall see what my gift brings when we sing together."

Madeline shook her head. "I don't sing. Great sense of rhythm, but can't make a tune come out right."

He raised her hand to his lips. "Then perhaps we shall dance together."

The image she got, however, was definitely not one of dancing. She swallowed. "Ah, like I said, lunch is ready, if you're hungry."

He released her. "I shall join you after I return my oud to its case."

Back at the counter, she picked up the knife and

sliced the bread while she surveyed the spread. "Mustard, lettuce, tomatoes. Needs something else," she muttered. "Maybe some grapes. Celery?" An unexpected breeze ruffled the hair at her nape.

"Grapes would be a pleasure." The masculine voice sounded so close it clung to her like dew.

She shrieked and whirled around. The knife flew out of her hand, straight toward Zayne, then abruptly clattered to the floor. He must have batted down the blade in a reflexive move too fast to see.

"I'm sorry. The blade didn't scratch you, did it?"

"I am uninjured, but I thank you for your concern."

Zayne stood at her side, his body heat enveloping her with a spicy scent that scrambled her insides. He was so close that she could see the thin gold thread that wove through the cord at his neck, the subtle pattern of flames in the silk of his shirt, and the intricate braiding at the side of his head.

She drew in a shuddering breath, then bent to pick up the knife. "Mercy, Zayne, you startled me. You do move silently."

"All my people move thus." He settled onto a stool and laid a slice of cheese on a piece of bread. "I find I am hungry now."

"Help yourself." She glanced again at the closed door, curiosity returning. "Have you seen the cats? They weren't bothering you, were they?"

"I believe the one called Vulcan is sleeping on one of my pillows."

"Would you like me to get him out? Or open the door so he can get out if he wakes? They scratch something fierce if they're trapped." She stepped toward the door.

Zayne crooned something under his breath, too low for her to understand, or perhaps in another language.

"You may not enter without invitation," he commanded softly, and the brush of his voice stopped her. "Come back. Eat."

She tried to will her foot forward, but it felt like pushing through mud. Only when she turned around did movement seem possible. A frisson of unease wormed up her spine; then she shook her head. What she wanted to do—pry into his room—was wrong and she knew it—*that* was what stopped her.

Yet she couldn't resist commenting, "You sounded busy. What were you doing?"

"I shall show you. First, come and eat. I know you are hungry. We will talk."

With one final glance at the door, she returned to Zayne's side. The wary instinct that something was not quite right here nagged her. She picked up a piece of bread and chewed it, her eyes never leaving his. "Talk about what?"

"Tell me of yourself, Madeline. Tell me of your beliefs and fears and desires."

Desires. That single word became all she could hear and see and feel. Hot, needy, she imagined the touch of lips to ear or neck or breast. Images tinged in flame burst across her at the musical word. She leaned forward, until her breath touched the cord at his neck. Her lips longed to follow.

The tune of "Dixie" suddenly burst into the room, breaking the mood.

Zayne eyed the offending source, his eyes narrowed. "What manner of instrument is that?"

"Just my cell phone. And if you don't know about smoke alarms, I'll bet you don't know about cell phones either." She flipped it open. "Madeline Fairbanks."

It was Brendan from The Mystic shop in the French

Quarter, returning her call. "No, love, haven't seen him in ages," he said in answer to her question. "How's your mother?"

"The same." She took a quick bite of her sandwich.

He sighed. "Oh, I do miss her energy. To see Irena Cromwell perform once more would be bliss."

"I'd like to see that, too. Brendan, do you have any idea where Cyrus might have gone? Anyone he might have gone to?"

Brendan was silent a moment. "Sorry, I don't—Oh, wait, I almost forgot. Right before he disappeared, he had me order something. I put the box on the shelf and forgot about it, waiting for him to pick it up. Would you like it? I don't even remember what's in it anymore."

At last, possible leads. Madeline drummed her fingers against the counter. "Yes, I'd like to pick it up."

"We open at three," he reminded her. "And stay open until two a.m."

For a retail business, The Mystic kept decidedly unusual hours. Then again, The Mystic had a decidedly unusual clientele and stock.

"I'll see you this evening." Madeline closed the phone, then found a phone book. One other lead she hadn't tried. A hypnotist crony of Cyrus's she remembered seeing backstage several times. His voice mail answered, saying he'd be in the office until five, so she left a message that she'd meet him then.

She glanced at her watch. Time to get to work.

Time to put some distance between her and Zayne. To give her reactions a chance to steady again.

Finishing her sandwich in record speed, she stood, put her plate in the dishwasher, and dried her hands. "Are you done? If not, just put things back in the fridge when you are. I've got to go out for a bit. Get some work done. Here—would you like to listen to my mother's CD?"

Before he could answer, she flipped on the music and was off to her bedroom to change.

Zayne stared, astounded at her boldness. Madeline had left. She had spoken to others during the meal, then had simply turned her back on him and left. How did she dare? The Minstrel was never treated with such disrespect.

He lifted his arms, ready to shift to her side, for he saw no signals outside her door demanding privacy, when suddenly the music she had begun claimed his attention. The sound was unique, filled with odd rhythms and strange vocals, but he found the music appealing.

Particularly the woman's voice. She sang with beauty, with a clarity almost as remarkable as his own. Not quite—she still needed a richness of timbre—but he had never expected a human to attain this quality.

Still, something about it was not quite right. Something grated, like a sound that was felt but not heard. Unable to decide what exactly bothered him, he glanced around, seeking the chanteuse, but saw no one. Puzzled, he followed the sound to the source, a black box Madeline had poked before her departure.

He peered closer at it, prodding the small flap. How had music gotten inside this? Was the singer captured inside? He did not think Madeline so cruel, but perhaps she did not realize the plight of the singer. He poked the black box, and as suddenly as it had started, the music stopped. A shelf with a silver disk slid out.

He picked up the disk, peering closer at its rainbow sheen. Had the essence of the singer been captured in this? If so, the wizard had used a poor spell, for it captured not the scent and taste, nor the sight and feel of music. Only the sound.

Sliding the hole at the center of the disk over his finger, he lifted his hands and transported to Madeline's side.

She had her back to him. Although she had removed her red shirt and the blue bottoms, she still wore two narrow strips of white. The strips did little to conceal, and much to entice. Instantly, familiar tension gripped his body. Her skin was a delicate tan, with a small blue decoration on her bottom. The whirlwind of his entrance ruffled the edges of her hair, and she spun around, her eyes widening at the sight of him, her hands automatically covering herself.

His mouth went dry as sand. Her breasts were plump and smooth; these the divination had not shown either, but they were as stirring as the rest of her. Ah, but he could not wait to touch her, taste her, smell—

"What the hell?"

Her anger recalled him to his purpose. Zayne planted his feet and lifted the disk. "You captured the singer on this?"

"Get out! You have no right to barge into my bedroom."

He frowned. "There was no barrier; you lit no stones of privacy."

Her astonished gaze flew to the door, still shut and intact. "How did you get past that?" she demanded.

"Transport." He waved a dismissive hand.

"Leave now, Zayne."

Instead he lifted the disk and strode closer. "Who is this singer? How do you hold her on this?"

She backed away, then turned slightly, as if aiming for the door. "It's a CD of my mother. Everyone listens to CDs. It's one of the ways we get music. What's the big deal?"

"Her soul is not within this disk?"

She gave him a wary look. "Amenity-challenged," he thought he heard her mutter under her breath before she answered. "It's just a recording of her voice, with thousands of copies made. Her soul resides with herself still." She inched past him, her gaze flicking toward the door.

Her vehement assurance mollified him somewhat. He reached for her, then suddenly his hand dropped, as he saw more clearly beneath the sheer white strip she wore. The blue decoration! His blood chilled. "Do not go," he commanded in a low breath, and her sideways exit stopped. "Where did you get that?"

"Get what?" She peered over her shoulder? "That tattoo? I've had it for years. Why?"

"Because of this," he said coldly. He lifted the turquoise tablet he wore at his chest and moved it aside, revealing the second tablet, broken in half. He had worn the tablet most of his life, his single legacy from his mother, but he had never known why, or where it had come from.

Madeline's tattoo was also half of a circle. He removed the broken pendant from the cord and placed it next to her half.

The edges and the pattern matched exactly.

Chapter Four

Madeline craned her neck to look in the mirror, and everything inside her grew still.

Her tattoo was the other half of his pendant.

"Where did you get that?" he asked, his voice a silky demand. "Where is the tablet?"

Her gaze still snared by the intricate patterns, one of stone, one of ink, she answered him automatically. "When I was sixteen I went crazy for a while, a streak of rebellion. I got a tattoo. And these." She touched her multiple earrings.

He brushed her tattoo with his thumb. Despite her anger, despite her wariness, a shiver ran through her at the intimate touch. "It does not vanish?"

"Permanent ink. Where'd you get your pendant?"

He ignored her question, his thumb still tracing the curls of turquoise. "The runes are difficult to read."

The chill inside her spread, a feeling that reality had realigned to new patterns, as she watched him. His bronze finger contrasted with her paler skin. He leaned forward, tantalizing her with a whiff of cinnamon. His long hair wasn't just smooth, she realized; there was intricate braiding on the underside, and the ends of it brushed across her skin with the softness of a kitten's tail. Sparks, winking colors of purple, silver, and orange, surrounded him. Zayne looked foreign, almost otherworldly, with the angles of his face and the brilliance of his eyes and the music of his voice.

Who was he? Was it mere chance he came now? How had he gotten past her locked door? Real questions, real doubts arose and demanded answers.

"I must see the runes clearer to read them." His fingers slipped beneath the edge of her panties as though to lower them. A mere brush against her skin, but the fiery touch was enough to break through her unusual passivity.

"Hands off." She jerked from his light grasp, pulled on a pair of linen slacks, and then added a tank top. With a quick gesture, she tucked the hem into the linen slacks.

"I must read the runes on your tattoo." Scowling, he crossed his arms.

"My panties are off limits, and if you can't remember that, then you'd better leave." Tildy had vouched for his character, she reminded herself. He wasn't some mad rapist. But Tildy wasn't here and looking at . . .

. . . A shower of sparks surrounding him? She squinted, blinked, then decided her vision needed a check when the colors winked out, one by one.

Zayne's head tilted as he studied her, but he had visibly relaxed. "I have caused you distress. My apologies."

Feeling on more equal footing now that she was dressed, she nodded toward his chest. "Does your pendant have anything to do with why you're here?"

"I did not think so. I never expected to find the other half. How did you know this pattern? Your choice was not random."

"Where did you get the pendant?"

He hesitated a moment, then leaned a hip against her dresser and smiled. It was not a smile of capitulation; it was a smile of challenge and assurance. "My mother. She told me little of its significance. No human, however, should have the companion."

She lifted her brows, feeling again that lick of fear, that dizzy sensation of standing on the brink of a cliff and not wanting to look over but knowing she would. "No *human*?"

"No human," he repeated. Before she could demand more explanation, he interrupted with another silky command. "Tell me, Madeline, of the source of your design. Tell me."

His musical, hypnotic voice slid across her, inside her, lulling her. A whiff of cedar brushed across her, adding to the sense of unreality.

"Cyrus Cromwell, my stepfather." To her surprise, she found herself answering readily.

"Step—father?"

"He married my mother when I was eight."

"Then you are not of his blood, this man who held the tablet."

"No."

He nodded as though pleased to discover that. "Why did your mother marry two males? Was she not united to but one?"

Madeline pressed her lips together, holding back the urge to answer each question. Wasn't she the one supposed to be asking the questions?

Instead, with an effort, she broke eye contact. She turned away, took a white gauze shirt from her closet, and shrugged it on. "Getting way too personal here, Zayne," she said with her back to him. If she was going to be sharing a house with this man who made her insides mush, she'd better get some barriers established fast.

And get some questions answered.

She started putting her hair up into the knot she wore when she was working, her back still to him. "My turn for questions. Who are you, Zayne?"

"I told you. Minstrel of Kaf."

"Which means absolutely nothing." She spun around. "How did you get past my locked door?"

It was a mistake to look at him. He was still lounging by her dresser, looking very masculine, very commanding. Very . . . alien. She swallowed hard, her heart hammering against her ears.

"How did I get in here? Would you like me to show you, Madeline?"

His tone drew her gaze to his magnolia-leaf eyes. The green had darkened now, as dark as deep bayou waters. "I can show you if it is what you desire," he murmured.

A dare or an eager invitation? Either made her cautious. Still, her heart sped with his nearness, with the honeyed warmth of his voice all around her. "Yes, it's what I want," she answered, breathless.

"Soon I shall, then." There was no maybe in his voice. "Now I would know more, Madeline. About this mother and this stepfather."

Again his voice, a voice of dangerous beauty and mesmerizing need. Cinnamon and cedar, faint but permeating, tickled her senses.

Answer. Answer all I ask. Answer with truth. The words, his words, his voice came from inside her, a command she could not ignore. Nothing in her room mattered but the green, ageless depths of his eyes and the commands of his voice. Yet he hadn't moved; he still lounged casually against her dresser.

"Why did your mother marry two males? Was she not united to but one?" He repeated his question, tenacious in the quest for an answer.

Something insistent and undeniable inside her compelled her to answer. "My father died; my mother couldn't bear to be alone, and Cyrus was good for her career."

"This is a trait of your people? To unite multiple times?"

"For some. Not all of us."

Not for you, Madeline Fairbanks. There was utter assurance in the thought. Or the command? She couldn't be sure which. Or which one of them the declaration had come from.

"Tell me of this Cyrus Cromwell."

"At first he was great. Then things changed."

"How?"

She gave a bitter laugh. "He found out I was adopted. I gather it came as a surprise to him. I was not of his blood, and not my mother's either. His rejection was subtle—no one else recognized it. But I did, and he was as cruel as he could be to me." To her utter mortification, she found herself telling this almost-stranger truths no on else knew. The words spilled out of her, iron filings drawn to the magnetic force of Zayne.

And a worm of fear grew. This wasn't right. *This was not right.*

"He was cruel?" The sparks around Zayne brightened, flashes of color that were gone so quickly she could almost believe she'd imagined them. Still, she could not drag her gaze from his, the green now dark as shadowed moss.

He shall pay for hurting you.

Confusion roiled inside her. Which thoughts were hers? Which his? What was imagination?

"This Cyrus, this stepfather, where did he get the other half of the tablet?"

Sweat broke out on her nape as she struggled to keep quiet, but she could not stop the words. "I don't know. He kept it in a locked leather chest. Most of the things in there gave me the creeps, but not the necklace. Such beauty among the ugliness fascinated me. So I stole it for the pattern."

"You still have it?"

"No. As soon as he saw the tattoo, he tore my room apart looking for it. He found it, but he was still furious."

"A turquoise tablet is not something to be taken lightly. Where is this stepfather? This Cyrus."

"Well, there's the rub. I don't know. In fact, that's my job right now, trying to find him. And I'm not having much luck, either."

He considered this a moment, then straightened. "We shall work together to find him. You wish to locate the man; I have need of the tablet."

"No offense, but I don't think you'll be much help," she said bluntly. "You're a stranger here; you'll just be in the way. I'll work on my own, but I'll let you know what I find out."

"That is not acceptable. I will work with you."

"What can you do to help?" she scoffed.

"This, perhaps," he said softly, coming close. His hand slid down her arm, turning her so they both faced the mirror. He wrapped his fingers around her wrists, first left hand to left hand, then right to right. The hairpins fell from her tingling fingers. He surrounded her, the tall, muscled strength of him at her back, the heat of his arms beside her and across her midriff and beneath her breasts. His hair brushed against her, then slid over her shoulder, like a silken rope tethering the two of them. Desire, hot and sharp and demanding, spread through her like flame through parchment. The tips of her breasts grew hard, visible through the thin fabric of her shirt and bra. She could see the flush of her skin and the motion of her chest as her breath sped up. Rainbow colors surrounded them in a strange, personal aurora borealis.

"Shall we work together, Madeline? Be together? Two as one?"

"No." *Two as one. Two as one.*

"Are you sure?" The question whispered inside her. He bent down, his lips grazing the skin of her neck, his teeth catching the lobe of her ear, his tongue outlining the diamond stud. He tightened against her. "Together, Madeline?"

"Yes." Her capitulation was a drawn-out sigh.

This was not right, her mind repeated. *Not right*, her heart echoed. Her gut tightened with a paralyzing fear, even as her mouth dried to cotton.

The desire—yes, that felt right. With each motion he made, as each kiss drew closer to her lips, she felt to her bones the symmetry and grace of him.

But not her ready agreements, not her loquaciousness. Those were wrong. She closed her eyes, fighting against his mesmerizing eyes and body, though she could not stop the hypnotic chant of his voice.

"No. This is not right," she whispered aloud in a last effort. Suddenly she was aware of the tips of his little fingers pressed against the pulse at her wrists. The pressure was warm and solid, an anchor, a penetrating heat. Suddenly she heard the crooning chant and smelled the scent of cinnamon.

Knowledge flooded her.

He was hypnotizing her. Manipulating her!

With all her will, she twisted, pulling away from the contact and freeing herself from his embrace. Zayne blinked, as though startled by her abrupt movement.

The scent of cinnamon disappeared. The thrumming in her head stopped.

"What the hell are you doing?" she demanded. "You did something. Something that made me blabber like an idiot." She grabbed his arm. "What? What did you do to me?"

He lifted one brow. "You think such a power is possible?"

"No. Yes." A shudder ran across her as anger and fear joined. Had her world gone mad? "You . . . hypnotized me. I don't talk like that to anyone, much less someone I just met. *What did you do?*"

"Merely a Truthspeak spell."

"Merely—" she sputtered with fury.

"You were remarkably aware of the effects. Most humans do not even remember speaking."

Spell. Humans. Too many strange pieces clicked into a picture she wanted to deny. "Yeah, and don't you forget that. I'm on to you now, and we're not ever going to repeat that scenario."

"There is no need," he said mildly.

Her temperature rose another few degrees, from anger that he seemed to feel no guilt about manipulating her like that, and from the brush of his thumb against the back of her hand. Her grip on his arm had loosened; her fingers ran across his skin with a sensual stroke. Abruptly she let go and backed away.

"Who are you, Zayne? And don't give me that crap about Minstrel of Kaf." *What are you?*

"That is who I am."

"Why have I never heard of Kaf? How can you do these things? Come into my locked room? Mesmerize me so quickly? Move so quietly?" *Sparkle like a rainbow. Move with such harmony.*

Inside, she was trembling. Nausea pushed at her

throat, but the anger and the compelling need to know proved just as potent as her fear. Those were the only reasons why she wasn't dialing 911 or fleeing.

Those and the fact she'd end up behind locked doors with her mother if she told anyone she thought she'd been coerced by magic.

"You will not believe the entire truth, Madeline."

"Try me. I've learned some strange things." That nauseating feeling grew stronger as dread and horrifying suspicion swelled.

He didn't answer right away. Instead, his green eyes searched her face, as though seeking an answer to his unvoiced questions; then he nodded. "*Ma-at*," he said.

"What the hell is *ma-at*?"

"*Ma-at* is how I came in here." He lifted his hands and suddenly a circling wind filled her bedroom and sent the three cats streaking under the bed. In the next instant, he disappeared.

"Zayne? Where'd you go?" Madeline whirled around the room, eyes blinking. She'd closed them for a second, but that wasn't enough time for him to have crossed to the door, not even running.

I am in my bedroom. His voice sounded in her mind. His voice, not some hallucinations. Nothing in her imagination could conjure up that full timbre and heated tone.

"Oh, hell, he's telepathic," she muttered.

I can only send you my thoughts. I can only hear those thoughts you would send me by choice. Provided you had the talent, that is.

"Where are you? Did you turn invisible?"

My bedroom.

She raced from her room, through the kitchen, then drew up suddenly, unable to take a step nearer to his closed door.

"I saw your curiosity about my surroundings. Now thou may enter, Madeline Fairbanks," he said aloud, even that simple statement sounding like a song.

She flung open the door. An odd sensation of walking through cobwebs brushed across her skin as she passed through the portal. Why did she feel that if he had not bade her to enter, she never would have gotten across the threshold? Her housemate definitely fell into the realm of—

—impossible.

Chapter Five

Madeline turned in a circle, unable to believe the transformation in the previously ordinary room. The circle of stones in the center held a small fire, but when she looked, it was clear the wooden floor beneath was neither scorched nor consumed. A small, exotic-looking brass-teapot floated an inch above the flames, and from its long, curved spout wafted a green-tinted steam scented like tea. Two handleless cups were set beside the fire. The walls seemed covered in iridescent silk, which shimmered and rippled with an invisible breeze, and gave an illusion of vast spaces within the room. The windows were open, but it was pleasantly warm, not thick with New Orleans humidity.

And, the bed—oh Lord have mercy—was pure sybaritic decadence. The frame and mattress had disappeared, vanished or buried beneath a huge mound of pillows, which were covered in soft, jewel-tone fabrics. Zayne sat in the center, dressed in a short robe of a green so dark it appeared almost black. The robe had no belt, but it stayed closed, revealing only the smooth skin of his chest and strong legs.

His long hair was pulled back, and at his side was a squarish, three-stringed instrument. His oud. He wasn't playing, only running his long fingers along the wood and the strings, like a man stroking his lover.

Filled with a poignant longing, she could only watch silently that caress. His gaze captured hers, and she saw sharp, relentless need in the green depths.

Then the emotion vanished. His slow, easy smile returned, but now it did not erase the frisson of fear skittering across her spine. Who was this man? *What* was he? For no power on earth could have transformed him and this room in the time he'd had and with no more than the contents of a single duffel bag.

"Madeline," he said, setting aside his oud and rising from the pillows with a languid movement. Just her name, but he made it a symphony in three syllables.

"Magic," she whispered, her insides growing cold.

"We call it *ma-at*."

"We?"

"I am djinn."

The blood left her brain, and her knees lost their strength. Madeline sank onto the mound of pillows, then immediately shot back to her feet.

"The pillows moved," she accused.

"They do but adjust to support you," he answered mildly.

She gave him a wild look. "You think you're a genie."

"Djinni," he corrected, giving the word a softer beginning and a lilt at the end. "And I not only think, I am."

She shook her head. "Genies are bald guys with black goatees who come from a lamp and grant wishes."

"I do not grant wishes," he said, his low voice suddenly dark and menacing. "Only a spellbound djinni, slave to the human, lost to the concourse of his people, can be so commanded. And do I look like I could live in a lamp?"

She was suddenly reminded of the spell she'd read,

the binding spell, and a shiver ran down her back. As for the other criteria—one look at his auburn hair and solid body dispelled those myths.

She couldn't deny her eyes. The transformations were impossible without the help of some unnatural phenomena, whether you called it magic, *ma-at*, or mind over matter. She'd been cynical about the effects of magic, believing only in what she could taste and touch and smell.

Well, here stood that evidence, six foot three of near-naked glory.

"Oh, man, what a story," she breathed, her treacherous knees weakening.

Zayne put his hand beneath hers, holding her upright and steady with the touch of his mere palm against hers. "No," he said softly yet implacably. "No one must know of me."

"You told *me*."

"Because I have no choice. Now, you wanted to know how I entered your room." His hand tightened around hers.

A Kansas tornado descended on Madeline. The room disappeared behind a spinning blur, and a giant roar sounded in her ears. For endless seconds bitter cold and fear stole her breath; then the whirling roar stopped.

She was plunked down in her kitchen.

Only when the room stopped tilting did Zayne let her go. Swearing under her breath, she gripped the counter, needing something solid and familiar as she stared at the djinni. He perched cross-legged beside her, floating in the air. Just one more impossible feat that had suddenly become as possible as instant transport and reforming rooms.

"So, you see," he said with confidence, "I have skills

that will benefit your search. Let us decide how we will find this Cyrus Cromwell."

Work with him? After all that? Madeline shook her head. Maybe later she'd doubt her senses and question everything that had just gone on. For now, her shock at the sudden transport had erased her fury. No more fear. No more anger. Just numbness at the quicksilver turnaround in her life.

And disappointment. Djinni or man, Zayne was one more person manipulating her to serve his own ends, whatever those mysterious ends might be. For she didn't believe for a minute that this gorgeous djinni had dropped into her life because she'd done a spell for charm and assurance or because he happened to be in the neighborhood and oh, coincidentally, she had the other half of his strange tablet.

"If you're going to turn me into a toad, then go ahead and do it," she said quietly. "But I can't work with you, not after what you just did."

"Why would I desire to turn you into an amphibian?" Genuine puzzlement crossed his face.

"You're missing the point. I'm talking about your Truthspeak spell. Obviously I can't stop you from doing whatever it is you want to do. I don't have any magic to counteract yours. I can't live with you, wondering when you'll throw another spell on me. I want you to leave." She stopped, waiting for his reaction.

"I am here at Tildy's invitation."

"Then I'll leave." She straightened.

He stretched out his hand. "Do not go, Madeline."

"You going to use your *ma-at* to force me to stay?"

"No." His fingers closed. "Are you not under obligation to Tildy?"

"You'll be here to watch the house. I'll come back when you're gone." She turned to go.

"Do humans value their promises so little?" His whisper stopped her in mid stride. Not because he used magic, but because of the depth of disappointment she heard in his tone.

She valued straightforward honesty, mostly because it was so rare. And she always kept her promises. She turned back to him, and discovered that at least he'd stopped levitating.

He drew in a deep breath. "Stay. Please. I am not your adversary."

"You didn't have to compel me to answer you."

"Would you have told me anything otherwise?"

"No. But you didn't even try another approach. And you didn't need to know all that."

"I am a stranger here, and your world seems very alien to me. How can I know what I will need?"

His quiet reaction nonplussed her a little. "You're justifying your actions, and you know it."

"I am sorry, Madeline. I had not realized you would be so offended. I will not coerce you again."

She had a feeling that apologies did not come readily from him. "Because I'll know what you're doing?"

He gave her a hard look. "If I desired it, you would have no knowledge of what I did. I will agree because you ask it."

"Right. What I desire, you do."

A ghost of a smile crossed his lips. "I am not so easily commanded."

Now, there was an understatement.

"But," he continued, "as you ask, I will not do anything to coerce you."

"Why should I believe you? Or trust you?"

His face grew stormy and the air around him crackled and sparked bright blue. "Once given, the word of a djinni is inviolate. We do not go back on a promise or a bargain."

"So, what are you promising? You won't do magic, or *ma-at*, again?"

"Of course not." He made it sound like the idea was inconceivable. "I will promise not to use a spell to compel your actions." He frowned, then added, "Unless you were to endanger my world. Kaf and my obligations to my people come first. Or if your action would place you in danger."

"Always a loophole," she muttered, wondering exactly what his world and his obligations were that they should be foremost in his mind and first in his loyalty. "Why are you here?" she asked suddenly. "Because of these obligations?"

"Yes," he said simply.

She waited, but when he offered no further explanation, she raised her brows. "Want to tell me about them?"

"It would be difficult to explain unless you saw my world." He ran a finger down the cord around his neck and gave her an expectant look. "Would you like to go there?"

"We're not talking the Sahara or Saudi Arabia or someplace on Earth, are we?"

"Kaf is the realm of the djinn, and it is not of this world."

"And you get there . . ."

In answer, he lifted his hands. That whirlwind spun through the room, and then he disappeared. Before she could draw a second, startled breath, he reappeared. In his hands he held a flower.

"We transport," he said. "Will you come to my world, Madeline Fairbanks?"

Transport through a whirlwind to a world not in this dimension? "I think I'll pass for now."

"For now?" That slow, lethal grin was making its way back. It lit his face with sensual power. "Then there is hope."

He held the flower out to her. This was no flower that Earth could produce. Silver glinted at the edges of the three shimmering aqua blooms. The petals seemed to be in constant motion, rippling like the surface of the ocean stirred by a demanding wind. The green stem shifted and stretched, as though the blossom examined its surroundings.

Zayne crooned something, and a clear green pot appeared, holding the roots and the dirt clinging to them. "In the meantime, here is a little bit of Kaf, which has agreed to come here."

"A sentient plant?" She took the proffered pot, eyeing it warily.

He frowned. "I would not transport and transplant her without her permission. A plant's experiences are by nature very limited, but this little one is different."

Madeline leaned forward and sniffed, wondering if there was a scent. There was, a rich gardenia aroma that stirred her insides. She felt a brush on her cheek and was startled to realize that one of the petals had touched her. A puff of air touched her nose, and the scent grew stronger, more redolent and beautiful. Her breath caught, and beads of sweat broke out on her brow.

"She likes you," Zayne said softly.

"How can you tell?"

"The scent. If she did not, the scent would not be filled with the essence of passion. It would be unpleasant."

"She communicates with odors?"

"How else would a flower communicate?"

Madeline shook her head. When did sentient flowers communicating with blasts of perfume become part of her world? "Where should I set her?"

"She will tell you."

As Madeline carried the plant about the room, the scent first acquired an acrid edge, then grew stronger and more irritating, like smoke, until she began to move in the opposite direction, when it took on a pleasing flowery aroma. At last, she set it on a small stand outside her bedroom where the afternoon light filtered onto it, and was rewarded with another brief burst of that rich gardenia.

Bronze, the orange marmalade cat, jumped onto the stand and began to sniff, eyeing the leaves as a snack.

"No, Bronze!"

She didn't have to worry. The silver edge of a petal slashed across Bronze's nose and a gagging stink filled the room. With a howl, Bronze, uninjured but startled, leaped down and careened around the corner. The stink disappeared.

"Okay, that was interesting. What kind of a plant is it?" she asked Zayne when she rejoined him in the kitchen.

"I know not that particular plant's name, but we call its species *frangipela*. Passion flower." He gave her that slow grin. "Djinn will sometimes set one beside the pillows on the first eve as *zani* and *zaniya* unite. If the *frangipela* approves of the match, it is said the perfume produced is the most exciting in the world."

And she had one sitting outside her bedroom door. Oh, the guy was smooth, she'd give him that. Smooth, and very effective.

Madeline leaned back in the chair, then gave the

levitating djinni an irritated look. "Would you stop that? It's disconcerting."

"Stop what?"

"Levitating. I'm used to talking to people who sit in chairs, not in the air."

A blink later, he was sitting on a mound of pillows that had suddenly appeared over the wooden kitchen seat. "Your chairs are much too hard."

"That's better, Goldilocks. Never mind," she added with a chuckle when he frowned in confusion. She shook her head, surprised that he could make her laugh. By rights she should be furious with him, but there was something about him that seemed so natural a part of her.

And she realized, somewhere between her anger and hurt at the Truthspeak spell and her acceptance of the plant, that she had decided to stay.

It didn't mean there weren't some boundaries needed, though. "Let's get back to what we were talking about before. Your promise not to coerce me with your *ma-at*. Unless I do something dangerous to Kaf."

"Or to yourself."

"How about to you?"

He gave a negligent shrug. "I can take care of myself."

Another understatement there. "I also want you to promise not to kiss me."

That slow smile returned. "Ah, Madeline, that I cannot promise." He leaned forward, and his voice lowered, a deep, flowing river of sensual sound. "For I would like very much to kiss you again. My response to you was honest, not a spell or an artifice."

She drew in a shuddering breath, filled with the images he could paint with simple words. "Then, no love spells?"

"Bah, love spells are misnamed. They are for attraction or for lust. Love cannot be commanded by ritual, Madeline."

"Then no lust spells."

He touched her with that smile. "I have no need of a spell in that."

"And if I say no, you'll stop?"

"Of course."

She got the distinct impression that a woman saying "no" to him was never one of his concerns.

"Although I keep the right to try to change your mind," he added.

"Of course," she echoed, smiling a little. She found herself enjoying this verbal sparring and bargaining.

"And"—his voice softened still further—"when a djinni makes love, *ma-at* is a part of it. We cannot help touching not only with the body, but with the mind and *ma-at*. I can make no promises in that."

"I . . . I wouldn't want you to." Madeline resisted the urge to fan herself.

"Good." His hand caressed her jaw. "For when making love, I want no restrictions, no boundaries."

"Stop, Zayne. You're going way too fast."

"But I have not yet made the promise. You may draw back if you wish. That I will honor." He leaned forward and touched her lips. Nothing too much, no teeth or tongue. He kissed her with the bare brushing of his mouth, and she felt it to the soles of her feet.

Mmmm, you taste of apricot and dew. His unfeigned pleasure, so intimate and honest, was oil to the flame. Heat licked along her veins. Air sparkled and crackled. For the life of her she could not draw back.

At last, he did. "That is a taste of lovemaking with a djinni."

"You are so arrogant." *But, oh, he had a right to be.*

"It is a trait of most djinn." He grinned. "But we have much to be arrogant about."

Madeline burst out laughing. "I can see I'd better get that promise soon."

Though his arrogance both amused and annoyed her, his refusal to promise no kissing made her believe his sincerity. If he had agreed to everything, she would have believed none of it. But his bargaining, and his admitting there were some promises he couldn't keep, lent credence to his claim that he would keep his word.

"So, back to that promise." The smile faded from her, for this was too important for chuckles. "You promise not to use a spell, like that Truthspeak, to coerce me."

He opened his mouth.

"Except if I endanger Kaf or myself," she finished for him.

"And in other matters I shall stop if you say no."

"Will you promise?"

He lifted one brow. "What do I get in return?"

Her insides shriveled. She should have known it was too good to be true. Some impossible demand, or some lewd suggestion, would that be his ploy? Damn, and she'd almost believed him.

She crossed her arms. "A promise is given freely."

He stretched out his legs. "For the djinn, bargains are a sacred art and inviolate. We consider them more satisfying and elegant than a mere promise. I would resolve this matter by our traditions."

"So, what do you want?"

"Cooperation," he said at last.

Her cold feeling began to warm to anger. "Like what? My warming your bed?"

"Well, yes, I would accept that offer, if freely given."

"Accept!"

"Although what I ask is your cooperation as we search," he continued as if she hadn't spoken. "You seek your stepfather. I seek the pendant he owns and answers to some questions." His eyes flamed. "Among other things. Should we work at cross purposes?"

Her cheeks flared with embarrassment that she had read him so wrongly. Or perhaps he was only playing against her expectations. "In other words you want to be partners. Equal. Sharing information. Working together."

He tilted his head, thinking, then nodded. "I will hear no more complaints of coercion, or threats of refusal and leaving, or convictions that I have naught to offer."

She pulled her fingers across her lips, indicating her lips were zipped, then muttered, "Never mind," at his puzzled look. She had a feeling "never mind" was going to be a ready part of her vocabulary for the next few days.

"What you learn, you will share. While we search, you will stay with me. Do you agree?"

"Yes."

"Then we seal the promises." He was suddenly at her side. If this partnership continued, she'd definitely have to get used to that. He lifted her hands and kissed the backs, his lips soft against the skin, the hint of spicy cinnamon wrapping around her. Then he leaned forward and kissed her cheeks. "Thus the bargain is sealed. May it be what your heart desires. Now you."

She repeated the action, noting his smooth nails and strong fingers. He had no calluses on his fingers—surprising considering the years he must have played the oud. His cheeks were smooth, too, no hint of a five-o'clock shadow here.

"Thus the bargain is sealed. May it be what your heart desires."

A shiver ran across her as she intoned the words. The bargain was sacred, not to be broken. She suddenly understood the power in those words.

Chapter Six

Cars, Zayne decided, were an unpleasant, inefficient method of travel. Too noisy and smelly and cramped. He felt as if he were crammed into the revolting bottle of the humans' myths.

A car had only one advantage that he could see. It could go to a place never visited before. Transport only worked for a place the djinni could visualize, a place he'd been before either through his own efforts or through transport with another. Since Zayne had never seen this "French Quarter," as Madeline called their destination, he could not transport them.

Hence, he was stuck in this bottle of a car as Madeline wove too close to the many other odorous, cacophonous vehicles, while thin streams of cold, stale air pelted him. At least, after this he would know where to transport. He closed his eyes to shut out the rushing crowds, so different from the space and leisurely pace of Kaf, and muttered a simple muting spell, muffling the discordant noises and dampening the stench.

At last she pulled to the side of the street, maneuvering with precision between two cars. Trees such as he had rarely seen shaded this area. Their rough trunks were wider than a man's arms could encircle, and thick limbs formed a green canopy across the uneven walk of solid gray stone. Beneath the trees was cool, fresh air. Now, this was a Terran bliss he had not expected.

Madeline stopped in front of another solid building, made of red squares with columns of white.

"Is this the French Quarter?"

"No, I took a quick detour to see my mother. I'm bringing her cannoli from Brocato's and a new calendar—she hangs them all around her room." Madeline stopped before the fence of metal posts and flowers. "You don't have to come in. This stop has nothing to do with our hunt."

He was not so sure, if she planned to visit the woman united to Cyrus. His eyes narrowed. Madeline stood still as stone, not looking at him but at the building in front of her. She gave no indication of feeling, and that in itself was interesting, for in the brief hours he'd known her, her eyes and face had hidden few emotions from him. The only sign of her feelings were the white knuckles where she clutched her voluminous leather satchel on her shoulder.

"Our bargain says we stay together. I will come in with you." He was curious to meet this mother who sang with such beauty yet was fickle enough to join with two males and heartless enough to allow cruelty to be perpetrated on her daughter.

He followed her inside, then behind a door that required her to tap in the ritual of opening on the numbered pad beside it. He had not been aware that humans so protected their domains.

His nose wrinkled. Strange smells here. All was clean and shining, but the mix of pungent ammonia and body odors beneath the soap and lemon was uncomfortable. Moreover, there was a scent of . . . wrongness. They passed a woman who sat in a chair staring blankly ahead, while another rocked back and forth, moaning softly to herself. Each had a second female companion, speaking some low chant.

"What manner of place is this? What do the guardians do to them?" Keenly aware that Madeline had placed her mother here, he tried to keep the horror out of his voice. Perhaps he did not understand the purpose of the place.

Apparently, he did not succeed. She gave him a sharp look. "It's a psychiatric care facility. One of the best, and one of the few that offers residential care; there's a long waiting list."

"What is the purpose of coming here?"

"Sometimes people become too incapacitated to function or be cared for at home. They need special help. This place provides that help."

"So they are like this before arrival? Did they cast wrong a spell?"

"They're like this before they come, yes, but not due to any spell. It's a chemical imbalance, which alters their perceptions of the world. For my mother, the diagnosis is paranoid schizophrenia. Voices no one else can hear tell her things, and she's irrationally afraid of people who mean her no harm."

They passed through another door requiring a ritual number to open, as well as the assistance of an apprentice, into a corridor of rooms. The carpeted floor softened the tread of their footsteps. He rubbed a hand along his arm, ready to leave this place. Something in the house disturbed him, the sensation of life askew.

Madeline stopped at one room. Outside the door, she hesitated and drew in a deep breath. She peered around the open door, then entered.

There was no one inside. He looked around. The room was more luxurious than others he had glimpsed, with a carpet and a thick quilted cover on the bed. On every spare surface of wall were what he assumed were calendars. Madeline found a spot for the one she had brought and attached it to the wall. She opened it to a picture of pink flowers next to a frozen man on a rearing animal. The man was labeled *June*.

"Statues of New Orleans," Madeline said, giving it a satisfied pat. "She likes pictures of New Orleans and Louisiana and places she's been. No people, though." She leaned down and opened a small brown box that was cool inside. "I'll leave the cannoli in the fridge."

A young woman with bright red hair peered into the room. "Hi, Madeline. I thought I saw you pop in here." She caught sight of him. "Who's your friend?"

"His name's Zayne. Zayne, meet Lucy, Irena's nurse."

He bowed. "I am pleased to make your acquaintance, Lucy Irena's Nurse."

"Ditto."

"How's Mom?" Madeline handed Lucy a box. "Here, I brought the staff some cookies."

"Thanks. Irena's much better. It's amazing. She's down in the solar, playing the piano and talking to the staff. Five days, her longest rational period since she's been a resident here."

"Do you think she's recovering?"

"She's making progress. Would you like to see her?"

Madeline hesitated, then shook her head. "You know what happens. If she's improving . . ."

"You come here yet you will not see her?" Zayne asked. Sometimes humans were puzzling. Was this avoidance some ritual that he was unfamiliar with?

"You don't understand," Madeline said tightly.

"You could peek into the solar," Lucy suggested. "When she's at the piano, she won't see you."

"I would like to see your mother," Zayne said, seeing

Madeline's indecision, admitting his curiosity about the woman who had raised her.

"Okay. Let's try it."

The room Lucy led them to was bright with sunshine and filled with trees held in pots. Madeline slipped behind one of the largest, her eyes fastened on the woman at the piano.

Irena Cromwell was a tiny woman. She should not have hands that could reach such a spread of notes. She should not have the strength of finger to express such passion, nor the depth of lung to give such power to her singing. Yet undeniably she did.

He did not know the song she played, nor could he always translate the words, but still the fine hairs on his arms rose, as though touched by an invisible wind. Hers was a voice not only beautiful, but one that commanded attention.

The beat of her song fluttered against his heart. This was not the desire and the pleasure he felt with Madeline. What was it? The tug was familiar, yet at the same time alien. It slithered along the paths of nerve and sinew. He glanced around, catching the enthrallment of all within the sound of Irena Cromwell's voice.

His gaze snapped back to Irena, who clearly delighted in the attention of the audience. Her singing grew not louder but more powerful, and at last he recognized what set his hair alive and what enhanced the wild power of her voice.

Magic.

Magic underlay the song of Irena Cromwell.

He stepped forward reluctantly, drawn by some inexplicable compulsion. The foreignness of Terran magic disturbed him, even as he acknowledged its power. Terran forces were as strong as *ma-at*, but humans did not tap into them.

Most humans, he amended, reaching her side. For certainly Irena did.

Was she wielding the power by instinct, unconscious of its workings? Was the power put upon her by another? Or did she willfully draw from the streams of Terran energy? He could not tell.

Leaning one elbow against the piano, he watched Irena. She looked up at him, her deep red hair flowing across her shoulders, her pale blue eyes fiery with the music.

"I do not know you," she said, her voice breaking out of the song while her fingers still played.

"No."

She turned back to the music, the song growing wilder.

A matching wildness rose in him, jolting him. He began to sing to the music Irena played. She looked up sharply at the first note, listened as he sang the first measures, then without another word, her gaze locked with his and she began to sing an accompaniment, interweaving her magic into their harmony.

His *ma-at* rose to repel the invasion.

The forces of magic and *ma-at* were each too strong, too different to coexist. One must give before the power of the other.

Madeline listened to the harmony of Zayne and Irena, as awestruck as the staff and residents. Her body moved instinctively to his rhythms, as a sharp blade of jealousy ripped through her.

Their house had always been filled with people, mostly musicians. Irena drew them like a magnet. She had been trained as a classical pianist, but she had gained fame by making the classics accessible, and her tastes were egalitarian. Rock, rap, country, soul, blues, trance, ska—all music was welcomed in the Cromwell home.

As long as the musician who played was the best.

Many an aspiring musician had tried to use Madeline as entry. She'd been devastated to learn that her first high school crush only asked her out so he could pick her up and meet Irena and Cyrus. Nor was it the last time she'd been fooled. A marketer trying to get Irena's endorsement for his clothing line, a songwriter wanting Cyrus to promote him, the writer who'd called this morning, had all pretended first to care about her.

So now she was living with another musician and what did she do? Bring him straight to Irena. Smart move. She had gotten used to taking a back seat to Irena's vibrancy, but she had never liked the role, she admitted.

This was one musician, one man, Irena could not have.

Never able to be still long, she stretched her legs with a demi-plié, then rose on tiptoe, shifting a little from her spot behind the potted ficus tree. Zayne did not look like a man besotted with Irena's fascinating complexity. Madeline frowned, hearing a shift in tones and a faint discord. Their voices and their songs clashed.

Outside, the winds picked up. The leaves and limbs of the surrounding trees swayed with a rustling of leaves and a cracking of limbs. The room grew hotter. Terran magic rebelled at the song of Kaf.

This was wrong, Zayne realized. Their voices did not blend; they clashed. Instead of joy, the song brought suffocation. Yet he could not stop. He felt as though a sticky web wove around him and between the words and the notes. A fireball snapped into view before his eyes. This battle was felt on Kaf as well, and both Terra and Kaf rebelled. Sharp pains shot up his legs and wrapped his gut. Sweat trickled down his back as the trees tapped accompaniment on the windows.

A shift of movement caught his eye, tearing him from the notes. *Madeline*, he thought. *Where's Madeline?* He stepped back, ripping a hole in the collecting web, abruptly breaking his portion of the song, and reached a hand out. *Madeline.*

Irena's eyes were wild, almost feral. Her gaze snapped from his face, to his hand, to where he reached. To Madeline.

Madeline. Madeline heard Zayne's voice, full of need, in her mind. *Madeline.* He wanted her. Not the song. Not Irena. Not the Cromwell magic.

Her mother's hands crashed down on the piano, a harsh, discordant note; then she leaped to her feet, her wild gaze fixed on the potted ficus.

Madeline's insides shriveled, knowing what was to come next. Yet she refused to look away, daring her mother to show some measure of sanity.

"You!" Irena shrieked, pointing at her. "Get away." She flung her hands up, covering her face and hunching over like a hag. "Get out. Get out." Rocking and sobbing. "Don't do this to me. It's all your fault, Madeline. All your fault."

Madeline could not move. She could not tear her gaze from the sight of her mother, shoved back into the insane world of unseen terrors by the merest glimpse of her daughter. The dust of guilt surrounded her aching heart.

"Leave me alone." Screaming, sobbing, arms covering her head, Irena slammed a fist against the piano. "Maddie, noooooo."

Lucy raced to Irena, a syringe in hand. With a single sympathetic look at Madeline, the nurse jerked her head toward the door.

Madeline backed away, watching the familiar but always heart-wrenching collapse of her mother. She tried to ignore the shocked looks of the staff and visitors who had never seen her mother's illness; tried, but managed it no better than she could mute the sound of her mother's cries.

The hall was quieter and cooler. She leaned flat against the wall and drew in deep, shuddering breaths. She wrapped her arms around herself as she tried vainly to warm her insides.

She had hoped. Hoped the improvement meant a real advance. Hoped that the sparkling musician was back. Hoped that this time would be different. That this time her mother wouldn't freak out when she saw her.

The questions whirled around again. What had she done wrong? What could she have changed? How could she have prevented this?

As a child she had always wished her mother would pay more attention to her, be as aware of Madeline as she was of her music or of Cyrus.

"That'll teach me to think a wish can solve problems," she whispered.

A warm hand settled on her shoulder and neck. "Do you grieve?" Zayne asked in a low voice.

"Grieve? We reserve that for death. I'm just so damn . . ." She shook her head, unable to give words to the tumult inside—that unnamed mix of guilt and frustration and worry and sadness.

"But with a mind so disturbed . . ." He broke off. His hand slid to the side of her arm, pulling her close in a comforting gesture. "I am sorry."

"Because my mother thinks I'm the devil incarnate?" Bitterness and regret coated her words, but she leaned into the warmth and strength of him.

"Because this visit has made you sad."

Two nurses came from the solar supporting Irena, who was softly sobbing. The tranquilizer injection had finally taken hold. Madeline shrunk back, hiding behind Zayne's solid body, fearful her mother would see her again.

Irena glanced in their direction, but Zayne drew a hand in front of them, and Irena's gaze fixed on Zayne.

"At last I have heard you sing," she said, smiling at him, her voice slurred from the tranquilizer.

Madeline's throat closed at seeing that smile. Her mother had always had such a stunning smile; it captivated audiences on stage and on film. She hadn't seen the smile for the past year. Hadn't even been able to look her mother straight in the face, eye to eye, without her mother's complete collapse.

Now that smile was directed at the djinni in front of her, while there was no recognition in her gaze for Madeline. A moment later, Irena disappeared down the hall.

"Did you just do something?" Madeline asked Zayne.

"For a brief span of time I raised a veil, hid you from her vision."

"Thanks."

He made a don't-mention-it gesture with his head.

Lucy scurried out of the solar with another staff member.

". . . finally got settled."

"Call Dr. . . ."

Madeline heard snatches of their conversation before Lucy came toward her. Madeline waited, embarrassed that Zayne had witnessed the scene, yet now grateful for the warmth of his hand at her waist.

"I'm sorry," she told the nurse. "I didn't think she would see me."

"Neither did I." Lucy hesitated, then continued, "Maybe you shouldn't come back to see her for a while. Give us a chance to help her recover and get stronger."

Madeline raked a hand through her hair. She'd been expecting this; every time Irena caught sight of her she took two steps backward. What shamed her, however, was the relief the suggestion brought. "You'll call if anything changes?"

Lucy nodded. "Give her more time. She's making progress. Her grasp on reality is growing."

"As long as I'm not here."

Lucy's silence was all the answer necessary.

She turned to go, then turned back again. "Lucy, has my stepfather been to see her? Contacted her in any way?"

"No. Not that I've seen."

"Does she still claim she talks to him daily?"

"It's one of the issues she's working out, but the delusion is highly resistant to therapy."

"Will you let me know if he does?"

"Sure."

Outside the building, Zayne paused on the sidewalk. The sun warmed his skin and his face, and it felt good after the eerie, hushed coolness of the building. He took in a deep breath, clearing his lungs of the stagnant air, then glanced over at Madeline.

Her eyes were closed and her cheeks pale. She turned her face upward, as though she, too, needed the fire in her blood restored by warmth.

Did she know of the magic? Did she use it? Other

than that brief moment when he had first come into Tildy's, he had not detected any signs of magic around her. Could it be only coincidence that she wore the other half of his tablet? He was not a strong believer in coincidence, not when a divination had brought him here. Was this why the divination had pointed him to Madeline, not because she was to be his *zaniya*?

Yet already his body hungered for hers. The flow of her shoulders and hips drew him in a way he had never felt before. He wanted to protect her against the pain of her mother's illness. Were these not the reactions of a male djinni upon finding the woman who would be his *zaniya*?

"It is good to be outside," he observed, delaying for a moment talking about the magic. "The air in there troubled me."

"Yeah. It's an excellent facility, but it's still an institution, not a home."

"You are doing what you can."

"That's what I tell myself."

"My mother had moments of . . . confusion," he surprised himself by admitting. It was a fact of his past he told no one. In fact, he rarely told aught of his past. On Kaf, where children were cared for by all, no one would understand a djinni whose earliest years were spent with a lone woman he called Mother.

Yet he thought Madeline would understand and perhaps find comfort in knowing he had shared a similar trial.

Sympathy softened her face. "Had? She's better?"

"She died. For the djinn, such confusion separates us from our *ma-at* and we do not long survive."

Madeline laid a hand on his arm. "I'm sorry."

"It was many cycles ago; I was very young."

"My dad died when I was seven, but I still miss him."

He continued. "While she lived, though, until she sent me away to school, only my mother and I shared our home on the open, windswept desert. We were alone. I still have an aversion to confining spaces," he admitted, then paused.

Normally, words flowed as easily as music for him. Why was it so difficult with Madeline? "I was never sure what her state of mind would be, however, and that was very difficult for a child. When she left me at school, I hated her for abandoning me. But, deep down, I was also grateful I no longer had to wake up wondering. Do not feel guilty for your choices or your emotions regarding your mother."

She said nothing, just laced her hand through his to share pain and comfort.

As they walked back to the irritating car, however, he could not shake the last image he had had of his mother—arms lifted, black hair whipping in the first whirlwind of transport, dark eyes fixed on him in sorrow. He remembered the gentle hands of the villagers, which held him back as he shouted for her not to leave him.

In one of her more confusing actions—or perhaps it had been a rare lucid moment—she had taken him to a village and left him there, telling him he was destined for more than she could give. Since he was still too young to have developed any powers, he was not able to follow her or to transport home. Cycles later, when he reached the start of adulthood and his *ma-at* strengthened, his first transport was to the remote region of Kaf he had once called home.

She was gone; not even a trace of bone remained. All that was left was the broken tablet. When he'd picked it up, fire letters appeared in the air, spoken by the voice he had not heard in uncounted cycles.

"By now, I am gone and at peace, Zayne. I cannot survive with this confusing battle inside me, this battle that takes me from my *ma-at* for too long. Perhaps I am wrong to give you this, but the tablet is all I have, all that remains of your heritage. Wear it and remember, or destroy it and forget—you shall make the choice I could not. Only do not forget this one thing. I love you, my son, love you enough to want more for you, love you enough to allow this wonderful gift I see in you to flower. Never doubt that."

The letters disintegrated and the voice faded; it was the last time he'd heard her speak.

He'd stared at the tablet for a long time before he slipped the chain over his head, where it had stayed all these cycles. Destruction, he'd decided, could always come later, but answers might not.

Zayne stood beside the car, still silent, still fingering the edge of the broken tablet. Madeline waited inside the car for him, her hands clutching the wheel. The wind from his open door blew wisps of her hair around her still pale face, and inside him rose a companion pain to her hurt. If he could have spared her that, he would have.

Had the divination led him to her, not just as his *zaniya*, but to answer the questions and doubts that shadowed his cycles? Were these answers he wanted to learn? Would they bring Madeline more pain?

Good or ill, he must know. He got into the car, then with a wave of his hand lowered the wind and expanded the space around him. He hated the narrow seat, hated confinement of any type. As soon as he had the vision of where they must go, he would transport them.

Madeline pulled away from the curb.

He stretched out his legs. "Your mother plays music with the power of magic."

Chapter Seven

"She and Cyrus were always dabbling . . ." Madeline pulled up at the stop sign and glanced at Zayne, who was sprawled beside her, legs outstretched. A hot breeze slipped in his open window. It plucked at her tidy twist, without ruffling his hair. Beads of sweat rose along her nape. Her eyes narrowed. "Is there more space around that seat?"

"*Ma-at*," he answered succinctly. "I dislike being crowded."

"Useful trick." Maybe having a djinni around could be useful. Zayne would be a handy companion on a rush-hour streetcar.

"I do not do tricks."

There was a clear warning in his voice. Magic, or *ma-at*, was not something Zayne took lightly.

"She did not dabble, Madeline. Magic was interwoven in her music."

"You're serious? Magic? Like your *ma-at*?"

He made a dismissive gesture. "Not so powerful, of course. Weaker than most djinn, but with a strength unexpected in a human. There are few human wizards, and I know of none who have mastered the forces of Terra. Even Tildy, who has studied for many years, does only the simplest spells."

The road before her tilted as a wave of dizziness

washed over her. A car behind her honked, and Madeline started. She waved a hand in apology, realizing she'd been sitting at the stop sign, and moved forward, headed toward Tchoupitoulas Street.

"Are you sure?" she asked, unable to digest the mind-boggling idea that her *mother* did actual magic. People didn't do magic that worked—company sitting beside her excepted, of course, but he wasn't human.

He threw her a "you're questioning *me*?" look.

"How do you know?"

"I can feel it. The energies are foreign; they pluck and irritate. And fascinate." The last seemed tacked on with reluctance. "With the magic, her song becomes irresistible."

"My mother is a great musician. She doesn't need some hocus pocus boost."

"I heard her talent; she has the heart of music. The magic supplements the fascination of her hearers, assures their acceptance."

She fell silent. The world of modern music was fickle. Many with talent weren't noticed or were cast aside for better-promoted but perhaps less-talented artists.

Despite the heat blowing in the windows, a shiver crossed her back. Her sweaty palm gripped the steering wheel tighter. Magic? Was that how a classical pianist developed into a best-seller phenomenon and stayed on top for so long?

"I did not say, however, that she practiced the magic," Zayne added evenly. "Only that magic infuses her music." He touched a finger to her shoulder, a brief touch, and smoothed the collar of her shirt, drawing her attention to the fact that he suddenly seemed very close to her in the small car.

Her heart lurched in her chest, and the reaction had

nothing to do with the driver who'd just cut in front of her with an illegal U-turn. Abruptly, gravel spitting beneath her tires, she pulled onto the shoulder, then twisted to face Zayne. "What are you saying?"

"Someone else could have conducted the necessary ritual. With or without her knowledge."

"Cyrus?" she hissed with a rush of anger. Cyrus didn't care what he did or who he hurt as long as he put Irena on top and kept her there.

"Does he have such power?"

"I didn't think so, but if somebody did it, then my money's on Cyrus." She clenched a fist. "This magic—could it be part of her mental breakdown?"

"I could not tell. I only felt her draw on the powers when she sang."

Magic to make Irena popular and establish his reputation as well? Had he pushed too hard, ignoring the costs, and broken her? Ahead, the city streets swam before her eyes. Oh, this had Cyrus's dirty fingerprints all over it. She slapped her hand against the steering wheel. "Dammit, Cyrus, what kind of a game did you play?"

"Magic is no game, Madeline."

"I'm learning that." Her vision righted itself, the world coming into a new focus. The stinging on her hand reminded her that she had work to do. "Let's go see Dr. Bellows," was all she said as she shifted back into drive and headed up the soaring ramp of the Mississippi River Bridge.

Dr. Marcel Bellows, the hypnotist, lived at the end of an isolated dirt road next to a cemetery. Madeline wondered if the choice was deliberate, for the atmosphere of the looming, above-ground tombs set amongst live oaks and hanging moss enhanced an eerie sense that the small, ordinary house was in truth set apart from the natural world.

Dr. Bellows was a short, thin man, whose languorous voice belied the twitchy fluttering of his hands. He rubbed his palms against his black suit, as he showed them into a curtained room. Madeline took a seat at one end of the sofa, while Zayne settled at the other, looking around him with curiosity. Dr. Bellows sat behind a narrow, ornate table and steepled his hands, his fingertips tapping.

"How can I help you, Madeline?"

Madeline had no patience for evasion. "I'm looking for my stepfather, Cyrus Cromwell. Have you seen or heard from him?"

"No, I'm afraid not."

"Do you have any idea where he might be? Or who might know?"

"No." His twitchy fingers rubbed along his lips.

She leaned back, eyeing him. Years of studying body movement and bodily expression of emotions told her he was hiding something. "You two were colleagues."

"Not exactly. Cyrus had an interest in my work." Dr. Bellows gave her a bland look, although his fingertips beat faster. "You should have waited until I returned your call, Madeline. I could have saved you the drive out here. I can't help you."

"What does a hypnotist do?" Zayne asked abruptly.

"Therapy. I use hypnosis to help stop addictive behaviors and to treat stress symptoms. In the altered state of consciousness, which bypasses critical or evaluative functions, we can reach further into the untapped strength and knowledge of the mind."

"Like a chant will focus power," Zayne said thoughtfully.

"Similar, I would imagine."

Madeline leaned back and absorbed the interchange, content to let Zayne play the good cop role for a while. Bellows might have the degrees in psychology, but Zayne's mind worked on a whole different level.

"Does it take long to reach this state?" Zayne asked.

Bellows drummed his fingers across the glass-topped table, and for the first time his remote facade cracked. "I'm conducting research into rapid induction methods that take only minutes. If you would like a demonstration, I could hypnotize you."

"I think you'll find Zayne a resistant subject," she interjected, uneasy with the idea of Bellows hypnotizing a djinni. The doctor's ethics might be questionable, but she doubted he was an ineffective quack.

Bellows pulled himself to his full height. "The ones most susceptible to hypnosis are not the gullible, but those who have the ability to focus and exclude the rest of the world."

"It is all right, Madeline," Zayne said gently. "I should be interested in learning more about this." He turned back to Bellows. "You may experiment with your technique."

Clearly excited, the doctor pulled up a chair and sat in front of Zayne. "Take a deep breath, hold it, now exhale, closing your eyes down. Let yourself relax. Get rid of the surface tension in your body, let your shoulders relax. It's okay to relax."

Even though Madeline wasn't being hypnotized, the doctor's soothing voice lapped over her, like gentle waves on a placid beach, urging her to rid herself of tension and open her mind. Yet some part of her was always aware of the voice and the technique, of the small creaks in the house and the tiny noises of inadequate air-conditioning.

"Open your eyes, Zayne."

Madeline jerked, realizing her eyes had drifted shut. She blinked once at the small amount of light in the darkened room. She didn't feel any different, she realized.

"I'm going to lift your arm," the doctor continued. "It will be totally relaxed, no strength in the muscles. Only I will be able to lift it."

Surreptitiously she lifted her hand, just to reassure herself. Bellows was even better than she'd expected. He had lifted Zayne's arm, she saw. The hypnotist slowly slipped his palm out, and Zayne's arm dropped to his side, as though it had no support.

Tension spread in her stomach, erasing any overlaid relaxation. Zayne sat calmly, blankly. He looked hypnotized.

The djinni didn't think or act like a human. What would he do with whatever suggestion was given him? Despite his willing participation, what would be his reaction when he found out he'd been hypnotized?

"Bring him out, Dr. Bellows," she ordered.

"One test."

"No—"

"Zayne, what would you like to do most at this very moment? Tell me, and then you may come out."

A slow smile came over Zayne, full of heat and mischief. "This is what I want most to do." He leaned over and kissed Madeline, his lips moving on hers with sensual abandon, while his fingers tangled in the tidy bun of hair. "You should undo this," he murmured. "I would see your hair down loose."

Then he returned his attention to her mouth, a lingering, we-have-forever kiss. His mouth was warm, with just-right firmness, and she felt the kiss clear to her toes. Slowly he lifted his lips away from her, but his hand cupped her chin, and his thumb traced her lips in an erotic rhythm that felt as natural to her as a heartbeat. "That is what I want to do while we are here. Were we elsewhere . . ."

Dr. Bellows cleared his throat. "You're out of the trance now."

With a tiny jerk, Zayne blinked and a singular flash of confusion momentarily appeared. He continued to stare at her mouth, though, and gave her a private wink.

"Well, I think this must conclude our time—" Dr. Bellows began.

Zayne drew his fingers across her jaw, then sat back, his arm stretched across the top of the sofa. "Not yet, Doctor." His voice was almost a purr.

The purr of a tiger. Wild, powerful, and unpredictable.

The hypnotist returned behind the desk, his fingers drumming. "Please, be quick. I have a meeting this evening."

"Did you hypnotize Irena Cromwell?"

"No, I did not," he said primly, his hands fluttering.

"I did your experiment," Zayne said softly. "You will answer our questions with truth."

"Cyrus didn't make friends," Madeline added. "He made contacts. And I doubt he would have allowed anyone to hypnotize him, especially someone with your skill."

"He refused," Dr. Bellows agreed.

"Then it was Irena. What did you tell her?"

"I don't remember."

Zayne leaned forward. "Tell us."

Bellows swallowed hard. Obviously, he too heard the unstated menace in Zaynes voice. "She sometimes got nervous about going on stage and performing. I merely offered her a suggestion that she listen to Cyrus's reassurances."

"Why use Cyrus as an intermediary?" Madeline asked. "Why not simply tell her not to be afraid of performing?"

A momentary confusion crossed the doctor's face, as though he wasn't quite sure; then it cleared. "She performed in a lot of venues, and I thought a single suggestion wouldn't be wide-ranging enough. Cyrus was always there."

Dr. Bellows might be convinced it was his idea, but he wasn't persuading her. Cyrus could have easily expanded on the general command, without the knowledge of the good doctor. "Did the hypnotism get rid of my mother's stage fright?"

"She didn't miss a performance, did she?"

She hadn't, hadn't cut one short either, until the last one. "Did you hypnotize my mother before her last performance?"

"Of course not."

"Think again." She leaned forward, bracing her arms on the desk. "Did you hypnotize my mother before her last performance?"

Dr. Bellows rose to his feet. "This interview is at an end."

"Dr. Bellows, I have no interest in suing you or reporting you to the AMA or your governing boards for any peripheral involvement you may have had in Irena's collapse. Unless an inquiry is the only way I can get the answers I need."

"Answer her," Zayne commanded softly.

The hypnotist's lips pursed, as though he'd swallowed something distasteful. "Yes, I did. But there was nothing different about that night from any other."

"Did Cyrus—"

"There was nothing different," Dr. Bellows repeated emphatically. "Now, Miss Fairbanks, I must ask you to leave."

He was turning belligerent and uncooperative. She'd gained all she could from the hypnotist. "Thank you for your time."

A moment later, she and Zayne were outside in the muggy air.

"The Truthspeak spell is much easier," Zayne observed mildly.

"Don't tempt me," she muttered, then glanced across the car. "Why did you agree to be hypnotized?"

"Because you wanted answers, and I wanted to learn his skill and whether he used any magic in his techniques."

"Does he?"

"He is quite skilled, but does not tap into any Terran magic."

"Were you really hypnotized?"

The smile he gave her was a repeat of the one he'd given her just before the kiss. "It was a state similar to one we enter for certain trances and Circles of Power. One I have mastered many cycles ago."

"So you were pretending?"

His brief hesitation made her wonder exactly where his willing cooperation ended and Dr. Bellows's technique began. "Not about the kiss."

It wasn't exactly the answer to her question, she realized. A frisson of unease passed across her, leaving her cold. The idea that someone could have the enormous powers of a djinni under his control, even if briefly, was not one she liked to entertain.

Cyrus Cromwell sat on the porch of his cabin, a luxury retreat he'd built in the center of the bayou. The retreat was well protected against the curious and the dangerous; its existence hidden from all save him. He stared into the gathering night. The still, black waters of the bayou meandered between the cypress knees and beneath the hanging threads of moss, while the heat and humidity enveloped him in their twin arms. Weather—hot or cold or wet—never bothered him, for it was all part of the nature that gave him his strength.

In his mind he replayed the voice-mail message he'd just listened to. His long fingers stroked his chin, while he considered what Bellows had said. And not said.

So, Madeline was curious about her mother. He'd expected her prying; the girl always was too stubborn, but she didn't worry him. What could she do? Tell the police her mother's illness was caused by his magic?

Still, perhaps he had left her alone too long. She could become an annoyance.

What about the man Bellows reported she'd brought with her? Unlikely that this was the one he sought. Not when he was with Madeline. Madeline had no musical gifts. An *adopted* daughter did not carry the blood of the House of Ninegal, once Minstrels to the ancient kings of Babylon. Only one of the blood could serve his purpose. Nonetheless, it wouldn't hurt to learn more about her companion.

A lance of pain sliced between his eyes. He clenched a fist, frustration biting at his gut. The debilitating headaches, a legacy of Irena's collapse, were rarer now, but they had not vanished. He was not ready to resume his pursuit; Irena was not ready. Careless pushing had ripped her fragile supports. He would not make the mistake of precipitous action again.

Abruptly he rose, went inside, and picked up the tattered diary, the broken turquoise tablet, and the scrolls of prophecy. After the headache passed, while he awaited more information from his myriad sources, he would reexamine the papers and see what else he might discover.

He stretched out on the bed and turned on Irena's last CD, enjoying his creation as the sound of her piano crashed into the room. As for Madeline? His hand moved to his groin. He had a more mundane purpose in mind for her.

Chapter Eight

Twilight had arrived by the time Madeline and Zayne returned to the city. With the falling of the sun came a small measure of relief from the humidity, and Zayne stretched in appreciation as he emerged from the confines of the car.

Madeline had pulled into a large square where many vehicles sat motionless, like beasts perched to pounce on the unwary. How many of these things did humans need? Their profusion was a reminder of how unpleasantly populous Terra was in comparison to the space of Kaf, and Zayne was heartily glad when she directed them away from the square.

The narrow bands for walking were also crowded. After being jostled and dismissed with a muttered "sorry" from more than one passerby, he rested a hand at the curve of Madeline's waist, keeping her near. He liked to watch her walk, so effortless and poised, but he loved to be close to her even more. With a quick wave of his hand, he created an invisible barrier around them. After that they glided untouched through the masses.

Madeline tilted her head. "You just did something again, didn't you?"

"Would you prefer the push of bodies?"

"Not really. But you should be careful about doing

too much *ma-at* out in public. You said no one should know you're here, and I agree."

Asking him not to practice his *ma-at* was about as useful as asking a human not to breathe. "I shall be discreet," he said at last.

"Good. The mob scene would not be pretty if these people knew what you were."

He glanced around, a shadow sliding down his spine as he remembered words from his mother. *Be wary of the humans, Zayne. They will use you and abuse your talent.* "I remember little of my mother, but she had few good words to say about your world. She warned me, if I ever came here, not to trust a human."

"That's pretty harsh, to condemn an entire world. She'd been here before?"

He thought a moment. He'd never really considered the matter; his mother's strictures had merely been part of the fabric of his days. "I don't remember her coming here, but she may have done so without my knowledge."

"With that warning, I'm surprised you came here at all."

"I had reasons." He glanced around. "I think you and I both have misconceptions."

"I don't have misconceptions about your world. I have no conceptions."

He lifted a brow. "Bald? Black goatee? Lamp?"

"Okay, maybe a few." She slanted him a glance. "So, do you think I'm untrustworthy?"

"No." He had no doubts about that. "Only the others do I mistrust."

She stared at him a moment, then, to his relief, laughed. "At least you're direct."

He gave a faint sigh, uncomfortable with the idea of all he had yet to tell her. Matters would be much simpler if she were djinn. As it was, he could not speak until he was assured she was his *zaniya*, that he had not misinterpreted the divination. He must hear her sing first.

Then he had the problem that her world was very different from his. He feared that until she knew him better, and trusted him enough for him to take her to Kaf, she would not understand the vital nature of what he did. She would not agree freely to the ceremony of union and to staying with him on Kaf.

Hear her sing. Earn her trust. Clear goals in a morass of uncertainty. He shifted closer to her, anchoring them more firmly together, compelled by an inexplicable urge to hold her close.

Madeline did not pull away. "Tell you what. We don't have to go straight to The Mystic to pick up that box of Cyrus's. The shop will be open all night. Let me see if I can't change a few of your opinions about Earth, and you can tell me about your world."

"I would like that," he agreed, and realized that he did want to see more of her world. Not the crowded world of unclear minds and smelly cars, but the Terra that could produce such a complex, interesting woman as Madeline Fairbanks.

"Then put yourself into my hands—"

"Most willingly." *Touch me anywhere*, he added to her mind.

She flushed. "It's an expression, Romeo."

"I am not—"

"I know, you're not Romeo. Another expression. I just meant, follow my lead."

While they walked, the warmth of her skin heated his palm at her waist, and the play of her hip as she walked was a delicate caress. He liked both sensations. Almost as much as he liked the faint vanilla scent of her skin, only discernible this close to her. A scent for him alone, as it should be.

Madeline proved an excellent guide. She glowed with enthusiasm as she pointed out small features of the area—the curved metal on the balconies, the porcelain and jewelry displayed in windows, the colorful paintings on walls and doors, the hidden spots of green behind the buildings. All of it began to intrigue him as much as did her liveliness.

He stopped at one window and pointed to a vest draped in the corner. The colors reminded him of the flames of Kaf, and the shimmering threads brought to mind Madeline's eyes and hair. "You would look good in that."

"Me? Really? Seems kind of bright."

"You should wear bright. And bold."

"What kind of blouse would look good under something so form fitting?"

"You would not wear a blouse," he said softly, suddenly picturing her in vibrant colors and little else. He touched her mind with the thought, and she flushed. The sparkle of desire spread between them, airy and invigorating.

"Don't," she muttered. "No *ma-at.*"

"I am being discreet." Still, he withdrew, sensing her discomfort with the intimacy. In truth, his spiraling fascination with her, while undeniable, was still too new to be comfortable for him either.

One day, however, he would see her dressed in colors of flame.

As they continued their walk, Zayne paid greater attention to his surroundings. He was surprised to discover he liked the French Quarter, now that he could avoid the brush of the crowds. The humidity he was not used to, but the warmth he liked. Since both heat and humidity formed part of the nature of this world, however, he chose not to judge the natural cycles. He would tolerate water for the pleasure of flame.

He breathed in deep of the Terran air. It was not fresh, like Kaf. Still, the outside air was better than the car. At least here the air was not stale. A whiff of old fermented grain passed across him, and he grimaced. The occasional unpleasant odors he could do without.

However, the air here also contained sweet scents of flowers and honeyed candies. The rich redolence of gravy and hot spice made his mouth water. From the shops came the familiar aromas of perfumes, candles, and incense.

He absorbed Terra through all his senses. His vision took in an interesting earring on a passerby, the colored beads draped around necks, and the shimmer of heat off the hard surfaces. He felt the rumble of traffic beneath his sandals and the touch of bodies on a crowded corner. Each sensation was imbedded in his memory, along with the sweet motion of Madeline's hands and the pleasure of her touch when she drew his attention to something.

One thing, however, he found disturbing. The stronger touches of magic.

This French Quarter was steeped in the powers of Terra. Currents of magic threaded through everything. These forces were too irritating to ignore, too foreign for acceptance. Unfortunately, he could do nothing to stop them.

Mostly, however, he listened. To voices, Madeline's voice especially. To vehicles. To the scrape of rocks and brick and to the whistle of the wind. He heard the song of birds, the chatter of insects, the barking of dogs, and the meowing of cats. Doors slamming, beads rattling, whistles blowing all wove together in a symphony of sound.

As he listened to the patterns and the play of notes, noise became sound, and sound became music. He hummed a piece of a tune, blending it with the melodies of life around him. For despite the drawbacks, despite the thick air and the water, despite the magic, above all else one thing made this Quarter very appealing. Music.

Music was everywhere. Bits and snatches of music came from the insides of the buildings and flowed onto the street. Performers stood on the sidewalk with their instruments and their dancing and their songs. Some of it was not good, none of it contained the full sensory experiences of djinn song, but, oh, there were flashes of pure beauty and intriguing rhythm. And for that he could forgive much.

"I did not realize Terra had so much music in the air," he told Madeline.

"New Orleans is a very musical town. Let me show you the true heart of the city." She took his hand, her smaller fingers wrapping around his in appealing contact, and led him past several corners to stop outside a building.

With her, he stood and watched and listened to the performers inside the dark and foggy room. Three males with skin darker than most djinn performed from a raised platform. Focused lights highlighted them and the sheen of their skin, the whiteness of their eyes and teeth, and the gray of their fleecelike hair. Two sat, one behind a collection of drums, one with a stringed instrument as tall as he. The third stood and played a golden trumpet.

High, clear, crisp notes spun into the room like glimmering fairies. The stringed instrument sounded a low countermelody, while the drums kept it all together with a constant beat. The rhythm was uneven, long-drawn-out notes coupled with a race of scales, but oddly compelling because of its sheer unpredictability. The melody wove through in small sequences of notes that hinted at the whole. Even the drums added variations while maintaining the integrity of the beat.

He absorbed the music, each note and nuance. This style so fresh and odd—could he use it? Could he feel this Terran music the way the performers did? How would the djinn hear this music? Could he touch Kaf with its sheer beauty?

A new melody took form in his mind as he listened. He stood, fascinated, until the musicians took a break.

"You like improvisational jazz?" Madeline asked in a low voice.

"If that is what this music is called, then yes. Very much."

"Would you like to meet the musicians?"

"Do you know them?"

"I know just about anyone who's played, sung, or danced in this town."

She wove through the narrow spaces between the tiny tables. The thick smoke in the room irritated his throat and eyes; he was glad when she waved to the man standing behind the long wooden table and they escaped to a short hallway. Remnants of the smoke lingered in the dusty, stale air, but at least he could breathe. She knocked on the warped wooden slats of a door; then, when a raspy voice bade them to enter, he followed her inside.

The three musicians were lounging on chairs and chaise. They passed a thin tube between them, each sucking on the end and then releasing a small stream of smoke before passing the tube. Two of them held metal cylinders labeled *Dixie beer*; one held a clear container labeled *spring water*. All three broke into wide smiles when they saw her.

"Madeline Fairbanks," boomed the one with the grayest hair, the horn player. "As I live and breathe."

"Hey, Earl. BJ, Lyle. How you doing?"

"Fine, fine, but we ain't seen you in a month of Sundays. Heard you was off to college."

"I was. Now I'm back, working for Feydor Blaze. You know—can't take the girl out of New Orleans."

"Ain't that the truth."

"How's yo momma doing?" asked the one who had played the strings.

"She has her good days, Lyle."

"Any chance we'll see her on stage any day soon?"

"One day, maybe. I hope. Congratulations on Lyle Junior getting his degree from Xavier last month. Bet you're mighty proud."

"Shor am. Thanks for the check you sent."

"You're welcome."

"How 'bout you?" asked the drum player. "Doin' okay?"

"I am, BJ. Thanks." Madeline smoothed her hands down her pants. "I was wondering if any of you've talked to Cyrus recently."

"No, sorry," was the general response as the conversation flowed around Zayne like an easy river. Madeline's voice, he noticed, changed as she spoke. The vowels got longer, the consonants less precise.

"Say, fellas, there's someone I want you to meet," she said. "This is my friend, Zayne. He's a musician, too, but he's never heard jazz."

"Never heard jazz?" Earl made it sound like he'd committed some disgrace. "You're not from around here?"

"No, I'm from Kaf."

"Never heard of it," said Earl, obviously dismissing as unimportant any place that he didn't know and that had never been exposed to jazz. "What do you play?"

"Mostly an oud."

"It's like a guitar," offered Madeline.

"What do you call that tall instrument you play?" he asked Lyle.

"Bass fiddle." Lyle took a deep breath of the circulating tube, passed it on to BJ, and then rummaged behind him. "Here, I've got a six string. Why don't you play a bit for us?"

Zayne hesitated, torn between his need to create music and his fear of the consequences.

"Try it," Madeline urged, her foot tapping as though eager to hear him play.

"I shall try." He took the instrument, fingering the smooth wood and taut strings. He plucked each one, listening to the sound. "This instrument is very pure in tone."

Lyle beamed. "Yeah, it's a good one. Now show us what you've got."

He got the feeling they didn't expect much. He played the first notes of the melody spinning through him. Earl, BJ, and Lyle fell silent, listening.

The song consumed him, but he carefully kept *ma-at* at bay, not adding the sensory experience his people expected. For now, only the song, the notes and tempos, mattered. The music and Madeline, sitting beside him, a smile lighting her changeable eyes.

BJ set down his metal cannister and began to thump his fingers on a table, keeping the beat as he had with the drum. Earl hummed, a pursed-lip sound that imitated the trumpet. Lyle watched him play.

Such a strange feeling it was to play with others.

Always, the Minstrel played alone, unless he was joined by his *zaniya*. Earl altered the melody a little, and Zayne frowned, not expecting another to take such liberties. Yet he played on. The variation was not so bad. Not what he would have done, but still . . . interesting. BJ slid his fingers across the table in an imitation brush. Zayne mimicked the sound with the guitar.

"Oh, ho," breathed Lyle.

The song ended, and the trio glanced back and forth.

"You're good for a white boy," observed Earl.

"You like to sit with us for a couple of songs next set?" BJ asked casually. "We're getting ready to go back on."

Reluctantly Zayne set aside the guitar. Those last measures, he had felt the *ma-at* and the strange powers rising within him, demanding release in the song. Indeed, they still swirled inside him, ready to join the battle for ascendancy. "We have a person we must meet."

"We have time," Madeline interjected softly. "A couple of songs. I would like to see you perform."

He glanced at her, reluctant to refuse her anything. He took in the light reflecting off her hair, the brilliance of her eyes, and the prim neatness of her attire. But beneath the very human exterior she wore the other half of his tablet. She decorated her ears with gems, and she should be dressed in the vibrant color of djinn passions. She desired to hear a Minstrel of Kaf play improvisational jazz with three Terran musicians.

Inside him, as he absorbed the complexities of Madeline, the powers of *ma-at* and of magic shifted and blended for a brief moment. A fragment of melody wound through him, the melody he had just played, but this time it contained not a battle of forces but a combination of the two.

Suddenly he was anxious to try once again the strange music and the stranger experience of sharing the music with these three men. "Two songs only."

"Let's go, then." Lyle held out the smoking tube. "You want a hit before we go?"

He gave a quizzical glance at the tube. Was this some kind of human ritual in which he should partake?

Madeline made the decision. "No, he doesn't. Not his style."

The threesome accepted the choice with nonchalance, stubbing out the fire at the tip of the tube.

"What was that ritual?" he whispered as they followed Earl, BJ, and Lyle to the stage. "If I am to appear part of your world, should I have taken it?"

"A high djinni? No, I don't think that would be a good thing."

He glanced at her, puzzled.

"I'll explain later."

The next moment, he found himself on stage.

Zayne was good. She had not appreciated how good when she heard him in the garden, Madeline realized. But seeing the way he had picked up on a music form strange to him, how he had embraced the unique sound and soul of jazz, she realized how talented he was. While he was on stage, he drew every eye of the audience. Normally, bars had a few devoted listeners while the rest of the audience carried on a dozen separate conversations and waiters snaked their way through the crowded aisles.

Not when Zayne was singing. Conversation ceased. A waiter set the glass of ice water she'd requested on the table, then stood, clutching his tray, rapt. Zayne seemed completely oblivious to the attention. His focus was on the music. Earl, BJ, and Lyle were some of the best, but with Zayne on stage they literally shone. Their spotlights took on a luminous glow, while an aura of sparkling white surrounded Zayne. Maybe he was using his *ma-at*, but if so, that was only an enrichment of his own essence. This was who and what he was.

He was a musician, she admitted as she sat alone at a tiny, darkened table off to one side. A musician as devoted as her mother had been. She smoothed a stray hair into the twist at the back of her head, tidying and neatening. She didn't want to get pulled back into that world. For her peace of mind, she couldn't allow it.

With musicians, the music always came first. She knew that. She accepted it. She'd lived it.

But she didn't have to live with that reality, not anymore. She couldn't. *Never get involved with a musician*—the motto had worked for a lot of years and she wasn't about to break it with someone who had the added burden of being from another world.

So, anything happening between her and Zayne was of the short-term variety, and she'd better remember that.

Then she gave a rueful shake of her head. Although it seemed forever ago, she'd met the man this morning. Already she was thinking in terms of ending a relationship? When one hadn't even started?

"A lot premature," she muttered, lifting the glass of water to drink.

Still, there was something about the way Zayne looked at her, something in the way he touched her that made her think of strings of endless days. And nights.

She took a slug of water. Maybe the ice would chill her down. Zayne was flamboyant, talented, determined. He could have the pick of any woman, including the gay female impersonators, in this room. Why would he be interested in her?

Of course, the flip side of that was, if his interest wasn't simply a powerful sexual attraction, what could he possibly want from her? He was a djinni, for mercy's sake. There wasn't much he couldn't do on his own. What could she have that he would want?

Admittedly, the turquoise tablet was a puzzle and maybe she was being foolish, but she believed him when he said he didn't know Cyrus and hadn't known about the tablet before he arrived. He hadn't even been coming to see her, he'd been coming to see Tildy. He'd been surprised to see her there.

He had a reason for coming, he admitted that, but it couldn't be because he wanted something from her. His business didn't concern her. It was probably some djinn, *ma-at* thing. Something that she'd have to know his culture to understand, as he said.

She glanced over the edge of her glass toward the stage. Zayne had looked up from the guitar, she found, and his gaze was fixed on her. He held out his hand to her.

Come, join me, his voice inside her mind urged.

Frantically she shook her head, the wings of panic beating at the mere suggestion she should step onto that stage. *No*, she mouthed back.

He hesitated a moment, then returned both hands to the guitar.

As you desire, Madeline. I shall join you there instead.

He didn't move, though. He smiled at her, his gaze never leaving hers. The trio faded; all she could see was him, sitting in the middle of a crystalline spotlight. Zayne's song did not miss a beat, but she knew he sang not to the audience or for himself, but only to her.

For the first time in her life she felt included, not

ignored, during someone else's performance.

Only when Zayne finished, when he returned the guitar to Lyle and acknowledged the applause with a tilt of his head, could she pull in a deep breath. He glided off the stage, paying no attention to the audience, straight to her.

Oh, damn, he was dangerous, and she'd better let her brain put a curb on her emotions. He was a musician; he was a djinni. Music and magic. This had heartbreak written all over it.

Wordlessly he threaded his fingers through her hair, cradling her head between his hands, loosening her careful hairdo.

Then he kissed her.

A kiss of heat. A kiss of strength. Need, desire, jubilation—the emotions danced inside her like sparkling raindrops, almost as if she felt what he felt and shared what drove him. Pinpoints of brilliant blue and gold and orange glistened against her eyelids.

Mine. The word was so faint she barely understood it. An echo from him? Or from her inner longing?

For all its intensity, the kiss was brief. So brief she had no time to react, only enjoy. Then he leaned his forehead against hers. "Thank you," he whispered.

"You're welcome." Tingling lips could barely form the words. "For what?"

"For giving me this music." He straightened; his fingers traced a pattern around her ear and neck, before he let them fall to his side. "For freeing my song."

The kiss must have scrambled her. What was he talking about? When she opened her mouth to ask, however, he continued very matter-of-factly, "I have kept my promise. Two songs. Now we leave."

Heart thumping against her chest, Madeline breathed, "Yes."

He didn't touch her again. He didn't need to. His heat and strength radiated across her, and as they left the bar, once more he enveloped her with his power.

Let her brain curb her emotions? The rest of her wasn't listening, and the brain was fast giving up the fight.

Joy. Freedom. Zayne embraced the rare sensations as they spun through him.

Madeline had given him this. He held her closer, shielding her from the small knot of youths who demanded the entire walkway as they came down the street. Absently he muttered a quick enchantment, and the two of them slipped between the youths, almost unseen. A minor inconvenience next to the pleasure that filled him.

For too many turns of the sun he had played beside the specter of uncontrolled power and disaster. For longer, he had played as Minstrel, one part of the fabric of *ma-at*. He had forgotten what it felt like to simply play. To sing for naught but the enjoyment of the notes.

Mindful of his world's safety, he had not drawn on his *ma-at* just now; he'd relied only on the power of his voice. Again unbidden, though, that strange force had risen, pulsing in time with the uneven rhythm and adding to the rich harmony of the jazz. As though this was the music the power had long waited for and finally had found its home.

Except *ma-at* was too much a part of him, too much entwined with his music and his soul, to be denied. His essential force had not waited to be summoned. It rose like a flame swirling within him, threatening to consume both power and jazz.

Until he had caught a glimpse of Madeline. Alone,

watching him, her face in shadow and smoke.

He had seen the rise and fall of her breasts in the rhythm he played, and from then on, he'd thought of nothing but her and the music. Madeline as she had shared the joys of her world, her easy grace, and her warm laughter. She had not joined him in song, but he had seen and felt and even heard the unconscious sway of her body in time to his voice.

The powers did not fade within him. Instead, they strengthened and flowed out and around Madeline, then back to him, now intertwined. Their battle became energy he controlled and used until he was left with the music and with Madeline, with creative freedom, unfettered pleasure, and hot desire.

Somehow Madeline had transformed the beast inside and helped him control his music.

His problem was not solved. The two forces were still opposed, and only a small bit of their strength had become part of the music, unlike when he played on Kaf. He still did not have the control and balance he needed.

He had hope, though. How much stronger would he be when Madeline sang with him?

For tonight, though, he had the echo of a melody, a hot sultry night, a quest, and Madeline. A woman who confused him by the contrast of her bound hair and plain clothes with her sensuous lips and fluid motion, who excited him by the mere touch of her scent or the unpredictable color of her eyes.

Tonight, surely, he could not question that he had found his *zaniya*.

One final proof remained—for her to sing with him.

Chapter Nine

As they walked, Madeline looked up at the night sky. Nighttime humidity was thinner and the air cooler without the rays of sun piercing it. "I like New Orleans at night. That's one of the nice things about working with Feydor; I don't think he's ever seen the dawn side of noon, so I don't have to get to work early."

"Night on Kaf is beautiful, too," Zayne observed. "We have so many stars."

She thought she detected a wistful note in his voice. Stars weren't visible here, the reflected lights of the city muted them, but the moon was near full. "Do you have a moon, too?"

"Yes."

"You miss Kaf, don't you?"

"It is my home," he answered simply, and that was answer enough. When she was away at school, missing New Orleans was a hungry ache that never really went away. She had missed the taste of boiled crawfish, the sound of rolling waves at the lakefront, even the daily rain showers. At least, though, she had been on her own world.

"Tell me of Kaf," she suggested. "What does it look like, smell like. What food do you eat? Are there a lot of djinn?"

He shrugged. "Many fewer than humans. Our land

is harsh, but beautiful with a sun that sets a brilliant red, vibrant desert colors, and the caress of a hot breeze."

"Flowers like the *frangipela*?"

"Many flowers. Fruit trees." He stopped a moment, to stare at the Mississippi River. "Our water is mostly in wells, ponds, and small streams. We have few large bodies of water. Our longest river is one of fire. To see all that water flowing is strange."

"I come here when I need down time. Get a café au lait and sit and watch the river. It can flow so lazy you'd think it was a pool. Other times, it's muddy and churning, ready to burst the banks, and sometimes the surface doesn't seem to move, but beneath it you can see the ripples of treacherous undertow."

"I never thought there could be such variety in water."

"While I think of deserts as wastelands of yellow sand," she said with a smile.

"The variety is as amazing as your water," he answered with a laugh, then glanced down at her. "I should like you to see my world."

His suggestion was casual, but Madeline bit back her automatic, breezy refusal, sensing it was important to him. She stopped in the center of the sidewalk, letting the night crowds flow around them. The wind ruffled across them, setting his earring moving, yet his hair stayed a smooth curtain across his shoulders. Kaf was a place of *ma-at*, another world. She was uncomfortable with the idea of letting him transport her to a place she could not escape without his aid.

This was the second time he had mentioned it, she realized.

As if sensing her doubts and fears, Zayne caressed her cheek. "It will not happen tonight, though."

The clutching of her stomach was part fear, part desire. And part hunger as her stomach gurgled, reminding her that other than stopping at a gas station on the way from Dr. Bellows's for Cokes and candy bars—Zayne had a sweet tooth and a fondness for Snickers, she'd discovered—she hadn't eaten since the luncheon sandwich.

"We should break our fast before we enter this magic shop," Zayne said.

"Are you sure you aren't telepathic?"

"Telepathic I am not." He grinned. "But my hearing is good, and my stomach also feels empty. Are there Snickers available?"

"We need something more substantial. Ever had an oyster po'boy?" All of a sudden she had a craving for one, and to hell with diets.

"It is a food I am unfamiliar with."

"You'll love it." A short time later she handed him half of the French loaf, laden with fried oysters and dressed with mayonnaise, lettuce, and tomato.

He twisted it in his hands. "Are all human meals served between slices of bread?"

She laughed. "No, not all. But I end up eating a lot of mine that way, it seems." She bit into the po'boy. "Mmmm, good oysters."

"Why?" he asked before taking a mouthful.

"Why are the oysters good?"

"Why do you eat your meals between slices of bread?"

"Busy, and I'm not much for cooking. Do you like it?"

He tasted another mouthful before answering. "The bread is crusty with much flavor, but there should be more spice to the rest."

"Next time I'll add Tabasco. It can be an acquired taste."

"This would be good with slices of roasted goat seasoned with pepper and curry."

"I'm not sure you'd have a po'boy then. Goat's never been on the menu."

"So, do you like spice?" His lids half lowered, sleepy, sexy, and inviting. "The more unique and potent the flavor, the more I like it."

She should be expecting the cayenne heat that flashed through her, but her unrestrained response whenever he looked at her like that, whenever she read more into his offhand comments, still had the power to startle. She handled it by taking him literally. "If you want spicy, you've come to the right town. Wait until you taste boiled crawfish and gumbo."

"You have not tasted roasted goat." He took another bite of crusty bread, somehow managing not to drop crumbs like she was. "The oysters are a new flavor for me. I like them. Thank you for sharing this."

While they were in the bar, the clientele of the French Quarter had shifted. Fewer families with kids roamed the sidewalks, and the tourists with Bermuda shorts and cameras had given way to Goth and vice. The denizens of the evening now claimed the streets of their city.

Zayne fit into either world, and drew the notice of both, she realized. Normally, she slid through crowds unnoticed. Not with Zayne at her side. Tension prickled down her spine and lodged in her gut with a twittering unease. She pulled at the collar on her shirt, suddenly finding breathing difficult.

A woman in a leopard-skin body suit and high heels slid her gaze across Madeline toward Zayne. Madeline pulled in a long breath. She wasn't onstage; no one noticed her at all. Her panic eased, replaced by embarrassment at her self-absorption.

The attention was all for Zayne. He wasn't overly tall or muscle bound, the kind that attracted attention with physical dominance. His leather pants and sleeveless indigo shirt weren't odd attire here, and even his long auburn hair wasn't out of place.

When had he added a dangling silver earring to his left ear? Her heart triple-timed as she drank in the subtle, sexy transformation.

Zayne's mutable attire, even when it gave him a greater exotic appeal, wasn't what drew attention to him, though. He glided through the streets with an assurance and a detachment that couldn't fail to be noticed. He had what Feydor had talked about, that elusive presence.

She caught a glimpse of the two of them in a window. If anyone looked at her, it was only to wonder what the lion was doing with the mouse.

"We need to turn there." She pointed to the corner ahead, by way of derailing her unappealing thoughts. "Brendan's store is two blocks up, on the right."

They passed two strolling ladies of the evening, but Zayne did not bother to look at them. His eyes were only for her. For all the attention he received, she realized, he paid it no mind. Like when he sang, his attention was on his actions. Or on her, and the rest of the world could go their separate ways.

A knot formed in her stomach. Being the focus of anyone's attention was difficult for her. Especially someone as intense as Zayne. A man with a mysterious purpose. A man who had used a Truthspeak spell without hesitation. A man who held the second half of her stepfather's turquoise necklace. A man who breathed sensuality.

"What is wrong?" Zayne rested a hand lightly atop her sleeve, drawing her attention. "Your eyes reflect brown."

Definitely disconcerting. She shook her head, tossing the last bit of her po'boy into the garbage. "Nothing. Nothing's wrong."

He hesitated, then apparently decided he shouldn't press her on the matter. Instead, he commented unexpectedly, "You move with grace. It is difficult to stay within the shield of another djinni, yet your movements mirror mine. Do you dance?"

"Not anymore." At least, not for anyone but herself, and ultimately, to remain vital, a dancer needed the presence of an audience.

He tilted his head, watching her a moment, then surprised her by not asking why she'd quit. "What styles did you dance?"

"Ballet." Ten years. "Modern." Five years. "A smattering of others." A childhood of lessons, an adulthood of dancing alone. "Once I even tried to learn *raqs sharqi*, as the teacher called it. Here, we call it belly dancing."

His lips curved into a warm smile. "Ah, *raqs sharqi*. The Dance of the Women. It is a rare privilege for a male to see such a performance in my world. I never have."

She smoothed a strand of hair back into place, suddenly embarrassed that she'd revealed so much. If only Zayne weren't so easy to talk to, even without that darn Truthspeak spell. "I don't think I was very good. Or authentic." The video she'd tried to learn from was good, but she'd missed the interaction of a class.

"I would believe you are better than you think, for your grace is natural, *si halika*."

Zayne trailed his finger from her lips across her chin,

savoring the feel of her. The pink in her cheeks darkened at his stroke, but she did not pull away. *Good*, he thought with sudden satisfaction, for he found he enjoyed touching her, craved it even. He hoped for more chances to indulge, to have her against him, cheek to palm, lips to neck, body to body. She had smooth skin and soft curves over a firm, feminine strength, and he had not merely flattered her when he said she had a grace he found appealing.

The longer he spent with Madeline, the more she intrigued him and the more his body recognized hers.

"What does *si halika* mean?" she asked, interrupting his increasing arousal.

"A *halika* is a honeybee." Actually he had said *my* honeybee, but perhaps it was best to keep that back until he could explain all.

"You think I'm a bee?"

"There are similarities. The sweet honey of your hair, a sting when crossed." He pointed to a small blue signboard painted with two eyes concealed by a misty veil. Curly gold letters at the bottom spelled out *Mystic*. "Is that where we go?"

"That's it."

They stepped up the two concrete steps, his hand resting at the small of her back. Ah, yes, she did move with a pretty grace, and the heat beneath his hand burned away the increasingly disturbing touch of magic as they neared the entrance. Madeline knocked at the door. A moment later it swung open, allowing them entrance, then shut behind them.

Mystic consisted of two narrow rooms made narrower by the volume of material packed onto the shelves, walls, and cupboards. Meandering paths between the towers of display were barely wide enough for two. A dusty, herbal odor clung to the air. He glanced around, curious and uneasy. "Strange energies reside here."

"What do you mean?"

"That is fake"—he gestured toward a plastic bag labeled *The Amazing Levitating Trick*—"but the crystal scrying bowl is truly powerful."

"Brendan runs an equal-opportunity shop," Madeline explained. "He caters to both the stage magician and the practitioners of the arcane arts."

"Hmmm." Deftly Zayne steered Madeline away from a shelf of vials. Some of the items were not only powerful, but dangerous, especially in unskilled hands. "The contrasts do not mix well."

"I never believed there was any actual magic in here."

"Your belief was wrong. Be careful should you come here without me."

"Zayne, I've been coming here for years without problems. Brendan's a friend."

"Good, for the man would make an unpleasant enemy."

"Sort of like you," she murmured.

He didn't answer; her observation was not far from the truth.

A man—gaunt and pale with colorless skin and blond hair bleached nearly white—waved a greeting, holding up a couple of fingers in a gesture Zayne interpreted as meaning he would join them in a few moments. Madeline gestured in return, agreeing, and the man—Brendan, Zayne assumed—turned back to his customer, who was studying jars filled with ground leaves and roots.

Zayne stayed near Madeline as she strolled around. She seemed more fascinated by the humans who populated the aisles than with the variety of stock.

A youth thumbed through a catalog of magic tricks. A mother with her baby and child waited while her companion stroked crystals. A long-haired man sniffed the array of candles, and two men argued whether a single vial of Pleasure-Enhancer would be enough to carry them through the weekend.

As long as Madeline's interest fixed upon no male, Zayne was content. He rested his hand again at her waist, emphasizing which male she accompanied, should any be of a mind to challenge his claim.

Still, unease tugged at him. The swirl of energies thrummed across him in irritating discord. Though weak and formless, their sheer number and variation were unpleasant. All of a sudden, something else intruded, something prickling the back of his neck.

A small display on a bookcase shelf caught his eye. Copper wrist bands. His wrists itched and his arms felt weighted with granite as he closed on the display. A knot of anger formed in his stomach, and bile etched his throat. Copper bands, the shackles of a bound djinni, and they thought to put them out for display? He picked them up, turning them over in his hands, and the knot eased. Engravings of flowers and vines, not the runes of binding, covered the surface. No powers tingled his fingertips; no constrictions settled across his wrists and throat. These were decorative only. Swallowing the nausea, he returned the bands to the shelf.

Something ate at him, though. What? He turned, looking for Madeline, who had flitted from his side. She waited at a nearby counter, while Brendan disappeared into the rear of the store. Probably getting the box they'd come for. Zayne joined her to wait. She gave him a smile; then her gaze flicked past him and an expression of sympathy settled upon her face.

He followed her glance to the couple he'd seen earlier beside the crystals. The couple with the two children. Amazing. They were actually blessed with two. Then he realized what was bothering him. The family did not look as though they believed themselves blessed.

The baby was crying with loud, frantic sobs.

The mother jiggled and crooned with ineffective efforts, while the toddling child clung to her leg, his thumb in his mouth. Obviously, the baby was distressed, but no human in the store made a move to assist. If they noticed at all, it was either with distant sympathy or irritation.

What manner of people let a child cry like that without offering assistance? Did they not know that children were a rare blessing, that all who knew the young one shared in the responsibility of care?

Well, he could not merely listen. He rounded a pile of books, just as the father turned from the crystals to snarl at his woman, "Can't you keep that brat quiet, Sharon? Let me look in peace."

Surprise stunned Zayne to a halt. When a djinn male found a *zaniya*, he swore to protect and cherish his mate; it was not a vow to be broken. Were humans not the same?

"I'm trying."

The woman's soft answer broke through his temporary freeze. He joined them.

The woman looked up at him, still jiggling the crying baby. "I'm sorry if she's disturbing you," she said breathlessly. "She's teething, and—"

Zayne shook his head. "I came only to help," he murmured. "As any should do." He touched a fingertip to the baby's sweaty cheek and began to croon a lullaby his mother had sung to him. He sang in the language of the djinn; the words would not matter to the babe. Only the softness, the tune.

The baby's cries softened to a hiccup. She opened her dark blue eyes, the last of her tears drying on her lashes, and stared at him. He felt the toddling child place a sticky hand on his leg, and he rested his palm on the boy's head, including him in the song. He sang of sleep and warm milk and comfort and protection. Slowly the babe's eyes closed, and a moment later she was asleep, her small mouth pursed and her breath a soft snore.

"She will sleep through the night," he said to the mother, still watching the baby.

"Thank you," the woman breathed. "She's been so cranky, and I'm so tired . . ."

He wondered if there was no one to help her during such times. Before he could ask, however, the other child drew his attention by patting his leg.

He crouched to eye level, taking in the lad's pinched face and faded shirt. The arms sticking out from the shirt were pale and scrawny as a willow branch. "Yes?"

"My name's Adam," the child whispered. "What's yours?"

"Zayne."

"I like to sing, too."

"Would you like to sing something for me?"

The child glanced up at the father, who was still intent on his crystals.

"Softly, just for me," Zayne said.

Adam nodded and began, "Twinkle, twinkle, little star . . ."

As expected, his voice was thin, with a just-out-of-babyhood lisp. Still, the little one had a good ear. He should be encouraged—

"What you doin' with my kid?" The man's ugly voice

intruded, and the child shrank back, tugging the hem of his shirt in a nervous gesture and ducking his face down.

It was then that Zayne saw the child's bruises. On the throat. On the legs. On the wrists.

Fury boiled inside him. He uncoiled from his crouch, pinned the abuser with a glare, and stretched out his hand.

Madeline paid for the box—the real reason Brendan was so ready to let her have it, she suspected. He was tired of carrying it on his books. Then, waiting for him to retrieve it, she turned around, looking for Zayne.

He was glaring at the man who had been looking at the crystals. She remembered seeing the woman and feeling sympathy at the hard time she was having with the cranky baby. Now the mother held her sleeping baby in her arms, and the toddler cowered nearby. Madeline's heart jumped in her chest. Zayne's hand was outstretched, and she saw the air around him dance with angry, glittering streaks of purple and amber.

Abandoning the counter, she hurried to Zayne's side. At once she took in the bruises on the child, the fear in the woman, the meanness in the man's face, the utter fury crackling around the djinni.

"Adam was just singing," the woman said, stepping between Zayne and her husband, causing the djinni to lower his hand.

"Well, he disturbed me." The man gripped the woman's wrist, then tugged her toward the door, ignoring her soft mewl of pain. "C'mon, Sharon, Adam. We're going, and before I found my crystal. You'll be sorry if you say another word."

Damn, she hated men like him. Madeline stepped

into his path, knowing what she was doing was really stupid—the man was a brute. Possibly coked up, too, she thought, noting his wide pupils and sweating face. But she couldn't just let him leave and take his anger out on his family at home. Not without trying something.

"Why don't you take a few more minutes to look over those crystals?" she said. "I saw some nicer ones down there. I'll just talk to your wife and kids while you look." *I'll give Sharon the number for the battered women's shelter and hope to God she listens.*

"Outta my way," the man snarled.

Zayne slid beside her. "Do not touch her," he said softly. The air snapped and crackled.

Unfortunately, the man took softness for weakness. "You going to stop me?" he challenged, shoving Madeline out of the way, apparently thinking his size was more than Zayne could handle.

He was wrong.

Zayne jerked his arm forward, spreading his fingers. Lightning, a flash so brief and bright it blinded, shot from his fingertips. The hair on her arms lifted.

The bully spun around and dropped to the floor. From another angle, it probably looked like Zayne had shoved him down.

He hadn't. He'd touched the man with nothing but his *ma-at*.

He strode forward, hand still outstretched, an avenging angel in leather and a silver earring. The man struggled to gain his feet, but couldn't. Madeline suspected that Zayne's outstretched hand was holding him down.

The bully's breaths came in sharp pants and his face turned an unpleasant shade of purple. As though Zayne were strangling him.

Madeline laid a hand on the djinni's outstretched arm. "Don't kill him."

Zayne turned to her, his green eyes so dark they looked like black pools. "You care what happens to him?"

"I care about you."

"Djinn do not kill," he said shortly, turning away from her. With his other hand, he grabbed one of the crystals from the shelf, an egg-shaped one of pure crimson. "You wanted a crystal," he said, his voice still low and etched with fury. "Try this one."

He crouched beside the man, who was now trying to scramble backward but making no progress. Zayne grabbed one of the man's hands, sandwiching the crystal between their palms. The man's struggles were no match for the djinni's strength.

He intoned a chant, his voice tight with fury. The words were foreign, exotic. All at once, there was a flash of red light, which spread from the joined hands to cover the man, then disappeared. Zayne loosened his grip and dropped the crystal.

It was now perfectly clear.

He pushed to his feet and stared down at the man, who scrambled upright.

"You're nuts," the bully snarled.

Zayne didn't bother to respond. He only watched as the man strode over to his wife.

"Sharon, I said it's time to go." He grabbed her right wrist, tugging her again. Suddenly he dropped his grip and grabbed his own right wrist. "Ouch! What the hell?"

Sharon was looking in amazement at her own arm.

"What you staring at?" he growled at Adam, giving him a slap across the cheek. Adam didn't even flinch. Instead, the man staggered sideways, and a red mark appeared on his cheek. He cradled his face and rounded on Zayne. "What the hell did you do?"

"As you reap, now will you sow," Zayne said implacably, feet planted, his hands fisted at his waist. "Touch them with pain, and it will be you who feels it. Twofold."

The man stared at Zayne in horror, then turned and yanked on Sharon's arm. All of a sudden he dropped it and clutched his shoulder in pain. "I'll sue," he said, glaring at Zayne. "I'll sue your ass off."

"And what will you say?" Zayne asked quietly.

The man sputtered and spewed, then stomped out, muttering only a "C'mon" to Sharon.

She did not follow. Instead, her eyes were on Zayne. "Thank you. I don't know what you did, or how you did it, but thank you." She turned to Madeline. "No woman has ever stood up to him like that for me."

Madeline hastily dialed the number of the battered women's shelter on her cell phone. "He can't hurt you, not physically, not anymore. Don't let him try anything else, though."

The shelter answered, and Madeline gave a quick explanation. "Talk to these people. They can help you. If you don't do it for yourself, do it for the children. Adam and the baby." She held the phone out to Sharon.

Dazed, Sharon hesitated, then nodded firmly. She took the phone and started talking to the counselor, the baby in her arms still sound asleep through it all.

Zayne crouched down beside Adam. "You may sing your heart now, little one."

"My daddy says I'm not very good."

"Who is the better singer? Me or your daddy?"

"You."

"Then whose opinion will you trust about your voice?"

"You?"

Zayne nodded. "I say your voice is pure and honest. It may not provide your life work, but it can be a joy. Let it shine so." While he was speaking, Madeline noticed his hands moving unobtrusively above the boy's legs and arms, not touching, but skimming across the air. The bruises slowly began to fade. "Will you do that?"

The boy nodded silently.

Zayne stood, just as Sharon handed Madeline back the phone, telling her, "They gave me an address to go to."

"Do you need a ride?"

Sharon shook her head. "I have a friend who lives nearby. She'll take me. She's been urging me to go for some time now. I guess . . . I guess it's time I listened." She gathered Adam close. "And thank you again."

As Sharon and her children were walking out of the store, Madeline heard Adam ask, "Who was that man, Momma?"

"An angel, sweetie, like in the TV show. Sent from heaven to show us the way."

Madeline cast a sidelong glance at Zayne. Sleeveless indigo shirt. Leather pants. Silver earring. Arms crossed at his chest. Waist-length hair. Shimmering sparks. Her heart was beating in triple-time again.

He looked at her, and his lips turned up in a slow, sensuous smile, which promised delights.

In all her born days, she had never seen anyone who looked less angelic.

Chapter Ten

The box was a bust. Literally. Inside was a two-foot-tall brass bust of Aleister Crowley, the infamous mystic. Madeline sat on the floor of Tildy's living room, cats stretched against her thighs, and turned the heavy sculpture around in her hands. No secret compartments or hidden surprises that she could see. Of course, a secret compartment wouldn't be too useful if it was easily found. Remembering how El Corazon had been hidden in *Romancing the Stone*, she tapped the ugly bust against the floor.

"What are you doing?" Zayne asked. He sat beside her, leaning against the chair, his legs stretched out in front of him as he absently petted Vulcan.

"Seeing if it will break apart and have some treasure hidden inside."

He watched a moment. "It seems quite solid."

"So it does." She stopped the futile effort and handed it to him. "Can you make anything of it?"

He turned it around, his agile fingers dipping into every indentation with an exploratory stroke. Madeline found herself staring at his fingers, at the careful caresses.

He would touch a lover with even greater attention. Her breath hitched in her throat, caught by the sudden heated image of Zayne's hands on skin, her skin, her curves. Did every thought have to turn to sex? She raked her hands through her hair, loosening the knot, trying to rid herself of this crazy fascination.

Another futile effort. As his thumb circled a small swirl at the bottom of the bust, her fantasy flashed white hot. *His thumb circling her breast, just at the tip.* He leaned closer to the bust. *His breath against her skin, his mouth suckling.* Could she actually feel the touch? Her breasts tightened, and the nipples hardened to a tingling awareness as her imagination conjured the sensations of an intense, consuming lover.

He turned his head, giving her a curious look. Oh, God, she hadn't broadcast that thought, had she? Broadcast like he could? Or had the images, the words come from him? She couldn't deny he was looking at her as though he were that intense, consuming lover.

She cleared her throat, trying to ignore the suffusing heat. "Zayne, thank you for helping Sharon and those children tonight."

"I did what any man should do." His hand brushed against her ankle. " 'Twas you who had courage. You had not the powers of *ma-at*, yet you faced him."

"Still, you could have ignored the problem."

"No, I could not."

"So, not only are you incredibly sexy, but you're kind, too."

"Do not mistake my protection for softness, Madeline. I can be quite ruthless if I must." Then his grin came back. "You think I am incredibly sexy?"

She laughed. "Yes, and I think you know it. Now, have you found something?" She nodded toward the bust.

"Perhaps." A second later, he pushed with his thumb and a small section of the base slid back with a click.

"How did you find that?"

"My fingers are perhaps more skilled to appreciate the differences than yours."

She *would not* make a double entendre out of that. Instead, she bent down, peering in the small hole. Zayne also looked, his hair brushing against her cheek. She caught the faint scent of cinnamon, and her shoulder warmed where his skin touched hers. Resolutely she ignored her reaction.

"I think there's something in there." She reached in and pulled out a small bundle of soft felt. When she unwrapped the cloth, at the center she found a tiny vial of aqua liquid. She started to lift the stopper, but he put a hand over hers.

"Do not open it."

"Do you think it's poison?"

He was frowning at the vial. "I do not know what it is. If it is a potion, then it is conjured by human magic, and this I have no knowledge of. We do not know what it might do. However, from what you have told me of your stepfather, he does not sound like a man who would go to so much trouble to attain a gentle power."

"You're right." She let out a breath, thinking. "We need someone who can analyze this and tell us what's in it. I know! Miss Tildy's nephew and his wife live not very far from here. He's a doctor and a professor at Tulane. If he can't analyze it, he might know someone who can."

Zayne nodded. "Jack Montgomery."

Once again he'd surprised her. "You know him?"

"We have met. I have known his wife, Leila, for a very long time."

Something about the way he said "known" caused her to give him a curious look. Leila was one of the most stunning women she'd ever met, and nice, too, as though good looks weren't enough of a blessing.

Had she and Zayne once been lovers? If so, it was in the past, for Leila and Jack were a devoted couple and absolutely nuts about their baby son. Still, the idea was painful to think about. If Zayne's past lovers were like Leila, then she was dreaming pipe dreams to think any of his teasing and flirting meant he was truly interested in her.

Suddenly the import of what he'd said hit her. "You mean Leila's a . . . ?"

". . . a djinni," he completed.

She sat back on her heels, stunned. She'd been living near a djinni for over a year and didn't even know it?

"She would not want that fact widely known."

"Yeah, I'll bet." She rubbed the back of her neck, still having trouble wrapping her mind around the idea that Leila was a djinni.

Zayne nodded to the vial. "Between them, Jack and Leila might shed light on what this is for. Is there aught else in the box?"

Madeline carefully set the vial on a table, then looked through the Styrofoam peanuts, while Bronze put her front paws on the edge of the box and looked inside curiously. "That seems to be all there is."

She glanced at her watch and yawned, then yawned again, suddenly realizing how tired she was. Too much had happened in the past forty-eight hours. She'd been put on notice by her employer, she'd given up her apartment, she'd started a quest for her mysterious stepfather, and she'd met Zayne.

Suddenly she was aware of the quiet, the late hour, the fact that she was alone with Zayne—even the cats had left the room—and their bedrooms lay only a few feet apart.

And his was a masterpiece of sensory decadence.

The bedrooms, however, were a lot closer together

than her world and the world of a minstrel djinni.

She raised her eyes to find him looking at her. No one had ever looked at her like that, with intensity and heat and admiration all at once. Her heart drummed against her chest. An exotic scent, both sweet and musky, curled around her, and the sensual aroma stirred her blood. She forgot about being tired.

"The *frangipela* flower is awake," Zayne murmured. A wealth of sparkles surrounded him, a brilliant rainbow of colors.

"Is it magic I feel?"

"The *frangipela* does not create our desire, only mirrors it."

His voice was a gentle, arousing caress of need. He leaned closer, and the sparkles around him spread out, bathing her in their shower. She could imagine the stroke of his strong fingers on her cheek and down her throat, the weight of his palm above her heart.

"Is that from you? Or is it my imagination?" she whispered.

"From me. When a djinni makes love, his *ma-at* is as instinctive and unstoppable as the sparkle of his emotions and the touch of his body."

"Is that what you're doing to me? Making love?"

"Not *to* you. With you. I want you and I thought . . ." His head tilted, the motion of the silver earring catching pinpoints of red and violet. "Madeline, do you not desire me, too?"

"I'm not into one-night stands."

That lethal grin flashed, for just a second. "I was not planning on but one night."

"But how many? How long will you be here?" She hated the part of her that wouldn't let her soar, that kept her from seizing this moment, even as her heart tugged to be set free and her body strained for the touch of his.

Oh, but if there was anyone who could tempt her past all caution, that person was Zayne. Sensual, charming, and he was looking at *her*, not what she could do for him.

He moved in a blink, his leg and hip touching hers. His masculine scent enveloped her, more arousing than anything the *frangipela* could conjure. His effervescent emotions fizzed against her, tiny pricks that stimulated skin and imagination and lulled caution.

"You think too much," he said. "My nights can be as numbered, or as endless, as you wish."

"Rub a lamp and get three wishes from a genie?"

Something hard and dangerous flashed in his green eyes. "We do not grant wishes."

"So you said. I only meant . . ." She shook her head, not wanting to tell him that he granted her wishes merely by being here. "Never mind. I just have trouble believing in fairy tales, and the idea that a man like you is attracted to me seems like one."

"Why should I not be attracted to you?" He touched her hand, not with his *ma-at* this time but with his hand, entwining their fingers together.

"C'mon, Zayne. You attract attention wherever you go. You'd have to be stupid not to realize how . . . beautiful you are, and I don't think there's a problem with your intelligence. You could have any woman you want. Why would you want me?" *Oh, God, why was she saying this?*

"If you believe I could not want you, then why do you believe I want to make love to you? To have you share my pillows?" He wasn't looking at her but at their hands, his larger one enveloping hers. His thumb circled with slow strokes across her skin, keeping her aroused with only that small touch.

"Because I'm here and the *frangipela* is doing its thing?"

"You think it would not matter this night who was opposite me?" He sounded almost angry as he looked up at her. That hard, dangerous light flashed again in his eyes. "That I do not care who shares my pillows?"

"No, that's not what I meant." But wasn't it? Wasn't that what she'd said? "Sorry. I guess it did come out like that."

"As you said, I could have anyone I choose," he said bluntly. "If I chose you, must it not be because I do desire you?"

"Humans sleep with one another for a lot of reasons besides desire."

"Djinn emotions are not easily hidden."

The sparks, she noticed, had dimmed to a shimmer. *Good job killing the mood, Madeline.* Even the scent of the *frangipela* had faded.

"Do you know what I see when I look at you?" he asked. "What I saw from the first? Your hair is the color of sweet honey, and your eyes are ever different, ever entrancing. Right now they gleam like sunshine on a dewdrop. I saw rhythm in the sway of your hips. I see now a woman of determination and wisdom and generosity. And caution."

He loosened their hands. Suddenly the warmth left her and she realized what a neurotic, insecure idiot she'd been. Seeing him with the child tonight had deepened her perceptions of him. He had so much more than a sexy bod, a magical voice, and the powers of *ma-at*. There was also a core of decency.

So what if it was only one night? Or a few? Being Zayne's lover, if only briefly, would be worth any later tears or regrets or doubts. Right now, she could have been with him, running her hands through the length of his hair and tingling in the center of an effervescent rainbow instead of watching him stand up.

It shouldn't matter that she'd only met him today, and that he was a magical being from another world, here on some private djinn business. It shouldn't, but it did.

It mattered, yes, but it didn't change one whit how much she wanted him.

He held a hand out, assisting her upright.

"Can I go back in time?" she asked. "Just ten minutes or so, and redo this whole scene? From the point when you're telling me the *frangipela* only mirrors our desire?"

He smiled, melting her insides to liquid chocolate centers. "Reversing time is one thing I cannot do."

"Pity. Zayne, I just need a little time—"

"A very little time, I hope."

She laughed. "Yeah, very little. It's just I—"

He laid a finger against her lips. "When we unite, you must have no doubts." Then he stepped back and lifted his arms. "Later, Madeline."

"Soon."

He grinned, then disappeared in the now familiar whirlwind.

Madeline's answer to frustration was movement. She had just finished a combination of pliés and petit battements when someone knocked. It was Natalie.

"Hey, Madeline. I was driving by, saw the light on, and remembered you told me yesterday you'd moved." She leaned one shoulder against the door jamb and took in the sweat and the leotard. "Oh, hell, you haven't been exercising? Anybody who exercises at midnight is in serious need of a friend dragging them out for a drink. Especially a friend with information."

Madeline laughed, feeling relaxed. "Information? C'mon in. I'll open a bottle of wine."

"I'd rather not stay here. I'll wait here while you change." Natalie stood just inside the doorway, glancing around and rubbing a hand along her arm.

Remembering her friend's aversion to magic, and Tildy's house was steeped with magical paraphernalia, Madeline nodded. "Be with you in five minutes."

Natalie was waiting uneasily, her foot tapping, when Madeline returned. Her foot stilled, and she held out a piece of paper. "I did a little snooping for you. Cyrus Cromwell is one secretive man, but he did make several phone calls to this woman."

"Thank you. I'd run out of leads." Madeline glanced at the name and phone number. "Swamp Suzette? The woman who does the bayou tours? Why would he call her?"

"Maybe he likes feeding marshmallows to the gators."

"Not bloody likely." She stuck the paper in her bag; she'd plan a visit tomorrow. "Now, where can I buy you a drink?"

"My brother's club? Drinks are on the house."

"Your brother's club opens at midnight and has some seriously creepy clientele."

Natalie made a face. "True. Too noisy to talk anyway. We'll figure it out on the way."

"Sounds good. Oh, wait, I have to leave a note." She didn't want Zayne returning and wondering where she was. Or popping in beside her, right in front of Natalie. Quickly she scribbled an explanation.

"The seventy-something widower Miss Tildy was expecting arrived?"

Madeline grinned. She couldn't say a word about Zayne being a djinni, and the way he made her feel was too private to share, but . . . "Do we have some things to talk about."

Naked, Zayne stretched out atop the clover of the oasis. He stacked his hands beneath his head, watching the stars of Kaf. Behind him, the silken sides of his tent made a gentle flapping noise in the night breeze. A fire crackled beside him, perfuming the air with thin, evergreen-scented smoke. His soul drank of the flame and air, replenishing his *ma-at* and renewing his connections to his world. Djinn could not leave Kaf for more than the span of a few cycles of the sun before returning to renew the bonds of *ma-at*, and as Minstrel he felt keenly his frayed bonds. The constant touch of Terran magic taxed his strength.

The winds and the heat had also soothed his raging arousal. Despite his certainty that Madeline must come to him without doubts, despite his utter exhaustion after the long day, had he stayed he would have been sorely tried not to bring her to his pillows this night. That strongly did he want her, and the depth of his need surprised him.

He expected that as the destined *zaniya* of a Minstrel, her harmonies would blend with his, a pleasure he had yet to experience and was eager for. He had not expected this obsession with her. The need to bury himself deep in her body, the desire to see that deep gold of wanting in her eyes. He knew that male djinn guarded their mates, but he had not expected this fierce well of protectiveness.

Nor had he expected to simply *like* her. Limited as the time was that he had spent with her, it was also . . . relaxing was not the word, not when clawing need for her was his constant companion. Yet in a way it was. She saw not only the Minstrel, but the man who was part of that essence, and it was the man she wanted. Being with her was like coming across a deep pool in the center of a harsh desert. The waters slaked thirst and replenished energy and relaxed the spirit.

Ah, he was too poetic. That he would save for his music. His reactions to Madeline fell more in the realm of primitive and primal.

He sat up, suddenly restless. At least his attraction to Madeline reassured him that he had interpreted the divination correctly. Once she got beyond the moonstruck notion that her voice would not blend with his, he would have his final sign that the time was right to tell her of their destiny, of his plans and his purpose. For a moment he considered trying his music, but he decided against it. Not unless Madeline was at his side. He did not wish to upset the fragile balances he had fashioned.

Instead, he stretched his hands to the fire, chanting the first Circle of Clarity, strengthening his *ma-at*, ridding himself of the fragments of Terran magic that clung to him.

A gust of wind blew his hair across his face and a flurry of sand pricked his naked back. He lowered his arms, waiting.

"You have returned, Minstrel." The deep, low voice of the Oracle sounded from behind him.

"Yes." He didn't turn around. If Alesander had wanted to be seen, he would have transported within vision.

"Your stay on Terra is incomplete." It wasn't a question. "You stay only long enough to renew your bonds to Kaf."

Zayne didn't bother to question how Alesander

knew where he'd gone. The Oracle knew much that was hidden from others. "I still have tasks there."

With the swish of fabric on sand, Alesander came into view. Sort of. The red hooded cape hid his body and left his face in shadow. As usual, all Zayne could see were the strong, tapering fingers.

He had known Alesander much of his life. The Oracle had heard him singing in the remote fringes where Zayne and his mother made their early home. Alesander was the one who had persuaded his mother that his young talent must be trained; it was he who had convinced her to leave her son at the school

It had taken many cycles before Zayne forgave him.

Since then, though, they had spent many turns of the sun studying *ma-at* together, sharing conversation. Zayne believed he knew Alesander better than anyone on Kaf.

Yet, in all that time, he had never had a direct view of the Oracle's face. He knew the mystic by voice, by motion, by shadow, by hands, by the *ma-at* he wielded.

"I hope those tasks will not take long." With a fluid motion Alesander lowered himself to sit on the sand. He lowered the hood, but the night shadows still hid his face. Zayne caught an impression of dark eyes, dark hair, dark skin, all blending into the evening. He tried to look no further, if his friend desired privacy, 'twas not his place to dishonor that wish.

"I do not know how long it will take," Zayne admitted. "There are complications."

Alesander laughed, a rich sound and a rare one. "Are there not always complications in a worthy task?"

Zayne smiled. "True."

Alesander picked up a handful of sand and let it trickle through his fingers. The starlight glinted off the grains, drawing the eye away from the smooth strength in the hands. "Do not tarry too long. Kaf needs you back soon."

"Have there been problems?" Fear tangled his gut, and he clenched his hands against the sudden trembling. Though he had hoped the separation of the worlds would prevent his Terran singing from affecting Kaf, he had stopped as soon as the message spells gave warning. The last time, in the bar with the jazz, though, there had been no warnings.

"A few unusual disturbances, but nothing so strong as the night you left."

That, at least, was a blessing.

"But," continued Alesander, "your presence, your song and harmony is missed. For now, the forces remain in balance, but this is a strange time for us. You are our only Minstrel. Should you be gone for long . . ." His voice trailed off.

The knot in Zayne's belly tightened further. The consequences to Kaf if there were no Minstrel was something spoken of only in hushed whispers. The fabric of nature unraveled. Chaos. A world in disarray.

In his voice rested the continued peace. Normally, more than one Minstrel and his *zaniya* toured the lands. Now, however, for the first time that any djinn could remember, only one Minstrel sang with the harmonies of Kaf. Him. Zayne.

Djinn were long-lived, not immortal. The two others who had sung while he came into his power had both met with rare untimely death. One was crushed under a slide of rock during a fasting time in the Towers, while the other had died beneath the hooves of an angry *madagon*.

For the cycles since, the harmony of Kaf had been Zayne's burden alone to bear. There were children of promise, children whom he would train as apprentice, but it would be many cycles before they were powerful enough to share the task.

He *must* get his problem under control. There was no other choice. He would not fail in his responsibility. He was Minstrel, and whatever it took, he would keep the faith entrusted in him.

Zayne glanced up from his brief musings. "I have until the moon cycle completes."

"I hope that will be time enough."

Time ran differently on Terra and Kaf; he would have enough time to be with Madeline until the deadline of her quest. But if that did not give him the answers . . . "Do you know why I went to Terra? What I seek?" he asked abruptly. "Do you know my path?"

Alesander didn't answer.

Zayne chuckled. "I do not believe you have ever answered those kinds of questions for me, my friend. You guide all of Kaf—"

"I do not guide all of Kaf," Alesander interrupted quietly. "Some must find their own ways. That is what makes them strong. It is why they are our leaders. Besides," he added drily, "you would question any advice I gave you, I do not doubt. This aggravation I do not need."

"Everyone needs a little aggravation, my friend."

"Perhaps your *zaniya* will give you that. You have been too long alone and too used to your own chosen paths."

"Says the man who makes his home in the forbidding Towers, and whom none will gainsay."

"Because I do not give advice to the likes of you. Only to those who will take it."

Zayne chuckled again, and Alesander joined him

with his rare, deep laugh. Then the Oracle rose. "I must be going; and you must be returning."

"Oh, I have brought you something, Alesander." Zayne rummaged through the small sack he had brought, suddenly reminded of a task he'd recently completed.

"You knew I was coming?" For the first time, Zayne heard surprise in the Oracle's voice.

"Let us say I had a hunch."

"Perhaps you should perform the task of Oracle."

"Not for all the waters on Kaf. Your austere lifestyle is not appealing."

"Sometimes I agree," Alesander's voice was no stronger than the whisper of a breeze.

Zayne glanced over in surprise, but the hood was back over the Oracle's head and his hands were clasped in front of him. There would be no answers to questions about that longing he had just heard. Instead, he contented himself with holding out the silver disk.

Alesander turned it around in his hands.

"It is how the Terrans keep their music," Zayne explained. "It touches only the ears, but still it can be beautiful. They use a strange device to re-create it, but I have fashioned this one for you. Your *ma-at* can bring it forth." He had included touches of the jazz, the voice of Irena Cromwell, his own new song. One thing he did know about the Oracle was that music was one of the few pleasures Alesander allowed himself. "I hope you will enjoy it."

"I am sure I will. Thank you." Alesander hesitated, then added, "Zayne, the divination you did was for your question. There are always other ways. Other paths."

"Advice, Oracle?"

"No. Simply a reminder. Should this path not provide what is necessary. You are too vital to Kaf for us to lose you." With that enigmatic caution, Alesander lifted his hands and disappeared in the whirlwind of transport.

Chapter Eleven

The dress was lying at the foot of her bed when she woke up. Madeline had no doubt who'd left it there. The giver was obvious, not only from the way it had appeared, but also from the design. He had taken the pattern of the vest they'd seen yesterday and fashioned it into something magical. Or *ma-at*ical, as the case might be. Even the cats recognized the power. They circled the dress, sniffing, but not one of them curled up on it for a bed or poked at it with a paw.

She picked up the dress. The cloth flowed across her hands like a hot summer breeze. Silk? Cotton? A blend? Most likely a fabric she had no knowledge of.

She stripped off her nightgown and slipped her arms into the short sleeves. The dress wrapped around her, fastening at her waist with a mere press of cloth to cloth. The design wasn't overtly sexual, with a shallow V neckline and a hem that reached her knees. One look in the mirror, however, told her she'd never seen anything more sensual.

She was wearing a flame, and it looked good on her.

The colors of fire—red, orange, yellow—blended across the soft fabric. Depending upon how she tilted her head, the predominant shade changed, but any view was a fiery shimmer. She swished her hips, and the full skirt rippled with teasing invitation.

The fabric caressed her and molded her like an attentive lover. Like Zayne touched her. Light, teasing, provocative. Each movement she made, the rise and fall of her chest as she breathed or the slightest motion of her hips, set the fabric swaying.

Now, this was flair.

Even the three cats were impressed. They sat at her feet and stared at her, unblinking, not purring or begging for a pet.

She circled her hips, a rolling movement she'd practiced from her belly-dance videos. The feel and the motion of the fabric delighted her. A beat thrummed in her ears; her feet took the first tentative steps of a dance. Her arms tingled with a need to join in, and she lifted them above her head. The brush of cloth urged her to move and to feel.

Humming under her breath, she began to dance, recalling the advice of the classes she had given herself. Head like a queen, still and regal. Weight centered in the flexible, fluid pelvis. Water springs upward, from the pelvis to each vertebra. Slowly at first, then faster and surer, her feet moved in the ancient steps and her hips and hands performed the ancient rites.

With each whisper of flame cloth and each fluid circle of hip and wrist, the advice and lectures faded. Joy overlaid, overwhelmed technique. She danced, oh, she *danced*. Without rigidly prescribed form. Without fear. Her body flowed, and with each step she slipped joyously into the fabric of the dance.

Despite the way the dance was often portrayed, *raqs sharqi* was a dance of women, by women, for women. A celebration of femininity. Never had she felt as sensual, as close to the earth and the flow of waters, as she did at this moment.

Alone in the room, she danced. Yet she was not

alone. In her mind, Zayne joined her and watched. He watched her, but she didn't draw back from the heat of his eyes or the blatant arousal he displayed. Nothing stopped her from dancing. For him. For herself.

She was dancing!

Impulsively she ran from the room, pulling up in front of Zayne's closed door and checking the stones flanking it. Stones of privacy, he had told her yesterday. If they glow, the djinni inside desires privacy. Without the glow, visitors are welcome.

They were solid white. Not glowing.

Still, she knocked lightly at the door. He had not been home yet when she'd returned last night. When he didn't answer, she took another look at the opaque stones, then pushed open the door.

Stepping into his room was like stepping into an oasis. A fresh breeze floated through it, rippling the iridescent silk walls. Hints of green made a random pattern like trees in the wild.

"Zayne?" she called quietly.

From one corner of the room she heard the rustle of skin on silk. It came from his bed of pillows, she realized, stepping nearer. He was still asleep.

Her mouth went dry and all coherent thought disappeared as she made another discovery. He slept in the nude. Not surprising, since he also communed with fire and attacked smoke alarms in the nude.

He was lying face down, affording her an unrestricted view of the bronze curve of his buttocks. The muscles in his back. The strong hand resting on the pillows. She didn't need him to roll over to remember that the front view was just as magnificent.

Her gaze locked on that sybaritic mound of pillows. Heart tripping, she inched backward.

"Do not go." *Do not go.* His quiet command hung in the air, spoke in her mind. *Come closer.*

Almost without her volition, her feet reversed her exit. Slowly she drew closer to that pile of pillows and the man sprawled among them.

"I didn't mean to wake you," she said, her voice breathless.

I like waking up with you at my side.

Sweet heavens. Simple words, but oh, what their intimacy seeded inside her. Him. Her. The pillows. Waking beside one another. Both naked. Zayne leaning over her with a sleepy smile. Zayne touching his lips to hers, starting their day with sensual abandon. The images burned, utterly clear, infinitely thrilling.

She leaned over, cupped his jaw in her hand, and kissed him. Full and warm, feeling the softness of his lips and the tingle of his power. Before he could respond, she pulled back and whispered, "Thank you."

"For what?" He rolled over then, sleek and sinuous as a cat.

No, not a cat. Cats were domesticated, and this man would never be tamed. Sleek and sinuous as a panther. Or a tiger.

Fortunately, the pillows bunched slightly, concealing his groin from view. Nothing else, however, was concealed. Not the strong line of his jaw and throat nor the light dusting of hair on his muscled legs. Not the indigo polish of his toenails, a dark color that did nothing to detract from his masculinity. His chest was smooth and firm. His nipples formed tight, cinnamon-colored buds. He smiled at her, his green eyes bright with interest. Apparently, djinn never woke up with bed head problems, either; his hair was as sleek and shiny as when he'd left her last night.

"For what do you desire to thank me?" he asked again.

Madeline started, realizing she'd been staring. From the curve of his smile, she knew he was enjoying every moment. "For the dress. I've never owned anything so wondrous."

"You are welcome." With a lithe movement, Zayne unfurled from the bed. He stretched, the muscles tightening and loosening with a natural rhythm. Madeline could no more look away than she could dance naked on a French Quarter stage. At last he grabbed a yard-wide strip of white linen and wrapped it around his hips. More as a sop to her modesty than to his, she guessed.

Not many men outside of Scotland could wear a skirt and look so masculine and so at ease, but Zayne managed it. If he had a pair of crossed scepters, he'd have looked the reincarnation of the powerful pharaohs of ancient Egypt. A moment later, he was cross-legged, levitating in the air beside her, the draped fabric at his hips preserving his nonexistent modesty and her disappearing sanity.

"Would you turn?" He made a circling motion with his finger.

She did as he asked, a slow circle with her hips, a shadow of the dance she had just done in private.

As he watched her display, Zayne swallowed hard. That dress! He'd chosen it for its appeal, knowing that Madeline's gleaming beauty and curved figure would shine in it. She would be noticed, admired, her confidence nourished.

He had not expected she would glow with such joy in it.

He did not want her noticed, he realized with a spurt of possessiveness. He did not want other men's eyes on her. When she wore that dress, she should be under his protection, wearing the turquoise of his people, with the runes of her tablet clearly announcing that she was bound with him.

Abruptly he made a decision. "I have a second gift for you."

"Another? No, the dress is really enough—"

Her protest was broken by the plaintive meows of three hungry cats, who surrounded them and gazed up with beseeching eyes. Khu's demanding screech sounded from the kitchen. Madeline laughed. "Time to feed the kids."

Zayne gave the cats an irritated glare. In the future, he must strengthen his guards to prevent unannounced entry of felines. "You may attend the animals; I shall return momentarily."

"I'll get us breakfast, too."

With a lift of his arms, Zayne returned to Kaf. Quickly he fashioned a turquoise tablet for her, then sat back on his heels to decide which runes to add. Glancing down at his still strong erection, he gave a rueful grin.

Waiting to take Madeline to his pillows was proving more difficult than the Nine Hundred and Ninety-Ninth Circle of the Adept. When he'd seen her in that dress—

In his cycles as Minstrel, he had shared pillows with numerous women. No djinni stayed with a single partner unless he or she had found a soul mate, a *zani* or *zaniya*. Sex was common and joyous, a celebration of life and the body. He had lost himself many times in the throes of pleasurable release. Yet always he had known, at the back of his pleasure, that it was he who controlled the union, he who dictated the rhythms and patterns, and who wove the music of passion.

Not so with Madeline. A fierce, hard arousal had gripped him while he watched her in that dress. On its heels swept a need and a hunger, which consumed like fire and stormed like the wind. In that moment, despite wearing the cloth of Kaf, she had never looked, nor seemed, more human. He had never wanted her more.

He had been sorely put not to take her to his pillows that instant, not to begin the rituals of unity that would make her his *zaniya*, and to Solomon with the niceties of telling her first. All that restrained him was the control gained from years of discipline while perfecting his *ma-at* and his music. She was reluctant, she had shown that last night. When they shared intimacy, she should be as eager as he.

He raked his hands through the sides of his hair, wondering whether his good intentions would hold when he returned. Behind him, the fall of water from the rocks strengthened, roiling down the sheer face in foamy waves. He glanced at it, then ignored it to add the runes he needed to the tablet. When he'd finished, he returned to Terra.

Madeline was in the kitchen. She spun about as he joined her, and her smile greeted him. "That was quick. I just got breakfast laid out."

"Not as quick as I might have been." At her questioning look, he explained, "I cannot go back to a time earlier than the last moment I was on Terra, but I could have come back in the next moment. Transport is easier without folding time, however."

"Less disconcerting for me, too." She waved a hand to the table. "Sit. Eat."

"First this." He opened his fingers. In his palm rested the turquoise tablet he had made for her, strung on a gold chain. The tablet was smaller than the one which had inspired her tattoo, but still it was carved with runes and symbols. "Your gift."

She drew in a sharp breath. "Zayne, it's incredible. But you've already given me too much. I don't have anything so valuable to give you."

Yes, you do.

Without waiting for further protest, he slipped the chain over her head. The small tablet rested below the hollow of her throat. His fingers slid with a delicate caress around her neck, slipping her hair from beneath the chain. For a moment he pressed against the back of her neck in an intimate caress; then he let her loose. A surge of satisfaction welled inside him that she wore his symbol, the symbol of his people.

"Thank you." Her smile was delightful, as she leaned over and gave him a quick kiss on the cheek. "I will find a way to show my thanks."

"Then I shall look forward to your gratitude." It pleased him that he had found two gifts that delighted her. "Now we eat."

Sitting beside him, she traced a finger over the etchings. "What do these mean?"

"Some are runes of protection. Some are symbols of identity. I have also given yours the ability to transport, since you cannot work *ma-at*." The last was added as an afterthought, when he reasoned Madeline might be more amenable to coming to his world if she thought she could return whenever she desired.

Her eyes widened. "You mean I can . . ." She spiraled her finger upward.

"Yes."

"Let me try it." She bounced to the center of the kitchen and waited. "Nothing's happening."

"Because you have to say the proper words. *'Abhn-ma-el.* By the great Solomon, I command thy winds transport me.' " He put his finger to her lips before she could repeat the words. "This power is strong enough only to transport yourself, and you can only go to a place you have been before. You must grip the tablet in your hand and hold the vision of this place firmly in your mind before you say the words."

"What if I've seen pictures? Is that enough?"

He shook his head. "The images will not be real enough in your thoughts. I also suggest you try someplace close the first time."

"Okay." She held the tablet. Her eyes closed and her face scrunched up as she concentrated. "*Abhn-ma-el*. By the great Solomon, I command thy winds transport me." She disappeared, only to call out a moment later, "This is so cool. I'm in my bedroom. You didn't warn me I'd land on my butt."

"Novice mistake. With your grace, you should do better next time."

Then she was back at his side, throwing her arms about him and kissing him. Thrice this morn had she kissed him. He would have to gift her more often. Before he could get properly into the kiss, she backed away and laid a hand on his shoulder for balance. "Whoa. Is dizziness also a novice hazard?"

"Yes, until you become used to the effort of holding the image. The dizziness fades quickly."

"Can I do that time-fold thing?"

"No, that is too complex to put into a tablet. Come finish your breakfast."

As she sat, she lifted the tablet to look at it again. "Is there a special significance to these tablets? I noticed Leila wears one, too."

He delayed by handing her a glass of cool mint tea, deciding what he should say. She must understand the tablet's importance and wear it continually.

"The tablet is an essential part of Kaf. It is the symbol of our place in the company of djinn. Every child receives theirs as a rite of passage into adulthood. Once the tablet is placed, no djinni willingly takes it off." It was only removed at death. Or if the djinni was bound by the spell of a human, forced to grant the wishes of myth. "You should not take off the tablet, Madeline. The runes of protection carved within the stone will provide you with a measure of shielding *ma-at* even if I am not present."

"Because of Cyrus?" She eyed him over her glass.

"What little I have learned about him does not ease my mind."

"I thought you said you could handle him."

"I can. It is you who must be protected." He gave her a steady look. "Also, the symbols of identity declare that the tablet is yours and that it was given to you by me. Do you accept this from me, without coercion?"

"Yes. I already did."

"Will you wear it always? To do so would please me, and ease my mind," he added, sensing her hesitation.

"Yes," she said at last.

"Good." Satisfaction settled across him. The acceptance of so intimate a gift was a good omen for her acceptance of him as her *zani*.

"Where does yours say you're Minstrel?" She touched a finger to the whole tablet he wore, her brief touch like a spark of lightning.

"Here." He pointed to the identifying runes, not needing to look at his tablet to know their location.

For a moment she looked closer, her hair brushing against his chest. The stroke, though soft and faint as a kitten's purr, elicited a powerful heat within him. With effort, he held himself still and kept his arms at his sides, until she leaned back.

"The other one that your mother gave you. Why is it broken?"

"I do not know. I know only that my mother owned it, but it was not hers. She said it was my heritage to discover. Or to destroy. I found it when I made my way back home after she left me at the school for education. She was gone. Only the tablet and those words remained."

She was silent a moment, then gave him a sympathetic look. "She must have known you wouldn't be able to destroy it. What child would destroy the one link to his past? Not to criticize your mother or anything, but knowing that, she damn well could have given you less cryptic information."

What a relief it was to hear his own unexpressed anger voiced by another. "I have thought so, too."

"So, each tablet is unique. Can you read who owned the broken one?"

"No." He took the broken tablet off his neck and laid it on the table between them.

"You don't mind taking it off?"

"This one is not mine." He pointed to a series of markings. "These are the protection. This says the owner was renowned for her voice and her mastery of the harp."

"A Minstrel?"

"Only males can be Minstrel."

"Chauvinist."

"Perhaps I should say that only males have the mix of voice, powerful *ma-at,* and bodily strength necessary in a Minstrel."

"I still think it sounds chauvinistic."

"Can we get back to the tablet?" He traced the runes to the end. "It is here that we would learn the identity of the owner of the tablet. But that part is missing."

"Not anymore." She set her glass down with a thunk, her eyes excited.

He nodded, pleased that she had so readily seen what he had seen. "Yes. Your tattoo."

"My tattoo," she agreed. "I asked the artist to be faithful, reproducing the original as exactly as possible. *That's* why you wanted to read it yesterday."

"May I look more closely now?"

"Um . . . yeah, sure." She stood with her back to him, then drew the dress up to her hip, just above the tattoo. His eyes drank in the tantalizing glimpse of her rounded bottom and the taut, smooth curves of her thighs.

"What does it say?" she asked, craning her neck as though she could read it herself.

He collected himself and lowered the flimsy fabric of her panties to reveal the marking. The edges were blurred, but they were easily read.

Easily read, easily believed. Had he ever truly speculated on the matter, he should have guessed. "Her name was Taraneh."

"Do you know who she was? Why her tablet was split?"

"Her name has never been spoken by the djinn that I have heard, but I am familiar with it."

Madeline spun from his grasp. "Enough with the cryptic replies. Who is she?"

A sliver of regret sliced through him as she adjusted the dress to cover herself again. He brought his attention back to the tablet.

"Although djinn are called by their common names, we are given full names, private names, at birth." Names usually chosen by the father in the naming ceremony, although his mother had told him she had chosen his. Private names were closely guarded, for it was only with the full true name that a djinni could be bound. Yet he didn't hesitate to explain to Madeline, knowing she would not play him false. "My name is Zaneyvei y Sholehaniya y la Tarnehya."

Madeline blinked. "Zane-what?"

"Zaneyvei y Sholehaniya y la Tarnehya."

"Zaneyvei y?"

"Sholehaniya."

"Zaneyvei y Sholehaniya?"

"y la Tarnehya."

"y la Tarnehya. Zaneyvei y Sholehaniya y la Tarnehya. And I thought Madeline Margaret Nadia Fairbanks was a mouthful."

"Our names reflect, among other things, our lineage. Sholeh was my mother. Taraneh was her mother." Normally, both the male and the female lineage were part of the name, but his mother had never said anything of his father, other than to say he was djinn.

Madeline picked up the tablet. "This was your grandmother's? Why doesn't anyone know about her? Why would it be split in two?"

"Those answers I do not know," he admitted. At first he had made inquiries, but none he asked had known what could split a tablet. Eventually he had stopped asking, his need to fit in with his society stronger than his need to know. His interest in the matter had waned as his music and his *ma-at* had consumed him.

"Maybe we should look for those answers."

"They will not be on Terra," he said quietly. "My mother had no use for Terra. They will be on Kaf."

Madeline sucked in a breath, and he knew she was still reluctant to go to his world, but he thought he saw a gleam of interest. Would the mystery and the ability to transport be enough to overcome her caution?

"Not all of the answers. How did Cyrus get the tablet?"

Apparently, her reluctance still won. "I do not know."

Quickly she finished her breakfast. "Then let's find him and get some answers. I have to shower and put on some jeans, then we'll head for the bayou. I hope Swamp Suzette has some information, because after this I'm fresh out of leads."

Zayne shook his head. "First we will give the potion to Leila."

Forty minutes later, Madeline found herself and Zayne at the home of Leila and Jack Montgomery. They were fortunate enough to find both at home. Or maybe not so fortunate, Madeline decided, seeing the enthusiastic greeting Leila gave Zayne. Still, Jack didn't seem upset, and Madeline knew her spurt of jealousy was misplaced.

The two djinn stared at one another for a moment; then Leila cast a speculative look toward her. Madeline got the distinct impression she'd been the topic of a mind-to-mind conversation between them.

"What can we do for you?" Jack asked.

Quickly Madeline brought out the vial and explained how they'd gotten it. "My stepfather ordered it, and concealed it just before he disappeared. Knowing what's in it might give us a clue where he is or what he's up to. I thought you might be able to analyze the chemicals, Jack, although I know it's a lot to ask."

"Since your ties are now to Terra," Zayne told Leila, "if there is magic within this, you are better able to glean its purpose."

Leila reached for the vial, but Jack intercepted it. "Let me check it out first."

"But—"

"We need to know if there's a poison in it."

Leila settled. "You are right."

Madeline nodded. "Be careful."

"I will." Jack deftly tucked the vial in his shirt pocket.

They chatted a few moments, but as soon as Zayne was engaged in conversation with Leila, Jack drew Madeline aside.

"I don't know Zayne well," he said in a low voice. "I've thought he was a decent man, but I suspect there are depths and secrets to him even Leila doesn't know. Djinn don't always think, or react, like a human would."

"I've been discovering that."

"His *ma-at* is very powerful." Jack cleared his throat. "He hasn't . . . ? I mean, if he controls . . . I have something that will counteract all his *ma-at* against you."

Madeline shook her head. She didn't want to counteract all Zayne's *ma-at*. There were parts of it she found useful and quite pleasant. "Thanks, but I'm with him of my own free will. We have a bargain; he will not coerce me with his *ma-at*."

Jack relaxed visibly. "If you have made a bargain, then he will keep it at any cost." His lips twitched in humor. "Although I warn you, those bargains have a way of twisting into unexpected paths."

"Since Zayne arrived, unexpected is a way of life."

"When you're with a djinni, that doesn't change," Jack said, and the look he gave his wife was sheer heat.

Madeline held out her hand. "Again, thank you for your help."

"I'll get you an answer as soon as I can."

Her cell phone rang. Madeline excused herself and answered it.

"Madeline, good, you're up." It was Lucy, the nurse at the care facility. "I know normally you're a night owl."

"What's wrong?" Her stomach curled. Only bad news would prompt that anxious note in Lucy's voice.

"Do you know how to get in touch with that man who was with you yesterday?"

"Zayne?" Hearing his name, he glanced at her. She held up a finger, delaying his questions, even as her sweaty hand gripped the phone. "Yeah, why?"

"Your mother is very agitated; the medication's not helping. She keeps saying she has to see him. I thought if we could find him, bring him here, we might not have to use restraints."

"He's with me. I'll ask him." Zayne gave her a curious look as she covered the mouthpiece. "My mother is extremely disturbed, and she insists she needs to see you—"

He took her hand. "We shall leave at once."

"Be there in a sec, Lucy. We're just around the corner."

Why did Irena want Zayne? She barely had time to wonder before she disappeared into the vortex.

An hour later, she still didn't know.

Madeline stood in the hall outside her mother's door, careful not to be seen, leaning against the wall for support and listening. She blinked back the tears in her eyes and swallowed hard against the lump in her throat. Irena sounded so normal, so lucid. She was like the charming, sparkling, intelligent woman she'd once been.

Zayne did that for her. He'd been speaking with her for nearly an hour, calming her with his soothing voice. He'd pitched his conversation low, but Madeline could still hear every word, a fact she believed he'd planned. At first he'd spoken only words of reassurance until Irena's agitation quieted. Then, as she'd grown more coherent, they'd spoken of music.

Now, though, Madeline heard him ask, "Why did you want me Irena?" There was a restless stir; then Zayne made a soothing noise. "Tell me only what you desire."

"You have to promise to bring Cyrus here," Irena said with a note of her familiar hysteria.

Madeline clenched her fists, her nails biting into her palms. *Please. Let this be a real breakthrough. Not just a temporary moment of sanity.*

"I cannot promise that now," Zayne said gently. "I do not know where he is. Do you?"

"No. No, I don't." The desperation in her voice tore through Madeline. "But he must find you."

"Why do you say this?"

"Because I have heard you sing. You wear a tablet?"

"Is that important?"

Madeline held her breath, waiting for the answer.

It never came. "I don't know. I don't know," wailed Irena.

Zayne calmed her again, then said, "Even if I should discover him, I cannot be sure that I will be able to bring him here. Thus, I cannot promise."

"You have to. I must see him. Only he can get rid of this . . . fog."

"Why do you say that?"

"He put it there. By magic," Irena whimpered. "I was suitable, but I'm not as strong as Madeline."

Madeline leaned her head against the wall and wiped away a tear with a furious gesture. Just as she and Zayne had figured, Cyrus was behind her mother's breakdown.

Somehow they would find a way to stop this madness.

"I had such a beautiful voice, he always said." Irena's tone grew dreamy and reminiscent. "I would make a beautiful mother, he said. He wanted a child, and I couldn't have one. So we adopted Madeline. I never talked about her adoption; she was our gift."

Irena had shifted to talking about her first husband, Madeline realized.

"Such a beautiful child. But she wasn't suitable, he said."

"Why?"

"She hasn't the voice. Only one of the blood," Irena said in a singsong tone. "Such a beautiful voice you have, Irena."

Madeline drew in a shuddering breath. Her mother's thoughts were drifting as her hold on sanity loosened once more.

"I love her, you know. I love Madeline."

Madeline leaned against the support of the wall. Eyes closed, tears streaming down her cheeks, she replayed the soft words over and over. How many years had it been since her mother had told her *I love you*?

Confusion slurred Irena's words, but each one shredded another piece of Madeline's heart. Cyrus had done this. Cyrus had come between mother and daughter, had caused Irena's breakdown.

Irena's voice grew drowsy. "I want to perform again. I have to, but I need Cyrus. 'No one will outshine you.' He told me that the day I hit platinum for the first time. 'No one will ever outshine you, Irena. No one.' "

Madeline froze. Irena didn't understand what she was saying. She'd only cared about music and had paid no attention to what Cyrus did to get her in the limelight and to keep her there.

Madeline did.

Singeing fury blasted away the cold and the tears. That slimy, despicable worm! She slammed a fist against the wall, not caring a bit about the sting in her hand. That bastard! Damn him. My God, all these years, and she was too dumb to see it.

Cyrus was the curse behind her debilitating stage fright.

Chapter Twelve

How *dare* he? How dare her mother not notice?

Madeline raced out of the care facility, fearing Irena would see her, fearing she would say something she would regret if she faced the mother who had failed to protect her against a monster.

Hot, sticky air bathed her in instant sweat, and the trees' shade offered no relief from her blistering fury. She stalked up and down the sidewalk. Her vision blurred, and she pounded her fist against her palm.

She'd been only fifteen. Fifteen! A dancer, not a singer. How could she have been any competition to her sparkling, charming, talented mother?

Nine years had passed, but she remembered those days with undimmed clarity.

Three events had come together in one week. Irena sold her first platinum CD, Madeline danced her first soloist role on the professional New Orleans stage, and Cyrus found out she was adopted.

The experimental ballet was a difficult one, and, although she was the youngest dancer to perform the role, she'd mastered it. Dammit, she'd mastered it! The cost was months of grueling preparation with painstaking—and painful—attention to each move and each nuance for a technically perfect performance. In those days, Cyrus pushed her and her mother mercilessly, but they both accepted his demands as necessary to their art.

The pundits made a great fuss over her youthful virtuosity. She devoured the newspaper articles, showing them to Cyrus and her mother, filled with awe and excitement and a teen's natural arrogance. One of the papers referred to her as Irena's adopted daughter—old news as far as she was concerned.

Cyrus had been shocked, though he'd tried to hide it. Madeline hunched over as she walked, arms wrapped around her waist, feeling the rise of nausea. Why her adoption was important to him she still didn't understand, but it was. After that, Cyrus's attitude toward her had changed, subtly but devastatingly. Guidance became criticism. Approval became disappointment. Barbs were hidden inside teasing. His unspoken, confident message that she would excel changed and she knew he expected her to screw up.

She drew a shuddering breath, the air so thick she could barely find oxygen in it. One week later, she'd performed daily to accolades, but she'd found it harder and harder to assemble the necessary confidence to overcome her natural backstage butterflies.

That night—God, she still remembered that awful night—Cyrus was backstage as always, giving her the nasty vitamin drink he insisted she take before every performance. The taste was particularly foul that night, she remembered. He'd put his hand on her shoulder right before her first entrance.

"Break a leg, Maddie," he'd said, giving her the traditional backstage wish for good luck. "Break a leg."

His grip had hurt. She rubbed her shoulder, still remembering the cramp that developed in her trapezius. She'd pressed on, but she'd been off balance during the entire performance. In the third act, she'd misstepped, a bobble normally easy to correct, but instead she'd fallen. In a one-in-a-million freak twist she had broken her leg.

Madeline squeezed her eyes shut against the jab of pain in her leg, the burn of nausea in her throat. She remembered the gasps of horror from the cast. She remembered hundreds of eyes staring at her from the audience, eyes that judged and pitied her. To this day, however, she could never remember whether the quiet, taunting laughs she heard in her nightmares were real or imagined.

Madeline opened her eyes and looked up at the hot sun. She'd been in a cast for several weeks, and someone else had taken over her role in the ballet. When the cast was off, she'd tried classes again, tried to get back on stage, only to see the horror, hear the laughter, feel the humiliation echo inside her. Each time she tried, the stage fright got worse and expanded until she'd been forced to give up first performing, then any kind of public appearance, then anything that drew attention to her.

As she withdrew, other things changed. People who once praised her now ignored her. Colleagues celebrated the loss of competition for scarce work. Acquaintances saw her worthy only as a conduit to Irena or Cyrus. She lost her innocent view of the entertainment world, then turned her back on it, no longer wanting to be consumed by that madness.

She no longer wanted to be on stage, but, oh, she still longed to dance.

For nine years, she had tried. She watched her diet, kept her muscles toned and the physical memory of phrases ingrained. Every dancer needed to dance daily, either in rehearsals or classes, so she'd done daily routines, watched instructional videos, danced in front of the mirror analyzing herself.

Ultimately, though, dancing was about performing, a celebration of the body's ability to bend, swoop, stretch, and leap. Without that audience, any audience, the demanding regimen grew pointless. She gave herself fewer classes; her strict attention to form relaxed; demands for technical perfection eased. Worst of all, the joy faded.

Fists clenched until her nails dug into her palms, Madeline paced the sidewalk. She hadn't believed in magic then; she'd been unable to see what Cyrus had done to her. Now she did. He had created a single incident, used an adolescent's confusion and a performer's natural nervousness, and then he'd magnified the fear, fed it magically. She swore and slapped her hand against the trunk of a live oak. "Damn him! Why?"

"Madeline?"

She spun around to find Zayne behind her, a quizzical look on his face. Embarrassed, she combed her fingers through her hair, trying to straighten the tousled mess, and pulled a Wet Wipe from her bag to wipe her face. "Sorry for bailing out like that," she mumbled.

At once, he gathered her into his arms. "What is wrong? What has happened?"

She leaned against the solid brace of his chest, taking in the steadying beat of his heart. "How's my mother?" she asked, the words muffled against him.

"She is sleeping." His hand stroked down her hair. "She said nothing more with coherence."

"She said more than I expected."

Standing in his embrace felt so right, so good. She leaned deeper into him, raw nerves calmed by his masculine strength, her emotional storm soothed by his gentle touch.

As her anger and embarrassment subsided, awareness and desire crept into their place. His spicy scent wrapped around her, and her breathing fell into the rhythm of his. Her skin tingled beneath the weight of his palm at her neck.

She leaned back a little to look up at him and with her fingertips traced the strong lines of his jaw and neck. His pulse quickened and arousal brushed across her. Oh, she'd been a cautious fool last night to refuse his invitation. The future was uncertain. Maybe they would have only a single night together, or a string of nights. Didn't matter.

Her heart executed a jeté inside her chest. What mattered was that she savored the joy in these moments, for joy could be too fleeting. She raised herself on tiptoe, bracketing his face with her hands and kissing him. "You're a remarkable man, Zayne. A good man."

"Very good," he agreed with a touch of arrogance, but the thought he slipped her was definitely a naughty one, and she laughed.

Zayne was pleased to hear her laugh again. When he had seen the evidence of her tears, his first instinct had been to comfort her, but now he delighted in her feminine overtures. Was her promise of "soon" to be this night? His body tightened at the mere thought. He erased a lingering tear with his thumb. "Do not cry over Irena. She is troubled, but she will find her own way."

"I wasn't crying over her . . . well, not entirely. I was angry."

He tilted his head, surprised. "Why?"

"Because I realized Cyrus not only messed with her mind, but with mine also."

"What? What did he do?" *The fiend would pay for this outrage.*

"He's behind my stage fright."

A chilly wash of apprehension drew him back. His hand stilled on her hair. Perhaps he misunderstood the words. "Stage fright?"

"Well, I call it stage fright, but it's stronger, weirder. The idea of being the center of attention . . ." She shuddered. "I sweat; I shake; I can't talk. I can't even breathe."

"You are confident with me."

"One on one, I'm fine. More than two pairs of eyes on me is a nightmare. I kept thinking I should be able to get over it, but every time I tried, it just got worse."

"You cannot perform?"

"No, and now I know why. Cyrus."

So, *that* was why she'd refused to sing with him. A knot formed in his chest, and a battery of conflicting questions assaulted him. Not only questions for Madeline about why Cyrus had done this, but selfish questions for himself. How could a woman with this stage fright be the *zaniya* of the Minstrel? How could the balance be maintained without a public performance of harmony? Could he have misinterpreted the divination?

No. How could he be wrong when every part of him—body, mind, soul—affirmed that she was the one he wanted to share his life with? When she met his challenges, then responded by smiling at him with desire and calling him good? He rubbed a trembling hand against his turquoise tablet. He must understand this. "What did Cyrus do?"

"Magic. He put some kind of spell on me."

"A very sinister magic. Why would he do such an evil thing?"

"I'm not entirely sure. Remember, Irena said he told her no one would outshine her? I guess he thought I was starting to, although I'm certainly no threat to her."

"Perhaps you were more dangerous than you realized," he murmured. As a Minstrel's *zaniya-e-na*, *zaniya*-to-be, her voice would surely rival the best. Moreover, Madeline had something more vital than technical virtuosity. She had passion.

Her shrug said she did not agree. "Weird thing is, I keep thinking he changed when he found out I was adopted. Why would that matter?"

"Perhaps his spells work best if he knows the line of your birth."

She looked up at him. "If this is some spell on me, is there a counterspell? Something to take it off?"

"I have not learned one." Fear of performing was not a matter he had ever considered. Singing for others was lifeblood to him. "I shall look, but the task would be easier if we knew how he fashioned the workings of the spell."

"One more question for Cyrus Cromwell to answer when we find him," she said fiercely. "I'm going to get rid of this fear. I have to!"

Hearing the desperate yearning in her voice, he leaned over and kissed her forehead. *I vow, Madeline, I will do whatever I can to help you.*

They transported home to get the car for the trip to the bayou. While Madeline went inside to wash the signs of tears from her face, Zayne waited outside. He raked his hands through his hair, giving vent at last to his agitation.

The weight of the two turquoise tablets pressed against his chest. The weight of confusion and responsibility to his world remained a heavier burden. Sweat stung his eyes and heat pounded his back, and he hummed under his breath, a wild melody, as he paced.

Suddenly a small red orb spun in front of him, chiming its alert. He halted and gritted his teeth. His message sphere was warning that his actions had unsettled Kaf. His music was his outlet, his vent, but for the moment he had forgotten this was denied him.

He knew the needs of Kaf. He would not fail the djinn's trust.

He also would not fail Madeline.

Their search for Cyrus had taken on a new depth and a new urgency. No longer was it just about Madeline's job, the mystery of the tablet, or even her need to cure her mother. They must find out the means Cyrus had used to weave his sticky web about her. They must free her of this shackling fear. For her sake as well as his.

"I'm ready," Madeline called, coming out. As she opened the door where the car resided, he drank in her trim legs displayed in those jeans that fit her like her skin did, the colorful scarf tied at her waist, the soft curves of her breasts beneath the buttonless shirt.

His body tightened in that now familiar rush of need. She backed out the car, then motioned him to join her. Could such mutual desire be wrong?

As he strode to the car, though, he could not deny one other doubt he had not shared with Madeline.

Spells like hers were not static shields, thin layers that could be peeled away and discarded without residual consequence. This spell had been with her a very long time and had woven itself into her life and her memories. Even if they could lift it, she would still remember the companion fear. Her body would remember, too, and might still react.

How could she be his *zaniya* if she could not perform and sing with him?

His fist tightened. They would find Cyrus, and they would break the curse he'd put on Madeline. She would soar free once more, the way she was meant to.

For he could not accept that she was not his *zaniya-e-na*, his soul and his life.

Zayne had seen this bayou place in his divination. He had seen the gnarled roots of the trees, the veils of hanging moss, and the ripple of life beneath the black surface of the water. He had seen; he had not experienced. No divination could portray the deceiving patterns of light that filtered through entwined leaves and branches. Mere vision did not convey the scent of rotting vegetation or the perpetual buzz of insects in muggy air.

The powers of Terra, raw and elemental, were generated in these primitive areas. He rubbed his arms, not liking the unease that cloaked his body like sweat. They were stopped on a narrow piece of road that dipped down and was swallowed by the water about a tent's width from their car. For once, he was glad for the barrier of the metal.

Madeline frowned at the paper printed with directions and a map. "That's the highway. Turn right at 10.3 miles. Turn left 2.6 miles." She eyed the dials before her. "Here we are, 2.6 miles exactly. So where's the road we follow for the final half mile?"

He looked around. "I see no road." There was only the wall of trees and moss, only the spread of stagnant water and tangled roots.

"Neither do I." With a quick jerk, she restarted the car and slowly backed it up.

"Wait." He pointed to a narrow path he'd just sighted. "Perhaps we are meant to walk."

"And perhaps MapUSA needs to update their records to take into account overgrowth and flooding," Madeline muttered as she parked the car as far to the right as she could manage. "Okay, let's trek between the cypress trees."

He liked walking through the bayou even less than he liked riding through it. The thick, solid trunks of the cypress hemmed the rise of muddy ground where he and Madeline trod. Brown or emerald leaves, ropy vines, and gray moss filled in holes between the trees. The humid air clogged the remaining spaces. Not a breeze stirred. No fire could survive the encompassing dampness. No, he did not like this place.

A swarm of insects buzzed his head, while a small biting one landed on his arm. Gently he brushed it off, then surrounded himself with a mild repellent.

His spine tightened at the brush of Terran energy. "This is not a good place."

"Afraid you'll see the *loup garou*? The Cajun version of a werewolf?"

"There are unpleasant things lurking here. This woman may be one of them."

Madeline stopped and faced him. She looked incongruous here, so feminine, clean, and honest. Yet, strangely, she seemed to belong here more than he ever could, and that he did not like.

"Zayne, we're going to see a woman who has lived in the bayou all her life and who makes a living by giving air-boat tours. She feeds marshmallows to the alligators so they will come near and give her clients a view. People come here all the time. No one has disappeared because of Swamp Suzette."

He was not reassured. "Humans do not feel the energies here. They come and go oblivious. That does not mean the wrongness does not exist."

Madeline slapped her arm and brushed the air around her head. "Gnats and mosquitoes. *These* are the scourge of the bayou." She glanced over at him. "You, on the other hand, feel the evil energies but are not in the least affected by the bugs."

"My *ma'at* can protect you, too, if you wish."

She gave him a quizzical look. "What would you do?"

"Little that you would notice. The repellent will fade by tomorrow." He waited for her decision, remembering his promise not to coerce her.

"All right."

"Stand quiet," he murmured. "Your feet apart, your arms away from your body."

She complied, her eyes fixed on his. Hers were green now, he noted, a deep, deep green reflected from the surrounding vegetation. It seemed as though here, in the bayou, she cast deep roots to her Terra. Became part of the earth and the water.

He would surround her with the power of the djinn.

He held his palms above her head, intoning the simple words to guard her from the bite and sting of the insects. His hands hovered above her, not touching her, but no more than the thickness of his turquoise tablet away from her body. Across her hair, her cheeks, her ears and jaw and neck, his hands glided past her skin, cutting away the stagnant air, protecting her with his *ma-at*.

The palms of his hands tingled with the power of *ma-at* and the powerful urge to touch. Except contact would break the flow of the shield surrounding her. Every point of her would be touched by his *ma-at* instead.

A flush of blood deepened the tones of her skin. Ah, but the sight was beautiful. He moved across her shoulders and arms, then lingered above her round breasts. Her nipples tightened through the fabric, and he heard the catch of her breath.

His breathing matched hers, deep and fast. The blood, too, rose within him. This was a spell with consequences he had not anticipated. Still, he had started, and by the love of Solomon, he could not stop.

Slowly he moved down her body, past the indentation of her waist, kneeling to reach her groin and the juncture of her legs. The urge to lean forward, to kiss her so intimately, shot through him. Before him, Madeline shifted restlessly.

"Be still. Do not yet move," he crooned, fitting the words between the chant of the spell. "Were I to touch you now, the protection would be incomplete."

"Ohhh." It was a single, drawn-out word of disappointment; then she whispered, "Can you touch me soon?"

Why did she issue the invitation now? His sharp hunger for her was almost pain.

With care, he finished first the right leg, then the left, his whole body now tight with the raging need to touch, to savor, and to claim. He shoved to his feet, sliding closer to her so his body was as close as his hands had been, though still not touching.

She looked up at him. Her lips parted, inviting his entrance and his possession.

Overhead, a bird flew, its shadow crossing over them with a moment of cool darkness and reminding him of the bayou steeped in the powers of Terra and of his duty.

She glanced up toward the disappearing bird. "A water turkey. Look at the tail feathers."

He had no desire to look at tail feathers, not when he had Madeline in sight. Yet he stepped back, away from the temptation of her. "You are protected by my *ma-at*."

Madeline gave a small sigh, acknowledging and accepting his withdrawal. She drew in a long breath, then gave a short sniff. "I smell orange."

"The repellent lingers with that odor."

She laughed, a hearty sound that fed his soul. "In other words, you coated me with the djinn equivalent of citronella."

He shrugged. "The spell is effective."

"Yeah, I guess it is," she answered, her head cocked. "No bites and no swarms. Thanks. Oh, look, a cabin. Let's go."

A water turkey. Could she have said anything more gauche? Madeline cringed, replaying the moment. She'd never felt so desired, so aroused, so alive as she had when Zayne finished his spell. And he hadn't even touched her! So, what clever response did she come up with? A damn water turkey.

She scratched at a bite on her arm, one she'd gotten before Zayne had banished the pests. Each pass of his hand had stirred the air, stimulated the hairs on her arm, caressed her skin until every inch, clothed or not, felt as though it glowed with starlight. The bayou was hot, but she was hotter.

He hadn't even touched her, she repeated, amazed. No feminine equilibrium was safe around a man who was a joy to the senses as well as being more effective than a can of Raid. He was exotic and unpredictable. She, on the other hand, was wearing cotton underwear and sensible cross trainers. He spoke in music. She responded with comments about water turkeys and citronella.

Apparently, she had a ways to go yet with that flair thing.

They reached the weathered gray board cabin. No one was in sight, but the rocker on the porch swayed back and forth as though someone had just left. "Suzette?" she called. "It's Madeline Fairbanks. I left a message on your voice mail."

Silence followed. "Suzette?" she repeated.

Be cautious, Madeline. Zayne's voice broke into her thoughts, startling her. His body seemed to loom over her, surround her, even though he still didn't touch her.

"Don't do that," she hissed. "It makes me jump."

I do not wish to be heard by any but you. There are forces here, old forces, primitive ones, but very strong.

"Suzette's not a witch," Madeline insisted. Yet some of Zayne's unease seeped into her, and she kept her voice low. After all, Suzette was a woman who knew Cyrus. Beyond the edges of the clearing, leaves rustled, as if a breeze had found its way through.

Except there was no breeze. Not a single breath of air.

The rustle grew louder. It spread out from a single point in front of them to an encircling arc.

"Come, Madeline." Zayne gripped her wrist. "We should leave."

"No, I want to talk to Suzette. Don't transport me away. No coercion, remember?"

"Unless you are in danger."

"I see no danger yet. Wait. Please."

Zayne muttered something under his breath that

sounded profane and let go of her wrist. He moved to her back and stretched out his arms on either side of her. Still not touching her, he shielded her with his strength. His *ma-at* tingled along her bare skin and to the depth of her muscles. In the distance a gator roared its defiance of the disturbance.

A snowy egret took off, emerging from the dense growth like a white feathered arrow shot from an invisible bow. The rustling increased, approaching them on two sides. A baying sounded, unmuffled by the dense foliage. Zayne's hands opened, fingers outstretched.

She laid a hand on his muscled arm. "Wait. Don't do anything. I think it's—"

Two creatures burst into the clearing, tails wagging.

"—a dog. Two dogs."

Electricity crackled around her. Sparks seemed to shoot from Zayne's palms, and the air smelled scorched and charged.

Two hounds froze in mid lope, their floppy ears caught straight out. One was liver and white and not much bigger than a skunk, while the coal-black one could have given the Baskervilles a good fright.

"Ohmigod, you froze them. That doesn't hurt, does it?"

"I do not harm animals. I merely stopped them."

"Can you unstop them?"

"Of course. Is it wise to let these creatures free? They have big teeth."

"They're dogs. They're pets."

He gave her a puzzled glance, and she wondered if he didn't understand "dog" or "pet" or both. Just then, the central rustling grew closer.

"Zayne, please," she warned. "I don't think we should let Suzette see your power."

NAME: ______________________________

ADDRESS: ______________________________

____

____

TELEPHONE: ______________________________

E-MAIL: ______________________________

____ I want to pay by credit card.

__ Visa   __ MasterCard   __ Discover

Account Number: ______________________________

Expiration date: ______________________________

SIGNATURE: ______________________________

Send this form, along with $2.00 shipping and handling for your FREE books, to:

Love Spell Romance Book Club
20 Academy Street
Norwalk, CT 06850-4032

Or fax (must include credit card information!) to: 610.995.9274.
You can also sign up on the Web at www.dorchesterpub.com.

Offer open to residents of the U.S. and Canada only. Canadian residents, please call 1.800.481.9191 for pricing information.

If under 18, a parent or guardian must sign. Terms, prices and conditions subject to change. Subscription subject to acceptance. Dorchester Publishing reserves the right to reject any order or cancel any subscription.

He snapped his fingers, and the dogs fell to the ground. They gave a yip of surprise, then continued to lope toward the strangers. Madeline hoped the waving tails were a good sign.

"If they bite me, you can freeze them again," she whispered as the small one ran around them in a frenzy of barking. The other had size on his side, and he could afford to be sedate. He went to Madeline and shoved his face against her groin for an identifying sniff.

"Does that count as a bite?" Zayne whispered back.

"Not yet." She shoved the dog's face away, scratching behind his ears. The dog sat on his haunches almost atop her feet and let her scratch. "So what's your name, fella?"

"Zayne," answered the djinni at her side. "Have the forces taken your memory, Madeline?"

"I was talking to the dog."

"They speak?"

"Not words, but we understand each other, don't we, fella?" The dog's tail thumped in answer.

A woman came into view. She wore wader boots and carried a shotgun and two dead, furry rodents, each about two feet long. Nutria, Madeline guessed. They were taking over the bayous, lawns, and parks, much to the dismay of the locals. Even the local sheriff took his deputies out nutria hunting to practice their shooting skills.

Suzette was a six-foot, large-boned woman with dark hair and surprisingly few wrinkles on her weather-browned face. Despite her size, the woman moved with absolute silence.

"*Mais*, Butcher and Eel, *venez ici. Maintenant*. You leave them folks alone. 'Allo, Madeline. I hope the hounds done not scared you."

The hope did not sound sincere. "You recognize me?"

"*Oui*. I got your message." Suzette shook the nutrias at her. "I left you one. I tole you, no tours today. Why you come anyway?"

"I don't want a tour. I want information."

"I live in a swamp, *chère*—what kind of information you tink you gonna get offa me?"

"Cyrus Cromwell," Madeline said succinctly.

The woman drew up, and her eyes narrowed.

Do you not believe in a subtle approach? Zayne's reproachful words slid inside her.

She made a dismissive gesture behind her back, keeping her focus on Suzette.

Avoiding the question, Suzette nodded toward Zayne. "Who's your friend there?"

"His name is Zayne. I heard Cyrus called you right before he disappeared."

After a long, interested look at Zayne, Suzette turned back to Madeline. "*Non.*"

"When did you last see him?"

Suzette raised a brow. "Who says I ever saw him? Why you wanna find Cyrus anyway? Everyone knows you two 'bout as friendly as the snake and the bunny."

Madeline had no doubt which one of them Suzette thought was the bunny. "I have my reasons."

"Oh, you are a prim one. Well, you wasting your time. I never seen Cyrus Cromwell, and you can take that to the bank." She turned away. "Now, I got me some nutria to skin."

Madeline decided to take a gamble. "If I took it to the bank, I'd be overdrawn."

Do you want me to use the Truthspeak on her? Zayne offered.

This dual-conversation stuff, one verbal, one mental,

was a pain. She gave an irritated shake of her head, hoping he understood that human gesture.

Suzette inhaled sharply and pivoted back to face them. Her finger caressed the bore of the shotgun. "You calling me a liar?"

Of a sudden, everything around them was utterly still, as if life itself had taken a pause. No insects swarmed or buzzed. The black surface of the water turned to obsidian rock, without even a faint ripple. Even the leaves and vines stopped their small vibrations.

Her stomach clenched. They were isolated out here, and Zayne thought it was a place of magic. He shifted closer to her, bracing her with his heat and a whiff of cinnamon, so foreign in this place of verdant dampness. From the corner of her eye, she saw him make a subtle gesture with his hand and heard him intone a serves of words, so low she knew Suzette wouldn't hear. What he'd done she didn't know, but it was reassuring to have him here.

"Liar?" she answered Suzette, shaking her head. "Just forgetful. I know Cyrus. He wouldn't have skipped coming to a place as steeped in magic as this is."

A gator roared again, sounding closer than ever. Thin ripples skimmed across the water, as though something stirred in the depths. Butcher and Eel whined.

Suzette's finger curled around the trigger. Her gaze shifted from Madeline to Zayne, and her lips tightened. "Stop whatever you're conjuring. The swamp don' like."

"Zayne isn't the issue. This is between you and me."

Madeline! Zayne's shock intruded. *Do not underestimate her. She is more than she seems.*

Madeline was coming to realize that Suzette wasn't

the Swamp Suzette rustic she had portrayed to him. What depths the woman had, however, were as concealed and muddy as the bottom of the bayou.

The ground beneath their feet vibrated, and a strange rustling whispered through the cypress. Suzette lifted the gun, pointing it toward Madeline but speaking to Zayne. "You stop, or you'll find out if you can be faster than a bullet."

Behind her, Madeline felt Zayne tense. His muscles bunched.

"Zayne, stop," she warned.

"She would harm us."

"Not if you stop. She won't tell us anything otherwise."

She waited, breath caught, until she felt him relax and the low chant stopped. The vibrations ceased and the winds died.

"We did what you asked," she told Suzette. "Now put the gun down."

After a long minute, the woman lowered the barrel. But she kept her finger by the trigger.

"I told you straight out what I wanted," Madeline continued doggedly, trying to keep her gaze from straying to that trigger finger, trying to keep Suzette's attention from Zayne. "Now I'm going to tell you what I think. You know Cyrus, and you may not know where he is, but you damn well know how to contact him. I want to see him. So here's a message for him." She leaned forward, her lip curling. "You tell my bastard of a stepfather I know what he did to Irena, and I know what he did to me. I'll find a way to break his hold, and if he wants to stop me, he'd better show his damn face."

"Cyrus always did say you were too bloody transparent." Suzette tilted her head. "Would it shock you to learn we were lovers?"

"No." Surprise her a little, maybe. Cyrus's tastes were very sophisticated, and Suzette would never move with elegant ease through the cocaine and tuxedo crowd.

Then again, her stepfather was known to partake of unexpected and forbidden pleasures. He'd even tried manipulating his way into her bed one summer. She'd moved out the next day and never returned to the Cromwell house.

"Nothing my stepfather did could shock me," she added.

"Ah, *chère*, don't be so sure of that." At least her finger had finally relaxed on the trigger. "I don't know where he is, that's a fact. I do know if Cyrus don' wanna be found, then he's not going to be."

"But . . ." There had to be more. Why else would Suzette have gotten so chatty?

"You don't find Cyrus. You let him find you."

"How?"

"By offering him something he wants." She gave a low whistle and the two hounds came to heel.

"What would that be?"

"*Mais, chère*, that's for you to figure out. But you might start by looking at that man beside you." A second later she, the hounds, and the nutrias disappeared into the bayou.

Chapter Thirteen

The ride from the bayou back to New Orleans was not a pleasant one for Zayne. Too many emotions beset him: fear for his chaotic music and endangered world; doubts about Madeline's stage fright; anger that she had so suffered. Questions about his tablet, a biting need to exact retribution against Cyrus Cromwell, and hungry desire for Madeline on his pillows all billowed about him as ungraspable as a sandstorm.

"What do you think Suzette meant about looking to you for something Cyrus wants?" Madeline's question interrupted his silence, and he was grateful for the distraction.

"I would guess my music or my *ma-at*, since those are the essence of a Minstrel."

"Cyrus is interested in both."

"Do you believe she told him of our visit?"

"If she did, the question is, will that bring him out of seclusion? I wish I knew why he disappeared. There was no reason; no one blamed him for Irena's collapse."

"For Cyrus to control your mother, there would have to be a connection between them. Mind to mind. When she collapsed and fell into madness, he could have experienced repercussions."

"You mean he's sitting out in the bayou, also incoherent?" She sounded pleased by the idea.

"I believe he is stronger than that. I meant the break could have disrupted his strength, left him with residual confusions or symptoms."

"Cyrus wouldn't want to be seen at anything less than full strength, but it's getting on to a year. So, maybe he's just waiting for a reason to reappear. Like you." Suddenly she snapped her fingers. "Like a performance. Even when you're not using a spell, I can't resist that voice of yours."

Zayne hesitated, a flutter of doubt keeping him silent. Madeline had never heard him sing while drawing on the full measure of his *ma-at*. In the garden, with Irena, even at the jazz bar, he had tempered his songs and sang only briefly. She had never experienced the wild forces that battled inside him; he had never allowed them full rein while on Terra. Yet even though she did not know it, that was what she asked him to do.

If he tried more, if he sang as a djinni with his *ma-at*, and with the competing forces, what would be the effect on Kaf if he could not control the music? From the warning beacons, he knew his actions still reverberated on his world.

His insides knotted. With Madeline, he had managed a small amount of control at the jazz club, enough to give him hope for the future. But an entire performance? When she was still too spellbound to sing at his side and be his balance? Could he do that? He did not know if he had the strength by himself.

At his continued silence, she cast a quick worried glance toward him. "Yeah, that isn't such a good idea. It could be dangerous for you."

"I do not fear Cyrus Cromwell." Although pleased that she thought of his safety, he was not thrilled that she believed he hesitated for that reason.

"He's capable of nasty things, and we don't know how much power he wields."

"His power will not match that of a djinni, especially not one who is Minstrel. No human sorcerer could."

"Are you sure about that?"

"Yes." Few on Kaf could match his power and ease with his *ma-at*. He feared the workings of no human.

"Could you turn him into a toad?"

His brows knit. "What is this fascination you have with turning someone into a toad? The spell is difficult and does more harm than good." Although for Cyrus Cromwell, he might make an exception.

"I was just joking. Sort of."

Abruptly he made a decision. He had promised Madeline to help her find her stepfather, and he needed Cyrus to erase her stage fright. Madeline's presence seemed to offer a measure of control, and he needed to use only enough *ma-at* to attract Cyrus's attention. The balance would be delicate, the task difficult, but he must try.

He had to know if, with Madeline, he could control the battle within.

"I will do it. Do I perform where I sang last night?"

She shook her head. "You should be solo. One of the local musicians owns a music club. He has the stars in, but he also features new acts, and he's particular about who he lets on his stage. The talent has to be damn good. Cyrus used to go there a lot." She reached over to her cell phone, which was attached to some device at the front of the car, and punched in a couple of numbers. After a few rings, a man answered.

"Hi, Wilson. It's Madeline Fairbanks."

"Hey, babe, long time no see."

"Working for Feydor keeps me busy."

"You calling to tell me Irena's coming back?"

"Not yet, but I hope someday."

"Don't we all."

"I have a favor to ask. I have somebody I want you to feature on your stage."

"I'm booked until August, but I could audition him for September."

"It's got to be this week. No later."

"Sorry, impossible. Richie Aquina's singing next."

She made an annoyed grunt. "You wouldn't say impossible if you heard Zayne."

Wilson gave a soft chuckle. "Madeline, baby, you're a sister, but you don't have a gifted ear."

Zayne frowned, not liking the easy endearments from this Wilson. Nor liking Madeline's ready acceptance of them.

"I know that. I also know if you feature Zayne, your second night will be double from the word of mouth."

"That good?"

"Trust me."

There was a moment's pause. "Tell you what. You and this Zayne come down tonight for an audition. Eleven, after the first show? I'll listen to him. If he's as good as you say, then I'll cut the current act off early."

Audition? I will listen. If he is good! Zayne stared in astonishment at the phone, anger rising. His palm tingled with the urge to melt this phone and this man's temerity.

"Thanks, Wilson. You won't be sorry." She turned off the phone. "We're all set. I know you'll wow—" She broke off as she caught sight of him.

The air crackled and sparked with his anger. "I am Minstrel. I do not 'audition' for anyone."

"This is the only way we can get you on so quickly."

"I will not." He crossed his arms.

"It's not really an audition; we both know you'll wow him."

He refused to say another word. He had given his answer.

"Just think of it as another performance."

No answer.

"I know you're thinking about it. There are fewer sparks in the air around you."

By Solomon, she was right. Despite his righteous anger, he was listening to her.

"Please," she said softly. "It's the only way I can think of to find Cyrus."

Her simple plea cut through his anger and his pride. When Madeline looked at him like that, there was little he could refuse her. Still . . .

"I will."

"Thank—"

"On one condition."

"What?" she asked warily.

She was wise to be cautious of an angry djinni. "When I perform, you will be there beside the stage, and you will wear the dress I gave you."

"That's two conditions."

He glared at her.

She drew in a long breath. "All right."

They were approaching New Orleans when Madeline's cell phone rang and she answered.

"Madeline, you must come back." Virginia, Feydor's researcher, sounded frantic. "Tonight. Mr. Blaze has been in such a foul mood."

"Why?" Virginia was like a computer when tracking down and remembering research facts, but in dealing with a man like Feydor, she was about as effective as rubber legs on a ballerina.

"The St. John's Eve party. All the decisions. The decorator says we need a touch of red in the black and silver scheme. The florist called to say tiger lilies were in short supply. Now the caterer needs an update of the guest count, and I can't find the list."

"Tell Feydor the party's his bailiwick now, since he practically fired me."

"He told me to handle the decisions."

Oh, hell, Virginia would make a mash of it.

I would like to meet this Feydor. Zayne's voice sounded in her head.

Madeline cast a quick glance at him. "Why?"

"Because he's in the throes of a deadline, and he says there's no one else," Virginia wailed, thinking Madeline had spoken to her.

Zayne just nodded toward the phone. *Tell her you will be there soon.*

She couldn't resist Virginia's plea for help. "If I show you the computer tracking for the replies, can you call the caterer with a weekly update?"

"Yes."

"And the other matters?" Feydor interrupted from the extension, his tone perfectly even and ice cold. "You need to straighten out this mess you left, Maddie."

"Call me Madeline, sir, and it wouldn't be a mess if you hadn't told me not to darken your door unless I had Cyrus."

"I was precipitous."

"Is that an apology?"

"Yes."

"Change your mind about the job?"

"No. How does your hunt go?"

She glanced over at Zayne. "There've been some unexpected twists."

"I'll expect you in fifteen minutes for a report."

"If you stop badgering Virginia, we'll be there in ten."

"*We*?" The word was a drawn-out ice cube. "I made myself clear—"

"See you." She hung up, then turned to Zayne. "Why do you want to meet Feydor?"

"He started you looking for Cyrus, did he not?"

"Yes, he wants to interview my esteemed stepfather. Oh, hell, you don't think there's some other reason, do you? I've worked with Feydor for six months. He can be a pain in the butt, but he's a straight shooter. No magic there."

"You did not recognize the true magic in Brendan's store or the bayou either."

This home of Feydor Blaze was oppressive, Zayne decided, even by human standards. The thick stone block walls were more solid than most human structures, and the dark overhanging roof pushed the whole structure against the ground. Stagnant humid air wrapped around the house like a barrier.

The house interested him less than the man they met inside, however.

While Madeline was hunched over a device explaining something to Virginia, Zayne studied the man who had just stalked into the room.

Feydor Blaze was as solid and dark as his house. He was taller than Zayne, with the bulk of a man of strength. But he moved with the grace of a *chi-zhao* master, and keen intelligence shone from his eyes.

He would be a dangerous adversary.

What Zayne could not decide, precisely, was whether he was an adversary or not.

There was tenderness in the way the human touched Madeline's shoulder, even as his words were forbiddingly cold. "Who's the companion, Maddie? No, never mind who he is. Tell him to wait outside."

Zayne crossed his arms. His mood, already darkened by the prospect of auditioning and by the time at the bayou, was not enhanced by this man's attention to Madeline. "Speak to me directly."

To his credit, Feydor was not reluctant to take up the challenge. He stood in front of Zayne, his hands in his pockets. "You were not invited into my house."

Strange, it seemed of a sudden that some force nudged his feet, encouraging him to leave. A feeling of urgency, of something lost that he must go find, seeped through him.

A curious force, this. Not *ma-at*, for sure, and not magic. Not sinister either, but insistent. A human might not recognize the external source of the urge, but he did, allowing him to easily resist. All that training with the Chant of Purpose was finally of benefit.

"I do not wait for an invitation," he said calmly. "I go with Madeline. She is under my protection." He waited for Feydor's response.

A spark of interest rose in Feydor's flat black eyes, and the force receded. Zayne's nostrils flared, catching the scent of something dry, like leaves before the monsoon, and something sharp, like the aftermath of a lightning storm.

"About that 'under my protection' bit—" Madeline began, turning from Virginia.

Feydor quieted her protest with a wave of his hand, his gaze never leaving Zayne. "A self-appointed guardian?"

"Yes."

"Her lover?"

"Yes." Zayne saw no reason to deny the inevitable or to lessen his claim.

Madeline stalked over to them. "Entirely too macho and personal, you two."

They both ignored her.

Feydor nodded. "She's needed that, and I wasn't the man."

"Good," Zayne said softly. Although djinn never worried about past lovers with their partners, he found a strange satisfaction that he was not facing one of Madeline's. He was not entirely sure what his reaction would have been had the human held her, or been one of those who had hurt her in some way. He just knew it would not be pleasant.

Feydor stepped back, and Zayne got the impression he'd passed an unspoken test.

"You may stay. Introduce us, Maddie."

Her lips tightened; then her hands fisted at her waist. "Feydor, this is Zayne. He's a friend of Miss Tildy's and is staying at her house while he's in the country, and it's none of your damn business whether we are lovers or not. You're my employer, not my father, and you stepped way over the line with that question. Zayne, meet my boss, Feydor Blaze. He writes creepy vampire novels that take the reader on a real emotional roller-coaster ride. He can be a bastard, but he treats everyone that way, so at least he's open about it and won't back-stab you. And you also stepped way over that line, too. I am an adult, and I do not need a guardian." She stopped and drew in a deep breath, then leaned back, crossed her arms over her chest, and waited.

She was truly annoyed, Zayne realized with astonishment. He played the conversation over in his mind. He had but spoken the truth. Ah, but he had reacted with the instinct of a male djinni for his mate, while he and Madeline had not declared together.

He pressed his palms together and inclined his head

toward her, giving her the rituals of apology. "You are right. My actions were hasty. For that, I request forgiveness."

Madeline gave him a suspicious look, then evidently decided he was sincere. "All right." She gave Feydor an expectant look.

He was rubbing his chin. "You're right, Maddie," he said absently, his gaze flicking between the two of them. "Sorry."

Apparently the apology mollified her, for she gave a satisfied nod. "Considering you're grumpy as Grumpy on deadline, I'll accept that. Feydor, the people hired for the party are all professionals. They know the budget, and they know the effect you want. If they suggest a change, agree to it. If there's a major problem, call my cell phone. Virginia, you set with the computer?"

"Yes."

"Then I'll see you on St. John's Eve."

Outside the house, though, she paused at the car to ask Zayne, "Well? Is Feydor a wizard or a sorcerer or a warlock?"

"No." He was not sure who or what Feydor was, but he did not draw the forces of Terra. Most importantly, and the only thing that interested Zayne, he intended no harm toward Madeline.

Back home, Madeline finished her dance exercises, then showered in preparation for going to Zayne's audition. Dressed in a robe and towel-drying her hair, she stepped from the bathroom into her bedroom.

"When do we leave?"

At the masculine voice, Madeline shrieked and whirled around. Zayne was waiting in her bedroom. At least he was fully dressed and sprawled on a chair, not levitating at her side or lounging naked in the bed.

Not that it made much difference in the way her

heart raced and her hormones kicked into high gear. Not when he wore form-fitting, sleeveless, black leather with the turquoise tablet and silver earring.

"I need those privacy stones," she muttered. "Or my nerves will never survive."

He disappeared, then a moment later returned, carrying one of the stones from outside his door. "Here."

"How do I light it?"

"With *ma-at*," he answered, his lips twitching.

Madeline laughed. "No wonder you're so generous." She spied Mardi Gras beads heaped in a basket. Selecting a shiny purple one, she wrapped it around the white stone, then deposited the stone outside her bedroom door. "When the bead is wrapped around the stone, consider it lit." Pointedly she held the door open, waiting.

"Are you sure you do not wish to remove the bead?" he asked hopefully.

She shook her head.

"I could help you dress."

By the heat in his eyes, getting her *dressed* wasn't part of the plan. Now, that was a tempting offer. Except her first time with Zayne was not going to be quick. "We only have half an hour."

"How long is that?"

Making appointments with a man who had no concept of minutes, watches, or schedules was not always an easy task. "Long enough for you to put the cover on Khu's cage and put out cat food. Okay?"

"Very well."

When he'd left and shut the door, Madeline turned to her closet trying to decide what to wear. The flame dress she would save for his actual performance. Her dressier wardrobe of linen slacks and suits was too dowdy. Jeans were too casual. Tonight she wanted to look sexy and provocative. She wanted to issue an invitation he could not refuse.

Her blood thrummed in her ears, and her bared breasts tightened. Tonight she would show Zayne she wasn't afraid anymore. Her eyes went to the back of her closet. Grinning, she extracted the outfit buried amidst the dross. Oh, bless Natalie for talking her into buying this.

Zayne paced in front of Madeline's room, the cats Bronze and Silver weaving through his feet and sharing his agitation with their flicking tails, and Vulcan waiting by the *frangipela* plant with feline patience. He glared at the purple beads wrapped around the stone. By custom, he should not even speak to her mind. He had about decided to consign the niceties and conventions to oblivion when she opened the door.

He forgot entirely about nice as his body kicked into instant desire. Gone were the prim hair and stiff clothes. This Madeline was sexy, feminine, alluring.

Her tight, green, leather skirt exposed both her navel and firm legs. A white top stopped just short of her waist, so each time she moved or breathed, a tantalizing strip of skin peeked at him. Her loosened hair begged for his hands to rake through the silky strands and hold her still for his kiss.

He swallowed, mouth as dry as rock. For one who lived by his voice, he was decidedly mute.

"Have you been waiting long?" she asked in innocence. "You should have knocked."

Silently he pointed to the stone.

She gave him a delighted grin. "Privacy means no knocking? None of that mind talk?"

"Sometimes such strictures are ignored," he gritted out.

"But not by you?" She tilted her head to look at him. "For all your flamboyance, Zayne, you sometimes show a very conservative streak."

He wasn't interested in talking about himself. Silently he stalked toward her, backing her up until the wall stopped her. He spread his legs on either side of hers, braced his hands against the wall beside her head. "Stop me now if you do not want me to kiss you."

If you do not wish to be in my pillows.

Her eyes widened, and her breath came in hot little pants. "We don't have much time. Traffic—"

"—will not affect our transport."

"Zayne, we can't just appear in the middle of the sidewalk."

"I shall be discreet."

"You keep saying that, but people keep noticing you."

He fixed her with a look. "I will not be confined inside a vehicle when there is no need."

She opened her mouth to argue, then shut it.

"Good." He lowered his head.

"I want your kiss. I want your pillows." Her breath echoed his need.

"Good," he repeated fiercely. His body hardened to readiness. The audition could wait a short while.

"I don't want to be sandwiched between appointments. Not for our first time."

Something in her voice checked the raging beast of his need. A quiet determination, a plaintive request. He looked at her, her eyes wide and deep golden, her white teeth biting her lip. And he knew the path to his pillows had been interrupted once again.

"Have you lain with a man before, Madeline?" he asked abruptly.

"Yes."

"Many?"

"That's none of your business."

He searched her face and guessed not. Whereas he had been eager, driven to take her then and there against the wall, she wanted wooing and seduction. Where was his finesse and skill when he needed it most?

Lost, whenever he was around Madeline, he admitted.

She lacked experience, but she was wise in this matter. The first time together was a moment that could never be captured again, and it should be memorable. Quick and frenetic was fine, but only if driven by utter need. Not by necessity to be somewhere else.

"You are right," he murmured, then gave her a gentle, lingering kiss, allowing himself to cool in the sweet spring of her lips. "When I have you on my pillows, I want more time than it takes to feed the cats."

She was still laughing when he whirled her away on the winds of transport.

Chapter Fourteen

Cyrus didn't bother to knock. He strode into Suzette's weathered shack as one who took his welcome for granted. She spun around, and before her startled look could fade, he wrapped his hand in her hair and jerked her head back, exposing her to his brutal kiss. Butcher and Eel whined from the corner but made no move to protect their mistress. They remembered past encounters with his power.

He devoured her lips and neck, ignoring her whimpers of protest and her hands pushing at his chest. All part of the game. Past of his appeal to Suzette was the fact that he could overpower her and satisfy her at the same time. He ripped open her shirt, then shoved down her pants, stopping her from touching him and his zipper by shifting his grip to her wrists. When he had satisfied himself at her breasts, he let go of her wrists.

"Turn around," he growled. "Put your hands on the table and keep them there."

She did as he commanded. He opened his pants and freed his erection. "Spread your legs." With a single thrust he entered her from behind. Ruthlessly he controlled the encounter until she shuddered around him. Only then did he allow himself to come.

He withdrew, righted himself, then eyed her, still

leaning against the table as he had placed her and panting. "I want details," he said.

She took that as her release. She refastened her clothes, then turned to face him. "You want some gumbo, too, *ma cher*?"

"Of course." She served him a bowl at her bare table and set a glass of cold beer beside the gumbo, the imported brand she kept just for him. He took an appreciative mouthful of gumbo. Suzette's dishes weren't elegant, but they were flavorful and satisfying. Like her. Not something he wanted on a daily basis, but good for the occasional diversion.

"Tell me about Maddie," he said, still having trouble believing she had come into the bayous looking for him.

Suzette sat beside him with her bowl. The room darkened as evening shadows spread, but she didn't bother to light a lamp. He had no trouble seeing her, and she knew he enjoyed the surrounding dark.

"You took her too easy, Cyrus. Ignored her too long. She's different. She said to give you a message."

"Which is?" he asked, knowing Suzette liked to dole her information out in pieces. He would allow her the illusion of command until the gumbo was gone.

"You being a bastard, for one."

"Tell me something I don't already know."

"She says she knows what you did to Irena and her, and she's going to stop you."

He leaned back in the chair and sipped the beer. "Is she now?"

Suzette chuckled. "Now that surprises you. I think maybe you got some learning to do about her."

He frowned, then laid a hand on her head, chanting beneath his breath.

Her eyes clouded in pain. "Don't."

"Don't speculate, Suzette. It's not healthy." He lifted his hand, and her eyes cleared. "I'd like more of your excellent gumbo."

Without a word, she refilled his bowl, then sat and crossed her arms. Mutiny? he thought with amusement. Suzette had the raw connections to the powers of Earth that anyone who spent a life outdoors had, and she thought that put her on equal footing with him. She had no idea of the powers he actually wielded. If her rebellion continued, he might have to do something about it, but for tonight he was content with her information.

For she had been right. He was surprised at Maddie's spine. Not that it would help her to rid herself of the spell. After all this time, her responses were so firmly entrenched, she would never get free. "What else?"

A small, triumphant smile curved Suzette's lips. "For one thing, she was with a man."

Thanks to Dr. Bellows, he didn't react with the surprise she expected. "I know."

"Did you know he also has power?"

"Now you are getting interesting, Suzette."

"*Mais*, I'm always interesting, *cher*. Just read the writeups 'bout my tours."

He laughed. Suzette could be unexpectedly amusing.

She poured them both cups of strong chicory coffee and added warm milk. "This Zayne, he was almighty protective, surrounded her with this power he did."

He took a sip of the hot brew, savoring the bitter taste that came through despite the milk. "He acted like a lover?"

She shrugged. "She wore a necklace that matched his, not like one I ever seen."

His fingers tightened around the cup; then he forced

himself to relax, to erase the visible signs of his excitement. "What kind of necklace?"

"Carved blue stone. Turquoise, maybe. It was on a cord." She looked at him with troubled eyes. "The bayou don't like him."

"What do you mean?"

"When he shielded her, the gators roared. The grounds rumbled at him being here. I don' want him coming back no more."

Cyrus's gut tightened as excitement sped through him. He forced himself to speak calmly as he pushed to his feet. "I doubt he liked the bayou any more than it liked him. He won't be back."

"You going? Already? Can't you stay?" She tilted her head toward the bedroom.

"Sorry, my dear. There are some matters I must attend to." He gave her a swift kiss, as though promising more.

"Don't be so long away next time," she warned, standing in the door as he departed.

"I won't." He disappeared into the familiar bayous. As soon as he was out of her sight, he broke into a run. Next time, he was going to have to do something about that growing independent streak of hers. Remind her who controlled their relationship.

As he ran, his step never faltered on the uneven terrain. His eyesight was as good in the dark as it was in the day, and he passed through the cypress trees as a blur. He drew up to his retreat slightly breathless and covered with a comforting sheen of sweat.

Inside his house, he pulled a jar from the refrigerator, poured a glass of the dark green liquid, then drank it in a single swallow, chanting the words of the renewal immediately afterward.

If his speculations were correct, he would need the strengthening.

Muggy heat enveloped Madeline as she walked beside Zayne through the French Quarter. Overhead, dark clouds gathering for a late night shower blotted out the stars. The rain would not be a relief; it would only add to the humidity. At least they should be inside the Luck Club for Zayne's audition before the downpour started.

Clouds, heat, humidity—tonight none of it bothered her. Despite the looming choice of unemployment or a meeting with her slimeball stepfather, she felt . . . lighthearted. A perfect word. She felt light, as though chains she'd long carried, so familiar she no longer felt them, had been lifted from her. Maybe the freedom was temporary, or illusory, but for tonight she walked through the streets with a soft leather skirt brushing her thighs, a turquoise necklace resting against her bared skin, and Zayne's hand at her hip as he guided and shielded them through the crowds.

This time, the attention they drew wasn't all for Zayne. Whether it was the peekaboo skirt or her new attitude or the no-bra look, something drew eyes toward her. Even as the notice pleased her, though, her cheeks heated, and her mouth grew dry. She felt the urge to lower her head, to shrink inside herself.

If you care enough, if you try hard enough, you can do anything. Her favorite dance teacher had told her that once, and she believed it. *This is only a spell*, she reminded herself, although her body had difficulty remembering that.

"Their notice is brief," Zayne said in an undertone.

Damn, she hated when he read her mind like that. "Can you make me invisible?"

"If you were invisible, they would run into you. 'Tis

a veil, so their notice of you and their memory is brief. Most people are self-absorbed; this is enough."

As she delved deeper into the bustling French Quarter, her tension eased. She attracted fleeting attention, yes, but as Zayne said, most everyone here had more to think about than some stranger in green leather. She let out a long breath. She wasn't on stage here. She was merely a woman with an incredibly sexy man beside her, enjoying the sultry night.

"What do you like to do when you aren't being Minstrel?" she asked.

He frowned, puzzled. "I am always Minstrel."

"Always? It's a twenty-four seven job?"

"I don't understand."

"Twenty-four hours a day, seven days a week. All the time."

"Being Minstrel is not . . . a job. It is who I am. I am the balance of Kaf, her soul and her harmony."

A tender ache spread across her as she looked up at him. Did he truly only see himself as a Minstrel? Once she had thought of herself only as a dancer. Until she had lost that identity and been forced to recognize new ones. Godmother to Virginia's kids, outfield on the softball team, a reader of historical sagas, an indifferent cook, but one who could make a *très* fine jambalaya.

Minstrel. She wasn't clear what that entailed, but when she looked at him, she saw more. He was the man who got rid of the mosquitos for her, who defended a child, and who saw not a tone-deaf woman with stage fright but a woman who had grace. He had seen her as beautiful and polished enough to wear a dress of flame.

She saw a man who needed a little fun and a little relaxation. "Tomorrow, Zayne, let's just have fun. No Cyrus, no jobs or worries. Let's go to the beach."

"Beach?"

"Water. Sand. Sun."

"Beach sounds like my world." He smiled. "I would like that."

"Me, too." She glanced up at the thickening clouds. "The weather report said no rain tomorrow, but tonight if we don't get under cover soon we'll be soaked."

About a block from the club, however, the twang of a guitar drew them to the corner where two performers—a harmonica player and a guitar player—entertained a small crowd with an enthusiastic version of "Your Cheatin' Heart." Zayne moved closer to them, and she followed in his wake. Apparently the style of music mattered little to him. If it was music, he was interested.

When the song ended, he asked the musicians, "Why did you choose to raise the notes instead of lower them here?" He hummed a passage of the song, reproducing it perfectly, although she knew he must have heard it only once.

A lively discussion ensued, ending with the duo asking Zayne if he'd like to sing a verse with them. He glanced at her. "Have we the time?"

Since they'd transported instead of driven, they had a few extra minutes. "Enough for a song, but I'd like to be inside before that storm breaks and soaks us."

"We shall not get soaked." He turned to the duo. "Let us sing."

She didn't think Hank Williams was part of the normal djinn repertoire, but Zayne didn't miss a note or syllable. His eyes were open, but she doubted he saw any of the gathering crowd. His long hair hung over his shoulder, and the streetlight glinted off his silver earring. He stood behind the other two, allowing them the leads, but there was no way he faded into the background. Not with that bad-boy look. Not with the sensual motion of his mouth and hands.

He was dangerous and spellbinding, but as usual, he took the crowd's attention in stride. His focus was on the music.

Don't forget it, either, Madeline. Whatever happened between them tonight and in the future, she would never forget that his first love was the music; she expected nothing different. What made Zayne special, however, was that when he looked at her, he saw *her*. Not Irena's daughter, not a route to Cyrus, not someone he was with only because he wanted something from her.

She felt a warm glow in her belly. They were working together as partners in a quest to find Cyrus and they were dancing on the path toward becoming lovers. It was as simple as that.

Yet was it? As she continued to watch, a frisson of apprehension spread through her. Even as he lent his voice to this musical essence of Americana, there was something undeniably exotic about Zayne. He was of a different culture, a different world even, and she would be foolish to assume they thought alike, that they wanted the same things.

She forgot caution, however, when he looked up, saw her, and smiled. His smoky invitation enticed her nearer, and she swayed to the beat of his song. He stopped singing to touch the corner of her mouth. "Sing with me," he asked under his breath.

"I don't sing."

"Then will you dance with me? I promise, none will notice us."

The automatic "no" died in her throat, as his two musical companions switched to a toe-tapping version of "Small Town Saturday Night."

Zayne held his hand out to her. "Show me one of your dances."

Could she defy the terror of the spell? She took a deep breath and put her hand in his. His strong, polished fingers closed over hers. The heat from his body spread across their joined palms, up her arm, to touch her chest and heart. Hesitantly, her heart in her throat, her stomach threatening, she laid her free hand on his shoulder. "This is the two-step. Your other hand goes on my waist."

He complied, and she demonstrated the simple steps, quick, quick, slow, slow.

Not one person looked at her.

Still, the familiar well of panic made bricks of her feet. She stumbled and would have given up had Zayne not kept moving. Grimly she pressed her lips together, determined that she would not throw up. She kept her eyes down, risking only brief glances at the surrounding crowd.

Still no one looked at her.

Slowly, a second at a time, she relaxed. They touched no one. No one's eyes followed her. They danced alone in the middle of a sidewalk on a hot summer's night.

Well, he danced. She clomped.

To dance with someone who moved with such fluid grace was a true pleasure, and a distinct rarity. Her body loosened as her muscles remembered the earliest joys of dancing, and that light feeling returned to her heart and her feet. Gradually, she lifted her gaze to his and melded to his rhythms as though they'd danced together forever.

He led—there was no doubting that he commanded the dance—and he also had no trouble rapidly adding his own variations: a swing, a dip, a circle. Yet he never lost touch with her; his hands were anchored to her at palm and waist. His body charmed hers with the sway of hip and the brush of thigh, and his green eyes remained fastened on hers.

He led, but she surprised him now, she could see. She smiled as hot desire widened his green eyes when she stepped close enough that her breasts brushed against him. He led, she followed, yet it was a dance of equals.

Madeline could dance, Zayne acknowledged with delight. Her steps were full of grace, as he had guessed they would be, but he had not expected her to match his rhythm so perfectly.

Dancing was always a pleasure, but he had little time for it. Never had it been like this, as though their bodies could read and anticipate one another. Dancing with her was effortless, fluid, entrancing.

If she could dance like this now, was there not hope for her stage fright? Even if he must veil her at each performance when they sang?

He circled through the crowds, urging her closer, hoping for another brush of her body against his. Had he the power, he would keep her in his arms for an eternity. He inhaled, taking in her scent. She wore his turquoise tablet, and seeing the symbol of his attachment worn so close to her throat and heart brought a surge of heated satisfaction.

So many sensations bombarded him. Although he shielded them from prying eyes, he felt as though the last remnants of a veil had been lifted from him, a gauzy covering that filtered and muted. Each sensation was of Terra or Madeline, and the two intermingled. Thick moisture-laden air parting for their dance. Madeline's delicate hand in his. Her hips moving beneath his palm. Petal skin. Hard-poured rock beneath his feet.

Power, strength, and connection flowed through him.

Zayne effortlessly avoided the crowd circling the singers, moving Madeline gradually away. She smiled at him, as though she'd felt the shift of his muscles and liked it. His body tightened and hardened. A fierce need to take her, to join with her, body to body, mind to mind, raged through him. Would they create too dangerous a stir if he were to simply transport them out of here, back to his pillows?

Madeline leaned closer, her honeyed hair brushing his cheek.

With a smooth twist, he dipped her backwards, then up again, deeper into his arms. She didn't falter at the quick move, her body matching his perfectly. The movement brought his hips against hers, and from the catch of her breath, he did not believe she had failed to notice how much he wanted her.

A sudden cooler breeze swirled at their ankles and shoulders. A crack of thunder was his only warning before the rain dropped in a deluge. Swiftly Zayne wrapped his arms around Madeline, drawing her into the shield of his *ma-at*, as his protective spell warded off the rain.

"This is strange," she said, humor tinting her breathless voice. "Standing perfectly dry in the middle of a shower."

"Not to me."

The sound of her laughter slipped inside him. He gathered her close. Standing on the corner, the cooler air prickling their skin, with the heavy rain emptying the streets and shielding them from curious eyes, he kissed her at last.

She felt so right to him, her pliant body molded against his harder muscles. She smelled like vanilla and desire, and she tasted like rich cream in honeyed tea. His desire for her snapped and sparkled around them as he tilted his head and deepened the kiss. He teased the seam of her lips, and with a soft sigh she opened to him.

Slowly he caressed her. With the tip of his tongue. With the stroke of his fingers along her shoulder blades. With the whisper of his mind against hers, and with the touch of his *ma-at*.

She wrapped her arms about his waist, holding him as fiercely as he held her. She caressed him with as much demand and as much care as he touched her. "Zayne," she breathed against him.

Zayne. She was not a woman desiring the power of the Minstrel or the strength of his *ma-at*. 'Twas Zayne she kissed, and Zayne alone. He opened his eyes, drawing slowly back from the kiss, then touched her at the corners of her eyes. Her passion-heavy lids opened slowly. Not brown, not green, her eyes were a rich gold now, so opaque he could barely fathom their depths. And she was looking straight at him.

Something inside him rose, powerful and wild. Like when he sang, the undeniable tempest swept across him and into her, obliterating all thoughts but one.

Mine.

"Mine," she echoed, breathless.

Colorful sparks flared around them.

"Colored lightning in our cloud?" she asked.

"Djinn emotions." His voice was clipped with need, but there was a single promise he must keep first. "This audition, Madeline, will be brief."

* * *

Cyrus changed into his black silk robe, then went into his workroom. The smells of acid and herbs were more pleasing to him than the scent of a lily or the aroma of chocolate, for in these resided his power. Inside a box labeled "Maddie" he found the lock of hair among the other items, then selected a single strand. He laid it in a glass dish, sprinkled on blue crystals and the necessary herbs, and then set the collection on fire. He leaned over, inhaling the intoxicating smoke. The transition from corporeal body to ethereal spirit was the smoothest he'd ever made. Spirit walking, some termed it. Useful, he called it.

Find the match to this hair, he commanded himself.

He sped along the vapors, swift as a bullet, into New Orleans, then settled gently into the Luck Club. Maddie was shaking hands with Wilson Luck. Since she wouldn't be getting on the stage, she must have arranged something for Zayne. He drank in his first sight of the mysterious companion, who stood with crossed arms and a mutinous look. Cyrus moved closer.

Zayne whipped around, staring in his direction. Cyrus withdrew swiftly, back to his body, not wanting to reveal more of his presence.

Back in the retreat, he sank into a chair, his fingers caressing his chin. Yes, this Zayne could be the one, although why he was with useless Maddie was still a puzzle. He would have to do a little research into that matter.

He would call Wilson Luck and find out when Zayne was performing, see for himself whether this man was the one he wanted. Wilson wasn't one of Cyrus's small band of followers, but the musician would be eager for his attention. Cyrus Cromwell's talent at making a star of anyone he chose was well known within the industry.

A headache started to blossom behind his eyes. One telephone call to make before he could give in to his fatigue. Brendan at The Mystic answered after the fifth ring.

"Brendan, it's Cyrus Cromwell."

There was a moment of shocked silence before Brendan stammered, "Cyrus. I didn't expect—"

"I want the box I ordered."

"The box?"

"You know which box. The one I ordered just before I left."

The silence stretched out. At last Brendan whispered, "I don't have it." Cyrus didn't say a word, waiting for Brendan's capitulation.

"Maddie was looking for you, and the box had never been paid for, so I—"

"So you gave it to her," he finished coldly.

"Sold it. I didn't think you were coming back, and I needed the space. We're doing so well that the stock room is full, and . . ." His frightened voice trailed off.

"Give me one reason why I shouldn't punish you, Brendan, for selling what I entrusted to your keeping."

"She was with a man," he said quickly. "A man who activated the Judgment Crystal."

So, this Zayne had a deeper power.

"What do you want me to do?" whined Brendan.

"Do you still know the Ritual of Seeing I taught you?" he said at last.

"Yes, every word."

"I want you to perform it inside Maddie's apartment—"

"She's staying at Tildy Maehara's. I think this man is staying with her."

Interesting, and annoying. Tildy would likely have some protections outside and too many inside, and who knew what this stranger could detect? "Then do it just beyond the perimeter of Tildy's property. You will have to use the thrice regimen. Do it when Maddie isn't there, and do not let anyone know what you do. I will come for the mirror." The Ritual would allow him to watch her comings and goings. Pity it would only be on the outside.

"Do not fail me this time, Brendan." He hung up before Brendan could reply.

The headache was nearly blinding by now. He would have to make the replacement potion later. As he stretched out on the sofa, preparing to ride out this pain, he stuck his hand in the pocket of his robe and pulled out the broken turquoise tablet. His thumb stroked along the smooth edge of the shattered stone.

The pair of copper bracelets on the mantel caught his eye. Time had dimmed their brilliance, but time had only sharpened his determination.

To remove the curse on his family, forged centuries ago by a vengeful genie.

To be the first Cromwell since Naomi to command that awesome power.

Chapter Fifteen

The audition went as Mådeline expected.

Zayne was irritated, and the selection was brief. Yet his voice was as strong as she'd ever heard, while his talent and his love of the music was unmistakable with every note.

Wilson was entranced. He tried to persuade Zayne to play two sets a night for the next week, but the djinni agreed only to a single performance tomorrow, holding out the hope of more if all went well.

Now they had but to wait. Wait for Zayne's performance tomorrow night, then wait for Cyrus to find them.

Outside the club, Madeline drew in a breath of smoke-free air. She held Zayne's hand, intertwining her fingers with his warmth. "What now?"

"This." He leaned over and kissed her. Brief but thorough, the kiss was from a man who no longer questioned whether he had the right to kiss her or wondered if she would welcome his touch. "For a start."

She smiled, her lips and body tingling from the sparks he ignited inside and out. "One-track mind."

"I want to make love to you, Madeline." Sparks flared around him, and he reached for her.

"Wait."

His fists tightened. "Do you but tease me?"

"Tease a man who could turn me into a toad?"

"We do not—" The sparks grew brighter.

"*That* was teasing," she said softly. Definitely a man who had been teased very little in his life.

"Oh."

"No transporting from plain sight," she explained. She drew him into a small alley, hiding them from view, then wrapped her arms around him, pressing herself against him. "I want to make love to you, too, Zayne. Take me back home."

Before she could blink or doubt or choose, he gathered her in his arms and kissed her. His body was hot and strong, smooth skin over hard muscle. Leather-clad thighs enveloped her, bare arms wrapped her waist, and talented hands cupped her head. She rested her hands against his temples, her fingers tracing the braided pattern of his hair there.

His lips were soft and gentle, though, teasing her mouth open, tempting her tongue to taste his. Then he tilted his head to deepen the kiss and took command, leaving her only to feel. The silver earring brushed delicately against her cheek, while his hair fell across her shoulder, binding her to him with a silken veil. His arousal pressed hard against her belly.

His emotions popped against her skin like champagne bubbles and they careened inside her, tinted with fire red and diamond brilliance. A companion wildness arose inside her, fueled by the murmur of foreign words in his sensual, caressing voice. Words that could not be understood by the mind, only felt at an elemental level.

The whirlwind spun around her. Dizziness, disorientation, a whoosh of roller-coaster motion, but still his mouth did not lift from hers and his body did not release hers and his *ma-at* did not leave her.

The kiss exploded around her and through her, as the whirlwind died. He lifted his head from the kiss, and she opened her eyes.

They were in Zayne's bedroom. Though it was too dark to see much, Madeline felt a cool breeze, heard the rustle of silk, and breathed in the surrounding spice of cinnamon. Zayne snapped his fingers and a single brass lamp lit, illuminating them and the sybaritic mound of pillows beside them.

Without pause, his powerful hand trailed up her arm. He traced her neckline with the barest scrape of his manicured nails against the upper curve of her breast. Her nipples tightened, as though he'd commanded their attention and demanded their invitation to be tasted.

For the moment, though, he ignored their need. Instead, he cupped her jaw, his fingers threading through her hair, his thumb whispering across her lips.

He bent over and kissed her. An enveloping kiss that scattered rational thought to the winds. His lips possessed hers. One hand held her head, anchoring her close, while his other hand clasped her fingers. His muscled body molded against hers; then he stood utterly still. His breath came in shallow pants, and his mouth deepened the kiss. Nothing else moved. Not Zayne, not the air around them.

He ignited her with wild expertise, while his stillness kept the raging inferno bound with no escape or relief. His *ma-at* touched her like the hot sirocco, which fed the fires until they consumed her. She burned with the need to touch him skin to skin and heart to heart, to take him deep inside her and erase the years of his loneliness.

With a moan she wrapped her arms around him,

breaking through his stillness. The dance of her body rubbed across him in exquisite need. Sparkling lights twinkled behind her eyelids, a kaleidoscope of color and excitement. Her sensitive skin felt the tiny, kneading pressure from his fingers.

Come, si halika. *Join with me.* Zaniya-e-na. *Mine. Lover.* His disjointed, ragged words echoed in her mind, filling her with his need.

Shalian mir ad'n rajiana. As though he could no longer manage the foreign English, he switched to his native language. Strange phrases flowed over her, enchanting and spellbinding. Their meaning was clear. Clear from the erotic voice and the passionate touches and the hardness pressed against her.

Slowly he lifted his head from the kiss, taking small tastes, as though he could not bear to release her. His hand stroked across her cheek and down her neck, a feathery touch that felt like the brush of fire.

"Ah, Madeline, I have so wanted you," he breathed.

Without waiting for the answer she'd already given, he lifted her into his embrace. His arms were muscled, his body hard. A brief, disorienting wind heralded their transport; then she found herself sitting on his lap in his pillows, his arousal pressing against her bottom.

"I could have walked," she said, her protest breathless, for she still clung to him.

He kissed her again. Claimed her with a rainbow of fireworks. "We have delayed before. I take no such chances now."

She had no breath for a laugh, barely the strength for a smile. "Arrogant djinni."

"Grow accustomed to it."

"And if I said 'No, stop' and held you to our bargain?"

She held her breath as he froze. She'd thought his

arms hard before; now they were like ice. The rainbow became blinding white bolts of lightning. "You are refusing?" The musical voice became the feral growl of the tiger.

She was playing a dangerous game, but she had to know. Tonight Zayne was so assured and demanding. She felt powerless before his strength and the awesome might at his command. She had to know that she could trust this very powerful, arrogant, utterly masculine man.

"Would you stop?"

"Remember, I reserved the right to try to change your mind."

"How?"

"Like this."

He kissed her again. Powerful as his last kiss had been, he'd definitely been holding back.

He consumed her. She was overwhelmed by the pressure and taste of his lips, sweet chocolate and cinnamon. The mating of his tongue. The fiery heat of his skin. The power of his body. The iron band of his arms. All she could feel was Zayne. Her hands ran across him, trying to draw him closer. Their breath mixed, and her body ached with need of him.

His *ma-at* caressed her belly, the sole of her foot, nipped her earlobe and finger, drew long strokes up her thighs, like the damp touch of a tongue, while her breasts tightened from a moist, rhythmic suckling. Not illusion—the myriad encompassing touches were so very real—but not one of them was generated by his hand or his mouth.

And his voice. His captivating voice spoke to both her ear and her mind. His voice roused matching primal rhythms and elemental needs.

"This is the kiss of the Minstrel," he growled, lifting his head and withdrawing slightly.

She opened her eyes and realized she was flat on her back, deep within the mound of pillows. Zayne sprawled atop her, covering her body with his, his legs on either side of hers. Her arms were over her head, and he encircled her wrists.

"Have I changed your mind?" he asked fiercely.

"If I said no, would you stop?" She could barely form the words.

His eyes closed and a spasm of pain crossed his face. She felt the jerk of it within his muscles. "I have never forced a woman in my life. Nor have I ever broken a bargain." The words were shards of agony, clipped and brittle. His body shifted, as though he tried to release her, but was not yet capable of the sacrifice. He shifted again, this time letting go of her arms.

"Zayne." She didn't move. "Look at me."

He opened his eyes. Their green was muddied, confused.

"That was a hypothetical question."

He shook his head. "I—I do not understand."

"I wanted to know if you would stop if I asked you to. You've answered that. I didn't ask you to stop."

His eyes narrowed. "What exactly are you saying, Madeline?"

"I want to continue. I want to make love with you." She took a deep breath, amazed at her own boldness. Zayne was so powerful. He was dictatorial, always arrogant and mesmerizing. Yet she didn't fear him. He wouldn't harm her, and he wasn't using her.

The only way he would hurt her was if he broke her heart.

That, she would not dwell on. For she wanted tonight as much as she had wanted anything in her life. Even to dance again.

"Continue to speak," he ordered. The remnants of pain and anger were still there, but she could see she'd also piqued his interest. "What else do you want?"

"I want the kiss of the Minstrel. I want the kiss of Zayne. I want to be with you, skin to skin, naked. I want your body to be part of mine. I want to share pleasure and climax and afterglow. I want to sleep beside you and wake up beside you and start the cycle all over again."

"Not the part about you asking me idiotic hypothetical questions?"

"No."

"So why, by Solomon, did you ask it in the first place?" he exploded.

"Because I had to know you'd do it."

The look he gave her was one of sheer incredulity. "I made a bargain."

"I . . . never mind." She lifted her head to kiss his cheek, hoping she hadn't just killed the mood. "I wouldn't be averse to more of that persuading, however."

He shifted, moving with lithe grace until he sat upright. He straddled her, although she felt no uncomfortable pressure from his weight. His leather pants brushed against her leg where her skirt had pushed up, and the bulge of his arousal pressed her thigh. Heat flared between them.

He fisted his hands at his waist. "Is this the final delay, Madeline?"

"Yes."

"You are ready, *zaniya-e-na*?"

"Yes."

"Good." The next instant he was sprawled back across her and kissing her.

She returned the kiss. She didn't have *ma-at*, but she had passion. She could not speak directly to his mind, so she spoke the words aloud. She held nothing back, nothing in reserve. She matched his touches with feathery strokes. Her body danced with his.

He ran a hand down her side, and suddenly she was naked except for the turquoise tablet, while her clothes were draped across a carved wooden chest. Zayne still wore his silk and leather.

"Ah, your skin, it is so soft," he said, sliding the back of his hand over her hips. "It is like the thistle, soft and sweet-scented. I cannot stop touching you."

"I should like to feel you," she told him. When he started the brief chant that would undress him, however, she laid a finger on his lips. "I will do it. The human way."

"How is that?"

"Like this." She squirmed, rubbing against him as she shifted from beneath him.

"Mmmm, I like the way of the humans."

"I haven't started undressing you."

"I know. Slow human," he added with a grin.

"Speedy djinni."

"Not in all things," he murmured, bringing a flush to her cheeks.

How well she knew he could draw out the pleasure.

She managed to free herself at last, but not before she was breathless and her skin was exquisitely sensitive to his least touch. She straddled him, feeling the caress of his soft leather pants and the power in his legs on the inside of her thighs, then stroked his shirt, finding beneath the pattern a seam where it overlapped and fastened. "Now, the human way is to use your hands."

"I think I like this human way," he said, reaching up to ring her breasts with a light caress. Her nipples tightened. He gently thumbed them. "Yes, I definitely like this."

Distracted by him, she fumbled, but finally managed to get his shirt open and the sides shoved back. She inhaled sharply as she drank in the sight of him. She had gone a whole day without the chance to run her hands over the bronze smoothness of his skin. To feel the sleek chest muscles beneath her palms. To watch his nipples tighten, and listen to his sharp inhale as she teased the flat abdomen above the leather pants. To watch the bulge grow more prominent.

"Do humans employ the adept use of their mouths?" He sat up suddenly, sending his shirt away with a wave of his hand, and splayed a hand at her back, bracing her. Then, bending her back a little, he took her breast in his mouth, repeating the rhythmic suckling his *ma-at* had teased her with earlier.

Madeline clutched his shoulders, lost in a maelstrom of need and want, until he lifted his head to her other breast. She pushed him back a little.

"Remember." She held him back, and he allowed it. "I'm undressing you first. You still have your pants on."

He stopped, and the look he gave her was one of pure mischief. "You would remove my pants? With your hands?"

"Yes."

"Very well." He lay back down in the pillows, his hands stacked beneath his head. His legs spread, inviting her closer.

She reached for the zipper, then stopped. Blinked. There was no zipper. No buttons. No seam. No fastening that she could see. The leather fit like a second skin, revealing muscle and arousal, but with no way of removing it.

"Why do you hesitate, Madeline?" he teased. "Use your hands."

Maybe at the back? Kneeling beside him, she used her hands. Ran them over his hips, then reached behind to trace the curve of his buttocks and the waistband of the pants. She followed the edge to the front, where she stroked hard muscle and aroused flesh. She found she could slip the tips of her fingers beneath the waistband, and she teased the top of his sex until he groaned.

"Madeline," he warned.

"Where's the fastening?"

"There isn't one. I dress with *ma-at*." He laughed. "Oh, if you could see your face right now."

"Well, I'd say we have a problem, don't we?"

"No, we do not." His hips lifted against her as a chant tumbled from him. The pants disappeared, and he was as naked as she, leaving her palm resting on the length of his erection. Her fingers curled around him.

He groaned again. "No delays, Madeline. No more."

"No," she echoed, and the word was barely out of her mouth before she found herself once more flat on her back with Zayne on top, between her legs

"Now it is the way of lovers." He stroked her opening with his fingers. "Ah, such a sweet honey, *si halika*." Then he replaced his fingers with the tip of his shaft. "Look at me, Madeline."

Clutching his smooth shoulders, she stared at him. Though the light was dim, the green of his eyes shone bright against the pure white surrounding it.

With a single thrust, he surged inside her.

"Madeline." *Madeline*. His voice, spoken and projected, was a sigh of masculine satisfaction. His *ma-at* sparkled across her senses, stimulating and arousing, deeper, stronger than she'd ever felt it. Brilliant shards of color surrounded them. Her breath caught at the heat from the core of him, blazing across her. His green gaze never left hers. Everywhere, all, was Zayne.

"Ah, Madeline, you are so beautiful." He started to stroke, so slowly, nearly withdrawing before plunging back. "This . . . feels . . . so . . . good."

His rhythm was innate and elemental, the dance of male and female across ages and dimensions. He saw her as beautiful; she felt beautiful. She held him close and matched his pace and flow. His moans were her music. His touch was her fire. His breath was her air.

Pleasure engulfed her, and she exploded, keening her release.

"Ah, Madeline," he whispered, still hard inside her, gathering her tightly against him, "sing for me."

She collapsed, boneless, in his arms, her breath rasping. Her fingers combed through his silken hair. Until he kissed her neck and started his rhythmic thrusts again. Started the waltz again until she found new energy, new heights, new pleasures, and new release.

"Again." His low voice sounded against her temple. "Encore. I can never tire of your sweet giving."

She bracketed his face. "Not alone this time. Come with me, Zayne."

"I do not believe I could delay again."

A third time he began his strokes. No gentle waltz this time. This was a fiery *pas de deux,* a whirling tarantella. His demanding strokes took her with him on his flight of fire.

She gripped his sweat-slicked arms. "You sing for me, Zayne."

"Not for you, with you," he gasped and gave a powerful thrust. Fireworks burst around her. *Ma-at* exploded inside her. Zayne shouted his release. "Ma-de-line!" *Zaniya-e-na, si-halika.*

She held tight to him and shattered in his arms.

The pillows shifted and wrapped around Zayne, allowing him to drift deeper into their soft comfort. He snuggled closer to Madeline. Though he had slept a little, he was still too tired and satiated to perform the ritual that would cool the sweat from their bodies. His fingers played with the strands of her hair, even as he enjoyed the pleasure of her head nestled in the crook of his shoulder and her smooth legs tangled with his. Every muscle was relaxed, every fiber of his being contented.

He was happy, he realized. Happier than he had been in many cycles of the moon.

Madeline brought him this happiness. She had made love with him, with Zayne. She had not claimed the attention of the Minstrel. She had not cared that he was a male legendary for his endurance. He smiled a little at that conceit. There had been little of endurance or finesse in this first loving. Only the eager need to join with her.

He buried his nose in her hair. She had taken all he gave with uninhibited joy. But she had not just taken. She had given. Given her eagerness that he find his pleasure. Given her unconcealed delight in his loving.

From her even breathing, he guessed Madeline had fallen asleep. She shifted slightly, rolling away from him. He followed, enveloping her in his embrace, reluctant to allow any distance between them. Gradually sleep registered its claim.

One last thought brought the smile again.

Tonight they had forged the physical bonds.

I want to sleep beside you and wake up beside you and

start the cycle all over again. Madeline's words echoed inside him, and despite his fatigue, he felt himself stirring again. Waking beside her, even now in the midst of deepest night, holding her—he had not envisioned what joy that would bring. He would wake beside her, not just tonight, not only at tomorrow's sunrise, but every day.

Tomorrow and every day. Finally the true significance of the bonds of male and female, *zani* and *zaniya*, washed over him, filling his heart and his soul. He stroked her warm, bare shoulder gently.

The divination had sent him to her not just for the balance he needed.

It had sent him for love.

She was his *janam*, his soul.

He had fallen in love with Madeline Fairbanks.

Such a short time he had known her, yet to him time made no difference. He loved her. His body hardened with the sweep of fire at the realization, and his arms tightened around her even as his hips began to move against her. She had to feel the same way. He had learned enough of her to believe she would not have slept with him, would not have abandoned herself to his loving, had she no feelings for him.

Madeline turned in his arms and gave him a sleepy smile. "Are all djinn as insatiable as you?"

"How another djinni makes love is something you will never find out," he said with hard command.

"No, I suppose not." She cupped his cheek.

He turned and kissed her palm. "Is it too soon again for you?"

Her smile widened. "Fifteen seconds ago I would have said I was too exhausted. I find that is no longer the truth."

"Good," he declared and bent to kiss her.

As their lips met, the blood inside him rushed from his brain to pool in heart and groin. He kissed her again, and coherence fled. Now was not the time for matters of import. Now was only the time for loving.

Chapter Sixteen

Madeline stirred in the pillows, waking up a little when their support adjusted beneath her. Zayne gave a drowsy murmur of protest, and his arm tightened around her waist. She snuggled closer, her body pleasantly aching and replete.

She gave a small sigh of contentment. Zayne was as she imagined, an aggressive, demanding, inventive lover. Like everything else he did, he filled each moment with sensation. His spicy scent. The rhythm of his heart against her chest and his strong body inside hers. The slick contact of skin on skin. His sexy laughter and wicked grin. The silk of his hair binding her and the brilliant green of his eyes devouring her.

Yet, her wildest and most creative fantasies had never imagined the sparkling touch of his *ma-at* or the intimacy of his thoughts inside her mind. She had never dreamed about making love at the center of fireworks and the heart of a flame.

He hid nothing. He opened himself completely to her, and he demanded her honest responses.

She looked over at her djinni lover, at the strong back, the bronze skin, and the fall of hair. At the silver earring and the cord of his tablets. Even in sleep he exuded an exotic appeal. For a moment, she considered waking him up as he had woken her during the night, but a certain tenderness of her body told her they needed to wait for a while. After their visit to the beach, perhaps.

What time was it? Zayne's room altered one's perceptions, she realized. It was filled with illusions of the outdoors, but no clues of light or sound entered from the real world. She glanced at her watch. Nine A.M. Time to get up and shower, get things ready for the beach, then wake him.

She slipped out of the bed and gave one last glance back, unable to shake the feeling that she was stepping away from a dream. This room and these pillows were a place of *ma-at*, but outside them waited stark realities.

Zayne woke, stretched, and immediately knew that Madeline had left their pillows. The sound of running water told him she was in the shower. Though the room was shadowy, his internal clock told him that it was midmorn. She was probably preparing for their day at the beach.

While he would as lief stay amongst the pillows all day, Madeline had been looking forward to this beach trip. So, to the beach they would go.

Smiling, he rolled to his back and stacked his hands beneath his head. Nothing he had ever experienced on his pillows compared to last night. Madeline had found pleasure, too, he believed. Several times, he added with a twitch of masculine pride. His body was filled with a pleasant fatigue, and his soul was filled with contentment. She was so beautiful in both giving and demanding, meeting his *ma-at* with human creativity. His grin widened when he remembered how she had used her mouth.

His body sprang to life again. Perhaps he could persuade her to delay their trip to the beach. His grin faded, though, when he realized the shower was still running. Could she be sore? At times, he had been rather vigorous.

Deciding not to simply transport to her since she sometimes complained when he did, he rose from the bed and walked toward the showering room. His brows drew together as he heard a muffled sound. Madeline? Talking to herself? Or—He stepped inside.

Despite the hot steam filling the room, he froze. His *Are you all right?* died unspoken in his throat. Madeline was not talking. She was in the shower. Singing with happy enthusiasm.

Singing off key. Quite off key.

He could not deny the evidence of his sensitive ears. Madeline had not lied or evaded his request out of modesty or fear. She had told him a simple truth.

She could not sing.

Oh, she warbled with great vigor, but her voice slid off key and was too shallow for the complexity needed to sing with a Minstrel. He staggered backward, remaining upright only by bracing himself against the wall. Pain lanced deep and sharp, and he could barely take a breath, his chest hurt so badly.

She could not sing.

How could she be his *zaniya* if she could not sing? All *zaniyas* of the Minstrels sang. All of them.

The shower stopped, and the towel laid across the shower bar disappeared behind the curtain. Zayne knew he should leave, but he could not move. A moment later, the curtain was shoved back, and Madeline stepped out into the steamy room, the towel wrapped around her body.

Spying him, she gave a startled shriek, then relaxed. "I've got to get used to that little habit of yours of just appearing. Of course, you could have said something."

He didn't say a word, just drank in the sight of her.

She tilted her head. "Is something wrong? You look . . . The colors around you aren't sparkling."

He pressed his lips together. He could not continue to claim her as his. *He could not give her up.* He needed time to think, but that he could not do while she stood before him, naked and desirable. "I must go back to Kaf," he blurted out.

Her hands that fussed on her towel stilled, and she stared at him. "For how long?"

"I shall look for a counter to the fright spell," he said, knowing he did not answer her question.

"Oh. Will you be back in time to go to the beach?"

"I . . . I shall try."

"Then I'll get the towels and a picnic together just in case. The performance tonight?"

He had made a bargain with her. "Yes."

She bit her lip. "All right." She hitched her towel tighter, then fingered her tablet. "I have to get dressed."

Suddenly he could not leave. Not like this, at least. He covered the distance between them in two steps, lifted her chin and kissed her. Briefly, passionately, possessively. Then he stepped back and disappeared.

Madeline stared in disbelief at the empty doorway. What had just happened?

Unlike most men, Zayne couldn't hide his emotions, even if she didn't always understand what caused them. She knew when he was angry. She knew when he was happy. She knew when he was thinking about sex. Well, something was bugging the hell out of him. Something that had sent him running.

Last night? She scrubbed a hand across her hair. Was he a man running from the specter of commitment?

No, she hadn't imagined the connections formed last night.

So, what was it?

His mysterious purpose for being on Earth? She relaxed. That had to be it. His djinn business. Probably something to do with his world and his people. What could be so vital to a minstrel singer? She didn't know, but then again, she didn't know much about his world.

Maybe she should find out?

Suddenly the idea of going with him to Kaf intrigued her. She traced a finger along her turquoise tablet. She had the means of coming back whenever she wanted.

In the meantime, she'd put on her bikini and pack a picnic.

She could not sing.

Madeline could not sing!

On Kaf, Zayne paced outside his tent, his bare feet kicking up tufts of sand that stung at his heels. He could have easily negated the discomfort, but for the moment he welcomed it.

This nightmare could not be true. Madeline was his *zaniya-e-na.* His balance and harmony. His destined mate. He would not feel this way about her were she not. Nor could he ever imagine claiming another as his own.

The divination. How could the divination be wrong? He stopped and raked his hand through his hair, remembering one of Alesander's parting comments. *The divination answered your question. There are other ways.* He had asked to find his *zaniya.* Had he asked the wrong question? Interpreted the divination incorrectly?

Denial formed a cold, hard knot in his stomach. No, he could not have been so misguided or so betrayed by his emotions. Last night was not wrong.

He pivoted, sending up a spray of sand. There had to be another answer.

This time, though, the protest sounded hollow and weightless. Amidst the turmoil, only one fact was irrefutable. His ears still ached with the truth. She could not sing. This was no spell they could counteract. This was Madeline.

Madeline could not be *zaniya* to a Minstrel.

He started to pace again, and his agitated stride ate up the ground rumbling beneath his feet. The weight of the two turquoise tablets pressed against his chest. The weight of confusion and responsibility to his world were heavier burdens. He cursed, and for the first time ever, he wished he were not the Minstrel.

Sweat stung his eyes and heat pounded his back, and he hummed under his breath, a wild melody of jazz and djinn, as he paced the shaking ground. Suddenly a small red orb spun in front of him, chiming its alert. Zayne halted, staring blindly at it.

Minstrel! The sharp voice of the Oracle sounded in his mind. *Your agitation is felt even here in the Tower Lands.*

He gritted his teeth. His music was his outlet, his vent, but for the moment he had forgotten it was denied him here. At least while his song held two forces. He forced himself to contain the tumult inside, to croon a delicate lullaby until Kaf settled around him. Only then did he answer the Oracle.

I know the needs of Kaf. I will not fail the djinn's trust. He swallowed hard, and the pain in his chest nearly stopped his heart. No matter what his own needs, no matter how much he wanted Madeline, or she wanted him, he could not betray his world. He could not allow the chaos to descend.

Wearily his shoulders slumped. He was tired of being alone, he realized, tired of being the solitary Minstrel. Giving up the duty, however, was not possible.

He had been wrong about so many things, it seemed. Wrong about the promise of sharing his life. Wrong about his *zaniya* being his balance. Wrong about Madeline.

He pounded one fist against the other. No. He was not wrong about Madeline. She was his *zaniya-e-na*. There had to be another way. In the bar when he played the jazz, something had happened. Something with Madeline. If only he could figure out what.

Abruptly he straightened. *I shall return to Terra.*

Zayne. Alesander's concerned voice was no comfort.

I have some time, he insisted. *Time to complete a bargain.*

You have some time, my friend, Alesander agreed gently. *But not much. Choose well how you spend that time.* With that, he severed the link between them.

There was no choice about how he would use the time. He would look for the counterspell to Madeline's stage fright as he had promised; then he would return to Terra. He would spend the day at the beach. Then, with Madeline beside him wearing a dress of Kaf, he would perform and he would discover how to control the music.

Madeline surveyed her gear. Picnic packed. Bikini on beneath her shorts and T-shirt. Sunscreen, water, towels—all stowed in a bag. She was ready for a day at the beach.

Except Zayne hadn't returned.

She took a sip of her coffee, then grimaced. Cold. She tossed the dregs remaining in her cup. Well, if the beach wasn't possible, then she'd look in Miss Tildy's magic room for information about djinn and a counterspell to her stage fright. On her way out, the harplike tones of the doorbell sounded and she detoured to the front door.

She was mildly surprised to find Jack and Leila Montgomery on her doorstep. Leila was carrying a smiling Phillip. Jack handed Madeline the vial of aqua liquid. "We've come to return this."

"Come on in. Would you like something to drink?" she asked. Jack declined, but Leila asked for water, so she led them into the kitchen, then drew up, startled.

Zayne had returned at last. He sat in the kitchen with the three cats at his feet, munching a piece of melon. Another mild surprise—this morning was full of them—he wore only a pair of low-slung denim shorts, the first time she'd ever seen him in such ordinary-looking clothes.

Of course, on him even ordinary was incredibly sexy.

"You're back," was all she could think to say.

"Yes. Good morning, Leila. Jack." He rose and gave Leila a hug, took Phillip in his arms while he nodded at the vial Madeline held. "You have found something about the potion?" he asked Jack.

"Not much," Jack admitted. "It appears to be a mix of herbs. Here's the list of what I could identify."

With a final kiss to the forehead, Zayne handed Phillip back to Leila, then took the paper. Madeline read over his shoulder. She recognized a few of the names like valerian, but most of them she'd never heard of.

She looked at Jack. "What does it do?"

"As a combination, it's hard to tell. There are a couple of soporifics in there, things that will make you sleepy. A hallucinogen. A local anesthetic. Probably not pleasant."

"Is it dangerous?"

"Could be, in a large enough dose."

"Did you detect any magic in it?" Zayne asked Leila.

She shook her head, shifting Phillip in her arms. "None that I could identify, although I get a strange feeling when I hold the vial. Very unpleasant, like utter despair. A spell, I believe, with its purpose well concealed. Even without that, however, it would be a danger to a djinni."

Jack gave her a surprised look. "You didn't tell me that."

"I was still studying it. I took precautions, but I did not want you to worry."

A look passed over Jack's face, half pain, half frustration.

"Why is it dangerous to a djinni?" Madeline asked Leila.

"I have been learning about the plants of Terra. Although, like Jack, I am not familiar with all those ingredients, I had unpleasant experiences with two. Reactions humans do not seem to have. Dizziness, my heart sped, and my feet disappeared."

"Do you mean that literally?" Madeline asked.

"I mean I could not feel them or move them. It was as if they had turned to smoke."

"Definitely sounds unpleasant," Madeline said, noticing that Jack's face had hardened and he'd moved protectively closer to Leila and Phillip.

"What are you going to do with it?" Jack nodded to the vial.

"I'm not sure. Destroy it probably." How, though, Madeline wasn't sure. She couldn't just dump it down the drain and into the water system.

"We have some haz mat facilities at work," Jack said,

as if reading her mind. "I can yellow bag it and have it incinerated."

"Burning may activate the spell," Zayne cautioned. "We must conceal the vial until we know what spell has been placed on it. After that is removed, you can destroy the liquid."

"So it's back into the bust of Aleister for you," Madeline told the vial, then left for a moment to return it to its hiding place in Tildy's magic room. When she returned, she gave Leila and Jack a final hug. "Thank you for everything."

"If there's anything else we can do—" Leila said.

Madeline shook her head and stroked the baby's cheek. "I don't want you anywhere near Cyrus. We'll handle this."

After another warning from Jack to be careful, the couple left and she and Zayne were left alone. She stuck her hands in her shorts pockets. "Any success on Kaf?"

"I have not yet found a counter to your stage-fright spell."

"I appreciate your trying, but I have a feeling it's something I'm going to have to conquer on my own. What do you suppose Cyrus wanted with that potion?"

"Nothing pleasant."

"Not with that mix. Do you—"

"Shhh." Zayne touched the back of his hand to her cheek, stroking lightly and sending sparkles across her skin. "Remember, today we do not think of Cyrus or any of the other concerns which beset us."

She found herself relaxing under his caress. "No Cyrus," she agreed.

"Today we share a day at the beach."

* * *

Zayne stared at the expanse of water on the other side of the sand. When Madeline had suggested a day at the Biloxi beach, he had thought of small, still pools shaded by the palms of a desert oasis.

This Gulf of Mexico was neither small nor still. He could not see the shore on the other side, and foam-capped waves rolled in with endless cycles. He did not think he had ever seen such volatile water.

Not a single tree or scrap of shade graced the beach, either.

"Surf's up today," Madeline said cheerfully. "There's a storm brewing in the Gulf."

"This storm—it comes soon?" He cast an uneasy eye toward the horizon.

"Not today. Just making some good waves. Here we are." She pulled into a place to park at the side of the road, then kicked off her shoes. "Ready?"

No. "Yes."

They retrieved a basket, a bag, towels, and a blanket from the rear of the car. Also barefoot, he followed Madeline across the sand, still eyeing the expanse of water. Did she mean to go in it?

The breeze strengthened the closer they got to the water, but it felt hot and sticky. He licked his lips, surprised at the taste of salt. The hot sun beat down on the top of his head, and the sand beneath his feet was coarser than he was used to. This place made him uncomfortable, like the bayou. Not because of any evil. Rather, it seemed to be the raw essence of Terra, just water and the bare land steeped in the forces of magic.

So far he was not enjoying this day at the beach, except for Madeline's obvious pleasure.

She spread the blanket on the sand, then took the basket and bag he carried and weighted the corners with them. When she finished, she unfastened her shorts. He followed suit, starting to lower his shorts as well.

She glanced over, and her eyes widened. "Stop, Zayne. Don't."

He paused, his hands on the waistband, the shorts lowered to his hips. "Do not what?"

"Um, do you have anything on under those shorts?"

He glanced at her, puzzled. "No. Why?"

"I forgot to tell you about swimsuits. We don't swim in the nude. Not on a public beach."

He frowned. "You wear clothes? In the water?"

"Swimsuits." She waved toward the beach. "Like those."

He noticed the scattering of people then. Up till that moment, the water had held his attention. The men wore short pants, some baggy, some quite tight, some in florid colors. He chose one pattern, then with a wave of his hand transformed his shorts. "Is this correct?"

"Yes." She cleared her throat, and he enjoyed the bright interest in her eyes. "Unlike some, you have the build for a black Speedo." She slipped off her shorts, then shrugged off the shirt.

Now it was his turn to stare. Heat pounded him from outside and from within. Two strips of purple cloth barely covered her, emphasizing the length of her legs, the curve of her waist, and the sweetness of her breasts. Last night he had seen, touched, and tasted every part of her body. He knew her movements, her curves, and the texture of her skin, and he found them all arousing. But this clothing, which concealed and called the attention at the same time, was undeniably erotic.

With an inconspicuous wave of his hand, he changed the style of his swimsuit to something looser, less revealing of his desire. "What do we do now?"

"We go swimming."

"Swim? Out there?" he asked, pointing to the Gulf.

"Of course. Where else?" She reached over and took his hand, pulling him up with a gentle tug. "C'mon."

Holding her hand, he followed her into the water. "It is warm!" Nearly as warm as the water he bathed with.

"Because it's so shallow here. We'll have to walk out a ways before it gets deep enough to be cooler."

As they waded deeper, the water crept up his legs, and the waves buffeted endlessly against him. Coarse shells in the sand scraped the soles of his feet. He gritted his teeth against the uncomfortable wash of Terran forces, forcing his protesting *ma-at* not to rise and simply clear a path before him.

At last they reached chest height, and Madeline dove in. Panic welled briefly when she did not immediately surface, then died when she burst upward a few paces from him.

She slicked back her hair, shedding droplets of water, then grinned at him. "Water feels good. Let's swim."

"I shall wait for you here." He crossed his arms, prepared to endure. A large wave splashed against him, and he could not prevent his involuntary wince.

She gave him a pointed look, then paddled closer. "Do you swim, Zayne?" she asked as she rose to her feet.

"I have bathed in our pools."

"Ah," she said, and he realized with chagrin that she saw through his evasive answer. To his relief, though, she gave him neither sympathy nor laughter. "Do any of your people swim?"

"Most children learn. I was too . . . busy."

She tilted her head. "I'll teach you to swim if you like, at least a little. This is a good place to learn because it's so shallow. Any time you're uncomfortable, just put your feet down and stand up."

"You enjoy swimming, do you not?"

"I adore it."

Then he would learn the skill, even if he doubted he would enjoy it. "Teach me," he said simply.

She smiled. "Floating first. Lie on your back."

"This I have done in our pools," he told her as he complied, enjoying the feel of her hands supporting his shoulders and back.

"With waves it's a little different. Oh, damn."

A large wave crashed against her, sending her tumbling into him and swamping him with water. He dropped beneath the surface, swallowing water, flailing until he remembered Madeline's instruction. *Any time you're uncomfortable just put your feet down and stand up.*

When he rose above the surface, he gasped a grateful breath.

"How are you?" Madeline asked from beside him.

He wiped his face clear of the water, then opened his eyes. "My eyes sting," he complained, squinting at her.

"It's the salt water."

He licked his lips, which now tasted unpleasantly of salt and raw fish. "You enjoy this?" he repeated.

"You don't have to swim, Zayne. It's about time for lunch anyway."

He would not be defeated by Terran water. He would swim with his *zaniya-e-na*. "I will learn."

"It gets easier. Just hold your breath when the waves come."

"They are constant."

"Hold it for the big ones."

Swimming did become easier, he discovered, just as

Madeline had promised. He much enjoyed when she cradled him for the floating, and although he was awkward when she taught him the basic strokes, he felt he acquitted himself well enough.

He found swimming simplest when she swam alongside him. Not because of her gentle reminders about form or warnings of an incoming wave. Rather, he watched her movements and discovered he was able to tune his motions to hers. As he matched her, his body fell into her natural rhythms. The strokes became easier, and he began to anticipate the rise and fall of the waves and the ebb and flow of the current. Through her, water became not a challenge, a thing to conquer, but an integral part of him.

At last she stood up. "I've never seen anyone catch on so fast."

"I have a good teacher." He gave her a brief, briny kiss. "Thank you."

"It's as much you as me." She glanced over at him. "You hungry?"

He was, he realized, and his body was feeling the onset of fatigue. They returned to the beach, ate the sandwiches Madeline had packed, played a game of something she called Frisbee, found no shells along the beach, then stretched out on the blanket. Madeline lay on her back, her eyes closed and covered with a dark shield she called sunglasses, her face worshiping the sun. He lay next to her, on his side, his elbow bent and his head braced by his palm.

As he watched her, he was surprised by the contentment inside him. Normally, he did not appreciate inactivity. His life was filled with too many responsibilities to waste moments. This did not feel like wasting, however. This feeling reminded him of the times on Kaf when he renewed his bonds of *ma-at*. The hot sun overhead. A warm breeze. Inner calm.

There were differences, of course. The scent of fish. The damp breeze. The sound of the waves. The occasional voices of the other swimmers. Madeline.

"What are you thinking about?" she asked.

"You. The water. Renewing my bonds to my world."

"Tell me about your home. Not your world, your home. The house, or whatever you have, where you live."

"As Minstrel, I travel. There are favorite spots where I enjoy leaving my tent, however."

"By tent, I assume we're not talking moldy canvas here."

"Indigo silk. The inside is much like the room I fashioned at Tildy's, except my tent is more spacious."

She gave a soft sigh, and he could see he intrigued her. "Tell me about one of the places you like to stay."

"Right now, my tent is at the edge of a desert, very isolated. There is a grove of almonds and cedar trees behind it, with a deep, still pool. You can swim there."

She grinned. "A different experience from the Gulf, I take it."

"Yes." He leaned forward, touching her very lightly with his *ma-at*. "There you do not wear clothes to swim."

"No fair, Zayne." A pink flush brightened her cheeks. "I think one of us had better move before I do something that's definitely illegal on a public beach."

He did not move, only teased her a little with a stroke of *ma-at* along her ribs.

"Up to me, then," she said with a smile as she rolled over and checked her watch. "It's getting late. We should go soon."

"Is this a feed-the-cats-Zayne soon or an I-have-to-get-dressed-Zayne soon?"

"The former," she said with a laugh and turned to gather their belongings.

He could not say he was sorry to leave the beach, but he was sorry the day with Madeline was ending. His brief respite from responsibility and confusion was over.

When they had their gear together, they walked back to the car and stowed it in the back. She paused before getting in the car, glancing across the street at a building labeled "Gift Shop."

"Wait here, Zayne. Please? I'll only be a moment." With that, she darted across the street.

He leaned against the car, waiting as she had asked. The metal was hot, but he did not mind. He gazed out over the beach, no longer feeling the reluctance that had beset him on the way here. Only now, he realized, did he begin to feel again the strong forces of magic plucking at him, touching inside him. Despite sand and water being the very essence of Terra, while swimming with Madeline he had not been bothered at all by the alien forces.

"Okay." Madeline's breathless greeting interrupted his thoughts, and he turned to her. She held out a brown bag. "I've got something for you. A gift."

"You already gave me a gift, the gift of swimming."

"Well, you gave me two." She opened the bag and pulled out a strip of woven leather. "Go ahead. Put it on. No, let me do it. See, it has symbols of the beach. Shells laced within the leather. Blue wavy lines like the water." She looked up at him. "I wanted you to have something to remember this day by. To remember me."

He touched a hand to her neck. "I will always remember you, Madeline." A keen resolve hardened inside him. Despite the fact that she could not sing, she was his, and he would find a way to keep her always at his side.

This gift to him meant she also recognized, on some elemental level, that he was hers, her *zani*.

She glanced down, as if uneasy under the heat of his need. "It's not as beautiful as turquoise—"

He tilted her chin up, returning her gaze to his. "It is to me. Thank you. Please put it on me." He held out his arm, then stopped her when she would have tied the leather band around his wrist. "On the upper arm."

"Yeah, it would fit better there." She wrapped it around his arm, knotting the ends together with trembling fingers.

Her hand was small against his muscle, her fingers pale against his skin. A flutter sped through his gut. In the ceremony uniting *zani* and *zaniya* there was a portion in which a scarlet ribbon tied around the arm symbolized the intermingling of two life forces, two sources of *ma-at*. While her fingers stroked the soft leather, he reached out and touched her turquoise tablet.

"Bind thy *ma-at* to mine," he softly intoned, recalling those words of ritual. "Let our fires burn together."

She looked at him, her eyes reflecting the blue of sky and water. Her fingers stilled on the tied leather band, completing the circle.

"I accept thy gift, Madeline, as thou accepted mine." *Ma-at* spun between them, quick as the path of a bee.

He would find a way to be the zani *she desired.*

Fevered arousal shot through him, along with the urgent hunger to unite with her. To complete the ceremony. He forced himself to step back, but some of his emotions must have touched her, for she blinked, then drew her hand back, shaking it a little. "I must have gotten more sun than I realized. My arm's tingly."

During the ride home, he stared straight ahead, for

to look at her would be to desire her and to touch her. If he touched her again, he feared that his willpower would shred and he would be lost to both his responsibility and his honor. That neither the promise of his performance tonight nor the bargain not to coerce her could stop him from sweeping her to Kaf.

And that he could not do.

Chapter Seventeen

The previous night, Zayne had paid little attention to either Wilson Luck or the Luck Club. He'd been too angry, too intent on leaving, for curiosity. Now he lounged on a small chair at the side of the stage, his oud slung over his shoulder, and looked around. The club was similar to the jazz club—crowded, smoky, loud. The visitors seemed to be younger than those at the other club, but he could not be sure. He had difficulty judging the age of humans.

Madeline was sitting at the table with him; she glanced around and shifted uneasily. "Lot of people here."

"Is that not what you hoped for? So Cyrus would hear of me?"

"Yeah, but . . . I'm just glad it's you up on that stage and not me."

He didn't answer. One day he would find a way to help her over this fear. Tonight, however, was not the night.

With the ease of long practice, Wilson Luck wound his way through the crowds to their table. Zayne found the musician more interesting than the club.

Wilson was taller than Zayne, dark-skinned and wiry. His black hair was shaved close to his head, and a narrow strip of beard bisected his chin. His eyes were large, round, and a deceptively soft brown, for there seemed little that escaped his notice.

He leaned his hands on the table. "You ready, Zayne? 'Cause it's a kick-ass crowd here tonight. They'll be a tough sell, especially for an unplugged singer."

"I am ready."

Wilson glanced at Madeline, "If he crashes, you owe me big time for this, sister."

"He won't."

"Then let's go." Wilson mounted the stage, and the crowd quieted to an anticipatory murmur. He raised his hands, and even the murmur stopped.

"You've heard soul on this stage," Luck began.

"How come we never hear you play, then?" yelled someone from the crowd.

"New talent, brother, only new talent. The best, the stars before they're stars. Jazz, hip hop, rap, blues, metal, and any other style you can mention. Never had a dude like tonight's performer, though. Some might call him New Age—"

Whistles and shouts interrupted him.

Luck held up his hands. "I said *some* might call him New Age. I don't. I don't call him anything except good. So give a listen, then tell your friends, because they won't want to miss . . . Zayne!" He flung out a hand, pointing straight toward Zayne.

A spotlight swung to focus on Zayne, blinding him with its hot brilliance. He blinked, clearing his vision, and took that as his cue to go to the stage.

There were a few raucous comments that he preferred not to interpret and a few whistles that he ignored. These people mattered naught to him. Only two listeners were important. Cyrus, if he were here. And Madeline.

Followed by the spotlight, he took his seat on the

stage. The chair was hard, and he wished he could add a pillow, or simply levitate, but he supposed that would not be a wise choice.

On the other hand, as their purpose was to entice Cyrus . . .

The necessary spell took but a moment. Yes, the pillow was much better. He braced his foot against a rung of the chair, swung his oud around, and began to sing.

The notes spun through the smoky room like fireflies through the night. The song was fresh as air, complex as an evening storm. The room quieted, he noticed from the back of his mind. Now was the time to discover whether the faint hope of the jazz club was true.

Now was the time to show them, and Madeline, the true mastery of a Minstrel.

He looked up from his oud, straight at Madeline, and then he fed the song, and the pleasure of the audience, with his *ma-at*.

Cyrus stood concealed at the rear of the room, unimpressed at first with Madeline's companion. Zayne had very little stage presence; he ignored the audience completely, first squinting into the lights, then staring down at his instrument.

Yet, surprisingly, the affectation was effective. The crowd did notice him.

Cyrus frowned as he watched Zayne sit on a pillow. Had there been a pillow there earlier? He didn't think so, and for the first time his interest was piqued.

As Zayne began to sing, a strange song in an unknown language, all Cyrus's criticism evaporated. That voice! That voice was spellbinding, a rare voice few were ever privileged to hear in a lifetime. Even this once-raucous crowd knew it.

But was it good vocal cords? Or magic?

He leaned forward, studying the singer. He had to be sure before he made his move.

Zayne finally glanced up from his strange instrument, but he still paid no attention to the audience. Instead, he looked only at Madeline.

The music shifted, so subtly only a trained ear could detect the change. Yet now the beauty of it clung to the air, so haunting even Cyrus felt his chest clutch. Pinpricks of light danced before his eyes. His heart tripped against his ribs as excitement shot through him. Magic.

This man was the one he sought; he was sure of it now. This man sang with magic.

Zayne was a genie.

At last the moment of centuries was here.

So where did Madeline fit in? Why had the genie come to her? Cyrus's gaze went back and forth between the two, and suddenly he understood. After all these years, at last he saw.

He slid unobtrusively through the crowd, not wanting to draw the attention of Madeline or Zayne. Not until he was ready. Not until he had everything set. Then he would watch for their return. He would fetch Irena, and he would spring his trap.

With a final glance at the stage, he left the Luck Club without anyone knowing he had been there.

Zayne glanced toward the back of the room, feeling the chill of a sinister shadow move across him, but he saw nothing extraordinary. The sensation soon faded, and he forgot about it, returning his attention to Madeline. She watched him, lit by a single candle on the table in front of her. Her hair looked like burnished gold. Tonight she wore the dress of fire.

She was a woman of movement and action; she should not be simply sitting. She was not, he noticed with a touch of humor. Beneath the table, her foot tapped to the beat.

His song shifted to a ballad. His *ma-at* deepened, and his voice ripened. He shaded the edges of the room with colors of passion, and he sweetened the air. Nothing obvious. Wisps and hints and shadows that enhanced the senses and heightened the music.

Throughout all, his gaze remained on Madeline. A faint smile lifted the corners of her mouth, and when she moistened her lips, he felt the tingling dampness on his own mouth. A compelling need arose within him to sing a new variation of the dense ballad. He wove in the melodies of Terra, of jazz and country. The flowing, sensual notes deepened.

The strange, alien power joined his song. It swelled within him, dark and feral, interwoven on the music. Demanding. Intense. Primal.

He captured his listeners, brought the sweat of hot passion to their brows. As he watched her, Madeline ran a hand around the nape of her neck, lifting her hair in a futile effort to cool herself. Her breasts rose and fell with each breath, and his song shifted to match her rhythm.

The alien power rose, fiercer and stronger, darker, trying to replace the *ma-at*. Yet no message beacon came from Kaf, warning of change and destruction. Instead, each force inside him strengthened, rising to meet the other.

Suddenly he recognized it. Recognized the force that battled against his Kafian nature and his powerful *ma-at*.

Magic. Terran magic.

Avoiding the forces of magic before this visit, he had not recognized them when they first arose. Only during these past days with Madeline had he gained enough familiarity to recognize them inside him now.

Magic. He sang with the seeds of magic.

His fingers shook, faltering on the strings of his oud, as denial rose in his throat. The warnings from his mother, the history of the djinn, crashed upon him.

This could not be. Magic and *ma-at* could not coexist. They were water and fire, air and earth.

His song continued, driven by the wild battle within, by the tumultuous refusal to accept. Complex and rich, disturbing and compelling

Was this some strange sorcery? How could two such forces exist within him?

They could not. As he sang, they battled within him now. His affliction had not ceased, only grown recognizable. The *ma-at* of Kaf. The magic of Terra. Two incompatible forces. His body ached from the strain of their competition.

There could be no doubt as to which one must triumph within him. He was of Kaf, he was her Minstrel; her harmony, her soul.

Only Kaf could remain.

Only *ma-at*.

A scarlet orb snapped into being before his eyes.

Kaf. Fear rose inside him. He was affecting Kaf, destroying the balance of his world. This was not the answer. He could not control the magic inside him this way.

Yet he could not end the song. Not when Madeline was smiling and swaying to the rhythm. Not when magic and *ma-at* both fed his raging need.

Blinking to clear his blurred vision, he looked out

into the forgotten audience. The pervasive smoke eddied around the room, driven by the winds of his *ma-at*, as he ruthlessly tried to subjugate the magic to his power. Buried in the cloudy depths were countless pinpricks of light, a rainbow of color that flashed and spun, almost too quick to be seen, like the spots of light after a too-bright flash. He held his audience spellbound, drawn by the raging power of the voice of the Minstrel.

It was Madeline he sought, however. Madeline. Only Madeline. She had not moved from beside the stage, and the honeyed circle of light from the candle still bathed her in its glow.

Beautiful Madeline. Graceful Madeline, who could not sing and who feared the stage. Intrepid Madeline, who barged into bayous and stood up to abusers though she had not the protection of *ma-at*. Madeline, who taught him to swim and who accepted not only the whole of him but every part of him.

Madeline, who had not believed in magic but who embodied all its best.

His body tightened and arousal shot through him, demanding her, demanding release. The song changed again. Sensual with the fire of *ma-at*, seductive with the relentless flow of magic. It became the erotic battle of lovers, not warriors. Of male and female.

Madeline swayed in her seat, an instinctive, primal dance of a woman on fire for her mate. Her body moved with such grace, and he was so aware of her that he could feel the brush of her hair on his cheek and the weight of her breast against his palm.

His body hardened with anticipation. Tonight she would be his. He sang to her and invited her to be his lover. Madeline, dancer of Terra, counterpoint to all that he had assumed about this world. Madeline, who had introduced him to the good of her world. To jazz and beaches and Snickers.

The fiery desire shot through him. Demanding and unrelenting.

Suddenly the force of magic within him altered and took on the graceful sway of Madeline's rhythm. The magic became the ebb of the waves and the trickle of sand. It flowed from him and surrounded her, attuning to her pulse. When it returned to him, he accepted it, a new, beautiful countermelody that gave *ma-at* its natural claim of dominance while enriching the song with a new depth. Note by note, the song of the magic blended into the *ma-at*.

The message orb disappeared. He blinked. It had disappeared!

For an unheard of second time, his fingers stumbled on the oud. His heart quickened. Kaf had settled. She had accepted his magic and this new harmony.

He was Minstrel. Because Madeline was at his side, Kaf accepted the magic that lived within him. *He had found the path.*

With pure elation in his song, he brought the music toward its end, still watching Madeline, still feeling her unconsciously draw and direct the magic by the dance of her body. Still being aroused until his body burned with the need of her.

She was his *zaniya* not because she sang, but because she danced.

He finished the song then, ignoring first the stunned silence and then the enthusiastic applause. He slung the oud over his shoulder and hopped off the stage to Madeline's side.

He held out his hand. "Are you ready, Madeline? Are you ready to join me in my world?"

* * *

Madeline stared at the outstretched hand, then at Zayne. "You've played for nearly an hour nonstop. You must be exhausted."

"It is not rest I need." His voice was a dark, sultry night, full of exotic mystery.

She flushed slightly. Still, there was no choice, no difficulty in the answer. She had shown Zayne her world.

Now it was time to learn his.

Without hesitation, she put her hand in his.

Effortlessly he lifted her to her feet. The green in his eyes deepened, and around him sparkled a red as bright as flames. He led her out of the club, the crowds no barrier to his goal. With him, she glided past the bodies without even brushing against them.

She had never seen or heard him like this, so foreign and enchanting. Tonight he had none of the overlay of humanity. He was djinn and could be nothing else.

He led her outside into the hot, damp air, then drew her into a secluded alley.

He gathered her close into his arms, his body hard against hers. He was aroused already. This was a male who tonight would not be denied.

He bent and whispered in her ear. "Madeline Fairbanks, of your own free will, do you come with me to share my world?"

She took a deep breath. Her heart pounded so loudly she could barely hear her own answer. "Yes."

Immediately the cyclone descended and pulled her away from Earth. She clung to Zayne, to the strength of his body and the reassuring steady beat of his heart, to his warmth and his solidity. Once, she thought he brushed a kiss against her cheek. Always, he kept her close and protected.

Then, as abruptly as it started, the cyclone stopped.

This time, there was no stumbling. One moment she was sliding along an ephemeral slide, and the next moment she was standing still, wrapped in silence and heat and Zayne's arms. Her face was buried against his chest, and for a moment she drew in his even breathing and familiar, masculine scent.

His arms tightened about her and he kissed the top of her head.

"Welcome to Kaf, Madeline. Welcome to my home."

Chapter Eighteen

Madeline opened her eyes, then pushed back slightly from Zayne's chest. He kept her firmly in his embrace, his hand drawing small intimate circles on her back. He only loosened his hold enough for her to see this strange new world.

Immediately she was entranced.

It was night on Kaf, just as it had been on Earth. There were stars and a moon, too, but there the similarities stopped. Each star shone as a clear, brilliant spot of white in the ebony expanse of the sky. The moon was a quarter slice of gleaming sliver. No reflections from city lights dimmed the grandeur or the vastness of the night.

The air was hot and much drier than she was used to in New Orleans. She should have packed some moisturizer, she thought with humor. That is, if she had packed anything. She drew in a long breath, then another.

That hot air was the clearest she'd ever inhaled. No pollutants or exhaust. Instead, flowers and fresh woods perfumed each breath, like a cleansing shower.

Strangest of all was the silence. Only their breathing and the night breeze had any sound. There was no growl of an engine, or rumble of tire on pavement, or blare of a boom box to break the quiet. Not a voice. Not a meow. Not a horn honk.

She twisted, sliding in the circle of Zayne's arms, and he shifted his embrace to rest a hand at her hip. Because of the dark, she could see little in the distance, but before her was a tent, if so mundane a word could be used for the elegant arrangement of indigo silk rippling softly in the night breeze. Boulders on waves of sand formed the primary landscape, with scattered trees dotting the area.

"This is the place you described to me," she breathed, almost afraid to break the encompassing silence. "Your home."

"The tent is. I rarely stay more than a few risings of the sun, but this is a place where I often return."

"I can see why. It's so beautiful, at least what I can see by moonlight."

"Would you like a glimpse of more?"

"Yes."

He stood behind her, his body close enough that she could feel his arousal pressed against her. He crossed his hands at the wrists in front of her, then chanted. A light flared out from him, flat and far-reaching, allowing her to see well beyond the features illuminated by natural light. Beyond the tent on all sides was desert. They were surround by rolling, curving mounds of sand, some as high as the dunes and cliffs of Earth. Only lone rocks and boulders broke the natural rhythm of the sand, their smooth surfaces polished and glinting with silver or gold. Nothing to hem him in or confine him, she realized. She caught brief flashes of color—pink, yellow, bronze, orange—before the light faded.

"Oh, Zayne." Her soft sigh spoke the words she could not. This world so reminded her of the man who stood behind her, as though he embodied the essence of his Kaf. Exotic beauty, hidden rhythms, solitary splendor. "I'll be anxious to see it in daytime."

"I am not anxious for sunrise," he said, his voice deeper and more alluring than she had ever heard it. "I am eager for the night."

With his hands on her upper arms, he turned her toward him. The lights of evening gleamed in his auburn hair, highlighted the planes of his cheek, but his eyes remained in shadow. He ran his hands between them, changing their clothes so that each wore a sleeveless robe and shorts of indigo silk.

Except shorts and robe were words too ordinary to describe what they wore. The silk flowed across her skin so lightly she felt as though she wore nothing but the breath of a caress. If the dress was like wearing a flame, then these shorts and robe were like wearing the wind.

His manicured nail traced up her lapel, his manner both possessive and confident. When he reached her breast, he circled it with a delicate touch atop the lustrous silk. Her robe did nothing to hide the tightness of her nipples, just as his shorts did nothing to hide his impressive erection.

He bent and drew the tip of her silk-covered breast into his mouth, replacing his finger with his tongue. His hands played across her arms, then met at her back, pushing her deeper into the velvet of his mouth. When he shifted to her other breast, the night winds blew across the damp, exposed silk, not cooling but exciting. Soft growls of pleasure came from deep in his throat.

She supported herself against his shoulders, grateful for the brace of his hands. At last he lifted from her and stepped back.

His turquoise tablet lay in the middle of the deep V of his robe, a visible symbol that he was djinn, not human, and she was part of his world now. His bare feet curled into the soft sand, anchoring him well. His bare, muscled arms seemed dusted with gold, but she could not see his eyes. He held out his hand.

"Come share my pillows, Madeline."

She swallowed, struck again by his exotic sensuality. This was not a man of her world, but he was the man she desired with every particle of her being. She put her hand in his, but to her surprise he did not transport them the short distance to his tent. Instead, he picked her up in his arms and carried her inside.

Zayne set her on her feet in the middle of his tent, filled with satisfaction. *She was here. On Kaf. In his tent.*

"No transport?" she teased. "I thought you were eager."

"I am eager," he murmured, "to take my time tonight. To be very slow and quite thorough in making love to you." Her flush pleased him. In truth, he had not transported because he had not wanted to lose the sensation of her in his arms for even those brief moments.

He bent back to her lips, driven by a keen need to taste and touch. Their tongues met and mated in a dance as hot and as ancient as fire. He traced the smooth column of her throat into the V of silk, his thumb marking her speeding pulse.

"Your heart's tempo matches mine," he told her.

The breeze from outside carried the musky, stimulating scent of the *frangipela* from the grove behind his tent. Even the natural elements of Kaf approved of this mating.

Ma-at spiraled from him, electrifying air and skin. He also caressed her with hand and mind, savoring the curve of her thigh, the dip at her waist, her expressive hands, each tiny piece of her. With his teeth, he nipped the tip of her ear and her shoulder. She responded with a purr of pleasure, and her hands stroked his back, scraping lightly with her nails. She cupped his buttocks, holding him as she slid across him.

Desire roared like a beast, lengthening and hardening him. He captured her between his legs, while his hand reached lower, playing with the dampness at the juncture of her thighs. He wanted to touch every portion of her, needing her touch on him. Perhaps he sent her the thought, for her hands reached to caress his silk-covered arousal with long, slow strokes that roused a growl deep in his throat.

"Keep that up, Madeline, and this will be over too soon."

"Too soon is impossible." She tilted her head back. "Can you give us more light? I want to see you."

He broke from her only long enough to kneel at the fire and quickly conjure the requested illumination. Then he gathered her close, standing behind her. His hips pulsed against her from behind, stroking the curve of her bottom, while his hand made lazy circles around her breasts and belly. The robe she wore parted for him.

She inhaled sharply. "You smell like spicy cinnamon."

"Do you like it?" His fingers delved beneath her shorts, teasing the curls, his thumb pressing against her taut bud, while his *ma-at* brushed her lips with tingling spice.

"Yes," she moaned as her fingers kneaded his thighs.

"Then I shall arrange for you to taste it often." He enveloped her with redolent cinnamon carried by *ma-at* in the wake of his caresses. His erection pressed against her rear cleft. One hand played expertly with her soft lower folds, while his other thumb traced the line of her mouth, and his teeth grazed her neck. He felt her cheeks flush and her breath quicken as he rimmed her opening. Her hands on his thighs tightened, and she widened her legs for him.

"I wish to taste honey," he whispered. He slid around her until he faced her, then down her front, never letting their bodies part. At last he reached his goal, but instead of pulling down the shorts, he kissed her through the fabric. First he used his tongue to push the silk inside her, then he circled his tongue to stroke her, then he sucked it out with a gentle pressure. Again he repeated until she was moaning and clutching his shoulders. Only when he felt the pulses of her first convulsion did he stand and gather her back in his arms until she quieted.

She looked up at him, her eyes bright. "Zayne, why do you still have your clothes on?" Her voice was a silken invitation.

He returned her smile, then leaned forward to trail tiny kisses along her ear. When he reached the lobe, he traced the gems in her ears with his tongue and whispered, "I shall be pleased to remedy that, *si halika*."

He stepped back, lifted his hands to his robe, and then paused. She expected a snap of his fingers and the clothes would be gone in an instant—he could see that from the eager expectation on her face. Instead, he planted his feet and captured her gaze.

Slowly with his hands he opened his shirt, exposing himself to her one small bit at a time. At the same time, with his *ma-at* he reached out to her, opening her robe and revealing her soft skin to his eager eyes. Her breath caught, and he felt the change of her rhythms as she realized what he did.

"Oh, Zayne, you are wicked." Her smile proved she enjoyed this brand of wickedness.

"No," he corrected, "I am very good."

With leisurely precision, he stripped off their robes.

"Your breasts are beautiful," he told her when they stood bare from the waist up. "Curved and golden with a hard, eager nipple at each tip."

She swallowed, and her eyes moved hungrily over his chest. "How do you make everything a song? All I can manage is, 'Wow.' "

" 'Wow' is sufficient."

Her admiration stoked his masculine pride. He rested his hands at the waist of his pants, and her breath quickened. But he did not move, did not take the next step. Instead, he caressed her with his *ma-at*, circling her breasts and ribs and lower with long, slow strokes.

"No fair," she said, breathless. "I'm not touching you."

"When you are undressed, Madeline, you may touch me in any way you please."

He held his breath, brows lifted, waiting and anxious for her response.

For a moment, her hands fluttered toward her shorts, but then she stopped herself. She lifted her chin in challenge, her eyes bright with promise. Her arms lowered to her sides. "Then please continue."

Though he touched her with only his *ma-at* and his sparkling emotions, he could feel the curve of her breast against his palm and her hard nipple in his mouth. He tasted the sweet salt of her skin and smelled the perfume of her arousal. All these he sent back to her with his thoughts, exposing his need as he exposed his body. Her skin darkened with desire, and he felt her heat to his bones.

Only then did he begin to lower their remaining garments. As his flesh was bared, his need rose. *Your legs are strong, well-shaped, smooth.* He sent her the thought, his mouth too dry to speak. *I cannot wait to feel them wrapped around me again.*

When his erection sprang free, however—just as his *ma-at* revealed the thin strip of her red panties, just as she sweetly moaned—a fiery, unquenchable arousal raged through him, burning away his control and carrying him to the brink of precipitous release.

He closed his eyes. His fists clenched. Breathe deep. Chant the boring Mantras of Serenity. Anything to beat back the demanding, blazing urge. Anything to prevent himself from spilling here, now, too soon.

Very slow and very thorough would have to wait until the sharp edge of need was blunted.

When a measure of control returned, he opened his eyes. She was waiting for him, holding her shorts where he'd left them. Pulsing her hips to her inner rhythms. Smiling, knowing, and accepting.

His control vanished, and he was surprised to find himself trembling.

"Madeline," he groaned with a desire-harshened voice. With a thrust of his hand, he removed their shorts. Just as fast, the panties he'd forgotten to remove when he changed her dress disappeared, leaving her wearing only a turquoise tablet and a blush.

As soon as the panties were gone, she launched herself toward him, tumbling them both back into his pillows when he caught her in his arms. "My turn," she demanded.

Amber, scarlet, emerald, and gentian silk surrounded them. Her heat and her lithe body covered him. They sank into sensual abandon as the pillows adjusted to cradle them. Crystalline colors winked and crackled around them.

His desire enveloped her. Her desire inflamed him.

Her hands, oh, they touched him. Forehead, chin, shoulder, crook of arm, spine, crease of thigh. Everywhere she touched, a fire spread along his nerves and muscles. Her tongue circled his nipple, creating her own form of magic to match his earlier *ma-at*.

"Send me these thoughts, Zayne." Her breath brushed across the dampness left by her mouth, arousing, not cooling. She licked above his heart; then her lips moved lower to encircle him. "What do you feel when I do this? I wish I could send you how good it makes me feel."

Unable to reply with words, he spread his chaotic thoughts and spiraling *ma-at* across her.

"Ohhh," she breathed, laying her cheek against his belly.

His last shred of control was exhausted. Abruptly he rolled over, pulling her beneath him and positioning himself between her thighs. His thickened erection was poised at her opening.

"I wanted to touch—"

"Do," he commanded roughly, "but I can no longer wait."

"Okay."

He thrust into her moist welcome, turning her agreement into a gasp of pleasure. He withdrew, then thrust again, seating himself deep. Oh, by the love of destiny, she felt so good.

His usual finesse deserted him. All he could see, think, experience, was Madeline. He lost himself in sensation.

She met him with equal passion. Her hips welcomed each full thrust. Her hands cupped him from behind, urging him deeper and faster. She lifted her head to rain kisses on his face, and he braced her while he gave her a single, demanding kiss.

Powers rose inside him. Forces that competed and matched. *Ma-at* and magic. Djinn, human. Male, female. Water and fire joined, and steam erupted.

Infinite rhythmic pulses surrounded him as she found her release. Oh, thank the fires that sent him to her! His thrusts quickened in the timeless cadence of lovers, and then he joined her in her pleasure as a powerful orgasm jolted through him.

Only gradually did they calm and settle into the pillows, their sharp breaths softening and their hearts slowing. The scent of the *frangipela* shifted to a sweet, soothing aroma. Drowsy and languid, he gathered her into his arms. She rested her head against his shoulder with a contented murmur. He stroked her hair, relishing the soft feel of her in his arms.

"Memorable," she whispered, her voice growing drowsy.

Zayne nestled close, his arms wrapped around her. How wrong he had been to persist in thinking Madeline was his *zaniya* because she would complement him in his role as Minstrel.

Yes, she balanced his *ma-at*, and allowed him to control the alien magic in ways he did not fully understand. Yes, with her he could be Minstrel and sing the necessary harmonies of Kaf.

Those facts were not why he wanted to wake up beside her each morning. Being Minstrel had nothing to do with why he could laugh with her and share his fears with her or why the scent of her—he kissed the back of her neck—and the taste of her were so important.

He wanted her for his *zaniya* because she was an

essential part of him, because he loved her. Come morning, he would tell her. Of the divination. Of his purpose. Of his need for her. Of his love. Tomorrow, he would ask her to be his *zaniya*.

Tomorrow.

Chapter Nineteen

Madeline awoke disoriented. Rich brocade beneath her cheek. Pillows around her. Behind her was a fiery heat, a man's body.

Zayne. With a rush, memory returned. She opened her eyes, and the facts still remained. She had made love with a djinni. With Zayne. Several times in fact.

This time, however, they were on Kaf. She lay quiet, needing to absorb how her life had turned inside out in so short a time. Magic, spells, whole other worlds, genies, all things she had believed did not exist, were now an indelible part of her. Last week she rode the streetcar. This week she could grab a necklace and Scotty would beam her up. Through all of it strode Zayne, solid and magical, every woman's fantasy come to life.

She closed her eyes a moment, smiling, realizing her life had been turned around in another new and fresh way.

She was in love.

Somewhere amidst this whirlwind, she had fallen in love with Zayne, perhaps from the moment he had looked up from the doorbell and smiled at her. She loved his kindness and his empathy. She loved his humor and his sensuality. He was so different from anyone she'd ever met, open and generous and honest.

She was in love with a minstrel djinni.

What the future held, she had no idea. Was it possible for her to find happiness with a musician? If the musician was Zayne, yes. He made her feel so good, and she thought that she pleased him too. Was it possible for two worlds to blend?

Or would the fairy tale end?

Big questions that she had no answers for. For the moment she was content to snuggle close and savor the precious time they did have. However enduring or however brief. For joy could be snatched away, and love was a rare gift.

At last, however, more mundane matters demanded her attention. She slid from the pillows, trying not to disturb her sleeping lover. Then she looked around, biting her lip uncertainly. Surely even a djinni had, um, other physical needs, other facilities.

"Behind the gauze over there."

Madeline whirled around at the sound of Zayne's deep, sleepy voice. She found him sprawled in the pillows, watching her, his elbow bent and his head propped on his palm.

"How did you know what I wanted?"

"Because I have hopes that you will be quick so I may also avail myself."

"Oh." She found the gauze veil, heard him say some unintelligible words for water to flow as she went behind it, where she discovered the necessary amenities to complete her business. As soon as she emerged from behind the veil, he disappeared.

The flame-colored dress had been draped across the carved wooden chest, while the indigo pajamas lay in a heap near the bed. She put on the dress, then looked around, taking advantage of the daylight to see what she'd been too preoccupied to notice last night. From her limited experience with tents, they were hot and close. Not so Zayne's home. The interior was cool and fresh. Everything was luxurious and harmonious, from the mound of pillows, to the circle of colored rocks surrounding the central fire, to the cut and curve of the various decorations.

She spied a break in the silk and guessed it was a door. After a moment's hesitation, she stepped outside, onto the sands of Kaf.

Overhead, the yellow circle of the sun blazed with radiant fire. On Earth she would say it was about noon, but she couldn't be sure that the days passed the same here. Despite the sun's heat, the sand was cool beneath her bare feet, and soft as cotton.

They were alone here. She could see no other sign of habitation. No indication that another soul was within view. As she had glimpsed last night, surrounding them was desert, stark and remote and beautiful. Behind the tent, though, was a smattering of trees. She heard a rustling of silk; then Zayne stood behind her, wrapping his arms around her waist, and resting his chin on top of her head.

He hadn't bothered with clothes.

"Breakfast?" He held his hand out to her and on it rested two slices of cinnamon bread drizzled with honey. She could smell the rich spice and the clover honey, and blushed, remembering last night.

"Thank you." She took a slice of bread and bit into it, realizing she was hungry.

Zayne took the other bread slice. "What do you think of Kaf?"

"Beautiful, awe-inspiring. Hot. So fresh. Quiet."

"Well, it is not always quiet when the djinn are assembled."

Silently, enjoying the peace of the day with him, she

finished her breakfast. As she licked the last crumbs from her fingers, though, she sighed. "We'll have to go back home soon to let Cyrus find us."

"Later," he answered, his hands cupping her breasts through the fabric of the dress, his thumbs stroking the nipples. He leaned over and trailed nibbling kisses up her neck, then over to her lips. "You taste like breakfast. Like cinnamon and honey." He gave a wicked chuckle. "But there is another honey I quite enjoy."

That quickly, that easily, she burned for him.

"Upon arising," he murmured, "it is my custom to greet Kaf with a song. I would like you to dance with my song, Madeline, and then we have matters to discuss."

She stilled. Perform her dancing? With him watching? Her imagination was one thing. Reality was entirely different. There would be no veil this time, like in the French Quarter. *He would be watching.*

The automatic denial rose alongside the insidious fear. Her stomach lurched, threatening to return her breakfast. She pressed her lips together and shook her head. "I can't," she croaked out at last. "I do not perform."

"And I do not do auditions."

"I don't dance in public. I told you that."

"Does this look like a public place? This is my home. None will see you but me." He turned her to face him. "This is not a performance, Madeline. This is not me judging you or waiting to applaud or hiss. This is a man asking his woman, his lover, to share joy. I will play, and you will dance. If my eyes bother you, then do not look at them. Look at my hands on the oud. Look at the creation of the music."

She couldn't meet his eye, couldn't agree, couldn't

say a word against the rising nausea. Instead, she trembled with competing needs. To dance as he asked or to hide.

Fear won again.

He cupped her cheek, his thumb caressing her temple. "I did not ask to cause you distress. Think no more of it. I shall sing." He pointed to the trees behind the tent. "Sit there while I get my oud."

Madeline did as he suggested, humiliation warring with disappointment and fear. Stupid stage fright. Damn spell. Why couldn't she get past it, when she wanted so much to dance? When she wanted to dance for Zayne?

She had barely made it to the sparse grove when Zayne joined her. He had dressed in a short sleeveless robe of red, and his oud was slung over his shoulder. "You can sit there." He pointed to a V created by the trunks of two trees.

She wedged herself against the tree.

"This is a song I began after I played the jazz, but the words are in my language, not yours," he warned.

"The words won't matter. It's the music I want to hear."

Zayne began to sing. The song flowed from him like streams of fresh water flow across rocks. She heard snatches of jazz within it, but the melody could only be Kafian. Colors winked around him in deepening shades of purple, red, and gold. Fleeting tastes—clove, honey, almond—teased her tongue along with their fragrant aromas. All created by the voice of the Minstrel.

Then the song quickened. She straightened, drawn by the irresistible urge to join in the smooth rhythms. Her shoulders swayed.

She gave him a quick glance. He wasn't looking at

her. He was bent over his oud, his long hair shielding his face, totally absorbed in his music. Her whole body joined in swaying, in the start of a dance, remembering the familiar joy. Of their own volition her feet began to move; then her arms joined. Eyes closed, she danced to the beautiful voice and the strange music.

At last she opened her eyes, to find Zayne watching her intently, his eyes hot. Abruptly she froze, stomach churning, sweat breaking out on her brow, eyes unable to focus. Zayne said nothing, did nothing but continue to play the compelling music.

Madeline bit her lip, drew in a long, shuddering breath.

This is not a performance. This is a man asking his woman, his lover, to dance. Zayne's words echoed in her mind. *Not a performance.* There was no one else here. Just Zayne.

Not a performance, but a gift of thanks.

A gift of love.

For the man she loved.

Gaze still locked with his, letting him watch every tiny motion, Madeline lifted her hands in the dance of women, in the *raqs sharqi* she had tried before her mirror, and began to dance.

Zayne had believed Madeline to be graceful. He had enjoyed dancing with her. What he had not appreciated until now was how talented she was. Her motions were supple and free-flowing, like the great river she lived beside. Her interpretation of his music was a delightful mix of technique and passion.

Nor had he realized what joy she found in the dance. Her body moved free and easy. Her eyes were alight with pleasure, matching her shining smile. Watching her made his heart sing. Madeline loved to dance as much as he loved to sing.

What a foul spell that stage fright was, to cut her off from this essential nourishment for her soul.

Her dance changed to one of enticement. As he had said, she was talented. One lithe rotation of her hips and he was hard. One sensual smile and by Solomon he was looking for the nearest soft sand. The little tease knew it. His *salika* had a sting indeed.

He set aside his oud and stalked deliberately toward her.

She gave him a teasing grin, still dancing as she hummed. Rhythmic, but off key. He didn't even mind, as long as she kept those hips swaying.

One stride later he stood in front of her. He ran his hands along the juncture of her thighs. "Open for me," he whispered.

"Are these the matters you said you wanted to discuss?" she asked, still teasing, dancing out of reach.

Her words washed out the immediacy of his need, for he had delayed all he could. The time was past due for him to speak. When they next made love, it would be with full knowledge, full acceptance.

"Matters to discuss," he echoed, then drew in a long breath, uncharacteristically unsure. Would she understand?

A discordant wind whistled across the desert, carrying before it a stinging swirl of sand. Beneath his feet, the forces of *ma-at* lurched through the sands. *By Solomon, no, not now, not yet*. In the distance came a lonely howl; and his fingers tightened. The unrest continued; he could not ignore it.

For too long he had sung with the uncontrolled magic. For too long Kaf had been without the necessary harmony he provided. The unrest touched on many areas of his world. His song on Terra last night was not enough to soothe them all. He must perform here as well, with his full essence. *Ma-at* and magic.

Kaf needed the song of her Minstrel.

Her Minstrel needed his *zaniya-e-na* to control the magic.

"Madeline, I—"

The color drained from Madeline's face and her dancing stopped, as her gaze fixed on something behind his shoulder. She stumbled backward, her body hunched. "Zayne, you have a visitor."

Madeline swallowed hard against the nausea, willing herself not to throw up. Surreptitiously she rubbed her sweaty palms against her dress, feeling the clutch of unreasonable panic in her lungs. Dancing for Zayne had not conquered Cyrus's insidious spell.

How long had the stranger stood there, watching? She could see nothing except the red robe and the elegant hands. Not seeing the eyes didn't lessen her fear. He had been watching her.

Only now, when she wasn't performing, when the stranger turned to Zayne, could she draw a breath. Gradually the nausea subsided, and her curiosity rose.

The stranger bowed. "Minstrel, you are needed."

She was vaguely surprised to hear the stranger speaking English.

"I know. Where? I could not tell."

"Jarbesh-en-i'llan."

Zayne nodded, looking more serious than she had ever seen him. Whatever news the man—and height, breadth, and voice said it was a man hidden beneath the robe—was bringing was not good.

Should she leave? Fingering the turquoise tablet, she sidled backward.

Wait. Zayne's imperious command stopped her. "You will come with me."

"Come? Where? What's going on?"

Zayne ignored her questions, continuing to speak to the man in the robe. "We shall be there shortly, Alesander."

"You have not told her about the divination?" The hood turned in her direction.

"I was about to explain."

"Explain? To me? What?" Madeline rubbed a hand down her arm, feeling a chill despite the hot sun.

Neither man answered her.

Alesander spoke. "I hope you have not left the matter for too long, for she must understand. There is some time; the unrest has not spread beyond the focus. I shall do what I can until you arrive." The sand barely rippled with his disappearance.

"Explain to me what?" Madeline asked again, her stomach knotting.

Zayne sighed; then he faced her directly. "What I had just started to tell you. I am Minstrel, the balance of my world."

She remembered his telling her that, but she was guessing now that she hadn't fully understood what he'd meant. Apparently she was about to find out.

"Of late," he continued, "strange forces broke that balance, disturbed my song. Strange, fierce, compelling forces within me that I could not control."

Her stomach lurched. Oh, my God, he couldn't be— "Zayne, are you sick?"

He pressed her hand between his palms and kissed the tips of her fingers. "No, but I thank you for your concern. Until I met you, I did not understand this force. Now, as the divination foretold, I do. It is your Terran magic, and as such is incompatible with my *ma-*

at. With you, through you, though, I can control it. I can be the Minstrel."

She stared at him, her heart shriveling, praying she had just misunderstood. He could not be with her just because some arcane ritual told him he could use her to control this magic so he could keep singing.

"A divination is some . . . fortune-telling thing?" she asked carefully.

"It is a ritual. A path to follow." He stroked her neck, giving her that sexy smile. "At first I could not believe it, a Terran and a Minstrel destined to be united as *zaniya* and *zani*, but you have proven the wisdom behind the guidance."

Foretold. Destined. *Zaniya. Now that I am with you, I can control it.* Each word carved off a little piece of her. Her arms wrapped around her middle. Her stomach and her heart clenched from waves of hot nausea and icy pain.

"What is a *zaniya*?" she asked, determined to know it all. To have no illusions. If only she didn't feel so cold and shriveled.

"*Zaniya*? Your closest word would be wife."

"*Wife*." She could barely speak.

"For the djinn, though, it is more." He reached again to touch her cheek, but she shied away. "*Zaniya* and *zani*, female and male, are mates of the soul. Few of the djinn ever speak the bonds, but when they do, it is forever."

A phrase he'd used earlier came to mind. "You've called me *zaniya-e-na*."

"The promised *zaniya*. The one who is to be."

Her heart felt like a hard knot in her chest. "Let me get this straight. You came to Earth not to visit Miss Tildy, but to find me. Because a divination said that I was to be your wife, your *zaniya*. You thought I would simply abandon everything in my life so I could come to an alien world and help you control this magical force that was disturbing your singing."

He frowned as if sensing this wasn't going as smoothly as his divination had foretold. "I would not put it quite so—"

"Yes or no, Zayne."

He looked straight at her, his green eyes dark as the bayou. "Yes."

She jerked back as though struck. All his sweet words, all his kindness, oh, dear God, last night. All of it to manipulate her?

She swallowed hard, forcing back tears. She'd thought she couldn't be fooled again. She'd thought Zayne was different, that he had no ulterior motive. Oh, damn, this hurt. "Anyone would have done, then? As long as the divination *decreed* her the one?"

"No!" Zayne gripped her shoulders, forcing her to face him. "No one else would have done. You are so beautiful, so incredibly sensual, talented, giving."

"But you just accepted this divination." Her hand pressed against her chest, trying to rub out the spreading ache. "You didn't know any of that when you first came to Earth."

"I did not accept it. I resisted what I had been told and tried to believe there was another answer. That is why I said nothing until I was sure. Until I knew you."

"Are we speaking in the biblical sense here?" She shook her head at his puzzled look. "Never mind. You've known me three days, Zayne, and you're ready to make me your wife?"

"*Zaniya*, yes." He took a deep breath. "I have fallen in love with you, Madeline Fairbanks. That is why I want you as *zaniya*."

She tore herself from his grasp, hot anger searing

through her, drying her tears, charring her heart. How many times had she been told "I love you" when what the person meant was "I'd love you to do this for me"?

"Don't. No more honeyed words. No more manipulating. Be honest. You don't want *me*. You want this balance. And if it comes with a spicy roll in the pillows, hey, all the better."

"I am not lying, Madeline." His voice was tight, reflecting her anger. "I love you. Does this not show it?"

With one of his lightning-quick moves, he embraced her and kissed her. A kiss of passion and *ma-at* with his mind touching hers, revealing all his desires and needs. Last night she had believed that kiss. This morning she couldn't.

But, oh, her traitorous body and her grieving heart wanted to believe. Involuntarily her hips moved against him, craving the dance she'd learned in his pillows. His scent intoxicated her. His body, his voice, his touch all held her spellbound. No magic needed. Her own heart forged the bonds.

Sweet Madeline. Ah, yes, yes, zaniya-e-na. His voice sounded in her mind with no polish, no seduction, only a deep-down need.

With her last ounce of will, she jerked away from him. "No, Zayne. Stop."

He froze, then slowly lowered his arms.

"I love you, Madeline," he said quietly. No coercion. No *ma-at*. Just stark honesty. "I thought you cared for me."

She pressed her lips together, refusing to lie and tell him she didn't care, refusing also to admit that she had fallen in love with him. She could not forget that he had come, he had seduced and charmed her, because he wanted to use her.

"You're expecting me to just give up everything. My

friends, my family, my work, my life, my world. That's a hell of a lot to expect. You said you love me," she added recklessly, knowing she was stupidly lashing out but unable to stop. "Could you give up your music for me?"

"*What?* Another idiotic hypothetical question, Madeline?" She saw the sparks of anger start to rise around him.

"Just answer it."

The ground trembled beneath her feet, like the harbinger of an earthquake. A bevy of birds took flight with raucous protest. Zayne snatched up his oud and slung it over his shoulder.

"I will not stop singing. I cannot."

"See? I know the show-biz world."

"You do not know my world," he said coldly.

She didn't bother to listen. "I know about manipulating and using, doing or saying whatever it takes to keep singing, to move up, to get the contract, the hit, the Grammy. To put everything else second." She looked at him and gave a hollow laugh. "You won't believe it, but there is more to life than music. I'm living proof that you can lose it all and still go on."

"Not for me," he said quietly. "Not for my world. If I stop singing, my world is destroyed. There is no other who can stop it."

"Oh, c'mon," she scoffed.

"That is why you had to come here, to understand."

"No, I'm tired of understanding. I won't be relegated to second place. Or in your case, third, behind the music and the *ma-at*. Not again. Good-bye, Zayne." She reached for her turquoise tablet.

He was quicker, capturing her wrist with one hand, covering her tablet with the other.

She tugged and shifted, but he held her fast. "Let me go."

"No." His face was hard, and his voice implacable.

She lifted her chin. "Coercion, Zayne? You're breaking our bargain."

"The bargain applied unless you were in danger or Kaf was."

"The only danger I'm in is from you."

"But Kaf needs me, and I need you. Already we have wasted too much time."

Before she could draw a breath to argue, the whirlwind descended. The tent, the rocks and sand, all disappeared in the disorienting spin of transport. Seconds later they had arrived.

Chapter Twenty

Madeline had barely taken in the ground heaving beneath her feet and the spurt of an orange geyser before Zayne bracketed her face and forced her to look at him.

"I need your promise, Madeline, that you will not leave while I work. While I sing. Later we can talk, but not now. You must stay at my side for these moments."

The automatic argument died as she looked at him. This was a Zayne she'd never seen before. Not the charming djinni, not the mesmerizing singer, not the sensual lover. Not arrogant or imperious. This was a man of purpose and quiet determination.

The man who had, however briefly, given her back the gift of her dance.

She swallowed and nodded. "I promise."

"Thank you." He leaned over and kissed her, fierce and quick. "That is just one of the reasons I love you."

Before she could reply, he released her, turned, and strode away, pulling his oud off his shoulder. His long auburn hair swung behind him as he settled onto a flat boulder.

Sit beside me, Madeline.

Part request, part command. The arrogant djinni hadn't disappeared. Still, she complied. This place prickled the nape of her neck, with a warning that things were very wrong. Zayne began to sing as soon as she sat beside him, and Madeline looked around.

She knew too little of his world, a world of illusive *ma-at*, so she had no idea what was normal for Kaf. She didn't think this was it, however.

They were in the center of a jagged rock outcropping, and the land around them was in violent turmoil. Beneath her feet, she felt the rumble of the earth. Kaf was not quiet here. Pieces of rock sliced off with loud cracks. Other times the rock vibrated with a sound so high-pitched that it hurt her ears and shattered the stones. Ungodly howls rent the air, and steam hissed all around her, sometimes erupting into scalding geysers.

A large crack fractured the air, and a fissure spread from the base of the rock into the land below. Steam billowed from the opening. The unrest was spreading.

A few hardy souls popped onto the tableland and either perched on a rock or levitated in a circle around Zayne. All looked tense. All looked at Zayne, as if they expected him to have the answers. They listened to his music with utter attention.

Madeline stiffened and slid to conceal herself behind him, away from the listeners, even though they paid her no mind.

Gradually, to keep her mind off the audience, she listened instead to his song. The music drew her into the weave of its notes. It tugged at her heart, so poignant, so soothing. The song cajoled and yearned both at once, and her throat ached with the beauty of it.

The longer he sang, the more the land around them settled. Her mouth dried as she realized Zayne was singing not to the audience but to his world, calming Kaf with nothing but the powers of his *ma-at* and his music.

I am the Minstrel. I am her soul and her harmony.

The memory staggered her. He had told her straight out who and what he was. Even what he wanted.

This was not easy for him. His chest was damp with sweat and his voice harshened from use. Still, he sang on. Her gaze shifted from Zayne to the upheaval around her. From the set of his jaw to the cautious hope of the people surrounding them.

If I stop singing, my world is destroyed. There is no other who can stop it. Without the song of the Minstrel, this world would slip into chaos? She believed in the djinn and instant transport; why not a land that needed the harmony of her Minstrel?

Zayne was right. She could never have understood if she hadn't come here. If she hadn't seen how very much a part of this world he was. How he could never be taken from it.

But why was she here? What was so vital that he needed her sitting beside him?

As if hearing her question, something new entered his song, a strange rippling like the winds across the ocean. The melody changed, grew wilder, more intense, darker. A change she felt more than heard. The force crashed against her like the storm-fed waves at the beach.

Tiny cracks spread out from the fissure below. More steam spurted up, filling the air with the reek of sulphur. The quieting land erupted again.

He had lost control of the harmonies.

The shadow of his voice echoed in her memory. What had he said earlier? *It is your Terran magic. Incompatible with my ma-at. Now that I am with you, though, I can control it.* "Magic?" she whispered. "You play also with our magic?"

This time the answer was not memory but Zayne speaking to her, mind to mind, his voice sounding disjointed and strained. *Control. Easier if you danced.*

One more bizarre fact, each one easier to accept than its predecessor. Inside him were the alien forces of magic, and he needed her because she somehow was his control, his balance, just as he balanced Kaf. She was Terran, that was the difference. Somehow through her—and her dancing?—he controlled the foreign magic.

But she could not dance, not in front of all these people.

Instead, she leaned against his back, her hand on the leather band she'd given him. If she could not dance, she would do what she could. The power of magic pulsed against her, demanding entrance. In trying to conquer her stage fright, she'd done a lot of meditation. Would that help? She closed her eyes, chanting one of the mantras.

Do not hum, Madeline, came Zayne's quick retort.

"Sorry."

The land erupted around them, and the cracks grew longer. Zayne's muscles were hard with tension and his body was coated in sweat. His voice rasped with a violent tumult.

She had to help. Terra. Earth. Her world. Magic wasn't a violent storm to be opposed. It was the natural power of her world. Hers. She embraced the storm he generated. Its rhythm became a part of her; her heartbeat and breathing tuned to its tempo as it curled inside her. She did not control it; she could not use it. She only felt it with muscle and sinew. Her body pulsed against his, transmitting the beat. "Remember the waves at the beach," she murmured. "Let them flow. Remember the two-step and the earth beneath your feet."

The melody and the counterpoint shifted, and the

two threads intertwined. With each rich, soothing note, harmony returned. Slowly the land settled. The sheering rocks stayed solid, and the geysers burbled quietly in their pools. Fissures and cracks closed. Harsh sounds became the soft murmur of the watching djinn and the soughing wind.

Zayne's song altered also to an airy tune that tickled like champagne. Momentarily freed form the burden of being the Minstrel, he merely entertained.

His song ended. He rose, rotating his shoulders, and for a few seconds, Madeline saw the fatigue that sat upon him, before he hid it as he turned to greet the first of the djinn who gathered around him. Zayne was well liked, she could see, and it didn't seem to be simply because of his talents as a Minstrel. She'd seen groupies and fawners, and these people were neither. Yet he was set apart from them by the respect on their part and the solitude on his.

She tried to ease out of the gathering circle, but he caught her hand, and the look he gave her was hot and sensual. Rather than draw attention to herself with a scene, she slid behind a standing rock, enduring by hiding from the curious looks.

One youth, just entering the first years of manhood and already with a smile that would charm a female into forgetting all her good sense, tried to engage her in conversation.

"Sorry," she said, "I don't speak your language."

He leaned forward, clearly delighted "I know English. I visited your world when I was younger. I am Jared, Apprentice to our Protector."

"Pleasure to meet you." She held out her free hand.

Jared raised her hand to his lips, then continued to hold her fingers. "The pleasure is mine."

"Hello, Jared." Zayne's greeting was friendly, but his

hand shifted to encircle Madeline's waist as he placed himself closer to her side. The gesture was a blatant one of masculine claim. The glitter in his eyes was a warning.

Jared grinned, then inclined his head. "Kaf has been restless of late. We have missed your song, Minstrel."

Zayne's hand tightened on her hip. "I know. A problem now remedied."

At his casual assumption, Madeline's anger rose again. Witnessing his dedication and devotion to the people and the land, learning new depths and new kindness in him, she loved him more. But how could he simply assume she would give up her life to spend the rest of her days sitting on a rock and letting him channel his untamed magic through her?

This was his world, not hers.

He hadn't even asked her. What she wanted. Or didn't want.

She wanted Zayne to be with her because he desired her, because he liked her, because his heart gave him no other choice, not because some weird divination ordered it and some strange power demanded it.

She didn't want to be used as anyone's magical control. How could she tolerate a lifetime of loving him so desperately and deeply, forced to sit in his shadow, behind his power and his song? Would she always wonder which touches were given only because he needed to harness this foreign magic inside him?

More and more glances turned her way as the atmosphere grew more festive. She felt raw and exposed. She couldn't stay here. She couldn't. Stomach churning, she pulled back from both men and grabbed her tablet with a sweaty palm.

"I'm going home, Zayne. Don't worry about Cyrus; I'll find him myself. You've helped me and fulfilled your portion of the bargain. Stay here, learn to control your magic now that you know what it is. Good-bye."

Quickly, before she lost her courage, she said the words she needed to and left Kaf. Moments later, she was in her bedroom on Earth.

Before she took a breath, Zayne was beside her. That fierce glitter was still in his eyes, and his body was strained. He fisted his hands at his hips. "Why did you leave?"

"Won't your djinn wonder where you've gone?"

"To Solomon and the Towers with what they wonder. Why did you leave?"

"It's over, Zayne. I can't do it. I can't live under that scrutiny. I can't live with you, knowing I'm just . . . an anchor."

"It is not over. I need you."

"Need me, not want me. You need a channel. For how long? Now that you know what this magic is, you'll learn to control it without me. Then what? You'll be stuck with a Terran who can't sing and is afraid to dance and can't even work a lick of magic."

All her life she'd been in second place to her mother's music. She couldn't live that way, not again. Not with the man she loved.

"A channel? Do you truly believe that is the only reason I need you?" The sparks around him were explosive crackles of light. All colors, each impossibly brilliant. "Do you not believe I love you?"

"I . . ." Oh, God, he sounded so angry, so hurt, her traitorous heart wanted to believe in more than magic. She wanted to believe in miracles.

"What about this?" he asked silkily. Before a thought could pass or an answer form, he had her in his arms, and then he kissed her. A hot, expert, frenetic kiss with tongue and nips of his teeth intermingled with endearments whispering in her mind and his *ma-at* sparkling around her.

He lifted his head from the kiss, his sensual lips moist, his green eyes dark. "Are you saying no, Madeline? Do you tell me stop?" There was no music in his voice, only harsh need.

Anger vanished before passion. "No. Yes. No. I mean . . . More, Zayne."

He tumbled them both backward onto the bed, while his hands ran down her body, removing clothes with frantic haste. By the time she stretched beneath him on the mattress, they were both naked.

His body blanketed hers with fiery hot muscle. His auburn hair was a silken tease as it brushed against her cheek and shoulder. His fingers entwined with hers as he raised her hands above her head.

With no more invitation but the slickness of her body, he surged inside her. No finesse, no charming or teasing, only the raw and elemental need of a man for his woman.

His strokes were long, demanding that she meet each one with her hips. He filled her with his body, his *ma-at*, his mind, and finally, uttering a drawn-out groan, with his seed as she came with him.

Zayne collapsed atop her, still inside her. Only their slowing gasps sounded in the silence of the room. Only their pounding hearts moved. At long last, however, he rolled to his side. Solemnly he traced a finger along her turquoise tablet.

"Is this the only reason you are with me, Madeline? Because I pleasure you? Because I give you things like transport?"

"No!"

"Then why should you believe I only want you because you channel the magic?"

"I shouldn't," she admitted, unable to find a remaining spark of her anger while her body was so relaxed, satiated and warm. She shouldn't doubt him, especially not when Zayne's emotions surrounded him in brilliant Technicolor. "Except a divination sent you to me. You pursued me before you even knew me. It didn't matter who I was."

"Ah." He was silent a moment, then rolled to his back. Before she could feel his loss, however, he wrapped an arm around her, gathering her to his side. She rested her head on his shoulder. "You have the matter reversed. I did not fall in love with you because the divination sent me to you. The divination sent me to you because I was in love with you."

"Zayne, you didn't know me."

"My mind did not, no. But my body did. My soul did. The rest of me soon followed."

She lay back, stunned by his simple but profound explanation. Age-old question: Which came first? The divination or the love? Still, he had been rather single-minded about the matter. "You never thought you should stay on Terra?"

"I cannot, Madeline. I would die if I were cut off from Kaf. My world would die without me."

He meant both of those quite literally, and a shiver ran across her at the idea. "What if I can't leave Earth?"

"Humans do not have the bonds to magic that the djinn do to *ma-at*."

From his point of view, his choices and actions weren't about using her. They were about saving his world with a mix of common sense and the craziness of love. A divination led him to the woman he was destined to fall in love with, and because he could not live on Earth, then ergo she was destined to come with him to Kaf.

Last week she wouldn't have understood. She would have held on to her hurt.

Today she couldn't. Anger passed, leaving joy in its wake. Joy and a deep tenderness for this special man. "Stay there," she commanded abruptly. "I'll be right back."

"What—"

She put her fingers to his lips, silencing him. "I said I'll be right back." It only took her a few minutes to assemble what she wanted from the kitchen, but when she returned, she found him pacing the room.

"Right back," he accused, rounding on her. "You said right back. This was not right back. Your concepts of time, Madeline, are quite mixed up."

She laughed. "Coming from the man without a watch? Here." She handed him the steaming mug she'd prepared. "Sit on the bed and drink this."

He sniffed the tea, even as he sat cross-legged on the bed. "What is it?"

"Hot lemon tea sweetened with honey. Your voice sounds a little raspy. I thought maybe this would soothe your throat." She knelt behind him and began to knead his shoulders.

He glanced over his shoulder. "What are you doing?"

"Giving you a massage." She pressed her thumbs against the back of his neck. "You take care of Kaf, Zayne, but who takes care of you?"

He didn't answer. She didn't expect him to, for there was no one to care for him, she suspected, and there had not been for a very long time.

"You looked tired when you finished singing," she added. "I thought this would help."

"Maintaining harmony can be fatiguing," he admitted. "Especially with the magic."

Her hands made slow, lazy circles across his back.

"Why does magic come when you play, Zayne? I mean, that's not the norm, is it?"

"Definitely not. I do not know why I am different."

"Any theories?"

"One. A human sorcerer somehow used the broken tablet to bridge our worlds with his magic. Since I wear the other half, I feel the intrusion."

"Cyrus is evil. Do you feel that, too?"

"I did not say the theory was perfect."

She shifted her massage to his lower back. He gave a sigh of pleasure, leaving the mug floating in front of him while he leaned forward to give her better access.

"Maybe you're part human," she suggested.

He stilled, his muscles tensing beneath her fingertips. "What do you mean?"

"Maybe your father was human."

"My father was djinn; my mother told me that many times. He just was not part of our lives."

Personally, she didn't put a lot of stock in many of the things his mother had told him. "So maybe it was your grandmother. Or someone further back. If so, I'll bet your mother knew that human blood was there. Hey, maybe she had it too and didn't know what to do with it. Maybe that's why she was so anti-Terra."

His silence told her that her theory shocked him. A reaction not exactly flattering to her race.

She ran her hands up his ribs, back to his shoulders, and changed the subject. "How long have you been Minstrel?"

"I do not know how to answer questions like that." He moaned softly as she massaged his neck, right at the base of his hairline. At last she began to feel him relax. "In one sense, I have always been Minstrel. In another, I began when I got out of school and had sufficient power."

"There are no others?" She glanced toward the front of him. Well, his back and shoulders might be relaxing, but other parts were definitely stirring to life.

"Uh, what?"

She smiled at his distraction. Obviously, his attention had wandered elsewhere. "Are there other Minstrels?"

"Not now. Normally there are several, but djinn are not immortal. The two who would have companioned me each died in an accident not long after I came into my responsibilities. There are youths of promise, but it will be many cycles before they are ready."

So, he had borne this burden alone since he was but a youth. She pressed against his back, reaching around him to massage the length of his arms and give him a quick kiss at the corner of his talented mouth. Her heart ached for him. Zayne had lived a lonely life. First an isolated childhood. Then schooldays too filled with learning to be Minstrel to spare the time for swimming. Now, as a man he was aloof, separate, driven by his power and defined by his duty. His *ma-at* and his music were his whole world.

Until now. "You're not alone anymore," she whispered against his lips. She didn't know if she was making the right decision. So many things about it terrified her. The suddenness, his unknown world, being with him when he performed, the possibility that he would turn from her when he no longer needed her.

He stilled, then turned in her arms, threading his fingers through her hair. The mug of tea hovered forgotten beside him. "What you are saying, Madeline?"

"I want to be with you."

"As my *zaniyā*?"

She hesitated. Too many steps, too fast. He said that union was more than wedding vows. It was a uniting of the souls, eternal and unbreakable. Was she ready to give the promise of such a commitment and all it entailed?

He sighed. "So, there are still some doubts?"

"Concerns," she answered him, wanting honesty between them. "I have to be very sure." It would help matters if she believed in destiny and divinations as he did.

"I am not an easy man to live with," he admitted. "I am not used to being gainsaid."

"Oh, really?" she said drily. "I hadn't noticed your dictatorial attitude."

She forgot that sarcasm was wasted on Zayne. He smiled. "Good."

"But I love you and you love me—"

"You love me?" Sparkles danced about him, revealing his delight. The man had a terrible poker face.

She looked at him as he straddled her but made sure his greater weight did not harm her. She took in the planes of his cheekbones and the tiny cleft in his chin; his sleek, muscled chest and nipples taut with his desire; the dusting of soft hairs on his bronze thighs. His erection jutted proudly. Emotions danced around him like colored sparks. Her beloved djinni.

"Yes, and—"

With one of his disconcerting, blink-of-an-eye moves, he shifted her to her back and rolled on top of her, settling between her legs. With a single thrust, he surged inside her, joining them once again. He took her wrists and stretched her arms above her head.

"Leave them there," he commanded.

"Zayne, about that dictatorial attitude . . ." Her protest trailed off as he reared back, bracing himself on his hands. The movement pushed him deeper inside her, and, amazingly, she felt him swell more, setting off her cascade of desire.

"Shhh, *si halika.*" Zayne was surprised to find his hand shook as he brushed Madeline's hair behind her ear. He wanted to erase any uncertainties and he knew of no other way.

"There are spells I could do," he told her. "Rituals I could chant that enhance our loving or multiply the pleasures of touching each other. I say none of them. This is me, Madeline, only me loving you." He knew of no other way to convince her that what sparked between them was not an illusion but very, very real.

He withdrew from inside her, then soothed her whimper of disappointment with kisses to the lobe of her ear and the corner of her lips. He trailed his fingers along the curve of her collarbone; remembering intimately the dips and textures of her soft skin. Her most sensitive places were secret no longer, and he took full advantage of the knowledge. His licks and kisses had her moaning and dancing beneath him.

He explored her, knew how she would nestle into his body as his feminine counterpart. Not a fragment of her did he leave unattended. Her breasts fit like perfection in his hands and his mouth. He stroked the bud of her sex with his thumb and tasted her desire.

Her skin turned a delicate pink when he whispered what he wanted, where he would touch her, how he would touch her. The colors of her skin fascinated him. The darker bronze of his body did not change much, but her flesh turned a delightful rose when he excited her. There was some red on her nose from the sun, and brown outlining where her swimsuit had been.

He traced the lines of demarcation. "When you swim on Kaf you will be brown all over."

She flushed again, still looking at him. "Really? It

looks as if you covered up and forgot a few parts." Her bold gaze swept down to his sex, darker than the rest of him from the engorged blood.

"Oh, Madeline," he said with strangled laughter. For though she left her hands above her head as he commanded, she was not passive.

She used her mouth—told him what she liked, asked him where he wanted to be touched, made erotic promises of future pleasures. Her strong, supple dancer's legs and feet stroked his thighs and calves and tickled his feet. She used her entire body, rubbing against his hand, moving in enticing rhythms that showered them both with a firestorm of his glittering need.

Now she ignored his commands and reached for him. They touched as humans, but they made love in the middle of stars. For his *ma-at* and his music were too innate, too much a part of him for him to avoid them forever. Not when he was all instinct, all emotion, all love. Not when she took him into her arms and her body and her soul.

The room was still darkened when Madeline awoke. She glanced at her watch and discovered it was early evening. Nearly a whole day had gone by since Zayne's performance.

The cats would be needing food. She slipped from beneath Zayne's grasp and out of bed. Her lover didn't stir. He slept like he did everything else—with his full attention.

She threw on shorts and a camisole, then headed to the kitchen for her java fix. While the coffee perked, she filled the empty pet bowls with food and water, ran through her routine of warmups, then poured a cup. Sitting on a stool, sipping the first of the brew, she glanced around the kitchen, an uneasy sensation that something was wrong stealing across her. What was it? What was off kilter?

The cats, she realized. They were nowhere to be seen. Strange—usually the rustle of the food bag brought them running. "Bronze? Silver? Vulcan?" she called softly, heading down the hall.

A soft meow in the hall caught her attention, and she relaxed. Tildy's magic room. The poor kitties must have gotten caught there behind the closed door. "C'mon out to freedom, boys," she called as she opened the door.

The room was dark inside, too dark for the afternoon. Curious. She stepped in, and an overwhelming sensation of *wrongness* froze her. Too late she remembered. The cats had eaten the food she'd put out before she left. Impossible if they'd been locked inside here all day. She turned, ready to run, but she was yanked into the room. The turquoise tablet was ripped from her neck. The door slammed behind her, while a light flared in front of her.

A face appeared in the center of the light. A sophisticated face with black hair and cruel eyes. A face she'd sought, but had secretly hoped never to see again.

"Hello, Maddie," said Cyrus Cromwell, snapping his fingers and lifting the darkness.

"Hello, Maddie," echoed a dreamy, slurred voice.

Madeline spun around. Her mother leaned against the door, locking her in.

Chapter Twenty-one

"*Maman*, are you okay? Should you be out?" Madeline rushed to her mother's side.

"I'm fine." Irena patted Madeline's cheek. "Cyrus says I'll soon be back on stage. Performing like I want."

"No, he's using you. Let's get out of here." She undid the lock and tugged the door, but it refused to open. She tugged harder.

"You won't be going anywhere for a while, Maddie." Cyrus sounded pleased. "That door is quite impenetrable until I say you can leave."

Madeline spun to face her stepfather.

"Irena, come here," Cyrus commanded, and at once Irena glided to his side. He stroked her throat with a sinister grace.

"What are you doing to her?" Madeline clenched her fists, her nails biting into her palms.

"Nothing she isn't used to." He gave her mother a carnal, open-mouthed lick with his tongue. "Nothing she doesn't enjoy."

Madeline's stomach turned over. Irena was never this docile; Cyrus's hold over her was strong. She couldn't expect any help from her mother. She forced an appearance of calm, but fear fluttered in her belly. Cyrus had more power than either she or Zayne had imagined.

He lit a thin cigar. The match flare revealed that he wore a half turquoise tablet with a silver crescent moon pendant atop it. Her tablet chain was wrapped around his hand. "I understand you've been looking for me. So, here I am. What do you want?"

"For you to go to hell."

He smiled. "Not for a very long time."

She took a deep breath. She and Zayne had planned to lure Cyrus to them, had trusted that Zayne's *ma-at* could overcome the human, but Cyrus has sprung his own trap. Panicking now wouldn't help. "Feydor wants you to attend his St. John's Eve party. And he wants a no-holds-barred interview."

"I'll attend the party. No interview." He took a drag on the cigar. "I heard you were quite a spectacle at the press conference."

Anger rolled through her again, hot and cleansing, burning away the fear and leaving a sharp-edged fury. "What did you do to me?"

He didn't pretend to misunderstand. "Enhanced the natural fear of a performer. It strengthens every time you get on stage. The combination makes the fear quite unshakable. You'll never be rid of it."

"Oh, I will be, Cyrus. I will get rid of it." She could see that her calm bravado startled him a little. "Why'd you do it? I was just a kid."

"I had my reasons. Erroneous ones, as it turns out. Pity all the years I wasted, when I could have had you both. Mother and daughter."

"You'd never have had me."

"Perhaps. You always were stronger than your mother." He rested one hip on a table. "Anything else?"

She glanced at Irena, standing quietly to one side. "Free my mother from the hell you put her in."

"No." He smiled, a thin, cruel smile. "Unless you cooperate with me."

Fear broke through the anger again and trickled down her spine. "How?"

"Sit down while we wait."

She matched his casual pose, bracing her shoulder against a small armoire. He intoned a low phrase, and sharp, debilitating pain shot through her leg. The exact same pain as when she'd broken it, and the panic welled in behind it. She moaned, her knee buckling in reflex, and she dropped into the chair.

"I said sit," he said calmly and stopped the chant.

The pain left, and the panic was reduced. "Wait for what?" she gritted out.

"For Zayne to come looking for you."

Her stomach clenched. Oh, dear God, what had she led Zayne into? "Long wait ahead. He's gone for good. You might as well leave." She didn't really think she'd convince him, but it was worth a try.

She didn't. Cyrus took another drag on the cigar. "Oh, I don't think so. I saw how he looked at you. Who would have thought that scared little Maddie had the guts? So tell me, what's it like?"

"What's what like?"

"Fucking a genie."

Oh, God, he did know, all of it. "You're nuts."

"I don't think so."

She didn't bother to answer. His slimy innuendos and crude talk turned her stomach, while his cocky confidence sent fear spiraling through her.

Whatever happened to her, though, she couldn't let Zayne walk into this room. She'd felt the touch of magic before and she felt it now. Except this magic was perverted. Cold and dark and evil. And much stronger than she had guessed. Cyrus wanted Zayne in here;

that was reason enough to keep him away.

If only she could get her tablet.

"Irena, kneel at my feet," he commanded suddenly.

A flash of Irena's old spirit sparked in her mother's eyes. "Really, Cyrus, I don't think—"

"You don't think." His voice was a lacerating whip. "You do what I tell you. *Adaleske e duk hir.*"

Irena's protest was cut short as she squeezed her eyes shut in pain and her hand flew to her forehead. "My head. The pain!"

"Kneel, Irena, and let me relieve it."

Without protest, Irena did as he commanded. Cyrus stroked her brow, easing the wrinkles of pain; then his hand curled around her neck, his thumb resting on her windpipe.

Madeline bit her lip, her insides shredding. The warning was clear; Irena was also in danger.

"You may stand." Her mother did as he commanded.

Then she heard it. A faint call. At the back of the house, where her bedroom lay. Zayne. She had to warn him. She couldn't let him come in here. She lunged for her tablet.

Cyrus was faster. He grabbed her in an iron grip, covering her mouth at the same time. She fought him, fought him with everything she had. She even managed to get the tablet free, but he flung it across the room before she could use it. In the end, she was no match for him. He'd always been a physical-fitness nut, but this strength and speed was unnatural. His enhanced power held her helpless in his embrace.

Oh, God, she'd been too casual about poking the sleeping snake. His power and his cruelty were greater than she remembered. She heard him call out, "Tildy's magic room," in a credible imitation of her muffled voice.

Zayne, don't come. Leave. Now. Cyrus had her effectively gagged, but she tried to send her thoughts though she had no such talent, hoping some inkling of her desperation would get through.

It didn't. The familiar whirlwind of Zayne's arrival squeezed her heart in terror.

No! She saw Zayne materialize in front of her.

At the same time, Cyrus shouted. "*Assur-bani-al*," He threw something toward Zayne. "By the great kings of Babylon, I do tie thee. *Nulush!*" A brilliant green light flared. "*Rashan. Arshah. Narash.*" At each word a beam of light shot from the floor, one yellow, one white, one blue, and formed a pyramid around and above Zayne.

Madeline blinked, clearing her vision. Zayne stood before them, perfectly still, while a golden light that looked like a knotted rope coiled from his feet to his neck. Only his eyes moved. Furious eyes that stared at Cyrus with green hatred.

"What have you done?" she whispered.

Cyrus held up a vial of aqua liquid, twin to the one they'd found in the bust. "I think you recognize this. It's used to create the rope that binds him. It holds him in a . . . stasis, I guess you could call it. He can see us, but that's it. He can't hear us, can't move or speak. He can't work his magic."

"I don't believe it."

"Would he stand there if he had a choice? No, I rather think he'd be carrying out some unpleasant revenge, judging by the fury in those eyes."

She ran over to the pyramid, only to be bounced backward by a lightning bolt of excruciating pain when she hit the shimmering barrier. "Zayne, can you speak to me, to my thoughts? Can you hear me? Blink once if you can."

His eyes remained wide open, his green fury unchanged.

She whirled back to Cyrus. "What will it take to release him?"

"There's only one way. You must bind him, bind his power to grant you wishes." He held up a pair of copper bracelets, old and battered. Held them so Zayne could see them.

The tendons on Zayne's neck tightened, as though he suddenly fought even harder against his bonds. The green in his eyes grew as dark as the bayou and the fury in them deepened. She remembered how furious he'd been at the idea of being forced to grant wishes. How he detested confinement.

"Don't do it, Cyrus. Please don't do it."

"Oh, I'm not going to," he said softly. "You are."

She stared at him, the fear spreading. "I won't."

"Are you sure?" He murmured something to Irena, who immediately turned toward her daughter and gave a high-pitched wail of terror. Her head bowed and she braced her hands on the table. "Please, don't. Don't! Not again! No."

With mere words, he tormented her mother, the woman he'd married.

Irena lifted her head to stare at her daughter, looking for a brief second like the clear-eyed mother who loved her. "Don't," she repeated with a drawn-out moan. "Don't do what he asks, Madeline." Then she bent over, sobbing.

Madeline looked from Irena to Cyrus to Zayne, biting her lip, tasting the copper tang of blood. She steeled herself against the sobs of her mother, though everything inside her ached to stop them. She couldn't bind Zayne. Could not do it. Even Irena, in her confused state, recognized they could not give Cyrus that power, for he must have some plan to get control of Zayne once he was bound. She could not do that to the man she loved.

"No," she repeated.

"I see you need more convincing." Cyrus held up the vial, looking at it. "There are some rather unpleasant herbs in this, particularly for a genie. Too long a contact and I'm afraid . . ." He shook his head, making a small tsking sound. "Genies are not immortal."

She didn't believe it. She just had to stall for time, let Zayne free himself. He was so powerful; Cyrus couldn't be a match for him. The stasis spell had to be temporary. It had to wear off eventually. The potion was a mere stopgap irritant.

"You still don't believe me?" Cyrus said, as though reading her mind.

"If you're so strong, why don't you bind him?" She didn't think she was giving him ideas. If he could have, Cyrus would have done it.

"Now, there is a story, and I think I will tell you it. Take the time we need for you to see I'm telling the absolute truth. You can watch your lover die before your eyes. Or you can bind him."

He stubbed out his cigar in a glass bowl, then lit another one. "The story starts over four centuries ago, with a distant ancestor of mine, Graeme was his name. He was married to Naomi, not a beautiful woman but a very powerful one, and he had a child with her. But Graeme was weak. He fell in love with a beautiful woman, a heartless genie who seduced him with her sultry voice. When she got pregnant with Graeme's child, though, she abandoned him, her human lover. The fool began fading away, heartbroken," he spat.

Madeline's stomach knotted, and she crossed her

arms. Oh, she had an ugly feeling about where this was heading.

Cyrus continued. "Graeme's wife, Naomi, knew the dark arts, and she found the secret to binding a genie. While learning the ritual, she discovered that the full true name of the genie is needed. As I said, Graeme was weak. He readily gave Naomi the name of his lover, as well as her spoken name. Taraneh."

Madeline couldn't stop her involuntary glance toward Zayne. His grandmother. He had human blood in him. No wonder he had the power of Terra inside him, a power that could not coexist with his *ma-at*.

She turned her attention back to Cyrus, who was looking upward and blowing a stream of smoke. When he looked down, he gave her a hard smile.

"Naomi bound Taraneh and for many years enjoyed extended life, power, prosperity, and revenge against her enemies by commanding the genie's power. Before she died, she transferred the knowledge to her son, and the cycle of servitude began again for Taraneh. For the rest of her days, she would be at the mercy of the line of Naomi."

Revulsion brought a sour taste to her throat. Madeline looked again at Zayne, almost glad he could not hear how his ancestress had suffered.

Had he faded? Was his skin sallower? Or was she imagining it, giving in to the power of Cyrus's suggestion?

Cyrus continued his vile story. "At last, Taraneh got free in the only way she could. She cursed Naomi, then broke the tablet that connected her to her world and her power. This tablet." He held up the turquoise tablet he wore about his neck. "She rendered herself powerless. In the last seconds before her power faded and she died, she returned to her world and the child she had abandoned there."

Sholeh. Who had raised her son Zayne. Alone, isolated.

"What was the curse?" Madeline asked.

"No one of Naomi's seed could ever again bind a genie. None would ever again know that kind of power, but each would be eaten by the knowledge that it existed." He ground out his cigar. "There have been many suicides in my family. I refuse to be one of them."

"So you decided to break the curse."

"I am the most powerful Cromwell sorcerer since Naomi."

"And obsessed with binding a genie."

He dismissed her evaluation with a wave of his hand. "I will command the power, but I had to find the enticement that would draw the genie back to our world, where I could work the necessary spells. At last I got the final two answers I needed, one a deduction, one serendipity. I remembered that Taraneh was a singer, and believed one of her seed might be drawn to music, especially music I enhanced. Then I met a very powerful psychic. One with an uncanny gift for prophesy." Cyrus stroked his beard with the tip of his finger. "He died, quite soon after I had finished with him."

The fear in her hardened. Cyrus had killed in this insane quest for power. He wouldn't hesitate to kill again. She glanced at Zayne. Oh, dear God, the light in his eyes had dimmed. His skin was paler. She turned back to Cyrus. "What did the psychic tell you?"

"The house of Ninegal, Minstrels to the Babylonian kings, would bring my heart's desire."

Madeline glanced at her mother. "Irena is of this house?"

"Yes. At first I thought you would be the one to entice the genie. A child I could mold to do my bidding. You proved unsuitable. You were more resistant than I expected. You couldn't sing, although I decided your dancing would suffice."

"But I was adopted. Not of the blood. You created the fear in me as punishment?"

"So you wouldn't compete with Irena. All attention had to be hers. That's where I made my mistake. She collapsed under the pressure of my magic. After all these years, I've just now learned my mistake. The ancients would often adopt an heir if no child of the marriage survived or proved worthy. To them adoption made a child part of the house." He looked at her. "You were the one I needed all along, Maddie."

She swallowed hard against fear and denial. She was the one who knew Zayne's true name. The name he had entrusted to her. "I can't help you. I don't know his name."

"I think you do. And you remember every name you hear."

She shook her head.

Cyrus lifted his brows. "Pity. Then you will see him die."

Futilely Zayne strained against his bonds. Cyrus would pay dearly for this temerity. He glared at the human sorcerer. *Beware. My revenge will be swift and unmerciful, djinn justice in its fullest measure, human.*

Rage at himself fueled his coursing anger. He had underestimated the powers of the human. A mistake he would not make again.

Again he fought the anchoring rope of magic. The bonds were not as permanent as perhaps the human believed. *Because of the human magic in my veins?* But as yet the nauseating confinement had not loosened, and he could feel his strength going also.

The insidious potion weakened him. It muddied his mind and created strange visions before his eyes. He could not see well, nor could he focus the powers of *ma-at* for a spell of reversal. Not yet, though he felt the ill effects diminishing. Once free, he would find a way to reverse the other effects—the slowly lethal ones.

He must, or Kaf would die.

For he knew, from the moment Cyrus lifted the ancient pair of copper bands, what the snake planned.

Cyrus thought to bind a djinni?

He would soon learn the folly of such ambition.

What Zayne could not fathom, though, was why Madeline stayed. Why did she talk so long with Cyrus? Why did she not transport away?

Why was she still here?

Madeline could barely breathe past the ache in her chest as Cyrus confidently strolled over to Zayne, who watched him, still radiating an undimmed fury. He poured a few drops of the aqua liquid onto the magical rope. It rose higher, curling around Zayne's neck. Tightening. Tightening.

"You will bind him," Cyrus told her. "Then your first and only wish will be to transfer that power of command over to me. If you even think of double-crossing me, remember, I hold power over Irena and only I know the antidote to this poison, which has gone into his body now."

Her gaze flew to Zayne. Oh, God, every word of it was true. She could see him fading. Though the fury in his eyes had not abated, their clarity dimmed. His chest moved in shallow, rapid heaves. His feet—she couldn't see his feet, they were like fog, as though his body were drifting apart a molecule at a time. She reached for him, but the barrier shoved her back again with an explosion of pain along her nerves.

Tears welled from her eyes. Her throat clogged so that she could hardly breathe. She could see him die. Or she could bind him and watch his love turn to hatred, watch him be commanded by Cyrus's evil.

I would rather die. She wasn't sure if he actually managed to send her the thought, or if she only knew in her heart what he said.

"But I can't let you," she whispered, the tears so thick she could barely see his beloved face. Her stomach knotted and heaved. How could she have ever doubted their love or questioned their being together?

She loved him so much, but Zayne would never, ever forgive her for this.

Still, she made the impossible choice, which was no choice at all. He would not die. She turned to Cyrus. "I'll do what you ask."

Cyrus lifted his hands in a graceful gesture. "What did you say, Maddie?"

"I'll bind him."

Cyrus waved his hands, and suddenly Zayne could hear. "What did you say, Maddie?"

"I'll bind him."

Zayne's gaze flew to Madeline. Acid fury erupted through him at her horrifying promise. The woman he loved and trusted would not so betray him.

But she did. She took the scroll from the ensorcelling snake. She lit the candles, then walked backwards inside the circle of seven stones. His silent roar of anger drowned her words. Nothing could still the evil wind she conjured. The Spells of Reversal were still beyond his speaking, hidden beneath a swirling well of fog.

"In the name of Solomon, the great builder, I do tie thee to me."

She continued. A violent wind whipped through the room, spun about him. His arms grew heavy, his blood sluggish. Bile burned his throat.

"*Ash hadu inna illaha ash-Shaltan*. Do thou be with me, Zaneyvei y Sholehaniya y la Tarnehya."

His name. His full true name. She spoke the evil spell that would bind him. She used his trust against him. Raw pain tore his gut. Raw fury scoured him. *Do not, Madeline. Do not say the final words. Trust in my strength.*

She wasn't looking at him. Wasn't trying to listen to him. "*Ash hadu inna illaha ash-Shaltan*."

An earth-bound weight wrapped around his wrists. He could barely breathe for the great pounding in his chest. Over his screaming denial, he heard her chant the last words.

"I do bind thee, Zaneveyonar y Sholehanya a la Toletarnehi."

The hurricane wind roared around him. His turquoise tablet, the visible symbol of his djinn status, vanished. He was as one dead to the djinn. Inside him, he felt the agonizing scream of Kaf. He tried to lift his arms, but the powers held them down for the copper bands fashioned about his wrists. As the last bit formed, as the circle was completed, the wind vanished in a deafening roar, pulling with it the golden rope.

That binding was no longer needed. He stared in horror at the etched copper bands around his wrists. Nausea roiled inside him. Hot fury and cold revenge flashed through him. He could barely stand from the pain.

The runes of the bands told him this binding was designed with particular cruelty. He was bound for one thousand wishes, unable to work any power except to benefit his master.

Zayne raised his gaze to Madeline, utterly cold, all emotion save anger scoured from him. "What is your first wish, mistress?"

Chapter Twenty-two

Madeline knew Zayne would be furious; she expected blazing emotion and riotous sparks. Instead she got icy rage and a hard-eyed, unforgiving stranger. She stiffened her spine. "What can you do?"

"I cannot raise the dead, nor alter time. Use your one thousand wishes for personal gain alone." His words were bitter, clipped, cold. His deep green eyes, glittering with anger, never left hers.

"Enough!" Cyrus grabbed her wrist in a painful grip. "In the name of Naomi, who bound the seducer Taraneh, you will return the power to my family."

Zayne didn't look at him. "I answer only to my mistress's wishes."

My mistress. His words carved pieces from her soul.

"Madeline, transfer the command now," Cyrus demanded. "No delays, no tricks, or someone dies."

"Very well." Madeline lifted her hand, the one Cyrus held.

Zayne caught it, lacing his fingers with hers, then raising their three joined hands. Still capturing her gaze, he gripped Cyrus's wrist. "Your wish, mistress?"

There was only one way to reverse this nightmare. The snake said he knew the antidote, and she trusted that this once he spoke truly, for he would want Zayne alive if he commanded him. She prayed Zayne would be fast enough, before Cyrus could retaliate.

"I wish . . . to transfer all Cyrus's powers and magical knowledge to me," she said, completing her command in a rush.

Zayne's breath rushed out in a hiss. *So that is your aim, Madeline Fairbanks.*

"You traitorous bitch! May the curse of—"

"Powers of darkness, of life, of the cosmos, grant this wish," thundered Zayne, interrupting Cyrus's counter curse. "Through me come to her. Know, learn, take. Be this done!"

Lightning flashed from the copper bands, arcing from metal to metal in ear-splitting cracks. A hot gale wind whipped around them.

Power and knowledge surged into her in a dizzying, uncontrollable rush. Sinister knowledge. Vile spells. Evil chants. Too much darkness and sordidness. Her heart threatened to burst under the strain. Her head pounded with agony. Sour bile etched her throat, and crimson droplets of blood beaded on her skin. Hideous things she learned and did not want to know—they ripped into her, and her knees buckled. Only Zayne's unrelenting grip kept her from collapse.

Endure. Endure. You're not finished, she repeated to herself. She focused on Zayne, his green eyes, the intricate weaving of auburn hair at his temples, the smooth skin of his chest where only the half turquoise tablet remained. *Endure. You cannot leave Zayne bound.* He alone kept her conscious and sane.

At last the wrenching transfer slowed, and she felt the last tingle of power. Zayne let go of them both. Madeline stumbled backward, bracing herself against the armoire, barely able to stand or breathe. Her insides heaved from knowledge no decent person should ever have.

"You whore," Cyrus snarled, launching himself at her. His fingers curled around her neck. "I'll kill you for this."

Madeline was too weak to fight him; even without his magic-enhanced muscle, he was stronger than she was.

She didn't need to. Zayne's hand shot forward, and a stream of fiery light sliced between her and Cyrus. Cyrus was flung aside, prevented from attacking her by a shimmering shield between them.

"Irena," he pleaded, stretching a hand to her. "Help me."

Irena flattened her hands against the table, her arms shaking. "No," she whispered, her gaze flitting between her husband and her daughter. "No."

"You will not harm my mistress," Zayne said, still in that cold, emotionless voice. He turned to Madeline. "Do you wish for revenge? I can banish him to the summit of the remote mountains. I can turn him into a toad. If you command it, I can destroy him."

She shoved her hair back with a sweaty hand. Her mouth tasted like ash. Zayne's strongest beliefs were against harming another, yet when bound he could be compelled to do just that.

And he believed that she could, that she would, so command him.

"I . . . our justice will deal with him."

It was painful to speak. Her throat was so dry, her head pounded so much. She could barely see as the darkness that had lived inside Cyrus spread through her. Still, she pushed herself erect, refusing to let Zayne see what each motion cost her. Using Cyrus's knowledge, she plucked a rust-colored vial hidden at the center of Tildy's collection of fragrant oils, then handed the vial to Zayne.

"This is the antidote to the potion."

"Are you commanding me to take it? When I might prefer death to being bound for a thousand wishes?"

"I give you the choice, Zayne."

He glared at her. With a quick jerk, he drank the antidote, then tossed the vial away.

Sweat stung her eyes. She was so hot. Squinting, straightening, she memorized the planes of his face, the curve of his brows, the small cleft in his chin. "I have but one more wish. I wish . . ." She stopped, swallowed to moisten her sandy throat. If only she could have a drink of cool water. "I wish you free of the copper bands, your turquoise tablet returned. Never again shall you be bound."

His eyes widened then, the first sign of emotion since the bonds were placed on him. Sparks shattered round him in brilliant shards of living fire. He lifted his hands above his head, electricity arcing between the copper bands. "By the wisdom of Solomon and Azazel, let this wish be fulfilled."

The bands disappeared in a flash. His turquoise tablet reappeared around his neck.

She gripped the handle of the armoire. She would not collapse before him. "You are free to go, Minstrel of Kaf."

"Not yet." He turned to Cyrus, his hand circling, and the shimmering barrier began to swirl like a whirlpool. "Cyrus Cromwell, no more shall you conspire against the djinn. Let Solomon, Azazel, and Kaf be avenged," he said fiercely. His musical voice was dark, simmering with fiery retribution. "Let thy voice wither, let thy fingers fuse. No longer chant. No more the motions of thy magic perform. Think only on wisdom to reverse your fate." His circling hands jerked open, the fingers wide.

Madeline saw Cyrus's horrified look as he grabbed his throat with hands that resembled clubs, then disappeared in a swirling rainbow.

"Where did he go?" she croaked out.

"To a remote monastery. Even without power he was dangerous, for he would start the quest again. If he learns the kindness of the brothers, all will be restored. If not—" He shrugged, as if the matter interested him not. Then he turned.

Would he now exact his djinn justice on her?

He picked up her turquoise tablet, which Cyrus had thrown from her, and closed his fist around it. He looked at her, his face a mask, his voice flat. "You cannot use this. Kaf will not tolerate and the djinn will despise any human who bound the powers of *ma-at*. Stay on your own world, Madeline."

She didn't answer, couldn't answer. Black sickness washed across her. She tried to blank out the foul, insidious whispers of sinister magic. She saw only that he lifted his hands, then disappeared on the whirlwind.

"Live well with your magic, Madeline." His last words lingered but a moment before disappearing with the winds.

At last she collapsed to the floor. Her whole body ached. She felt so hot. So dry. Oh, dear God, she hurt so much. She bent over, retching.

Only when the spasm had passed did she realize someone was stroking her hair, crooning soft comforts. She looked up into the face of Irena Cromwell.

Irena's eyes were still clouded with confusion, but for the first time in over a year, she did not turn away in fear. Sobbing, Madeline fell into her mother's arms.

Naked, Zayne paced outside his tent, unable to go inside where the air still held the scent of Madeline and the pillows still bore the imprint of her body.

He'd lit the stones of privacy as soon as he returned. The djinn would have felt the ripples of *ma-at* from both the binding and the release. They could not have failed to notice the magic that had infused his song during his last visit. For a time, the stones would keep them away, but soon he would have to face their myriad questions and their demands for retribution against the human who had dared perform the abomination of binding.

His fist closed tighter around her turquoise tablet. Solomon be blessed, he did not want retribution against her. By all djinn laws and histories, he should. She had bound him. She could have destroyed his world, had he stayed bound. He should extract his vengeance without mercy or thought, but he could not. Not against Madeline.

He hated what she had done.

Yet he would stop any who wished to carry out such revenge for him.

Confusion roiled inside him. Across the night sky, lightning bolts flashed between the scattered clouds. The hot air was charged with the beginnings of a storm. Solitude did not bring the calm he craved, for the true storm was inside him.

Softly he began to hum, unable to deny the music that had always been his refuge against loneliness and the confusion of too many unanswerable questions.

He had one answer now, though he did not like it. He tugged the half tablet off his neck and set it on the boulder, laying Madeline's tablet beside it. She had suggested he was part human, and from something Cyrus had said, he deduced how.

Taraneh, mother of his mother, had been bound by an ancestor of Cyrus. "The seductress Taraneh," Cyrus had called her, so guessing how Sholeh was sired was not difficult. He ran a finger along the tablet. What pain Taraneh must have felt to believe that severing herself from her *ma-at* was her only choice.

Zayne spread out his hands. He was part human, and the human blood that flowed in his veins came from the same distant ancestor as the blood of Cyrus Cromwell. It was a bitter taste to swallow.

Yet he found the idea easier to tolerate than he would have before he met Madeline. He had thought Terra a foul land with naught to recommend it. He had taken his mother's warnings as his belief and her fears as his hatred.

Aching, he lifted his eyes to the moon, a barely visible smudge behind the veil of the rain. The moon on Terra was also a beautiful sight. With Madeline, he had shared sandwiches and Snickers and laughter. They had danced with a harmonica player. Before Madeline, he had assumed that all humans were like Cyrus and the abusive man in the magic shop, but there were also people like Feydor, Tildy, Jack, and Lucy. On Terra there was jazz.

The rhythm of jazz altered the song he hummed. Tendrils of magic joined his essential, innate *ma-at*. Every time he felt this, would he be reminded of her? Would he never stop wanting her? His throat tightened with a yearning ache. Abruptly he stopped humming. Instead, he drew in deep the strength and solace of Kaf's *ma-at*, renewing his tested bonds. His voice and his body were too tired to fight the need for Madeline and the alien magic.

Except it wasn't alien. It was him.

His mother had been unable to bear the burden of two powers in conflict. For the sake of Kaf and his people, he could not afford to take the route she did. He did not want to; life was too precious.

Looking at the two turquoise tablets on the rock before him, he rubbed the shell-and-leather band Madeline had tied about his arm He could only assume that as his *ma-at* had increased in strength, the dormant magic had also grown, until it broke through the powerful *ma-at*.

He sank onto a flat boulder, still warm from the sun, and stretched out along it, his toes buried in the sand. The strength of Kaf renewed inside him as he watched the growing tempest.

Madeline had betrayed him. How had he missed that she wanted power? A woman who could do what she had done was a world away from the *zaniya-e-na* he loved and who had given so freely and joyously on his pillows. Despite all, his body still hardened with the memory, and he closed his eyes against the pain.

With a loud crack, the clouds opened. Rain on Kaf was a rarity, but when it did come, it was torrential. In mere moments he was soaked, but he did nothing to stop the pounding of the drops against his bare skin.

Zayne. Alesander's deep masculine voice broke into his disturbed musings.

Yes?

Would you want some companionship? Your stones of privacy are lit; thus I apologize for the disturbance if you are set in your solitude.

He did not want to be completely alone right now, Zayne realized. He just did not want a crowd clamoring for answers from the Minstrel. *You would be welcome Alesander, although I have more need of the friend than the Oracle.*

"Like you, the man and the Oracle are impossible to separate within me." Without warning, Alesander was walking toward him. His red robe glided across the sand, while a shimmering halo kept the rain from him. "But I shall endeavor to be the friend first." The hood of his robe tilted, giving the impression that he looked upward. He added, with a hint of humor Zayne had rarely heard, "I should, however, prefer to be friends within the drier confines of your tent."

The night had grown chillier, Zayne realized, with the advent of the rare monsoon. He rubbed a hand down his bare arm. "It would be more comfortable," he agreed, knowing it would not. For reminders of Madeline were everywhere there.

Retrieving the two tablets, he followed Alesander into the tent, where he quickly dried off and donned a green robe. He offered the ritual tea and honeyed cakes, then resumed his pacing.

"Zayne, your energy is fatiguing," Alesander said with a laugh.

"Sorry," he muttered, running a hand through his hair. He rounded on Alesander. "How could she have bound me? Why?"

"I do not know," Alesander said quietly. "Tell me about her."

Tell me about her. Zayne words tumbled out, a litany and a song of the details he had learned. Her care for the mother who could not care back. Her smile. Her fears of dancing and her utter grace. Her friends. Her city and the flow of the river and the magic around her. None of it made logical sense; it was all just bits and pieces that were part of Madeline.

Alesander listened without comment until the end. "So, will she use this new magic to clear the mind of her mother? To remove the fear inside herself?"

"Cyrus has an evil power. She should have wished . . ." he broke off, stunned, then sank to his knees before the fire. He stared blindly into the flames. "She *could* have wished for those things."

"She did not, because she had the power to wield."

"Madeline has never wielded power. She never wanted it."

She did not want power. Not the woman he loved, not the woman he'd hoped to make his *zaniya*. His raging temper and hurt had left him blind and muddled.

He shifted to face Alesander, and for the first time he thought he saw light dancing in those dark eyes, deep inside the hood. His fist clenched around Madeline's turquoise tablet. "She should have channeled the magic into me." He shook his head. "No, she knew the difficulty I have had. She would not have given me more."

"Why did she not simply erase his gift?"

Now that he opened his eyes, the answer was clear. "The potion. She wanted the antidote. Leila told her of the strange effects, and only Solomon knew how else Cyrus embellished the tale." He rested his hands on his knees. "Her wishes were all for me, Alesander. The only way she knew to set things right."

Regret was a bitter companion. He opened his hand, the gold chain of her tablet spilling through his darker fingers. His gift to her had not protected either of them. He leaned toward the fire, trying to remove the chill inside him. "I was too arrogant. I took my opponent lightly and did not take proper precautions. We fell into a trap, and she believed Cyrus had the power to destroy me."

"Could he?"

He shrugged, feeling empty. "Cyrus was stronger than I thought possible, but not as powerful as he believed. He required the aid of potions to work his will.

Potions wear off. I believe I would have gotten free in time. But then, maybe that is my arrogance talking."

"It does not matter now. What was done cannot be undone."

Zayne tried to see into the hood before him, tried to see the shadow of his friend, but it was the pronunciation of the Oracle he heard.

"She bound a djinni," Alesander said softly.

"She cannot be purified," Zayne said tightly. "She cannot be on Kaf."

"And you cannot leave your duty, Zayne." Alesander's voice was a mere breath. "Kaf has no other Minstrel. She will be chaos without you."

"But there is magic inside me. Without Madeline, I cannot control this magic. My singing no longer harmonizes."

"There is another way."

Little by little, as Alesander repeated what he already knew, Zayne shriveled inside, died. Two choices. "If I cannot control the magic, I must eliminate it."

"This will show the way." Alesander's robe rippled, and he held out a scroll.

"Why did you not give me this before?" Zayne asked warily.

"Because you were not ready to make the necessary choice."

Zayne unrolled the ancient parchment. The cold inside him spread, taking over until he knew he would never be warm, despite the hot Kafian sun that would be his light.

"It is a poem, and a ritual," he said at last, then read aloud the poem.

"The battle enjoined, the forces unleashed.
Only one as victor, the other sheathed.

Embrace the night, the flow, the balance.
Wield the knife, the severing, the ritual of one."

"The ritual is a complicated one," he said dully, rolling up the scroll. "I will need some preparation. At the end, all ties with magic are cut. Only *ma-at* remains."

Alesander laid a hand on his arm, the first time they had ever touched. The hand was white, with elegant tapering fingers and polished nails. "You can never return to Terra, Zayne. You will always have human blood, and any connection to Terra will only reinforce that."

"I understand." He took the silver earring from his ear and sent it back to the world where it had been created. Every link forged during his time with Madeline must be sliced away from him. The taste of Snickers, fried oysters, and briny water. The sound of waves on a beach. The heavy feel of humid air. The aroma of vanilla.

Jazz.

Madeline.

He braced a hand against the ground, bent over by agony. Once done, he could never return to Terra, could never allow the least reminder lest the magic regain its hold in his music. "I must at least send her a message. Let her know I understand."

"Zayne." Alesander's concerned voice was no comfort. He sighed. "Very well, then you know what you must do."

"Yes." He knew what he must do, and he knew what he would become. He would be Minstrel of Kaf. And nothing else.

Chapter Twenty-three

Utterly weary, Madeline leaned her head against the steering wheel of her car, gathering strength to get out. She'd taken Irena back to the care facility, for her mother was still confused and anxious. Without repeated reinforcement, Cyrus's hold on Irena should slowly fade. The spell he'd cast was over, but the memories of him were still intact. Irena's psychic wounds from years of manipulation by Cyrus would not be quick to heal. Finally, though, there was hope.

As for her own stage fright problem . . . the counterspell that Cyrus had told her about involved draining the blood from two puppies, making it an impossible solution. She raked her hair back from her face. Even if she found another way, her fearful reactions were so familiar and ingrained now, she might never be rid of them.

Finding cures for herself and her mother were the only two things she might have used this vile knowledge for, and she had helped neither.

At last she got out of the car. She braced a hand against the side, fighting dizziness from dehydration and a desperate need for sleep. She would get rid of this knowledge, but for the moment, concentrating on putting one foot in front of the other took all she had. She trudged the short distance to the house.

Glancing up from the sidewalk, she froze. As morning approached, the mysterious gray of predawn concealed and altered substance; however, there was no mistaking the rainbow of sparkles ahead. Djinn emotions.

"Zayne." Her heart skipped a couple of beats. Then the waiting shadowy figure strode forward, and the heaviness returned. Not Zayne. Leila, her djinni neighbor.

Her furious djinni neighbor. "You bound him," she snarled. "Our Minstrel!"

Madeline was too tired to deal with an angry djinni and too heart-sore to talk. She shoved her hair off her sweaty face. "Leila, get out of my way."

"No. You—" Leila grabbed her wrist, then snatched her hand back. "You feel like you are burning up."

"Which is why I want to go inside to the air-conditioning and get a big glass of ice water." She pushed past Leila.

It wasn't that easy to avoid a djinni. Leila followed her into the house. "How could you have done this abomination? The retribution of the djinn—"

Madeline rounded to face her, suddenly angry, still hurting, needing release. "Cliff Notes version. I bound your Minstrel, yeah, then I used my first wish to take all the power from my stepfather."

Leila's breath hissed in. "Why?"

"Because it was the only way I could think of to save Zayne's life. Cyrus gave him that poison, and I needed the antidote. My second wish was to free him. Now I'm going to find the book with the ritual to get rid of these vile powers. Any more questions or accusations? If not, then *adieu*." She pivoted and stalked down the hall.

Still sparkling, Leila barred the door to Tildy's magic room. "Zayne was dying?"

"I thought so." Her shoulders slumped; she was too damned tired to stand up straight. "Look, if you're going to do your retribution thing, then do it now. I'm tired."

Leila's cool hand touched Madeline's brow. "You look like you've been scattered by the seven winds of Kaf."

"It's been quite a day."

"You took in too much, too fast. You are not trained in the control and the disciplines of magic. That is why you burn and tire."

"Plus this knowledge is not the kind you want mucking up your brain."

After a moment's hesitation, Leila took her arm and steered her into the magic room. "Sit a moment."

Madeline sank gratefully into a chair, exhausted.

"I'll be right back." The djinni disappeared, then returned a moment later with a tall glass of ice water, which she handed to Madeline. "Here."

Madeline took a grateful sip, then pressed the cool glass against her forehead.

"You love Zayne," Leila said gently, sitting beside her.

"Yeah."

"I already knew he loves you."

"You did?" Madeline gave her a curious look. "How?"

"A djinn male who has found his *zaniya* is . . . obvious to others of our race." Leila rubbed the back of her neck. "The heightened protectiveness. The constant shimmer of arousal. The energy can be most fatiguing to watch."

"Oh." The sudden flush on Madeline's cheeks had nothing to do with the fever of magic.

"A purpose is served with the display. Males know not to approach her, and females know he is no longer available to them."

Madeline blinked back tears, angry at the fatigue that brought weepiness. Zayne's protectiveness had sometimes irritated her, but she would give anything to have the arrogant djinni back at her side. "Zayne believed we were destined for one another."

"Destiny can be as tricky as prophecies or bargains with a djinni. There's always some hidden snag or loophole. Destined for one another does not mean the fates will allow you to be together. You bound him," Leila added softly. "A human who bound a djinni cannot stay on Kaf, and Zayne is our only Minstrel, our only balance."

"So he can't leave," Madeline agreed, her fist tightening against the clutch of pain. She drained the water, then leaned forward, resting her elbows on her knees, the empty water glass dangling from her fingers. "Helluva fix, isn't it?"

Would she ever be able to hear his name without that stab of yearning? Would she ever see sparklers or fireworks and not think of a hot, dry desert and a beautiful man who sang with the voice of angels?

"At least he's free. He's with his people; he's singing. He will be happy." She had to believe he could live happily and well. She set down the glass, then got up and started searching the bookcase.

"What are you looking for?"

"A book of spells and incantations, kind of old looking. *Powers* it was called, and I remember seeing a ritual for removing power." What had she done with it? She'd read through the spell for Charm and Assurance, then Zayne had rung the doorbell, and—"There it is. On the table."

With Leila looking over her shoulder, she quickly thumbed through the book until she found the right page. "This is it. Ritual of Dissolution."

"The Ritual should be done at a high time," Leila said.

"What's that?"

"Times of power. Noon and midnight. You will have to do it at midday."

"Only a few more hours; then I can be rid of this."

"Would you like me to stay with you until then?"

Madeline shook her head, setting down the empty glass. "Thanks, but I'm tired; I think I'll try to get some sleep."

"Would you like me to come back at noon?"

"If you don't mind. You can make sure I do this right."

"You will do fine." Leila rose and patted her hand. "Rest well, Madeline. Drink your fluids." A moment later she'd disappeared, leaving a row of filled water glasses on the table behind her.

Madeline smiled and picked one up to sip. Despite her fatigue, sleep was impossible, she knew, but she didn't want to be with anyone right now. Anyone but Zayne, and he was beyond her.

A blue ball suddenly popped into view just above her head, where it hovered in a lazy spin that sent beams of light rotating about the room. It seemed to be waiting for her to do something.

She reached up to grab it, but it settled itself into her palms. "For Madeline Fairbanks," said a tinny voice as soon as the ball touched her flesh.

"I'm Madeline Fairbanks."

"Ah, Madeline, my beloved *zaniya-e-na*." The ball spoke with Zayne's voice.

Her fingers convulsed around the ball, and her heart sped. "Zayne?"

"This is a message orb. Unlike with your cell phone, I will not hear anything you say. But I wanted you to hear this. I understand now why you did what you did. My temper is hot, but it is brief, and eventually I do think. I thank you."

She pressed a hand against her mouth, holding back a sob. She did not want to miss hearing a single syllable or breath.

"As I have forgiven you, I hope you can find it in your heart to forgive me. I, too, made hard choices I thought were best. If I were there now, I *would* ask you. To be my *zaniya*."

His voice broke off, as if he could no longer continue. Tears streamed down her face, but she didn't lift a hand to wipe them off. If she let go, the orb might stop.

"But I cannot return to Terra. For the sake of my people, I can now allow only *ma-at* in my song. The magic must be . . . eliminated." His voice faded to a mere whisper, then returned. "Yet the memory of you will always reside in my heart."

She swallowed against the hard knot in her throat. He no longer had her with him to balance him. In order to save his people, he was cutting off all ties to magic, to his human half, to her.

"If I could give this up for you, I would, but I cannot abandon my people."

"I know," she whispered, even though he couldn't hear her. "If you could, you wouldn't be the man I love."

"This orb contains a gift. I know now it will be safe in your keeping. I will continue to sing, *si halika*. It is my wish for you that you will continue to dance. *T'dost mi dara. Fresho, janam.*"

The lights in the orb winked out, and it split down the middle in her hands.

The orb wasn't a Memorex tape. There was no replay mode. The only way she'd hear his voice again would be in her dreams.

Her chest was so tight she could barely breathe. She dropped the orb, and out of it tumbled her turquoise tablet.

Madeline slipped the tablet over her head. Oh, dear God, she remembered when he'd given it to her. He had looked so . . . satisfied. So happy. He'd kissed her there—She bent over, clutching her legs to her chest as once more huge sobs were wrenched from her.

The ritual was almost completed. Zayne knelt before the roaring fire. Naked, he faced the sun as it made its slow rise to the horizon, the crimson sky a herald to its arrival. Beneath him was a cloth of white linen; and nine candles of red, orange, and yellow surrounded him. He had fasted as required, donned the robe of white silk, and set the necessary guards. The scroll lay open beside him. One final sequence remained.

Zayne, you near the end. Again I ask you if you would like company. Alesander's voice.

No, Oracle, I know my duty. I feel the unrest of Kaf. I know I must sing soon. You do not need to be here to remind me.

There was a moment's silence, although Zayne knew Alesander had not broken the connection. He almost thought he heard a soft sigh, before Alesander spoke again.

Not duty. Only companionship at a difficult moment.

Then you will be welcome.

Zayne wasn't surprised when Alesander appeared at once. He knelt outside the circle of candles. The robe he wore, however, was purple, not red. "Whatever your choices are, know always that you have my friendship, Zayne."

"Thank you."

Zayne turned back to the fire. All that remained was to remove the last physical connection to Terra, the shell-and-leather band Madeline had given him, and then cast the oils on the fire and recite the final words to sever his link to the magic. To eliminate all connection to his human side.

To cut himself off from Madeline for the remainder of his days.

He fingered the leather, unable to force himself to undo the knots. His hands and body ached. The knots swam before his eyes, while his fist clenched on top of them.

Every fiber in him rebelled against this. It was wrong. Madeline was his *zaniya-e-na*. He had human blood. How could he deny that part of him? A new complexity enriched his singing from the music he had learned on Terra. There was a new balance and peace in his life from his love for Madeline.

How could he deny his love?

He bent over, hands fisted before him, pressing into the silk. The knife edge of denial sliced inside him, cutting deep, cutting out confusion. "I am partly human," he said aloud. "This I cannot deny." Yet beneath his palm he could feel the rumble of Kaf, waiting for the song of the Minstrel.

"I love Madeline."

He waited for Alesander to remind him of his duty, but the Oracle remained silent. Zayne glanced over at the dark robed figure. "Do you not tell me I must continue?"

"I come in friendship only, and your choices do not change that."

"I cannot do this," Zayne whispered. Yet he must.

I love you, Madeline.

The morning sirocco rose with the coming sun. Hot and dry, rich with the power of Kaf. The scroll fluttered in the gusts of wind. He committed to memory the final stanzas. He read the poem too, though he had memorized the terrible words:

The battle enjoined, the forces unleashed.
Only one as victor, the other sheathed.
Embrace the anchor, the flow, the balance.
Wield the knife, the severing, the ritual of one.

He looked at it again, the words suddenly shifting in meaning. He read the final two lines, then cast a startled glance toward Alesander. *Whatever your choices are, know that you have my friendship.*

Choices. Always choices. The final two lines were not a sequence. They were a choice. Sever or embrace.

The powerful Terran magic had caused turmoil because he had never accepted it or his human blood. He had never welcomed either. Yet Madeline had taught him the joy of Terra. She helped him embrace his humanity. Through Madeline, his love and his balance, he filtered out the bad, leaving only the richness of earth and water for his song.

Madeline was not here.

He glanced down, seeing the band on his arm. She was here. She was here in the gift she'd given him. She was here in his memories, in the knowledge of Terra she had given him, and in the good he had found there.

She was in his heart and in his soul and, mostly, in his love.

If he fully accepted the human in him, both good and bad, would these intangibles be enough? Could he sing and control the magic through his memories? If he could, then there was hope. There was a way that one day they could be together on Terra.

Zayne shoved to his feet. "I will not do this."

"Do you choose your desire for this woman over your duty?"

"I am human, Alseander." It was the first time he had said it aloud.

"A small part," Alesander said drily.

"But the Minstrel creates balance, and to deny this part of myself is wrong."

"So what will you do?"

Zayne waved a hand, clothing himself in leather pants and silk shirt. His oud appeared over his shoulder. He retrieved the broken turquoise tablet and hung it back around his neck. "What will I do? I will be Minstrel, and I will sing."

Zayne chose a mountaintop where water tumbled in a sparkling fall and the wind whistled of solitude and strength. He squinted at the sun nearly overhead. Midday. A potent time. He gathered a circle of stones, set a fire blazing at their center, and then sat down to sing. No audience did he need, only the deep, powerful connections to his world.

Sweet harmony spread across the fires and winds, while his *ma-at* danced through the notes. Slowly, as his *ma-at* strengthened and flowed, so too did the powers of magic rise inside him. A rock cracked beside him, loosening a scarlet flame. The ground vibrated beneath him.

No. There would be no battle. He acknowledged the

forces of magic; they were part of him. He recognized their wildness in the tumble of the waterfall and their darkness in the depth of the green bayou.

Yet his was the soul of Kaf.

Sweat burned in his eyes, and his tense muscles vibrated as he sought to weave the conflicting powers. He focused on the shell in the leather band, remembered swimming beside Madeline, her scent and taste, and what she had shown him of her world. He shaped the magic through his memories.

Kaf trembled beneath him. Anguish gripped him as the battle raged on. He was not going to be able to do this alone.

Desperate, he called up the image of Madeline in the red dress. Madeline dancing in flame. Madeline of Terra. Flame of Kaf. He loved them both. He was part of both. His love joined the music, indelible and undeniable.

The magic soothed. No longer an angry child, but a precious companion. He embraced it, gathered it, then with controlled precision intertwined it with his *ma-at*. His control was restored, and Kaf welcomed his song.

Zayne finished the final notes, then sat in solitude on the rock, fatigue keeping him still. He had done it. 'Twas much easier with Madeline at his side, her scent embracing him, the flow of her body drawing him into the beauty of Terra. Right now, his body felt as though it had been battered by a *tsuahnam*, a wall of sand, and his throat ached.

But he had done it.

And now he had hope.

He could train the youths who would be the next Minstrels, raise them to take his place. He could take as long as needed, for djinn aged slower than humans.

Once there were others, he would transport back to Madeline. He would shift through time arriving back at her side within moments after he had left. Long, lonely years would pass for him, but he would spare her the pain of waiting.

He took a deep breath, his trembling fingers tracing the rune of Minstrel on his tablet. Then, no longer would he sing for the harmony of Kaf; his time would be spent on Terra with Madeline. He would only return to Kaf for brief visits to renew his bonds.

His gaze spread over the vast, isolated landscape. There would be plenty of time in the years ahead to commit Kaf to his memory.

This plan could work, and it was the only way they could safely be together.

Too long had passed since he had felt at peace with himself, with his music and his *ma-at*. Too long had the harmonies of Kaf been discordant. He raised his eyes to see a company of the djinn scattered around the rocks before him, listening to the true song of the Minstrel, their silence a testimony to the awesome power. When he gave them no sign to approach, however, they slowly left, and at last he was alone.

He rose, stretching his muscles and slinging his oud over his shoulder. Oh, how he longed to go to Madeline, to hold her in his arms, and tell her again that he loved her. But if his plan was to work, he could not go to Terra, he could not see her and indulge his needs, not for a very long time.

Chapter Twenty-four

Madeline knelt in Tildy's garden and squinted up at the sky. The sun was almost directly overhead. In a few more minutes she could get rid of these noxious spells. Until she'd had this unwanted glimpse into his mind, she hadn't realized what a sick man Cyrus was. She could have gone through life quite happily without ever knowing how to ritually dismember a goat.

She picked up the Book of Powers and read through the ritual again, making sure she had everything. Flowing water in the fountain in front of her. A linen bag filled with camphor, lavender, ginger, and salt. Two white candles, one brown one. Wristwatch off. Stomach empty.

Her hand was trembling as she tugged the hem of her tank top over her shorts, and her heart raced in her chest, the beat occasionally erratic. Her thoughts were a little erratic, too, she realized, jumping around like water on a skillet. Sizzling. She sizzled, too. Her skin was so hot, the fountain would probably steam when she put her hands in it.

Damn, she had to get rid of these spells soon or she'd end up in either CCU or a locked ward. She glanced overhead again. A minute or two more. She wasn't going to risk failure because she'd gotten too eager. To keep herself occupied during these final moments, she paged through the Book of Powers, nagged by the thought she'd read something else in there, something she needed to remember.

Smiling, she remembered going through the book that first day in Tildy's house. The spell for the Power of Charm and Assurance. Maybe a little bit of it had worked.

Her smile faltered when she reached the pages about binding a djinni; she peered at the look of cold anger on the bound man's face. She was about to flip past quickly, when a brightly shaded drawing on the bottom caught her eye. A tormented man surrounded by blue hot flame.

There *had* been something else she'd read that day. Something that now struck her as very important. She read aloud the final warning. "Beware, oh, foolish one, to be so bold. For the fury of a genie is mighty and his retribution fearsome to behold. Protect well thyself, for offenses cannot be undone except by purification in the Ordeals."

For offenses cannot be undone except by purification in the Ordeals. What had Leila said yesterday? Prophecies, bargains, and destinies were tricky things because there was always a snag or a loophole.

"Are you ready?"

Madeline screeched, and the book slammed shut. She rested a hand on her hammering chest. "Damn, Leila, you startled me."

"Methinks thou art a little jumpy." Leila pointed upward. "Time to start."

"Yeah." She didn't want to miss this window of opportunity to get rid of Cyrus's last legacy. "I've got something to ask you afterward, though."

As instructed by the book, Madeline lit the white and brown candles, setting the brown one in front, the two white on either side. She sprinkled the contents of her linen bag into the water. The pungent aroma of camphor wafted toward her, tickling her nostrils, and she held back a sneeze.

Just as the sun reached the zenith, she stuck her hands in the lukewarm water and chanted the spell, repeating the single phrase. "Water of Earth, take this from me. Wash clean for me, oh, Water of Earth. Water of Earth, take this from me. Wash clean for me, oh, Water of Earth."

At first she felt nothing different, only the soothing flow of water. Then, as she chanted, something stirred and collected inside her, like a gathering storm. She focused on her chant while bits of ceremonies and pieces of spells were dislodged from her mind and tumbled free. As the knowledge shredded away, it fled down her chest and arms, into her hands, and then out into the life-sustaining waters. The fountain hissed, and steam rose and dissipated. Still she chanted, drawing out all the poisonous knowledge and power, until at last the tumbling shreds were gone, and the waters settled, and the mist disappeared.

She knelt, listening to a lone bird warbling in the otherwise silent afternoon. She drew in the aromas of camphor and lavender. Inside, she was . . . Madeline. Just Madeline. The powers were gone. The knowledge gone, too. She felt the shadows of it, the faded remembrance that she had once known more than she desired, but the words of the rituals and chants had vanished.

She was tired and her muscles ached, she realized, but it was a clean fatigue. There was none of the lethargy or the sensation of being burned from the inside out. She lifted her hands from the water, amazed at how steady she held them, and took the towel Leila handed her.

"Are you okay?" Leila asked.

"Yeah." Madeline stood and stretched, checking her pulse. Her heart beat slow and steady. "Pretty good in fact. Hungry."

Leila handed her a granola bar from her pocket. "Here. I thought you might be."

"Thanks." They sat on one of the benches and munched granola. "Leila, what does *T'dost mi dara. Fresho, janam* mean?"

"It means 'I will love you. Forever, my soul.' "

Madeline looked away from Leila's sympathy, closing her eyes to hide tears, and her hand convulsed around the granola, breaking it into sticky crumbs. Only when she was composed enough that her voice wouldn't shake did she turn back to Leila, recalling what she had read in the book. "What are the Ordeals for purification?"

"The Ordeals of the Oracle?" Leila drew back. "Do not even think of that."

"I have to." She fetched the book and opened it to the page in question. Leila quickly averted her eyes. "It says here, 'for offenses cannot be undone *except* by purification in the Ordeals.' It's a loophole, an out."

"Close the book," Leila said in a strangled voice.

Madeline closed it. "What are the Ordeals of the Oracle? Tell me, or do I have to go to Kaf and ask someone?"

"No!" Leila gave a sigh. "The Ordeals are both test and purification. They test worthiness and resolve and . . . whatever the Oracle deems needs testing."

"What do they entail?"

"Each test is different, for the Oracle knows things beyond our ken. He will delve into your deepest terrors and your greatest failures and he will force you to endure both."

Madeline swallowed hard. This was not sounding good. "If I pass, I can stay on Kaf? The binding will be forgiven?"

"You will not pass, Madeline. These are tests of *maat*. Even among the djinn, few are brave or foolish enough to attempt them. Fewer still triumph. A human could not so endure."

"But if I pass," she repeated through gritted teeth, "I could stay on Kaf?"

"Yes."

Madeline scrambled to her feet. "I have to try."

Leila grabbed her wrist. "I do not know the consequences if a human fails. You do not know what you risk."

Madeline closed her eyes, scared spitless from what she was about to say; then she opened them. "What would you risk for Jack?"

Leila stilled, her gaze searching Madeline's face; then she stepped back. "You will need to be able to speak our language," she said. "Will you accept this gift?"

"Yes."

Pressing her fingertips against Madeline's temples, she chanted a few lines, then said. "Repeat after me. By the fires and winds of Kaf, grant me the knowledge I seek."

"By the fires and winds of Kaf, grant me the knowledge I seek."

"This boon I ask, great Solomon. This boon freely given."

"This boon I ask, great Solomon. This boon freely given."

"Now think of taking in the voices of Kaf."

Suddenly a cacophony of voices and sounds whirled

around her, then was sucked inside with a mighty whoosh, leaving behind silence.

"Do you understand me?" Leila asked.

Madeline blinked. Weird. Leila spoke in strange words, yet she understood every one of them. She answered in the same language. "Yes, I do."

Weird, but convenient. She gave Leila a hug. "Thank you for all your help."

"My pleasure." Pressing her palms together, Leila inclined her head. "May the benevolence and wisdom of Solomon be with you, Madeline Fairbanks. May the wind at your back and the sand at your feet soon carry you back to me."

"Thank you." Madeline clutched her turquoise tablet. Before she lost her courage, she pictured Kaf and chanted the words of transport.

A strange unsettling ripple spread across Kaf. Zayne felt it from his soles to his brows. A disturbance, but not like the ones he calmed. This was different. This was—

Madeline! Madeline was on Kaf.

He allowed himself one moment to pound the trunk of a tree in frustration. Oh, for the benevolence of Solomon, she could not have been that reckless.

Where would she be? She knew of but two spots to visualize. He made a guess and transported to the mesa rather than his tent.

He had guessed right. She stood alone, slowly turning around, looking so beautiful, but so very human, in her tank top, shorts, and athletic shoes. Her hair was pulled back into a tail.

"I'm here, Oracle," she called.

Zayne strode over to her, feeling the rumbles of Kaf. His gut tightened as fear lodged in his throat. His advantage of knowing where she was would be a short one. Soon, other djinn would appear, drawn by instinct and word passed from mind to mind. They would gather, and they would despise. Should they collectively turn on her, even his position and power could not stop them.

"Madeline!"

Zayne's furious shout brought Madeline spinning around. Damn, how had he found her so fast?

"Get out of here, Madeline. Before anyone else discovers exactly where you are."

He reached for her, but she spun out of his grip. "No, I'm going to do the Ordeals. Why didn't you tell me about them?"

"Because you will not survive."

"You don't know that."

"You will not take that risk."

They were dancing around each other, feinting and evading. Zayne was quick, but she was no slouch in the reaction department. He couldn't read her mind, and she wouldn't still to let him pounce and take her back to Earth.

"I won't live a lifetime without you," she said. "Not if there's a chance for something else."

"I have another plan."

"What?" His announcement was so startling, she almost let him catch her. At the last second she slid from his grip. "What plan?"

"Return to Terra. I will join you momentarily and tell you."

"Okay." If there was another option, she was all for it. Truth to tell, she wasn't all that keen on the whole Ordeal of the Oracle thing, if she could avoid it.

Something stopped her, though, and roused her suspicions. Something in his eyes. Resignation behind the fury. She was a good reader of body language, and this was not the look of a thrilled man. Her eyes narrowed. "Why won't you come with me right now?"

"I will tell you when I arrive."

She saw him start to chant under his breath.

"Don't you dare use a spell on me, Zayne. I'll transport right back. Tell me your plan."

"Madeline!" His voice was strained, and they were both panting from exertion. "We have about one 'right back' before they start to come."

"So be quick."

"I have found that with the memory of you, I can control the magic. It is more difficult, but I can do it until I train my replacements. Then I will come to you and we will live on Terra."

"I thought you said there were only youths who might one day be Minstrel."

He hesitated.

"We're running out of time."

"When they are grown, I will return to your side. I can fold time, and from your perspective, I will return only a few moments from now. Djinn age slower; you will see no difference in me."

"Except for those decades that you will be left alone, struggling. Then we'll have to live on Terra because I'm not welcome here, the place of your soul."

"I shall return here for brief visits to renew my bonds. There is also much I like about your world. My life will be there with you as my wife."

His wife. Not his *zaniya*. The change, the sacrifice he was willing to make for her, almost broke her heart with its loving spirit.

"This plan will work," he added desperately.

"If I would agree."

"The decision of a Minstrel shall not be questioned," he thundered.

"Then no wonder the divination sent you to Earth for a *zaniya* with the spine to stand by you. Zayne, this plan is the most precious gift anyone has ever given me."

"Good." He lunged forward.

She jumped onto a rock. "But I can't accept. You think I'm going to let you live alone for God knows how long, struggling to control the magic when I could make it easy? Then have you return, zap, as if nothing's happened, because nothing has happened to me, while you've been hurting and lonely? I'm supposed to let you give up Kaf because it won't accept me? Kaf is part of you—you have to keep coming back—and I can't even visit once in a while. You are her Minstrel. Giving up your duty would tear you apart, and seeing that would tear me apart."

"It is better than having you dead," he shouted. "You chose sacrifice over death for me. I am doing the same for you."

She stopped and stared at him. "You really think that will be the Ordeal's outcome?" she whispered. Until this moment, she'd thought he and Leila were being melodramatic.

Zayne could barely catch his breath, so much did his fear for her tear at him. "It is too possible, yes. Leave now, Madeline, before—"

Alesander appeared, standing on a platform of rock above her, his purple robe fluttering in the accumulating breezes of the arriving djinn. Even his hands were hidden, so no part of the man was visible. Only the Oracle stood above them. A heartbeat later Darius, the Protector of their *ma-at*, appeared, followed by King Taranushi.

Too late.

His mouth dry with fear, Zayne reached Madeline's side. He put his arm around her shoulders, his fingers resting against the fluttering pulse of her neck. He pressed close against her, giving her the heat and strength of his body.

"Could I transport out now?" she whispered.

"They will not allow it," he returned. "That is Alesander, the Oracle, Darius, the Protector of the *Ma-at*, and King Taranushi."

"Don't suppose you could turn them into toads."

Zayne pressed his lips together. How could he possibly think of laughing at this moment? But that was Madeline. She fought her tension with humor. In response he sent her a quick image—the crowd of djinn turning to toads and hopping away.

"Oh, Zayne," she said, half laugh, half sob. "I do love you."

The Protector and King Taranushi stepped forward. All humor vanished, leaving only fear.

The King looked down at them. "You would stand beside the human woman who bound you, Zayne?"

"Yes." He heard the murmurs of discontent and disbelief behind him, saw the shock of the King, the resolve of the Protector, but he paid them no mind. He would do whatever he must to protect and shield Madeline.

"Is she worthy of your loyalty?"

"Yes. Her binding was only to save—"

The Protector cut him off with a quick gesture. "Madeline Fairbanks, why do you dare come to Kaf?"

"I desire purification by the Ordeal of the Oracle." Her voice was quiet but steady. Zayne felt, though, the rapid beat of her heart and he could taste her fear as his own.

The Protector and King Taranushi exchanged a long look; then both stepped back and Alesander took their place. The Oracle would make the final decision.

"Do you know what the Ordeal entails, Madeline?" asked the Oracle, his voice echoing from the depths of his hood.

"Not exactly. Only that it's a test."

"It is more than a test. It is a trial."

A shiver ran through Zayne. Even as powerful as he was, he never wanted to test himself against Alesander. He gathered Madeline closer. She was strong, yes, but she was also fragile. She would have no defense of *ma-at*.

The Oracle turned toward the Protector and the King. "Will you accept the results of the Ordeal? Accept her presence here if she passes?"

"We will."

The Oracle looked out at the crowd of assembled djinn. "Are there any among you who will not accept this woman if she passes the Ordeal?"

Silence was his answer.

"Are there any among you who doubt that whatever trial I proclaim is a true Ordeal?"

Again, silence.

The Oracle turned to Madeline. "Madeline Fairbanks, do you freely accept the consequences of your choice?"

No! Zayne wanted to shout the answer for her. He wanted to transport her out of here, away from the danger. They could have a good life on Terra.

Do not interfere, Zayne, Alesander's voice boomed inside his mind. *The time is too late for you to stop her. Only she can do that now.*

Zayne's fingers tightened around her shoulder, ready to defy even the Oracle for Madeline's sake.

"Yes," answered Madeline.

Again too late. She was wrenched from his grasp, pulled up to the platform to stand in front of the Oracle. He saw her glance around, saw her eyes widen in blind fear as she wrapped her hands around her middle.

Her stage fright, he realized. Her magic-enhanced fear. Standing up there would be torture for her, and his insides tightened to a hard knot as he realized the Ordeal the Oracle would demand of her. What she could not do.

The Oracle glided closer, his purple robe brushing the rock. He stood beside her and lifted his arm, the long sleeve of his robe still covering his hand. No glimpse of the man inside gave hope of leniency. Madeline raised her hand to touch the hem of his robe. Lightning arced between them with a ferocious crack. Madeline staggered backward.

Zayne pushed forward, only to be stopped by the Oracle's power.

The Oracle lowered his arm. "Dance for us, Madeline Fairbanks."

Chapter Twenty-five

"Dance for us, Madeline Fairbanks."

Madeline barely heard the words of the Oracle above the roaring in her ears. So many people watching her. This fear was not irrational, for this audience despised her and longed for her to fail.

The frozen legs and knifing pain in her gut, however, were a legacy from Cyrus. She knew that, but rationality was no match for the multiplying terror. Nausea burned her throat, and only by sheer strength of will, and keeping her lips pressed firmly together, did she prevent the total humiliation of throwing up in front of everyone.

"Dance," Alesander commanded again. "Show us a dance worthy of the Minstrel."

Oh, God, she couldn't. She could not move a foot. Not a toe or a finger. Her belly twisted as she heard murmurs of annoyance ripple through the crowd.

Madeline, this is not necessary. Tell them you will return to Terra. Zayne spoke to her, privately and lovingly, without a hint of censure or blame. *Be happy with me.*

Be happy when she knew what he would have to give up? She slid one wooden foot across the stone. "I will be wife *and zaniya,*" she whispered. A dancer worthy of the Minstrel's songs. The other foot clomped onto the rock. The fear swept through her, leaving her panting. Two more steps of no grace, no talent. With an awkward movement, she shoved off her cross-trainers. Her arms waved in a pointless gesture, while her feet took two more Frankenstein steps.

The murmurs grew louder and more displeased. She looked up, looked out. Thousands of eyes swarmed before her, all filled with scorn. Thousands of mouths laughed at her. Their mocking derision deafened her. Panic filled her. Dizzily she turned her back to them and bent over, her stomach spasming in dry heaves.

The faces and laughter followed her, spinning before her eyes and filling her ears. The spell's grip was too strong. Tears spilled in great rivers down her cheeks.

"Do you stop, Madeline?" asked Alesander gently.

Wildly she shook her head. *No, no*. But her feet and her arms could not move.

"She needs music," Zayne called out suddenly. "Who can dance for an audience without music? I will play for her."

"No." The Oracle's voice echoed from his hood. "She does this alone."

Madeline. Zayne's anguished voice filled her. *You need not do this for me*.

"This is for *me*," she bit out. She was tired of that foul spell poisoning her life. "This is for us." She didn't know if he could hear her, if anyone could hear. It didn't matter as long as she heard. She turned and straightened, fighting the cramping pain. She could not move, but she could stand with head lifted. Her lungs gulped in the sweet air of Kaf.

Look at me, Madeline, Zayne commanded. *Not at them. Look at me and remember what is important. I love you*.

Notes sounded in her mind, sung by Zayne. The first measures of "Small Town Saturday Night." Along with the notes was a ridiculous vision of dancing toads.

The voice and the image cut off abruptly, compliments of Alesander, she suspected. Her gaze flew to Zayne. He stood, trying for a very innocent look and totally not succeeding. Trying to give her the strength of laughter. A chuckle almost broke through her blind terror.

"Oh, Zayne, I do love you," she whispered, buoyed by his support. She hummed "Small Town Saturday Night" under her breath. No matter that the Protector heard her and winced. This was for her. The two-step. Nothing more Terran than that.

Quick, quick. Slow, slow. Her steps weren't graceful, but at least she finally moved against the tide of nausea and terror. Quick, quick. Slow, slow. More steps.

Her muscles throbbed, then, like that horrible night, like yesterday, a lancing pain shot down her leg. For one wretched moment she swayed, trying to catch her balance, and then her knee buckled and she fell. Right on her butt in front of all of them.

She froze, staring, listening. The jeers. The laughter. The pity and condemnation in the sea of eyes. They fed her panic, each blast full and unrelenting. Oh, God, this was the worst. Worse than her darkest nightmares. Her heart raced, an erratic pounding against her chest, and unremitting pain split her forehead. She bent, hiding against her knees. Was this what a heart attack felt like?

The hem of a purple robe swam before her eyes. The Oracle. Leila's words rang in her ears. *He will delve into your deepest terrors and your greatest failures and he will force you to endure both.* The Ordeal magnified each sensation, each manifestation of the spell, she dimly realized as bile burned her throat. This was as bad as the fear would ever get. She looked up to see the faceless hood, the white hand outstretched.

Leave, Madeline. Alesander's voice offered no leniency. *You have fail—*

"No!" Madeline glared at him. This was no longer her worst fear. She had lived this before; she had survived and prospered without dance. Her worst fear now was losing Zayne; nothing matched that pain, yet she had even survived that hell.

"You have no power over me," she whispered, although whether she spoke to Cyrus or Alesander she wasn't sure. Grimly she pushed to her feet. She turned to the audience and forced herself to look at individual faces rather than a sea of eyes and mouths. But the individual faces became scorn, disdain, hostility, each one a piercing bullet.

Replace the many faces with one face. Zayne. She had no trouble finding him in the mass of djinn; his worry shone like a moonbeam amidst the stars. Her gaze locked onto his. If she didn't do this, he would follow through on that heartrending plan of his. She could not allow that.

She had washed away Cyrus's power.

She had Charm and Assurance.

She had the strength of her love for Zayne. Willpower and grit could not break through the spell, but maybe love could.

Keeping her eyes open, she started to hum and to dance. The image she forced herself to hold on to was of Zayne. His concern when she had cried for her mother. Quick, quick. Slow, slow. A broken smoke alarm and a frustrated, naked djinni. Two quick, two slow. His lazy smile when he rolled over on his pillows to greet her. Quick, quick. Slow, slow. One hand clutched her turquoise tablet, calming her irregular heartbeat; the other pressed against her stomach, keeping down nausea.

"Small Town Saturday Night." She had danced to this in the French Quarter, with Zayne on her arm. She had danced for him wearing a dress of flame. She twirled her hips, remembering the glide of the fabric and Zayne's delight at seeing her in the dress.

So much she remembered. Fearless Zayne afraid of swimming. The sparks when he was angry. Oh, the beautiful, glittering rainbow when he made love. Love crowded out pain and fear.

Two quick, two slow. The steps got easier. Lighter. Her heartbeat steadied. Pain backed off to an ache.

She watched Zayne as he swayed in perfect time to the notes she hummed. For the first time since the Ordeal began, she smiled. Sweat covered her body, but not from nerves anymore, from sheer exertion. The hot sun beat onto her head and the winds whistled across her. The stiffness left her. Nausea and pain vanished. Cyrus's last slimy hold on her slid away.

She danced.

In front of the multitude of djinn, she danced. Each step severed a strand in the unnatural bonds that had held her for too many years. Severed until at last she was free.

Madeline made a final circle and bowed to her audience. Zayne clapped with unabashed enthusiasm, but the rest did not join him. Besides her, only he and the Oracle understood what a triumph this was for her.

The Oracle stood beside her. "She has passed the test," he announced.

There were a few surprised murmurs, but they quickly died. The djinn were too respectful of the Oracle to gainsay him. Madeline knew, however, that she had not yet earned the respect that the *zaniya* of a

Minstrel should have. This first time was for herself. The next dance would be for Zayne.

"No," she said, her voice ringing clear. "I haven't passed. Not yet."

Madeline! Zayne's strangled voice sounded inside her.

Alesander turned. She got the impression that she surprised him, and she'd bet a case of Barq's root beer that Alesander didn't surprise easily. "Do you question the judgment of the Oracle?" he asked with deceptive mildness.

"You said a dance worthy of the Minstrel. I'm a dancer; I know that wasn't it." She lifted her chin. "Let Zayne play for me. Only then can you judge if my dance is worthy."

"Very well." The Oracle settled to the back of the platform with the Protector and the King. "Dance with the Minstrel."

Madeline Fairbanks, truly you are the woman for our Zayne. Alesander's approval sounded deep in her mind.

Zayne leaped onto the stage, covering the space between them in two strides. "Madeline, what in the name of Solomon has possessed you?"

"Let them"—she jerked her head toward the restive audience—"believe."

He glanced out at the company of djinn, then nodded. "You are right. But you should not have this." He tugged the band off her pony tail and tossed it aside. "And you should wear this." He ran his hands down her, and suddenly she found herself wearing the flame dress.

Madeline grinned and ran her hands through her hair, loosening it. "Let's dance."

He sat on the stage and began to play. His song

started soft and gentle, like a summer breeze. She poised, watching the motion of his talented hands and the green eyes filled with love. She had seen him play before and knew that his focus was always on the music, his head bent, his hair covering his face. But this time he looked at her.

She lifted her hands and began to dance. The dress spun around her as she executed a series of pirouettes, then arched her back, swinging up into a leap, the best elevation she'd ever achieved. His song speeded up, grew darker and more complex. She tasted and felt the yearning whispers of *ma-at* woven within the notes, and her dance gave them substance.

As she danced, she was struck by how free she felt. When she was younger, the instructors Cyrus chose drilled technical perfection into her. Her years away from their tyranny allowed her to develop something just as important. Style. She'd been freed to find her own heart in the dance, and it was with this that she now danced.

Zayne's song swelled again, dark and dangerous. The beat and rhythm of sensual jazz. She smiled. With a hint of plaintive country for good measure.

Fragments of his magic, now under his control, joined beneath the notes and the *ma-at*, flowing like the fingers of a river. Reaching out for her, the dancer of Terra. She swayed again with the sensations she felt in her bones. The rhythm of Terran rivers. The green mysteries of the bayous. The smell of vegetation and soil, the embrace of hot humidity on her skin, all of them carried to her as her lover sang. Her body and his magic were one.

Zayne watched Madeline as she danced with grace, power, and joy. His *ma-at* sparkled and resounded through the melody in a rich tapestry of color, taste, and aroma. Beneath it, his human side offered a new complexity. The song inside him swelled to a new crescendo, while she twirled in abandon. Her body, lithe and curved, created the difficult moves with a supple ease.

He hardened, responding to the feminine power she displayed. Desire gripped him, rapid and unshakable. He needed more than the union of voice and dance.

Now, Madeline, now.

She threw him a teasing, knowing grin. In perfect accord, she sunk to a bow, while he crashed the final chord.

The notes faded into the hot Kafian night. Zayne leaped to his feet, slinging the oud over his shoulder, while applause and the stomping of feet swelled across them. The djinn, and Kaf, were pleased. He strode across the flat rock, taking Madeline by the hand, bowing first to their enthusiastic audience and then to the three rulers.

"She has passed the Ordeal," he said, facing the Oracle, the Protector, and the King.

"She has," Alesander agreed. He turned to Madeline. "You are welcomed, Madeline Fairbanks, the dancer truly worthy to be the *zaniya* of the Minstrel."

She inclined her head in acknowledgment.

Zayne shook his head. "You have it backwards, Alesander. It is I who am worthy of the dancer of Terra." He made a formal bow to the three leaders of his people.

"May the winds and fires of Kaf be with you."

"May they speed your journey and grant you safe passage."

He lifted Madeline's joined hand to his lips and kissed the back of her hand, his body tight. "Are you ready?"

Are you ready to join with me, si halika? He embraced her, feeling the warm play of her muscles and the sheen of sweat from the exertion of her dance.

"Yes."

A moment later, he had transported her to his home. Instead of landing inside the tent, however, he visualized the small grove of trees behind, where the *frangipela* scented the night air and the hot winds were free to waft across the small stream. With the tiny corner of his mind and *ma-at* that was not entwined with Madeline, he brought pillows and silks outside.

His hands ran along her curves, feeling the supple muscles and the heat of her skin. His fingers tightened on her hips as he rocked against her, the pressure of her body against him a sweet agony. She wrapped her arms around him, returning his kiss with a frantic, willing need of her own.

He could not get enough of her, this woman who had turned him inside out and shattered every misconception. This woman whose body gave visual life to his music. Her love enchanted and spellbound him more thoroughly than any copper bands. She was *janam*, his soul, his balance.

She lifted her head from the kiss and smiled. "Are you always like this after you sing?"

"Often, so we shall spend much time among our pillows."

"Good. I like you on my pillow." A small furrow formed between her brows. "Before me, though, when you finished, how did you—"

"Later, Madeline." He bent to another kiss, silencing her.

But when he lifted from it, he knew there was one thing he must do first, before he took her to their pillows. He tucked the hair behind her ear, suddenly serious. "Madeline, will you be my *zaniya*?"

"I have always been yours."

"Will you share with me the ceremony of union?"

"Right now?"

"Yes. We can do the rituals of your world when you choose, but I should like our souls united before we share our pillows."

"This is the djinn version of a marriage ceremony?"

"Yes." He waited, his breath caught in his throat.

She smiled at him. "Yes."

He gathered her close to his side and led her over to the small stream. With a gesture, he brought out a scarlet rug and two robes of deep crimson, his threaded with gold, hers threaded with blue. They donned the robes, then knelt facing each other on the rug, the flowing stream on one side, a crackling fire on the other. He took off his leather and shell armlet and laid it on the rug between them; then he brought forth a scarlet ribbon. He handed her a parchment and pen and ink.

"Write your name on this and these words." He dictated the promises of union and fidelity, first in his language, then in hers, also writing on his parchment as she wrote on hers. Then he took the two parchments, rolled them together, and cast them on the fire. He sprinkled fragrant oils onto the fire, and the scents of vanilla, cedar, and cinnamon curled around them, carried on the thin smoke of the burning parchments.

"The old of one is gone. The new of two begins," he intoned.

"The old of one is gone. The new of two begins," she repeated.

"Put your hands on my shoulders."

She complied, and he did the same. His *ma-at* shimmered around them, a golden aura filled with the sparkle of gemstones. He surrounded her and embraced her with *ma-at* and mind and emotion. Her eyes widened, and her fingers tightened, and though she had not the ability of *ma-at*, he still felt her inside him.

He picked up the scarlet ribbon and tied it around her wrist. "I bind my powers and my life to thine. Let our fires burn together. This I do of my own free will."

She tied the leather back around his arm. "I bind my powers and my life to thine. Let our fires burn together. This I do of my own free will."

"Air and fire."

She paused, then said, "Water and earth."

"I desire now to be one with thee."

"I desire now to be one with thee."

"By Solomon, the vow is sealed."

"By Solomon, the vow is sealed."

The evening sun touched the horizon, bathing her in a glow of amethyst and gold. Zayne leaned forward and kissed her. "*Zaniya*," he whispered.

"*Zani*," she whispered back.

And their dance together began.

St. John's Eve

The night was sultry and clear, perfect weather for an outdoor party. Madeline took a sip of champagne and surveyed the crowds milling around Feydor's yard. "Your party's a success, Feydor, although I guess I'm out of a job."

Feydor perched at the edge of one of the tables, his legs stretched out before him and crossed at the ankles. He sipped his Jack Daniels. "Because Cyrus isn't here?"

"Yes. I got some of my questions answered, but he's not giving any interviews. Probably won't for a long time."

"Pity." He eyed her over the rim of his glass. "You've

changed in the past three weeks. You could do the job if you wanted."

She shook her head. "I'm quitting, Feydor." She glanced at him. "You don't seem too surprised."

"Let's say I had a hunch when I heard you were dancing again."

"As soon as Tildy comes home, I'll be moving. She said she'd take in Bronze and Silver for me."

"New York?"

"Let's just say away."

He took a drag on a cigarette. "I'm going to miss you, Madeline."

"You called me Madeline! But I didn't keep my part of the bargain."

"You could tell me what you learned about Cyrus. Not tonight, of course. But gradually over the next few months."

"I'll do that." There might be a few things she omitted, but it wouldn't hurt for someone on Earth to know about men like Cyrus.

He nodded and drifted away. A moment later Natalie joined her and gave her a hug. "I can't believe you're moving away. Who's going to join me for those midnight gab fests?"

"You'll find someone."

"Won't be the same. I heard your mother had a breakthrough."

Madeline smiled. "Yeah, the doctors are amazed at her sudden turnaround. It's only been a couple of weeks, but I think she's going to make it this time."

"Good. Sure you won't stay? Zayne's packed them in all week at the Luck Club."

Zayne had felt he owed Wilson that much. "We can't. Zayne has . . . other commitments."

"Speaking of which, I think he's looking for you."

Natalie gestured with her glass to Zayne moving easily through the crowd. "I can't believe you two got married so fast." She paused, watching Zayne a moment, then turned back to Madeline with a grin. "Then again . . ."

"Natalie," Zayne greeted her with a kiss on the cheek. "Madeline, we should be going."

They had another performance on Kaf, tonight. "All right. I'll keep in touch, Natalie."

They slipped away from the crowds and found an isolated spot among the trees. Before they transported, however, Zayne stopped her with a hand to the arm. He leaned down and gave her a thorough kiss. "I do love you."

"And I love you, too."

"Do not plan to linger too long after our performance," he commanded.

"Oh?" She lifted one brow. Life with an arrogant djinni, who had a strong protective streak and a bit of a dictatorial manner, was not always easy, but it never failed to excite.

His *ma-at* stroked across her, a lover's whisper. "The song I sing is a new one. While I formed it, my thoughts were of you." The grin he gave her was pure wickedness.

"I imagined you beneath a fall of water, naked, while I stood behind you like this."

He didn't move, yet she felt the slide of his damp skin against hers and tasted the drops of fresh water showering upon her. She felt the slick caress of soap and his hands upon her breasts and the pressure of his arousal from behind.

Without another word, he transported them away to the sands of Kaf and the gathered djinn, and she knew she would dance with the image still potent and fresh in her mind. Afterward, she would return with him to bring the fantasy to life.

The night air was hot and still, while overhead the myriad of stars formed their only spotlights. The murmurs of the crowd faded when the Minstrel strummed the first notes. Madeline lifted her arms. She gave her *zani* a tempting smile, letting the image linger with him as well, and began the first steps of the dance.

Stuck with her sister's two sets of teenage twins and a magic show about to go on tour, Dia Trelawny needs help fast. Her irresponsible sibling has disappeared as inexplicable as a rabbit in a hat, but Dia has learned of a man who specializes in finding missing persons, no matter how lost.

Hugh Pendragon's piercing green eyes appear to look right into Dia's soul, reading her anxiety about her sister, her unexpected attraction to him. Dark and mysterious, he seems a creature of moonbeams and nighttime, while she lives in the spotlight. But as he draws her into his web of seduction, she wonders which of them is the true magician. She may be a mistress of illusion, but Hugh has performed real magic in bringing her heart back from the dead.

___52465-1 $5.99 US/$7.99 CAN

Dorchester Publishing Co., Inc.
P.O. Box 6640
Wayne, PA 19087-8640

Please add $2.50 for shipping and handling for the first book and $0.75 for each additional book. NY and PA residents, add appropriate sales tax. No cash, stamps, or C.O.D.s. All Canadian orders require $5.00 for shipping and handling and must be paid in U.S. dollars. Prices and availability subject to change. **Payment must accompany all orders.**

Name ________________________________
Address ________________________________
City ________________ State ______ Zip ________
E-mail ________________________________
I have enclosed $________ in payment for the checked book(s).
❑Please send me a free catalog.

CHECK OUT OUR WEBSITE at www.dorchesterpub.com!